Daughter of the Cursed Kingdom

Daughter of the Cursed Kingdom

JASMINE SKYE

FEIWEL AND FRIENDS
NEW YORK

Content warning: This book contains fantasy violence, graphic depictions of injuries, discussions of trauma and PTSD, gaslighting and manipulation by a parent, death of characters, permanent disability, and suicide.

A Feiwel and Friends Book
An imprint of Macmillan Publishing Group, LLC
120 Broadway, New York, NY 10271 • fiercereads.com

EU representative: Macmillan Publishers Ireland Ltd, 1st Floor, The Liffey Trust Centre, 117–126 Sheriff Street Upper, Dublin 1, DO1 YC43

Library of Congress Cataloging-in-Publication Data is available.

First edition, 2026
Book design by Maria W. Jenson
Feiwel and Friends logo designed by Filomena Tuosto
Printed in the United States of America

ISBN 978-1-250-87261-6
10 9 8 7 6 5 4 3 2 1

This is for the Jasmine of 14 and 15 and 16, who scoured every library, bookstore, and dark corner of the internet, desperate to find a single epic adventure featuring queer characters.

Rosy & Shaw's story is for me, for you, and for all of us.

Chapter 1

SHAW

FOR ALL MY PREPARATION FOR SAMHAIN, NOTHING COULD have equipped me for how the night had gone. The specter beneath my fingers felt vile. My back screamed from the slashes it had so generously reaped upon me, but I couldn't dwell on the pain. Holding this monstrosity beneath me was like trying to cling to a wave. The tide wished to drown me and only Rosamund Holt was holding me afloat. She had the specter pinned by the neck, keeping it outwardly docile. Inwardly, it was anything but.

I'd always envisioned specters as especially horrible spirits. Angrier, meaner, and scarier, but fundamentally the same. I'd been wrong. The specter that had formed from Madam Dyer's curse—this unholy combination of bone witch, feral bone familiar, and ghost—was unlike any undead being I'd ever come across. The dark energy that flickered off the specter like tendrils of smoke was pure, concentrated death magic. A hundred times more powerful than an average bone magic ritual could produce. A thousand times more powerful than what the average bone witch could control.

There was no way to kill this thing. Not alone. Not even with Rosamund's help. I would have to simultaneously kill the living body while exorcising the dead inside. Maybe if I was bonded . . .

My gaze flicked momentarily to Rosamund. She was shifted into a badger, another new form, another casual display of power most familiars spent their whole lives dreaming to achieve. I'd tried to woo her for the majority of the fall term under the guise of a fake courtship. In the end, I'd been left cold and alone.

The specter's energy heaved up, and I returned my attention to containing it. I threw my leg over the back of its wolfish body, helping Rosamund physically hold it down while my magic did what it could to wrangle the specter's unleashed energy.

I didn't have the power to kill it, but perhaps I could unmake it. I dug my fingernails into the specter's skin. Its fur was sharper than a wolf's, even a bone wolf's, should have been. The death magic reacted as I began to bodily pull at the specter's shoulder blades. Black tendrils grabbed at my wrists, sinking into my veins.

Give up, the magic said. *Let go. I'll catch you. I'll give you peace.*

For one second, one terrifying second, I wanted to give in. For the briefest moment, I was tempted to die.

But I would not. I could not. I was Shaw Colchuck, heir to the Cursed Throne. Future Witch Queen of the Cursed Kingdom. My destiny did not end here, in the heart of the Bone Forest, at the hands of a blood curse gone rogue. My kingdom was on the verge of war with the Empire of Vinland, and I had a responsibility to my people to keep them safe.

I yanked at the specter's body, forcing the death magic to part underneath my fingers and reveal the entwined souls beneath.

The ghost was the first to come loose, releasing with something like a sigh. The specter grew more solid beneath me as one third of its power was removed. I reached back inside the specter with my bone magic. I pulled out Madam Dyer next, her soul flickering between rational ghost and disturbed spirit as I threw it into the open air. I didn't have time to worry about that. There was still the bone wolf. This was Ylva Holt's body. If I had any chance of saving her, I had to soothe her soul back in place before—

It was too late. Ylva's essence slipped my grasp, out the gap I'd formed in her body. The death magic that remained shook as though angry. Like it held all their agony and rage and now had nowhere to channel it. It lashed out with a massive push.

I landed hard on my back, only just managing to keep my head up. Fresh blood gushed from my wounds, soaking the dirt and bone shards below me. I rolled over, biting my lip so I wouldn't give in to the urge to scream. I sought out Rosamund instinctively and found her shifted back to her human form on the other side of the clearing. The bone wolf's body had collapsed between us. Even as I watched, the body began to disintegrate. Fur fell away as skin melted off the skeletal base. The death magic consumed what it could, and then, with a great shudder, it bled out in dark globs over the floor of the Bone Forest.

The Forest soaked it up like rain.

I wanted to collapse and rest my aching body, but it was still Samhain. The specter might have interrupted the ritual, but the clearing was full of angry spirits to calm and ghosts to help move on. I struggled to my feet. I wished that Yuyan, the flower witch of my entourage and our trusted healer, was here. But it was just me, the other senior bone witches, and the senior bone familiars. We'd have to tend to our wounds ourselves—once we dealt with the threat of the dead.

I took several unsteady steps, going slowly until I was sure my legs would hold me, then strode the rest of the way to where Rosamund still lay prone. My heart was in my throat, until I saw that she was awake—eyes fixed upon the place where her grandmother's body had disappeared. I reached out, and she let me help her stand. Together, we turned upon the spirits attacking the rest of our classmates.

Though Rosamund and I weren't bonded, touching her gave me a surge of energy. I didn't want to think about how compatible we were. It might have meant something before she'd torn apart my courtship necklace and thrown it at me. I'd gathered the pieces of that broken necklace and kept them. From the aching across the top of my thigh, I was sure they'd left a dozen little bruises from where I'd rolled over them during the fight against Rosamund's feral grandmother and the specter she'd become.

I'd always prided myself on logic over emotion, and tonight would be no different. No matter the pain I still felt over Rosamund's rejection, she was here now and I owed it to my classmates to use her offered help. She shifted into a bone wolf, and I anchored myself with a hand in her ruff. I lifted the other hand toward the remaining spirits and, pulling on Rosamund's intrinsic magic as a bone familiar and my own innate skills as a bone witch, settled them back into ghosts. I was strong enough to force a spirit to dissipate, especially with Rosamund anchoring me, but my people deserved dignity in death. If they'd lingered as a ghost, they'd held some unfinished business in their hearts strong enough that they'd felt they couldn't pass on without it being heard. I would give them the power to tell it to us and allow them to fade of their own accord.

Once all the spirits were calmed, I instructed my classmates to split into pairs and begin talking with the hundred or so ghosts scattered around the clearing. Rosamund and I made our own rounds. I was in my final year of schooling at Witch Hall—I'd trained for years on how to help a ghost move on. I barely had to pay attention as I listened to their stories, making mental notes about the ones with messages I'd have to try to bring back to various family members.

My lethargy sputtered at the sight of one of our classmates. Guanyu Cosho, born Guanyu Sun, was a flower familiar in our grade who'd been killed when Vinlander terrorists attacked the market at Multah. I hadn't been there, hadn't even had the chance to try to save him. I didn't know if that was better or worse. Rosamund had, and I could see the guilt weigh heavy on her shoulders as Guanyu told us his story.

Rosamund promised to give Guanyu's witch his final message, and like all ghosts without lasting business, Guanyu began to fade into motes of light.

"Will you grant me a favor too, Princess?" he asked, his translucent form already half gone.

"If it's within my power, it's yours," I said, the rote line given to every ghost. It felt less rote in the face of someone I'd spent the last six years of my life learning beside.

Guanyu smiled, and it was a vicious little thing. For just a moment, I understood why Shantie Cosho had been so enamored.

"Then, avenge me," he said.

I didn't hesitate before promising. War with Vinland was a terrifying prospect, but I refused to allow more of my classmates to be slaughtered so needlessly. Not while I had strength left to stand before them.

"Me too, Shaw," Rosamund said, once the last of Guanyu's light had faded. "I'll help get justice for Guanyu. I have to help."

I remembered how distraught Rosamund had been after Guanyu's death. How she'd floated like one of the dead herself, only barely clinging to existence.

Now it was as if someone had lit a spark under her. She'd finally woken from the half state she'd been in from the moment she'd come back from the Market Day fire. Even her anger the day she'd broken our courtship and run away from school couldn't compare to the fervor of her words now.

"I spent six years being afraid of myself, of my wolf," Rosamund told me. "Of the weapon I could become in the army's hands. But I don't care about that anymore. I won't be their weapon, but I will be yours."

I waited for the elation. I had finally won, hadn't I? Wasn't this what I'd wanted? The whole reason I'd tested Rosamund and Charles and all the other bone familiars last term? I was prophesied to lead us through the coming war. I needed to use everything and *everyone* at my disposal.

All I felt was cold. "I never wanted a weapon," I said, only just realizing it was true. "I wanted a partner."

Something broke in Rosamund's expression. Like her eyes were mirrors that had shattered and now reflected only fractal beings.

"I can't be your queen, Shaw," she said, too gentle. Gentle enough to make it hurt all the worse. "I won't rule this kingdom with you. I can't give you that. But I will make sure you live to rule it. We don't need a bond to work together, to fight together. Tonight proved that. So, let me be your weapon. Use me to win this war. And when we've won—because we must win—when the war is over, you'll gift me a ranch, like your grandmother did for mine. I'll raise horses and you'll find a familiar who can rule beside you. And that will be our victory."

I reached down and felt the outline of moonstone bones in my pocket, caressing those pieces of a broken promise. Why did her words hurt so badly? I'd known she wasn't going to be mine, hadn't

I? She'd run away as soon as the whispers of war became rumblings. I needed a familiar strong enough to stand beside me through it all.

But no, she wasn't refusing to stand with me in war. She was refusing to stand with me after. To be more than a tool to use and discard. To be the queen I knew she could be, if she'd only let herself.

The ice around my heart grew cold enough to burn. I wished I could believe I would win this war without Rosamund, but I couldn't. A bone wolf familiar? One I could pull energy from without a bond? I had to use her. I had to keep her close.

I had to harden my heart against this pain. To swallow down the disappointment and push forward. I would lead alone, against the might of an enemy so strong it seemed unfathomable that we could even beat them. That was my destiny. I'd always known it to be. I never should have believed any different.

Two of the final ghosts left in the clearing were Rosamund's own grandparents. Ylva Holt, known as Ylva the Red Wolf for her ferocity on the battlefield during my own grandmother's great war. And General Otto Holt, once my grandmother's top military advisor and the head of the Royal Company. He'd retired when I was still a young girl and died in a freak accident not long after I'd entered my first year at Witch Hall. I remember regretting that I'd never gotten the chance to meet him.

Now Rosamund's grandparents floated a few inches off the ground next to the back of the giant pine that made up the heart of the Bone Forest. Like most ghosts, they looked younger than they would have when they'd died. They held hands. Ylva was visibly delighted to be reunited with her husband after so many years. Otto seemed equally as besotted. I ruthlessly squashed the stirring of emotion that tried to rise just looking at them.

I cleared my throat. "If you're both ready, I'm sure Rosamund will be happy to take any final messages back to your family."

I was ready to be done with this whole wretched night. I needed to rest. Needed to bury my emotions in sleep and wake up with a clearer head and a harder heart. First though, I would need to get food and water and, above all, healing. The wounds on my back still hadn't clotted completely, and a fresh wave of blood streamed down every time I moved. I was uncomfortably wet, sticky, and sore.

"Rosy knows what to tell our family, I'm not worried about that," Otto was saying when I forced my attention back to him. "It's you we have a message for. If you're ready for it. We'll wait as long as you need."

That was enough to refocus me. "You can't linger. If your guilt consumes you—"

"Whatever guilt or regret I carry from my life is my burden to bear," Ylva said, a touch of the wolf's growl in her throat even now.

"We will do our duty," Otto said. "This is no easy thing to hear, and you've had a long night."

I had never turned from my own duty, and I wouldn't do so now. No matter their words, they needed to move on. It wasn't good for ghosts to linger. Every moment they risked devolving into spirits. I could already see the fracturing instabilities in their translucent forms, like thin cracks in a vase waiting for a single tumble to shatter wide.

"What is it?" I asked. "What message do you have for me?"

He met my gaze. The besotted husband was gone now, replaced by the war-hardened General Holt. I instinctively straightened. "Six years ago, I was murdered for the crime of knowledge. I'm sorry to tell you this, Princess, but the anti-magic protests in Vinland are no coincidence. This war was planned, deliberately, for years."

Rosamund stepped in close, drawing my attention. She looked suddenly anxious—as if this scared her more than having to break my heart. I nearly choked on my bitterness at the thought.

"Shaw, maybe not tonight," she said. "Tomorrow, you can summon them again."

"No," I replied, curter than I'd normally be. I was past caring. General Holt was dead, and ghosts couldn't lie to bone witches. He must truly believe that he was murdered to keep this secret. He must be certain that someone had sabotaged the relationship between the Cursed Kingdom and our northern neighbor. I said as much aloud, watching the general's face for any signs of uncertainty.

"Shaw—" Rosamund tried again.

My mind was racing, grasping on to the many implications of the general's words. "This is important, Rosamund. Don't you see? If we can prove the war was instigated maliciously, then we can take that evidence to Vinland. We can stop this war before it truly begins. We can save so many lives."

I was prophesied to lead my kingdom in war, but it did not have to be this one. Vinland was our strongest neighbor. To have to fend off the tens of thousands they could call to arms was a price I would not wish upon my people, even to see my destiny finally fulfilled. The idea that someone may have purposefully sparked this conflict, despite all we stood to lose, was infuriating.

Rosamund visibly bit back her protests. She nodded. "Okay. I'm with you, Shaw. I told you that. I'll fight for you. Whether to win a war, or to stop one."

Fight for me, but not with me. Be my weapon, but not my partner.

So be it. I turned to General Holt and demanded he tell me everything he knew.

General Holt beckoned us to follow him. We retreated farther into the heart of the Bone Forest, circling the massive pine at the center to hide away from the curious eyes of my classmates. The Forest began to sing, some strange amalgamation of noises that nonetheless came together into a chilling song. I shivered, and the wounds on my back protested fiercely.

"It began several years before my death, but so slowly I nearly didn't notice," General Holt started. "Only later did I realize I was no longer being invited to every meeting. One of my own thanes had the king's ear, and the king began to turn to them over even my own advice. I knew it was worse than I'd suspected when the king promoted that thane to general of the Royal Company and encouraged me to go home to my Ylva and our children and grandchildren, despite my personal expertise with war."

"Are you implying General Tepeh instigated this war against Vinland?" I asked, hardly believing my ears. General Kiwa Tepeh was the glass witch of my father's entourage—of course they had the king's ear. That was the whole point of the entourage system. It may have made more sense to keep an experienced general in charge of the Royal Company with the prophecy of my coming war, but just because my father had promoted General Tepeh early that didn't mean there was malicious intent behind it.

General Holt merely shook his head. "It was your father who ordered me killed, Princess," he said. His tone was soft, as if that could lessen the blow of his words. Apparently that was where Rosamund had learned it from. It wasn't any easier, coming from him.

All my cautious interest disappeared in an instant. Ghosts couldn't lie to bone witches, but that didn't mean they always told the truth. The disappointment of realizing that my hopes for stopping this war with Vinland had been laid at the feet of a paranoid dead man was hard to swallow.

I'd always reverted to a blank expression when upset—a byproduct of growing up in court—and this was no different. Yet somehow, General Holt seemed to read something on my face.

"I finally found proof, a few days before I was murdered," he continued, speaking faster now. "A map of Vinland, with the first targets already marked. I've been watching over my granddaughters for these past six years. I was there, at Witch Hall, when the village burned down across the river. The same village I once saw on that map, marked with a red circle. There can be no denying it now. Your father was the one who initiated this conflict."

Perhaps I was meant to feel something from his revelation, but all I felt was exhausted. That so-called evidence was circumstantial at best. A map of the villages that had been burned might be suspicious, but my father was an ice witch. It wasn't out of the realm of possibility that he foresaw the fires. He could have even foreseen that the fires would spark unrest in Vinland, leading to a rise of anti-magical sentiment and the brewing conflict we now had.

"You said he murdered you," I said. "How?"

"He insisted upon an escort home. I rarely needed one, but the Mountain was restless." General Holt shook his head. "The avalanche was human-made though. The men who'd come to take me home were well clear when the snow came down. I watched them after, as a ghost. They didn't even try to dig me out."

I nodded, but inwardly I wanted to shake my head. Negligence on the part of the soldiers, but that didn't mean my father had given the orders.

But still, there was something about General Holt's story that nagged at me. While I could believe most of it was the paranoid delusions of an old man being encouraged to retire—one whose accidental demise came as a relief to his soldiers—the idea of that map bothered me. If my father did know that the Vinland fires would spark enough unrest for this war, why not tell me before now? Before the Market Day fire that had killed Guanyu and a hundred other innocent citizens?

"Thank you," I told General Holt, and I forced myself to mean it. "I'll take your words to heart."

"The Witch King is ruthless," Ylva said. "Don't let sentiment stop you from doing what needs to be done, girl."

"I won't," I replied, and I meant that too. Just not in the way she wanted me to.

"Shaw," Rosamund murmured. "What does this mean?"

A few weeks ago, I might have told her. But Rosamund was not my familiar, and I had no obligation to tell her anything. "I'll inform you when I know more," I said. "You should say your last goodbyes." Her grandparents were already beginning to fade into light.

I slipped around the gigantic pine to check on the rest of my classmates. The Forest's song reached a crescendo. In the distance, a pack of wild bone wolves howled to match it.

I'd always had the luxury of knowing what my future held. Here, on the precipice of that destiny, I wanted to shake myself for falling into the belief that I could stop it. It was fanciful to let myself hope, even for a moment. I couldn't afford to give in to those kinds of childish desires, not when any hesitancy might cost the life of another of my classmates. Everyone in this clearing had signed up to fight this war with me. I had a duty to them to see it through.

Chapter 2

The Bone Forest was kind to us. After the final ghost disappeared into light, the bone pines at the edge of the clearing opened up to reveal a bubbling creek. We were able to clean our wounds and bandage them before collapsing into sleep.

In the morning, once we were up and fed, the Forest opened another path straight north. I whispered a thank-you to the nearest tree. If the Forest wanted, it could have led us on a winding journey. Bone witches and familiars like us were better at navigating the Forest's foggy maze than the average person, but even we were at the mercy of its strongest whims. Some three months ago, the Forest had trapped me and my entourage inside a clearing with a rampaging bull moose. I knew now that it had contrived to find a way to bring Rosamund Holt to my attention, but at the time, I'd been thrown by the apparent aggression.

Rosamund was a wolf familiar—the strongest anchor for bone magic. The Forest knew me, perhaps even trusted me, but it loved Rosamund. I watched as Rosamund asked the great pine at the heart of the Forest to please corral the herd of horses that had been let loose to distract the specter the night prior. The wind picked up, using the voices of visitors come and gone to give its agreement.

"She treats the Forest like a pet," Jingyi said to Chao, close enough for me to overhear. There was nothing but awe and respect in Jingyi's voice. I glanced out of the corner of my eye in time to see Chao nod, his eyes fixed on Rosamund.

A few weeks ago, I would have puffed up with pride. Chao was the heir to Jarl Hu—herself the bone familiar of my father's royal entourage. Chao Hu and his familiar were important figures to have on my side for the efficacy of my future rule. Their approval of Rosamund had been a blessing when I was courting her. Now it felt like salt rubbed in my badly bandaged wounds.

"Saddle up!" I called to my classmates. "We ride for Gravestown."

Rosamund left the massive pine and came to my side. "I'm coming with you. My parents are already in Gravestown selling the rest of our herd. I'll explain the situation to them, then I'll be free to come back to school."

I hadn't even considered the fact that Rosamund would expect to be allowed to return to Witch Hall after having fled before taking her finals last term. But of course, I couldn't use her as a weapon if she was on the other side of the kingdom.

I would deal with that problem later. For now, Rosamund's presence in our party solved a more immediate problem. "I know you have your shifts, but I need someone to ride Pyre."

Pyre had been Madam Dyer's bone horse. A beautiful sorrel mare that got along surprisingly well with my own horse, Cow. Bone horses did not take kindly to being pulled along on a lead. They didn't always take well to riders either, but I knew Rosamund was experienced enough to handle her.

With Madam Dyer dead, I hoped whoever she deeded Pyre to was willing and able to take in the bone horse. Pyre was all we had left of our former teacher. Madam Dyer's body had been gone when we woke up, but I hadn't been surprised by that. The Forest was built on death, and therefore the dead sustained it.

Rosamund went to find Pyre's saddle amid the pile of belongings that had survived the previous night. I followed to fetch Cow's, and within the half hour, we were on the road.

It was just past noon when we exited the pines onto the cobblestone streets of Gravestown. The high sun shone down on us as we traversed the bustling town to the large manor at the northern end. The pine-wood houses carried the same subtle vanilla scent that permeated the Forest itself. It would have given the illusion that the town was just a continuation of the Forest, if not for the difference in trees. The pines planted along the roads of Gravestown were inert—their branches did not contort into skeletal arms like the bone pines we had left behind.

Gravestown's various inhabitants stopped and stared as we rode past, no doubt because of our bedraggled appearance. I kept Cow's nose pointed north and did my best to ignore them. Them and Rosamund, who'd rode at Cow's heels throughout the entire journey. I might have asked her to keep watch over the back of the party if I hadn't known that Cow would try to kick any other horse who dared get as close as Pyre was.

Charles Almstedt had migrated to the front next to Rosamund by the time we made it to his mother's manor. The jarl of Gravestown was one of the most powerful people in the entire kingdom, and it showed in the intricately painted columns and elegantly carved arches of her expansive residence. A few soldiers stood guard outside the front door. They were dressed in the typical brown military uniform, Gravestown's crest sewn over the right breast. I stared at the embroidered stag, half listening as Charles demanded one of the soldiers go fetch his mother and the other get the stablehands to take the horses. Unlike Jarl Almstedt, Charles didn't officially have authority to command the soldiers of Gravestown's Company, but that didn't stop them from snapping to attention and doing as told.

The stablehands arrived first. I dismounted and didn't pay attention to who I was about to hand Cow's reins off to until I heard Rosamund exclaim, "Mama? Papa?"

"Rosy, baby," Rosamund's father said, rushing forward. Rosamund's mother was just a step behind him.

Rosamund's parents helped her off Pyre. Her mother was a deft hand with bone horses. She didn't flinch as Pyre tried to bite her and instead yanked on the reins to chide the mare. Mother and daughter had the same button nose, short stature, and curve to their smile. In contrast, Rosamund's father was a tall man, but she had inherited his thin blond locks and the shape of his chin. Glancing between the two of them, I could almost picture how Rosamund would look in a few decades.

"Jarl Almstedt was kind enough to offer us both positions," Rosamund's father was explaining.

"We planned to return for you and Ma and the horses on our allotted rest day," her mother continued.

Part of me wondered why they'd moved to Gravestown. The ranch Rosamund's family had in the village of Forest's Edge was bigger than anything they'd find in a city like this. The larger part of me couldn't care less. Rosamund's family was not mine to worry over, not anymore.

"Gran—" Rosamund said. Her voice broke. "Something happened while you were gone," she tried again. "And Gran—she—"

I stopped listening, distracted by the arrival of Charles's mother.

Jarl Almstedt's hair was the same striking red as her son's and tied together in an elegant updo. She was dressed in some of her finest clothing—the kind usually reserved for my father's court.

"There you are," she said brusquely. "I was waiting at the side gate." That was directed at her son. He looked sheepish, as if he'd been told many times to come through there instead of the main entrance. I felt a twinge of guilt that I hadn't asked, but didn't bother lingering over it. I stepped forward instead, and Jarl Almstedt redirected her attention to me. "Your father warned me you were coming with wounded," she said. "I've called the flower witches. Leave my son and his classmates to me, Princess. Your father awaits you in the blue antechamber."

It seemed I would have a chance to ask my questions sooner than I'd anticipated. Ice witches always knew when visitors were approaching their home. Jarl Almstedt's manor wasn't my father's home, but he was powerful enough at foresight that it didn't surprise me to learn he'd seen us coming regardless.

One of the soldiers beckoned me to follow. I handed Cow's reins to Rosamund and refused to glance back when she snapped my name. Even if she was mad at me for ignoring her, I knew she would take care of my horse.

The blue antechamber was an ornate room directly off the jarl's great hall. I'd been there before, but not in years. The soldier led me to a set of doors guarded by two more soldiers—these ones wearing the three-eyed raven crest given to those in the Royal Company. I vaguely recognized the woman on the left and gave her a nod of greeting. She bowed back before opening the door to allow me to enter.

My father was inside, but he wasn't alone. His entire entourage was present. Jarl Agalax Alki stood at his right shoulder, arms crossed and scowling at the far wall. Jarl Biyu Hu and her witch, Bao, sat on the couch opposite my father's chosen chair. General Kiwa Tepeh sat in the matching chair.

"Shaw," my father greeted me, and there was relief in his voice as he looked me over.

Though he would never dare show weakness in front of the larger court, his entourage was a different story. All rulers of the Cursed Kingdom were expected to form an entourage of advisors out of the other magical types. My own entourage had become my closest friends. I missed them fiercely. If Aklemin, Einar, and Yuyan had been able to join me on Samhain, we wouldn't have struggled nearly so much with the specter and the spirits it had created. Even though none of them were bone witches by design, their help would have been invaluable.

"Your visions must have been terrible if you asked your entourage to travel with you to check on me," I said.

I only realized my mistake after Jarl Alki snorted in derision. "Did you forget what day it was, Princess?" the flower witch asked.

Oh, of course. It was the day after Samhain. The jarls' council would meet tonight, just as they did after each of the cardinal holidays. Since Samhain was about bone magic, the meeting after always took place in Gravestown. After the council meeting, my father would preside over court here in Jarl Almstedt's manor for a full week—allowing select citizens of the kingdom to bring their concerns before the Witch King and his jarls.

"Come, my dear, sit. You must be exhausted after your ordeal," my father said. "Agalax, my daughter is wounded."

Jarl Alki stepped around the Witch King to approach me. I sat at the edge of the only open chair and tried not to flinch as he put his hands on my back. As a powerful flower witch, Jarl Alki had the power to heal injuries by touch. He'd been my primary physician growing up. But even as a child, I'd never been comfortable with his hands on me. That had less to do with his bearing toward me, for he'd always been a strict professional when I needed healing, and more to do with my suspicions about his treatment of his only child. I never could prove anything and Aklemin refused to say a word against their father, but I knew enough to worry nonetheless.

I glanced at the Witch King. I'd brought my worries to him once, sure that an ice witch of his strength would have foreseen it if Jarl Alki was, in fact, abusing his heir. But my father had seen nothing. I was sure that was only because of how much he trusted Jarl Alki. Ice magic was guided by questions. My father didn't *want* to ask the right ones, not when it would bring such a horrible truth to light about one of his own. Not when his entourage had already dwindled so much.

In truth, it had been my mother's entourage originally. She was the one with royal blood. The one who'd chosen my father as her witch and future co-ruler. He'd been a refugee from the Colonies with no standing in our kingdom at all. It was only later, once everyone had realized just how strong of an ice witch he was, that the grumblings had subsided.

Per tradition, my mother had put together an entourage of familiars first. She'd been an ice familiar, of course. Aklemin's mother had come on as the flower familiar, Jarl Hu as bone, and General Tepeh's former familiar for glass. A series of misfortunes had cut down that original entourage. General Tepeh's familiar had been the first. I'd never even met the man. Both he and General Tepeh had entered into the army together, but he'd died in a border skirmish some two years in. My own mother had been next, dead due to complications from my birth. Five years later, Aklemin's mother had abandoned us. Shifted into a fish and splashed into the river on a routine visit to Multah's docks—never to return. I wasn't sure if my suspicions about Jarl Alki began before or after that. If, in his familiar's absence, Jarl Alki had turned his anger on his remaining family member, or if that anger had sparked because of her abandonment.

Only Jarl Hu remained of my mother's original entourage, and as my father was the sole ruler of the kingdom now, the group had come to be known as his.

As much as I would rather not admit it, Jarl Alki's healing was effective. The massive scrapes along my back began to itch. I kept myself still out of sheer determination until the worst of the itching faded. Jarl Alki retreated to my father's side, and I leaned against the back of the chair in relief. I knew that if I looked, only thin scratches would be left of the once-gaping wounds. I would need to eat soon, and sleep, to make up for the energy taken by the healing, but first I had questions to ask my father.

My father was watching me when I looked back over. He had his chin propped on his fist, leaning just slightly to the left. Relaxed. More relaxed even than I could remember him ever being in front of others. What did he mean to portray? Was it meant for me, or for his entourage?

"My daughter and I need to talk," the Witch King said. "We'll reconvene later to prepare for the council meeting."

My father's entourage stood to leave.

"Chao should be with the rest of our classmates," I told Jarl Hu and her witch before they reached the door. "We wouldn't have survived without him. He's become a powerful necromancer."

"Thank you for saying so, Princess," Bao murmured.

"When you've had a chance to rest, we would love to hear the story of what happened over Samhain from your perspective," Jarl Hu added.

"I'm sure the whole council would," General Tepeh added. "Perhaps it can be added to the agenda tonight, Agalax?"

Jarl Alki nodded. "With your permission, David."

"Add it," the Witch King said.

That meant I had to make myself presentable before the council meeting. I wished I was comfortable enough with my father's entourage to be able to groan in front of them. I couldn't though. I knew that my grandmother's entourage had practically helped to raise my mother, but my father had kept me mostly separate from his entourage growing up. Maybe it was because of how coldly my grandmother's entourage had treated him, or maybe it was to encourage my own independence, but either way the result was the same. I respected my father's entourage, Jarl Alki included, for the work that they did, but I always felt an overwhelming need to prove myself in front of them.

Only after the entourage was gone, the servants cleared out, and the guards had closed the door to the antechamber did I relax my shoulders to mimic my father's posture.

"I am proud of you for how you handled the specter," my father said.

"You saw it?"

"I was able to watch pieces in my scrying glass. I haven't met that bone familiar fighting with you, so it wasn't as clear as I would have liked."

That made sense. Ice witches always had stronger foresight surrounding those they actually knew. Even a single meeting would be enough for my father to have a taste of Rosamund, but his visions would be clearer the longer he interacted with her. He obviously knew me well enough to have crystal-clear visions of my life, when he took the time and energy to ask his magic for them.

"And after, Father? When we talked with the ghosts?" I pressed, wondering if he'd seen the conversation with General Holt.

There was a pause. "No. You know that bone magic does not interact well with ice magic."

I shouldn't have asked. I did know that. Ice witches were completely unable to see or hear ghosts—not in visions, dreams, or scrying spells. The specter must have been just alive enough to be visible, but he would have lost sight as soon as I'd ripped the ghosts out of the wolf's body. "Yes, of course. Excuse me, I'm tired."

"Excused, my dear, but you should find time to rest before the council meeting. It wouldn't do for the jarls not to see your best."

"I know, Father. I have a question for you first. If you have time."

"Always, for you."

I hadn't been able to come up with a good way to broach the subject despite thinking on it throughout the entire ride. I knew the pause went on too long as I scrambled to think of the best wording, but my father waited patiently. He was always a patient man, especially when it came to me.

"I spoke with General Holt's ghost," I finally said. "He claims you knew about the war with Vinland."

"Ah," the Witch King said. He pulled his chin off his hand and straightened in his seat. "I'm surprised his ghost stuck around so long without devolving into a spirit. He was quite angry before his death."

"He seems to believe he was being manipulated. That you and General Tepeh forced his early retirement. That you removed him from meetings and planning sessions."

The Witch King shook his head. "Oh, no, we would have happily welcomed his voice on the generals' council, even without an active posting, as all retired generals are afforded. He was less enthused by the prospect. He never did like how your mother and I preferred to rule the kingdom. Too used to your grandmother's way."

I knew what my father was doing. Diverting the topic. Trying to distract me from the original question. Was there truth to what General Holt had said after all? I hardened my tone. "Father, did you know that Vinland would attack us?"

My father closed his eyes. When he opened them again, he looked tired. I'd never realized before how much he was aging. The gray at his temples had become more pronounced since the last time I'd seen him.

"Yes, my dear, I knew," the Witch King said. "Vinland was *always* your destiny."

"Then why—" My voice cracked. I cleared my throat, trying to calm my suddenly erratic heart. "Why not tell me?"

"Would you have wanted to know? You were already so young when you found out about the prophecy. I wished to spare you any further expectations until you grew into yourself. Into your power."

"But—" I didn't know what I was protesting. The future? I knew very well I couldn't change it. If my father said it was inevitable, then it was. He'd never been wrong before. "The Empire of Vinland will destroy us."

"They might," my father agreed. "But they might not. You are strong enough to face them, my dear, and so is our kingdom. Kiwa and I have done our best to prepare for it. Biyu and Bao and Agalax as well. We are behind you. You do not face this threat alone."

I pressed down on my temples. My head felt overly full. I needed rest badly, but I couldn't just let this go. Not now. "Did you tell General Holt that?"

"We meant to tell no one, but he discovered it on his own. He was determined to share it with the kingdom. No matter the ramifications of panicking our citizens six years before it was even relevant."

I blinked hard to clear my eyes, then looked up at my father. I hadn't thought it was true, but— "You did have him killed."

The Witch King inclined his head. "He was a threat. Any chance we have of defeating Vinland disappeared if he was allowed to reveal what he had discovered. I did try to explain so to him, out of respect for your grandmother, but he would not listen. We had no choice but to nullify the threat. Kiwa insisted we do it humanely. That we allow the man to keep his status as a war hero, instead of trying him for treason. It's simply unfortunate that his wife reacted as she did upon his death."

"She never recovered," I said. "And it killed her."

My father frowned, just slightly. For him, it was practically a grimace. "I thought I recognized her wolf form as the body of that specter. I would not have chosen that end for even my worst enemy."

The lingering guilt I felt at not being able to save Ylva returned. "Me neither," I murmured.

"I know this is upsetting, my dear," my father said. Unlike Rosamund and General Holt, he did not try to say it gently. It was a statement, not a plea. Acknowledging my feelings without expecting anything from me.

I inhaled, exhaled, and then did it again. It took a few more times before I felt calm enough to set aside my feelings and think through what I'd learned rationally.

"I hate that he had to die like that," I said. "But I understand your reasoning. I do wish you had let me know what kind of threat Vinland was before the Multah fire."

I watched my father's pupils dilate. Unlike my breathing exercises, the Witch King's silence was the result of visions. Whether they'd come on naturally after my words or because he'd asked his own magic to answer some question, I wasn't sure.

"Sometimes I still look at you and see the little girl who couldn't stop begging me for a horse of her own," he said finally. "Other times, I see the woman you've yet to become. I do you a disservice by not seeing who you are now. I am sorry, my dear. I should have told you. The tragedy at Multah was horrific, but we needed Vinland to make the first act of aggression. If not Multah, then Desertmouth. If not Desertmouth, then they may very well have found Witch Hall. There were so many possibilities, and none of them good."

I hated that. Hated his matter-of-fact belief that all those lives lost were necessary. "There was truly no other way?"

The Witch King shook his head. "War requires sacrifices. It always has, and it always will. I thought you too young to understand that, but I see now that I should have trusted you."

"Then trust me now," I said. "Tell me honestly, how much time do we have?"

"More time than we might and less than we should." The Witch King raised a hand, as if to ward off my coming protest. "You will have a chance to graduate before it truly begins, my dear. I can promise you that."

At least six months, then. Against all the horrible things I'd learned, that was something to hold on to.

Chapter 3

Though the Cursed Kingdom was a monarchy, many would argue that the true ruling power lay in the hands of the jarls' council. My father's voice held significant weight in council meetings, but all the kingdom's laws and regulations were voted on by the jarls themselves. The twenty jarls sitting before me controlled the towns and villages within the Cursed Kingdom. Even the royal palace sat inside a jarl's territory—though since that territory was ruled by Jarl Alki, my father had no reason to be concerned. I hadn't been aware of it as a child, but befriending Jarl Alki's heir was probably the single most important political move I'd ever made.

Standing before the council meeting that evening, I did my best to show no weakness as I began to explain the events of Samhain. Several of the jarls sitting in cushioned chairs along the large table at the center of the great hall had relatives among the bone witches and familiars who'd fought alongside me. Most notable were Jarl Almstedt—Charles's mother—and Jarl Hu—Chao's.

"As the esteemed council may be aware, Madam Moll Dyer took a group of bone witches and familiars on an expedition to the Bone Forest for Samhain," I began. "Though travel to the Bone Forest is an expected part of Witch Hall's curriculum during the fall break, this year it was decided that only the seniors would journey with her."

"Why?" Jarl Sandelie asked.

I knew I had to tread carefully. Jarl Sandelie's son was a powerful bone familiar in the year below mine. I wasn't sure if Jarl Sandelie would be mad his son didn't get to share in the glory, if it could be called that, of helping to defeat a specter—or relieved that he'd been far away from the danger.

"There was concern that this Samhain would be more difficult than previous because of the volume of restless dead expected after the Market Day fire," I said. "The youngest students didn't have the training to handle angry spirits. Those in their second-to-last year were asked to stay back on campus to help Misters Jostein and Tupso Voll lead a smaller Samhain circle while the seniors were sent to handle the hoard of ghosts and spirits we knew would be called to the Bone Forest."

Jarl Sandelie leaned back in his chair, seemingly satisfied by that answer. Jarl Tenas looked anything but. "How many of my people needed to be soothed?" he demanded. "How many were denied their peaceful rest because of those bastards?"

Jarl Tenas ruled over Multah—the largest and richest city in the kingdom—and was therefore one of the most powerful jarls on the council. He was also the jarl whose people had been slaughtered by the Vinlanders' attack. I wondered what he would have said about my father's earlier explanation. Multah or Desertmouth or Witch Hall. Those had been the options. There was no doubt Multah had the most resources to recover from something like the Market Day fire, but how many lives could have been saved if they'd been able to anticipate the attack?

Jarl Tenas's question was much more difficult to navigate than Jarl Sandelie's. He had an entire voting bloc of supporting jarls who all murmured their own anger at their leader's rightful upset.

"Let the princess explain what happened before you start demanding the details," Jarl Almstedt said. Charles's mother led the other largest voting bloc—the one that nearly always stood in opposition to Jarl Tenas's. The fights the two got into were infamous.

I cleared my throat before one of those fights could start. "The ritual began as expected. We were able to find the heart of the Bone Forest and, with its power, summoned a hundred ghosts into our ritual circle. I would estimate just about half were from Multah, though I don't have exact numbers, as I did not speak with all the ghosts personally. If you wish for a report, I will confer with my classmates and get back to you." Before any of the jarls could protest, I continued. "The complication began when we were attacked by a feral familiar."

The jarls did not stay quiet at that. Demands to tell them who and why and how echoed down from the arched ceiling of the great hall.

"Ylva Holt, whom this very council imprisoned in the Bone Forest some six years ago," I replied at large. "Denied human companionship or treatment for her grief-stricken rage, I can only assume she fell deeper into her wolf. Perhaps she saw us as intruding upon her territory, or perhaps we merely represented what she'd lost. Regardless of the cause, she attacked us. For reasons I cannot begin to fathom, Madam Dyer chose to curse her instead of merely subduing the threat. She was killed even as the curse took effect."

"But that would have turned it into a blood curse," Jarl Sandelie murmured, his face appropriately horrified.

"Yes," I said. "The blood curse consumed both Madam Dyer and the feral wolf familiar, as well as a nearby ghost. There three merged into one being. Into a specter."

Furious shouts rose from the council. Only my father and his entourage looked calm about my revelations. They must not have shared my father's scrying with the rest, then. Had Charles not had time to tell his mother either? Perhaps not. He'd been one of the more seriously injured. I wouldn't be surprised to learn that he'd been healed and fallen asleep immediately after.

Jarl Almstedt stood and turned to the Witch King. "We must send a party to the Bone Forest at once. If the specter is allowed to escape those pines and make its way here—"

"Calm yourself, Jarl Almstedt," my father said. "There is still more to my daughter's story."

I took my cue to carry on. "Having combined with a necromancer of Madam Dyer's power, the specter immediately forced all the ghosts we'd trapped to devolve into spirits. Chao Hu, with help from his familiar, Jingyi, worked to turn the spirits back to ghosts while I focused on the specter itself. Kalitan led a power-sharing ritual to aid him." This I directed to Kalitan's elder brother, Jarl Kwet. The youngest jarl at the table—only a few years older than I was—gave me a weak smile in return. I wondered if he, at least, had heard most of the story from his little sister already.

"Charles and Emma were instrumental in keeping the spirits at bay while my fellow witches worked," I continued, turning back to Jarl Almstedt.

She stared at me, as if trying to determine the validity of my words. I had nothing to hide. While Jarl Almstedt had high hopes for her son, she was still fond of her niece—a bone familiar in my year by the name of Emma Chambers, whose yapping dog shift had almost certainly done more to distract the spirits than Charles had. Jarl Almstedt finally retook her seat, apparently appeased.

"What of the specter?" That was Jarl Falk. Their daughter, Froya, was an ice familiar in my year, but they were one of a handful of jarls in the council who weren't magical. As a result, the other nonmagical jarls had formed the last voting bloc behind Jarl Falk. It was that small group that often became the tiebreaker on the many issues debated by Jarl Almstedt and Jarl Tenas.

I knew this would be the hardest part to say. How to explain the truly impressive magical feat I'd somehow accomplished, unbonded, without also explaining my unique connection to Rosamund? Or without sounding like I was lying to take all the credit?

I settled on the simplest version of the truth. "Ylva's granddaughter, Rosamund Holt, helped me get close enough to the specter that I could get my hands on it."

"How?" Jarl Snass snarled.

Jarl Snass was ruler of Rosamund's small town, though he rarely left his manor in its larger neighbor, Woodside. I wondered, a touch uncharitably, if he knew anything about the Holt family, despite them being obligated to pay tithes to him.

"She's a wolf familiar like her grandmother," I said. "And one with at least half a dozen other shifts. The specter was strong, but a wolf familiar of Rosamund's power is enough to subdue almost anything. She gave me the time I needed to rip apart the curse and release the souls trapped within the monster."

The jarls were silent at that. Several gave me visible once-overs, as if trying to see the evidence for that feat on my body. With Jarl Alki's healing, a quick wash, and a change of clothes, I knew there wasn't much.

"My dear, you truly have come into your own," the Witch King said. He stood from his makeshift throne to look across the council table, taking the time to meet eyes with each of the jarls. "I asked my daughter to come tell you of this experience with her own words, but I too watched it unfold. To have the power to unmake a specter while still so young . . . I admit I would have struggled to believe it if I hadn't seen it with my own eyes. I am so unbelievably proud of my heir. As I'm sure Jarl Hu, Jarl Almstedt, and Jarl Kwet are of theirs."

The effect my father's words had on the council was apparent. Several jarls applauded, as if I'd just put on a show.

"Might as well cheer now," said Jarl Tenas, one of the few who hadn't relaxed. "The real test will come soon enough. I hope you can bring that power down upon the Vinlanders, Princess."

"I will do what must be done to see our people safe," I replied, likely with a touch more bite than I should have. It wasn't that I didn't understand Jarl Tenas's concern, but I didn't need him questioning me in front of the entire council.

"There's time still," my father said soothingly. "Vinland is neck-deep in snow. It's no season to invade, on either side. We can increase patrols on the border and take the opportunity to prepare our army."

"There's not even six months until the seniors graduate. Most of the snow won't melt until then," Jarl Alki added.

"And Kiwa's going to lead the training for the students, won't they?" Jarl Hu said, referring to the army training I'd signed up for. That every senior except Rosamund had signed up for with me.

I watched as my father's entourage effortlessly manipulated the council. The rest of the jarls began to nod along. "Spring melt will give our scouts time to bring more news of Vinland's preparations so we can be ready to meet them," Jarl Falk said.

"And perhaps the princess will find herself a familiar to bond with in the meantime," Jarl Almstedt said meaningfully.

"Very well," Jarl Tenas said, though he obviously wasn't happy about the direction the council had taken. "Let her finish out her schooling, then. But you'd best make the most of these six months, Princess. We can't afford to have you turn your back on your destiny."

"I would never." I knew my tone was still too rough, but I didn't have the energy to cushion it. Jarl Tenas raised an eyebrow, but my father called for a vote before he could make any further remarks.

Unanimously, the council voted to wait until my graduation before addressing the articles of war. So there it was. Six months. Two more terms of Witch Hall, and then my graduation present would be a declaration of war between the Cursed Kingdom and the Empire of Vinland.

I SLEPT POORLY ON THE journey back to Witch Hall.

I'd grown up knowing I was destined to lead my people in war. As a child, I'd imagined battles where my entourage and I would sweep the enemy with our magics. I'd pictured all the accolades, the people who'd cheer my name as I came back glorious. I'd promised myself I'd do better than my grandmother. That I'd save my people from the hardship of the Crusades. There would be no decades-long war under my rule.

All those childish dreams had been shattered when word of the Market Day fire came to Witch Hall. War was not as fanciful as child's play would make it out to be. My nightmares were haunted by the fresh burns that melted Shantie's skin. By the deep slice that had nearly killed Rosamund. By the call of the dead, even hours away from Multah itself—so strong that I'd nearly taken Cow and ridden to the city to aid in the efforts to calm them.

In six months, my nightmares would become far more numerous. My father had said I was capable of beating Vinland, but I didn't fool myself into believing it would be easy. That I would be able to save everyone.

Rosamund wasn't helping my attempts at emotional regulation. It had been a week since Samhain, and even now, only a few hours' ride from Witch Hall, she kept trying to draw me aside to talk. I'd refused to let her no matter how many glares she gave me for it. Most of our classmates had noticed the tension and had taken to glancing between Rosamund and me—exchanging whispers when they thought I wasn't paying attention.

Worst of all, Charles had gone back to his old ways of standing just a little too close and making himself too readily available to my every anticipated desire. Obviously his mother had given him his own deadline. Six months before the kingdom was at war. Six months, then, for him to make himself invaluable enough to be chosen as my familiar. Provided he survived the war with me, he'd be crowned Familiar King and rule the kingdom at my side.

My heartbreak was still too raw to even consider it, and so I rode in silence until finally we arrived at the crossroads. To the right, it was half an hour's ride to Witch Hall. To the left, another two hours to Multah. I stopped Cow in the center of the fork and strained to feel any residue of the attack. I knew several circles of bone witches had planned to do Samhain rituals in Multah itself. Though a large portion of the ghosts had been called to the Bone

Forest during Samhain, those who'd lingered behind would have needed to be dealt with.

The rituals must have done their job. The lingering taste of death was gone from the air. If I hadn't known what occurred those few weeks prior, there would be no evidence of it now. Not from here, anyway.

The rest of my classmates waited, milling about despite how close we were to school. I couldn't decide if I was exasperated or touched by that. I made to turn Cow toward Witch Hall, when I caught sight of Rosamund. She'd faced Pyre in the direction of Multah, her grip on the reins so tight that I feared the leather might cut into her skin. Her face was in profile, but I could see how her pale skin had taken on an almost-greenish tint, like she was about to be sick.

For all of my nightmares, Rosamund had actually been in Multah during the attack. I knew it haunted her far more vividly.

"Go on," I said to the rest of our group, waving them in the direction of school. "We'll catch up."

Charles immediately scowled. "But—"

"Go," I repeated more firmly.

Charles visibly sulked, but he didn't argue any further. Farther ahead, I noticed Chao and Jingyi looking pleased. With the support they'd given Rosamund last term, they obviously hadn't been happy with the tension between us this past week. Kalitan and the other bone witches I'd grown up learning alongside nodded in easy agreement while the remaining bone familiars patted Charles on the back as if to say, *It's not your fault. How can you even compete?*

Rosamund Holt was a bone wolf, after all, and her place in the hierarchy of bone magic was absolute. She may have grown up on a poor ranch in a tiny town at the edge of the kingdom, but she had proven herself when she'd fought alongside us Samhain night. Not a single one of the students here would balk if I made Rosamund my queen, not even Charles. His mother might have words with him about it, but she knew the truth of his competition now. Even she wouldn't be angry if I passed up her son when a wolf familiar was on offer.

Not that a wolf familiar *was* on offer. No one else was aware that my courtship of Rosamund last term had been fake. Never mind that it had felt real to me, before the end. But it had ended and I wasn't the type to press where I wasn't wanted. No matter my own convoluted and bitter feelings on the matter.

I waited until my classmates had all started riding toward Witch Hall before nudging Cow closer to Pyre. "Rosamund," I said softly.

"I'm okay," Rosamund replied. It was so obvious a lie, I didn't bother refuting it. "Just . . . thinking of Shantie. Of Guanyu's final message."

Losing her bonded familiar had hurt Shantie more than all the burns on her skin combined. When she'd withdrawn from Witch Hall last term, she'd been practically catatonic with grief.

I had heard my father's explanations, but with the benefit of sleep and the nightmares that had come with it, I could admit to myself that they weren't truly satisfying. "My father knew the attack was coming," I murmured, soft enough that even the bone familiars riding away from us wouldn't be able to overhear. "Not the whole shape of it, perhaps, but enough."

That jolted Rosamund out of her stupor. She turned to stare at me. "What?"

I shook my head, preempting the demand for more. "I only want to explain this once. If Aklemin isn't too lazy to let the rest know we're coming, then the entourage should be waiting for us at school."

Rosamund frowned but didn't argue. She followed behind as I turned Cow toward Witch Hall.

My entourage was, indeed, waiting when we arrived at the school's stable. Though whether that was because Aklemin had told them, or because they'd heard the commotion of the others arriving ahead of us, I didn't know.

Twenty minutes later, we all sat at our usual table in the dining hall. Einar had carved runes on the underside that, when activated with glass magic, prevented any conversation happening at the table from being overheard or lip-read. He touched the runes at my nod, and I began the arduous task of explaining what had happened at Samhain for the second time. At least my entourage was an easier audience than the jarls, and I didn't have to be nearly so careful with my words.

There was a significant reaction at the reveal that Rosamund was actually a wolf familiar, especially from the newest member of my table. Toketie Holt, Rosamund's cousin, wasn't even part of my entourage, but she'd begun eating with us after Rosamund had been injured in the Market Day fire. Aklemin had gestured for her to join us for my explanation, which made me wonder if the ice witch was planning on offering her a courtship necklace soon. I'd almost expected to come back from fall break to one already sitting on her slender neck, but it was still bare.

Toketie's gasp caught Rosamund's attention. The cousins were sitting next to each other on the bench between Aklemin and me. Rosamund murmured something in Toketie's ear and the ice familiar quieted, but by her glower, she wasn't happy. Even without a touch of ice magic, I could foresee a long conversation in the cousins' futures.

The other side of our table had Yuyan Yao, Einar Ottosen,

and Einar's familiar, Oluk Blackwell. Unlike Toketie, Oluk wore a lovely necklace that Einar had inscribed with gold runes. He and Einar had begun courting last term, and he'd become a welcome voice in my entourage since. Our first official familiar, excluding my fake courtship of Rosamund, and now the only one. Oluk was wringing his hands, until Einar reached out to place his own large ones over his familiar's. Oluk clutched Einar's hand between his own, obviously calmed by the gesture.

"I'm sorry I didn't tell you all," Rosamund said. "I never told anyone. Gran made me promise to keep it a secret. She was drafted into the army because of her shift, back during the war against the Colonies. She didn't want the same thing to happen to me."

"It won't," I said. "I will not allow a draft. The only people who will fight in this coming war against Vinland will volunteer to do it."

Or be forced to by necessity of survival, if the Vinlanders crossed our border again. I tried not to think of that very real possibility.

"Those who do should be treated to proper wages and retirement options as well," Rosamund added quickly. I wasn't sure if the topic truly made her that heated, or if she was just glad for an excuse to turn the subject from her own duplicity.

"Yes, they should," I agreed. I made a mental note to bring it up with the jarls' council next time they met, over winter break. Not for the first time, I reflected that Rosamund would have made a great Familiar Queen. She cared so much and had absolutely no fear in sharing her opinions. I imagined her standing in front of the jarls' council debating some topic with Jarl Almstedt or Jarl Tenas.

Those thoughts weren't helpful. I needed to focus on the here and now.

I quickly explained the rest of what had happened. The more

important part for my entourage to know was what came after. I let Rosamund tell her cousin, with the rest of the table silently listening, about Ylva's death and the lingering ghost of their grandfather. Then I told my entourage what General Holt had revealed.

"My father confirmed it, at least in part," I said. "He did know the war was always meant to be against Vinland. He had General Holt killed when the man threatened to reveal the truth to the kingdom."

Toketie bowed her head, covering her face with her hands. Rosamund put an arm around her cousin, but her own face showed only anger.

"Why?" Yuyan exclaimed.

"He said it would have resulted in us losing the war," I said. "That the public didn't need to know until it was necessary. Until the Market Day fire."

"Then he knew about that? He knew all those people were going to die?" Oluk asked. He didn't sound as though he believed it.

I didn't want to believe it either, but it was the truth. "I won't let him get away with such a thing in the future. He has already promised not to hide things from me again."

Aklemin tilted their head at that. "He did?"

I paused, trying to remember that night. It was all a bit of a blur now. Hadn't he promised? I knew he'd expressed regret for not trusting me. "It was an implied promise, at least," I said. "I'll get a real one from him during winter break." For all his tendency to keep secrets, as all ice witches had, my father had never once broken a promise to me.

"And what if there's another attack beforehand?" Rosamund demanded.

"He said we had until the spring before things would truly

begin," I countered. "The jarls' council voted to discuss articles of war after our graduation."

"Oh good, what a thoughtful graduation present," Yuyan snapped. "Shaw, this is ridiculous. If your father knew Vinland was going to want to kill us, why couldn't he have done something to stop it in the last six years?"

"I don't know." I glanced at Aklemin. "He said it was inevitable."

My entourage went quiet at that. Most of what ice witches saw was mutable. Sometimes, very rarely, a thing was so unchangeable that it became known as prophecy. My war was one such prophecy. The war, I knew now, with Vinland.

Aklemin said nothing. They were looking off in the distance, seemingly unmoored from our conversation. I wondered, as I often did, what they were thinking about. We may have been friends for our entire lives, but I'd never been able to read them. I'd grown up learning to hide my emotions from court, but I had a suspicion that Aklemin had been forced to hide their emotions even in the comfort of their own home.

"What would you have us do?" Einar asked.

That was the question. "Finish our education. Learn everything we can from General Tepeh and the Royal Company. Figure out a way to win this war with as few casualties as possible. We *can* win. He may not have been working to stop it, but my father has been preparing for this war for years. We have a chance."

Even as I spoke, I felt myself grow more confident. I might not agree with how my father went about it, but I know he truly believed us capable of winning the war against Vinland. "My main goal is the safety of our people," I continued. "I don't want to wait for Vinland to invade us and risk more deaths like what happened in Multah. I will push the jarls to action as soon as I can."

Aklemin blinked a few times, jolting out of the trance they'd been in, and turned back to the table. "How?" they asked.

"That is what I'd like us all to figure out together," I said. "Let's see how General Tepeh organizes our Army Training and go from there."

No one looked fully satisfied at that, but they didn't argue. After a few more seconds, I gestured for Einar to deactivate the runes so that the rest of the tables at the dining hall didn't get suspicious. Taking my cue, Yuyan began to speculate about what classes we'd all have for the coming winter term. Oluk joined in, followed soon by Toketie—whose *nothing is wrong* mask impressed me, especially in the face of everything she'd just learned about her own family. No one looking over at our table now would be able to see a hint of her earlier upset.

In direct contrast to her cousin, Rosamund mashed at her food, visibly angry. Were we still courting, I'd take the chance to whisper some acknowledgment in her ear. Let her know we could talk later, just us, as we'd done so many times last term.

Weapons did not argue, and their wielders did not invite it. I turned away to engage Einar in conversation instead.

Chapter 4

My first class of the day, and therefore my first class of the winter term, was led by Mister Xian Xu and populated by all the senior bone and glass witches. The class subject was using bone magic to give power to wards laid down by glass witches—a highly experimental topic that Mister Xu said was a far more advanced field in his home country of Daming. We didn't do much that first day except talk through the plan for the term, but those plans had us buzzing with excitement by the time we walked out of the central longhouse.

Einar and I headed to where the second class of the morning would be held, followed by the rest of our classmates. All seniors were in the same course for the second morning block. It was held in one of the outdoor classrooms because that was the only space big enough to fit our entire year.

Halfway down the lawn, we were met by a group of senior bone and flower familiars. Jingyi was the first to bound up to us. She was dressed in the girls' school uniform today, hair loose down her back. She nodded once to me, then darted past to reach her witch. Chao gave her a casual kiss on the cheek in greeting.

"How was it?" I asked her.

I didn't immediately see Rosamund in the crowd, though at my request she had been allowed to stay a senior despite failing all her finals last term. Had the headmistress decided to drop her down a year after all?

Outside of the Friday workshops, all students in the same grade and of the same magical type and classification shared classes. According to Oluk's and Toketie's schedules, the senior glass and ice familiars would have just finished learning about organizational skills and spell management. Meanwhile, the bone and flower familiars were being taught how to perform rescue operations.

Flower familiars were often the first called to a scene, since their witches were healers. Bone witches and familiars typically arrived next, because we could sense death and needed to be on hand to help those who couldn't pass on peacefully. Additionally, bone familiars shifted into land mammals, which were overall more helpful than the aquatic shifts of flower familiars, or even the avian shifts of ice familiars and reptilian shifts of glass familiars. I didn't know all of Rosamund's shifts, but I knew she had wolf, horse, mouse, raccoon, and badger. Five animals that could be used in different circumstances during a rescue. Or in war.

"They started teaching us how to dig through rubble without causing it to collapse," Jingyi told me. "Some of the soldiers were helping instruct. Guess they have more experience than Madam Ipsoot at that type of thing."

I wondered what Rosamund had thought of that. Her distaste for the army was clear. Even though she'd agreed to help me fight, she still refused to sign the contract the rest of us had. We weren't officially part of the army yet, but we'd promised several years of service once we graduated. I only hoped that I could finish this war with Vinland in that time period. I did not want to lose as many years—or as many people—to war as my grandmother had.

Rosamund finally turned the corner of the eastern longhouse and jogged up to us. "Sorry, the soldiers wanted to give me a recruitment pitch," she said once she reached my side.

"That's what you get for showing off during class," Jingyi retorted, obviously teasing. "Your wolf really is impressive, you know."

Rosamund looked uncomfortable. After how long she'd hid her wolf, I could only imagine how she was feeling about it being so public.

My hand migrated inside the left pocket of my school dress. I'd placed the moonstones there, as I'd done every morning since Rosamund ran away last term. It had taken close to an hour to find all those iridescent stones carved into bones. They'd scattered when Rosamund had thrown the necklace at my face. Each piece was worth a hefty amount of money, but that wasn't the reason I'd kept them. They were meant to be a reminder.

I didn't even know what I wished to remind myself of anymore.

Aklemin and Yuyan were waiting for us with the rest of the senior ice and flower witches when we arrived at the classroom clearing. I sat down on the log next to Aklemin, leaving space for Rosamund to my right. It was shocking how quickly making space for her had become natural last term. So natural that I still did it, even though there was no reason I should.

It wasn't long before the ice and glass familiars joined us. Interestingly, Toketie sat next to Aklemin instead of on Rosamund's other side. Oluk sat between Einar and Yuyan. I was surprised, and glad, to see the rest of our classmates sitting in mixed groups. Not just witches with witches and familiars with familiars or bone students with bone and ice with ice. It hadn't been like this last year, even in our combined classes, but it seemed that bringing the three familiars to my table had opened the doors to more intermixing among the rest of the school. My fake courtship with Rosamund might have ended horribly, but at least it had sparked that one needed change.

Madam Kawak stepped into the classroom clearing only a few seconds after the last student found their seat. The headmistress of Witch Hall was dressed in dark blue, only a shade darker than the color of my royal house. The pale blue shawl wrapped around her waist served as a reminder of her status as an ice witch, much like the differently colored belts required by our school uniforms did. She'd let her white hair fall loose around her shoulders that morning. It softened her features compared to her usual bun or braid.

"I only allow myself to teach two classes a year, though in truth I prefer teaching to the administrative tasks that come with running this institution," Madam Kawak began, almost melancholy. "I hope that most of you remember your first summer here at Witch Hall and my Introduction to Magic?"

I nodded alongside most of the rest of the class. Though I had entered Witch Hall early enough to do the full eight years, I still remembered Madam Kawak's class well. It hadn't taught me anything new, but her manner of teaching had always struck me. Besides, I'd had private tutors since before I could walk, and schooling at Witch Hall hadn't diverged from what they had taught me until my fifth year.

Few of my classmates had entered school as young as I had, but they'd all been required to take Introduction to Magic their first summer at Witch Hall—whenever that happened to be. The earliest a witch or familiar was allowed to enter into schooling was ten years old, but many didn't manifest their magic until eleven or twelve. As such, the first three years of Witch Hall were all introductory, with students allowed to freely enroll into the second or third year without needing to do any catch-up.

It was only starting in fourth year that students could begin to fail out of Witch Hall's curriculum. A good half usually had by the time a cohort reached their eighth and final year—their senior year. My class was unusual. We'd be one of the largest to graduate once we finished the coming spring term. There'd been a few to fail early on, but many who would have been expected to purely because of the circumstances of their birth—Oluk Blackwell and Toketie Holt among them—had made it through to our senior year. Now I couldn't imagine completing my schooling without every single one of them.

"This course is a continuation of that," Madam Kawak was saying. "A bookend, if you will. In this class, we will begin the end of your time here by looking at the bigger picture of what it means to be witches and familiars." Madam Kawak met my eyes. I wondered what she saw in the stars, these days. "This class is titled Special Topics in Magic. It is about our way of life as witches and familiars. We will discuss spells and rituals, but we will also look at the way others have treated us, historically, because of our magic and the ways we have responded. Shall we begin?"

I dug into my bag for a notebook and graphite stick. My tutors had taught me plenty about magical theory growing up, and I'd learned even more in my last few years at Witch Hall, but I was interested to see what Madam Kawak had to say. The coming war with Vinland had been sparked through a building of anti-magical sentiment across the border. The same rhetoric is what caused the Colonies to attempt to wipe our kingdom off the map during my grandmother's war. If there was something the headmistress could teach me that would prevent the tragedy of my grandmother's war from being repeated in my own, I would learn it. With not even a full six months until graduation, I had to make the most of my remaining classes at Witch Hall.

I LET MY FRIENDS WALK in front of me on our way to that first afternoon of Army Training. I'd always admired General Tepeh the most out of all my father's entourage. They'd been young to the appointment, but then, so had General Holt once. I could learn a lot from them. I *needed* to learn a lot from them, if I had any hope of commanding the Cursed Kingdom's army to victory.

The army was split into companies, each officially led by the jarls. In reality, most jarls were not soldiers. Instead, they appointed a general to command their company, and the general appointed thanes to act as officers over the company's platoons. During times of peace, the soldiers within those platoons were guards and servicemen for the jarls to use. In war, the generals and their soldiers acted under direction of the Royal Company.

Though officially led by the royal family, the general of the Royal Company was a power on their own, and General Tepeh had transformed the Royal Company after they were given command of it. Slowly but surely they'd increased the number of witches and familiars in each platoon until the whole company was a magically fortified force.

General Tepeh now stood in the center of a group of thanes at the far end of the outdoor classroom where the training would take place. There were four thanes total, two on either side. Like

General Tepeh, three had black stripes down their military-brown pants, showing they were witches. The final one had the white stripes of a familiar. I wondered if there were any thanes left in the Royal Company who weren't magical.

My entourage paused at the entrance of the classroom clearing, looking back at me. All of them—my fellow witches, and the two familiars we'd gained. Only Rosamund was absent. I wished, somewhat unfairly, that she'd signed the contract after all. How could I use a weapon I couldn't even train with?

I stepped around Einar and led the group to the set of logs that made up the front row. I always sat in the front of my classes. I had gotten into the habit my first year of school when I'd realized I made my classmates uncomfortable and self-aware. They concentrated less when I was behind them. Only my entourage had gotten used to me enough that I could hang back and observe from the rear, like I preferred. Even Oluk and Toketie had been good about it, taking cues from the witches.

Rosamund never walked in front of me, even when I wanted her to. She never walked behind me either, even when courtesy would demand it—except for that one week where she'd been like a ghost, just after the Market Day fire, when she'd trailed after me like a shadow. Were she here now, she would be directly at my side.

I focused on the soldiers in front of me. "Good afternoon, General. Thanes."

"Princess," General Tepeh replied. "Will you introduce me to your entourage?"

"Of course, General Tepeh. You know Aklemin Alki, Agalax's heir. They are the ice witch of my entourage."

General Tepeh smiled. "Wonderful to see you, Aklemin. And who is this lovely lady next to you?"

I paused at that, not sure how to explain when I didn't even fully understand Toketie's presence myself.

Aklemin stepped in, putting a proprietary arm around Toketie's shoulders. "This is Toketie Holt," they said.

My inability to read Aklemin struck again. I didn't know if they were interested, truly interested, in Toketie. But if they weren't, they were making everyone think they were. It was more than just an arm around her shoulders. It was the way they had their head tilted ever so slightly in her direction. How their shoulders twisted to nestle against hers. It was all too deliberate to be an unconscious gesture, especially not from Aklemin.

Toketie's attraction to Aklemin had always been obvious, but I'd never seen her push herself on them. Not like Charles had with me. And yet, once Toketie had joined us last term, the ice witch had given her plenty of room to do so. Had deliberately opened up a space at our table so that Toketie would sit between them and Rosamund. Had taken to partnering with Toketie in their shared classes, from the rumors I'd heard. Yuyan had teased Aklemin about their blooming affection a few times, when the familiars hadn't been present.

I wasn't sure how Rosamund would react to the idea of her cousin bonding with a member of my entourage. She hadn't approved of Einar and Oluk initially, though she'd tried her best to hide it. But she'd done nothing to stop Aklemin and Toketie's growing closeness.

Unless this was all as fake as my courtship to Rosamund had been. If so, I just hoped Aklemin had talked to Toketie beforehand. The two of them were toeing a delicate line, without a necklace at Toketie's neck.

"I remember you, Miss Holt," General Tepeh said. "We talked

about your experience with supply logistics. I believe you're interested in the duties of our company's quartermaster?"

"Yes, sir," Toketie said, curtsying and dislodging Aklemin's arm from her shoulders in the process.

Aklemin's hand found her elbow, and they gently pulled her out of the curtsy. A moment of possessiveness? Or just an act, to sell the show? Sometimes I wished I could read minds, if only to know what went on in Aklemin's.

I cleared my throat, drawing the general's attention back to me. "Sir, may I also introduce Yuyan Yao, my flower witch. The tall one here is Einar Ottosen, my glass witch, and the familiar he's courting, Oluk Blackwell."

"A pleasure," General Tepeh said as the rest of my entourage bowed and curtsied. As they straightened, the general gestured us to our seats with a polite, "It looks like everyone has arrived."

I sat and my entourage followed. The general was right—all the logs had filled with the other students who'd signed the contract. No one under sixteen had been allowed, but plenty of sixteen-year-olds had signed up. Which meant it was more than just the seniors in the clearing. I caught sight of Jarl Sandelie's son and, next to him, the twins. Of course, they weren't actually twins but half siblings—a bone witch and familiar who held the most sway over the year below mine. I wondered how Mister Xu felt about his children being contracted to military service after he'd fled Daming for their protection.

General Tepeh looked over the gathered students and quirked a smile. "I thought to make some speech about duty. About our responsibility, as witches and familiars of the Cursed Kingdom, to guard this sanctuary of magic against the force who'd seek to destroy it. But I can tell I don't need to. You are all here because you already understand that duty. So instead, let's waste no time. I would like you to divide yourselves into four groups. The first, those interested in combat. You'll be learning under Thane Anders."

The only familiar of the thanes crossed his arms over his red thane sash. "Don't join me unless you mean it. Unless fighting's in your blood. There's plenty of work the army needs, and we can't afford deadweight on the front lines."

General Tepeh nodded. "To that end, the flower witches of the group may join Thane Beck to learn how to be an army medic. Even if you're stronger at potion making than active healing magic, you'll be much needed."

The thane to the left waved. He was heavily scarred, even more so than Toketie, with a whole chunk of his upper lip missing, but his smile was kind. "Should any other students here wish to learn the necessary skills to save the lives of the wounded, especially any flower familiars, you are more than welcome to join me as well. Anyone can stitch a wound with the proper tools and training."

General Tepeh acknowledged Thane Beck's inclusion, then said, "Thane Olhiyu will take those of you interested in intelligence work. A good scout can save an entire unit."

The youngest thane in the group inclined her head. She didn't speak, but the way her eyes roamed our group made me strangely wary. This was the same woman I'd vaguely recognized guarding the blue antechamber at Jarl Almstedt's manor. She hadn't been wearing a thane's red sash then. Had she only just been promoted, or was there a different reason she'd been chosen for guard duty that day? All I knew was that the thane in charge of the Royal Company's intelligence operations was not to be underestimated.

General Tepeh continued. "Thane Huang will take those interested in logistics. It takes a lot of hands to supply an army. Cooks.

Quartermasters. Glass witches interested in helping enchant better shields and swords and armor. She'll find a place for any of you."

The final thane smiled at Toketie, likely to acknowledge what the general had said about her potential to become a quartermaster. It was a valuable role, and I was impressed by Toketie's ambition to strive for it. I hadn't thought much of Toketie before last term, but despite the bitterness that welled within me at the idea that one of my entourage might bond with a Holt when I hadn't been granted the same privilege, I had no reason to tell Aklemin that Toketie was a poor choice for the entourage.

"As for me, I will train those of you with an aptitude for command," General Tepeh said. "I may pull any of you aside from any of the sections. We need squad leaders gifted in healing and logistics, as much as in combat and intelligence. You may make it known to your thane that you are interested in a command role, but you may not demand one. We do not have time to make mistakes with ill-suited officers. Is that understood?"

"Yes, sir!" the clearing echoed.

"Good." With a small gesture, the four thanes spread out. "Make your selection, though be warned we may move you if we find your abilities lie elsewhere. Remember, every position is important, every role deserving. We will only succeed if we all work as one whole. Now go."

I stood and turned to my entourage. "Einar?"

"I'll go with Toketie to logistics. I'm interested in the types of enchantments they use," he said, then looked to Oluk.

Oluk looked between Thane Anders and Olhiyu. "I'm not terrible at combat, but I was one of the best in Madam Bai's stealth class last year."

"I'll join you," Aklemin said, and left it at that.

Logistics and intelligence. Both valuable roles for members of my entourage to be represented in. "Yuyan, healing?"

"Yeah," she said. No surprise there.

"Then I will join Thane Anders for combat," I said.

"If you'll pardon me for interrupting," General Tepeh said. I'd noticed them watching us but had tried not to be bothered by it.

"Yes, sir?" I asked.

"You'll be joining me, Princess." The general raised a dark eyebrow. "Or did you not think I would take you for command?"

"I'm not afraid of proving my worth."

"You've done so plenty, most recently on Samhain."

"Yes, sir," I murmured, hoping the flush of pride that rushed through me wasn't visible.

I had wanted a member of my entourage in each of the sections, but I spotted Charles, Chao, and Jingyi stepping up to Thane Anders's combat group. Between them, I'd be able to pry for information. I would need to know what they were learning to be able to properly command them, after all.

"Then let us begin," General Tepeh said, and motioned me to follow them, away from the others.

"If I may, General?" I said as I fell into step beside them. "Will we get the chance to work together as a group? I know that specialized platoons do not always interact, but in wartime there needs to be cohesion in a company, doesn't there?"

"There should," General Tepeh acknowledged. "However, your classmates will have to find that cohesion in their assignments once they graduate."

"How do you mean?"

General Tepeh glanced sideways at me. We were out of the

clearing now and passing through the outer layer of the encampment the Royal Company had set up in the woods west of campus. "This way," they said instead of answering, and led me to a tent in the center of the camp.

We entered through the open tent flap, but General Tepeh was quick to close it behind us. I looked around. The tent was only just big enough to fit the large table in its center, a map of the Cursed Kingdom and its neighbors spread across it.

"This is the command tent," General Tepeh said. "We will have most of our sessions in here."

I turned to them, unwilling to be distracted from my earlier query. "I had assumed all the students who signed the contract would be placed within the Royal Company."

"They would have been," General Tepeh agreed. "The jarls' council, however, did not agree. With war looming so close, many jarls have requested that their heirs be allowed to join their home companies."

The implications were obvious. "They mean to give their heirs safe assignments and leave the other soldiers to die on the front lines."

General Tepeh inclined their head. "That was my assumption as well."

"And the other graduates? Why not put them all in the Royal Company?" I demanded.

"It was argued that a division of fresh blood was fairer," General Tepeh said. "In truth, I don't disagree. It will be easier for your classmates to learn among more experienced members of the army."

General Tepeh might not, but I definitely disagreed. How was I to keep the rest of my classmates safe if they were split among the twenty-one companies of the Cursed Kingdom? Would I hear later one had died in some distant battle, like Guanyu had? Furthermore, could I be guaranteed the jarls would put their full support behind the Royal Company, if they had no personal stake in its success? My entourage and I would be at the forefront of this war, just as my grandmother and her entourage had been, and it was easy to see how poorly that had gone. So few heirs had fought alongside my grandmother. The jarls had berated her for taking so long, for letting so many people die, without implementing any policies to actually help. Maybe the jarls with towns on the borders had, like Jarl Tenas's mother and the now-elderly jarl of Desertmouth, but the rest? When conflict arises, people too often turn to their own selfish interests.

My father had done a lot to win power back from the jarls' council in his time as Witch King, but all that would fall away once the war truly began. I needed the heirs on my side, *at* my side, along with the rest of our year group. Politics aside, I knew my classmates best. Knew what I could expect from them. Knew they would listen to my commands, where older soldiers might balk if they thought themselves more experienced than a freshly graduated eighteen-year-old witch, prophesied leader or not.

"Give us a chance to prove ourselves as a group," I said, only just keeping the plea out of my voice. "I can get the heirs to convince their parents otherwise if you give *me* the chance to show them the benefit of working directly under my command."

General Tepeh looked over the map on the table, obviously thinking through my proposal. "This Friday, we will be showing you all a mock company march. I will allow you to lead your classmates for this exercise, Princess, and we'll see how it goes before discussing this more."

"Thank you," I said. I made a note to make sure all my classmates had been properly trained in marching in formation beforehand. "We won't disappoint you."

General Tepeh moved around the table instead of responding. They took out a box of painted army units and scattered them over the map. "Come, let's discuss strategy."

I stepped up to the table to join them.

Chapter 5

ROSY

By the second day of classes, Rosy wanted to yell at her past self. If only she hadn't run away from school before finals last term, maybe she wouldn't be stuck in remedial classes all afternoon. At least she was still considered a senior, though a probationary one. Her morning classes with her fellow seniors were the highlight of her day. But then, after lunch, every single other senior went off to Army Training, and instead of being given a free period to study, she was stuck in classes with much younger students. All of whom stared at her like she was some newly sculpted statue in the center of the courtyard, made to be gawked at.

It was a relief to slip away after her final Tuesday class to the comfort of stable duty with Oluk.

"You could always sign the army contract," Oluk said when Rosy complained as they walked to dinner. "Then you'll be with us in the afternoons instead."

Rosy hesitated. Gran had wanted so badly for her to not tie her life to the army, but Rosy had promised to fight at Shaw's side and she'd meant it. She'd been a coward when she'd failed to save Guanyu, but she wasn't going to run away anymore. What did signing the contract matter now? Wouldn't she have to, in the end? Would she even be allowed to fight alongside Shaw without officially enlisting?

"Should I sign the contract?" Rosy asked as she sat down between Shaw and Toketie. "Would it be better if I did?"

Shaw tapped on the side of her soup bowl, and Rosy watched as Einar swiped at the runes carved into the bottom of the table. In seconds, the students who'd been eavesdropping on their conversation had turned away to talk among themselves—successfully distracted by the magic of Einar's spell.

"Don't sign up," Shaw said once their privacy was ensured.

"I could join the combat group," Rosy argued, since earlier that week Shaw had mused on which of their classmates she could most trust to report on the specific training that group was receiving. "It would be easier than asking the others for information."

Shaw visibly hesitated, which was unlike her. Another knot twisted itself into Rosy's gut. She wasn't sure where she stood with Shaw anymore. She hadn't realized just how much Shaw had opened up to her until she'd closed the doors. It wasn't that Shaw was freezing her out completely, but she also wasn't making space for Rosy the way she used to.

"Maybe next term," Shaw said finally. "I'm trying to prove something to General Tepeh, and I think your presence may weaken my case."

What did that even mean? Last term, Shaw would have told Rosy exactly what she was trying to prove to General Tepeh. Now she kept it close to her chest, even in front of her entourage. It made Rosy wonder how much Shaw had ever shared with her friends before Rosy and Oluk had started sitting at their table.

Rosy was still trying to figure out if she was relieved or

disappointed not to join Army Training when Shaw moved the conversation to the event happening that night.

Rosy wanted to groan at the reminder. Every full moon, the school held a massive assembly. There were competitions run by the teachers called feats, and visitors would come to assess what students they might want to offer jobs to upon graduation. Maybe the assemblies would have been fun if Rosy had done six or seven years of schooling here, but as an almost-eighteen-year-old, they were torture.

"There are always more jarls at assemblies during the winter and spring terms. We need to use that," Shaw said. "We *need* the jarls' support when the war begins."

"Why wouldn't you have their support?" Rosy asked, confused. "It's their kingdom too."

"If only politics were so simple, Miss Rosy," Aklemin said, a touch less airily than they'd normally be.

"How can we help?" Einar asked Shaw.

"I need the jarls to respect me," she replied. "As my entourage, you represent me. I need you to stand out at your feats. Don't enter ones you aren't sure you can win."

"What if a teacher requires it?" Oluk asked. Rosy figured he was thinking of Madam Xu, who'd forced them to do a number of feats last term for Advanced Shapeshifting and their Combat workshops.

"Then you do your absolute best," Shaw replied, voice hard enough that Rosy worried it would send Oluk into a nervous spiral.

Except Oluk seemed to take strength from her command. He pulled away from where he'd been leaning into Einar's side and nodded sharply.

"I have faith in all of you," Shaw continued. "When you win, be gracious to our classmates. Make sure to congratulate them on their own successes. Show the jarls that you are all leaders. Can you do that for me?"

"We will," Einar said.

Yuyan folded her arms in front of her chest. "You act like we weren't doing that already. Well, I suppose *some of us* weren't." She raised an eyebrow at Aklemin.

Aklemin groaned dramatically. "Slander, Yuyan. Absolute slander."

"Is it slander if it's true?"

Toketie leaned over to whisper in Rosy's ear as Yuyan and Aklemin began to bicker. "Do you think she means me too?"

It was a good question. Neither Rosy nor Toketie was officially part of Shaw's entourage, but they were both sitting at the table anyway. Last term, Rosy had allowed Shaw to pretend to court her because Shaw had asked for an opportunity to keep the other familiars at arm's length while she finished up the school year—to give her time to truly decide who she wanted to rule beside. And then Shaw made it clear the one she'd chosen was *Rosy*, and everything had fallen apart.

Rosy wasn't going to be Shaw's familiar, but she was aware what it looked like to the other students. She was aware of what the jarls would assume when she showed up at the assembly at Shaw's side. If she told everyone that she wasn't going to bond with Shaw, they'd start questioning what she was doing at Shaw's table. But the thought of separating herself from Shaw made all the voices in Rosy's heart cry out in protest. None of them wanted her to leave—not her wolf or horse or even her newest badger voice.

Rosy needed to stay. To keep Shaw safe and, with her, keep their classmates alive. She imagined Toketie being separated from her in the conflicts to come and nearly choked on her own breath at the terror that flooded her. No, she wouldn't leave Shaw's table unless Shaw demanded it of her, no matter what it implied.

Perhaps Rosy merely represented who Shaw's entourage *might* be. Even when they eventually went their separate ways, Rosy hoped that Shaw would bond with a familiar who'd be strong enough to hold their own. If Rosy could help pave the way for that familiar, she'd do it. And just like Rosy's presence, it meant something to people that Toketie was sitting at this table. The thing was, Rosy was pretty sure Toketie wanted what it meant far more than Rosy did.

"You're here, aren't you?" Rosy whispered back, deliberately looking from her to Aklemin.

Toketie glanced at Aklemin too. "Oh."

Her cousin was better at this kind of political subtext. She understood what Rosy had meant, what her own presence at the table meant. Rosy was close enough to see the way a blush darkened Toketie's sepia-brown cheeks.

Once, Rosy would have hated the thought of her cousin bonding with the ice witch, but she didn't want to diminish Toketie's choice. If Toketie wanted Aklemin and Aklemin wanted Toketie, then she wouldn't say anything against it. It was almost better to believe that Toketie had hitched herself to Shaw's entourage because of Aklemin and not because of Rosy. If it were the other way around and Toketie got hurt because of her proximity to Shaw, then Rosy wasn't sure she'd ever be able to forgive herself.

Not that it should matter. The whole point of her being Shaw's weapon was to prevent that happening in the first place.

They finished up dinner and headed out as a group to the assembly, but it wasn't long before they were all going their separate ways. As Shaw had predicted, there were half a dozen jarls wandering around the school grounds, observing the various feats. General Tepeh and their thanes were there too, though that was hardly a surprise.

Rosy ended up competing in one of Madam Xu's favorite feats—a competition over how quickly a familiar could shift. Charles's mother, Jarl Almstedt, was there watching with a smile that got smugger every time her son moved up the bracket. Shaw stood next to the jarl, nodding politely as the proud mother talked up Charles's accomplishments. Charles was a strong familiar, there was no denying it, and Jarl Almstedt obviously wanted to see him become Familiar King.

Rosy had shifted into her horse for the first couple rounds mostly out of habit—she'd pretended the horse was her first shift last term. But just before the quarterfinals, Shaw caught her eyes and gave her a meaningful look.

Rosy hadn't ever won this feat. She'd made it to the finals against Jingyi a couple assemblies prior only because Charles had been on page duty at the time. But she'd been competing at a disadvantage. Most familiars were fastest with their first shift, and Rosy had been hiding her wolf.

Her opponent in the quarterfinals was Froya Falk, an ice familiar with an eagle shift and Toketie's supposed best friend. Rosy wasn't sure she liked Froya no matter Toketie's insistence that she was *actually really nice and clever, Rosy, just give her a chance*. Part of Rosy wanted to use one of her other shifts, just to prove that she could beat Froya regardless. Still, Froya was the heir to Jarl Falk. Rosy didn't care about politics. The biggest reason she knew she'd make a terrible Familiar Queen was *because* she didn't care about politics. But if playing a little bit of politics meant Shaw had power to end the coming war as quickly as possible—and survive to rule after—then Rosy had to try. She had no idea if Jarl Falk was one of the jarls visiting Witch Hall tonight, but just in case, it would mean something for Rosy to show that she didn't underestimate Froya.

So when Madam Xu called for them to begin, Rosy reached inside her heart for her oldest voice. The wolf rose up to meet her, and she let it reshape her bones without hesitation. She sat like a dog after, ears perked up, and watched as Froya finished growing feathers.

"Winner, Miss Rosamund!" Madam Xu called.

The usual polite applause was intermingled with whispers and hushed exclamations. Those who hadn't heard about what happened over Samhain were now getting told the story by their more informed classmates. Rosy despaired at the thought of the renewed gawking she'd get during her afternoon classes tomorrow.

Jingyi ended up facing Charles in the quarterfinals, and it was close enough that Madam Xu had to call for a do-over three times, but eventually Charles emerged victorious. Rosy tried her best to keep a grimace off her face. She really didn't want Shaw to choose Charles as her familiar. He was better now than he used to be, but he was still a pretentious piece of work. Let him take over for his mom as a jarl and work with Shaw's entourage politically, but don't make him a king. Shaw needed a better partner than that if she wanted to lead the Cursed Kingdom to a brighter future.

Rosy ended up against a glass familiar by the name of Shugh in the semifinals. He had a snake shift like Oluk. Oluk had decided not to enter this feat, and Rosy could tell that had been a good choice by how quickly Shugh grew scales. It wouldn't have been a great comparison for Oluk, though Oluk's rattlesnake shift was more prestigious than Shugh's glass hognose.

Rosy's wolf won. She stayed in the form long enough to watch Charles handily beat the flower familiar he'd been up against before shifting back. The crowd around the field had grown significantly in the last few rounds. Rosy stood across from Charles for the final round and waited for his typical sneer to come.

It never did. Instead, Charles bowed. A little startled, Rosy bowed in return.

"Begin!" Madam Xu called.

Rosy didn't bother getting up from her bow. She put both hands on the ground to make it easier to turn four-legged, and called the wolf back.

The shift came over her faster than it ever had before. Several times last term, the wolf had begged to come out to challenge Charles, and Rosy had been forced to turn to a different voice to avoid giving away her secret. Now it took the chance to prove its dominance. Bones snapped, fur sprouted, and skin stretched in the time it took to blink.

By the time Charles finished growing the antlers on his stag, Rosy was crouched like a predator stalking its prey, ready to pounce. Charles bleated in shock and quickly shifted back to human. Rosy internally shook away the wolf's instincts and rose up out of the crouch. She let her tongue loll out, as if she'd just been playing.

"Final victory for Miss Rosamund Holt!" Madam Xu announced.

The applause that came was overwhelming to the wolf's ears. Rosy shifted to save herself and was relieved when Shaw jumped over the ropes to her side.

"Good job," Shaw murmured. "Now I just need to smooth things over with Jarl Almstedt."

Rosy frowned. "Was it too much? You said—"

"No, you did perfectly. That little display was exactly what I needed. Go ahead and watch the others compete. I think Yuyan has a feat next. I'll find you later."

Rosy resisted the urge to sigh. She *really* didn't get politics. "Good luck." And she left, to do as she was told.

INSTEAD OF NORMAL CLASSES, FRIDAYS had what Witch Hall called specialty workshops. Those were classes that took up two full blocks, one across the entire morning, and one in the afternoon. Rosy had been confused when she'd seen Intermediate Shapeshifting listed as her morning workshop—she'd been in Advanced Shapeshifting last term—until she went to ask Madam Xu about it and learned what her role would be in the class.

"You never did provide me proof for your senior project," Madam Xu scolded her as they talked outside the library Wednesday afternoon.

Rosy winced. She knew most seniors had made significant headway or even completed their required graduation projects. Between coming to school a term late and leaving a week early, she was horribly behind. Her idea was about helping familiars with only one shift figure out their second. She'd refined her theory about emotional connections to include proximity to the source magic—the Bone Forest for bone familiars, or the Obsidian Desert for glass, and so on. And she had an example to prove it. Guanyu had been able to find his second shift after their adventure in Lake Bloom. But then Guanyu had been murdered by Vinlander terrorists and everything had spiraled out of her control and she'd fled school before she could even take her finals, much less discuss her project with Madam Xu.

She explained as much to the teacher, unable to look Madam Xu in the eye as she stuttered out what had happened.

"Calm yourself, child," Madam Xu said, more gently than Rosy thought she deserved. "Madam Kawak agreed to push you through as a senior despite the end of last term. I am pleased to hear that you have a working theory, but I was prepared to work with you regardless. You are in Intermediate Shapeshifting as my assistant. Test this theory of yours and let us see if we can't improve upon education for familiars. I daresay getting them a second shift may even save a life by the end of all this."

Rosy thought of Toketie, stuck only with a swan shift. She was gorgeous in that form, there was no doubt, but the swan was hardly maneuverable in a fight. If Toketie had something like a songbird to switch between, it could indeed save her life.

It was with that in mind that Rosy tackled her first Intermediate Shapeshifting workshop as Madam Xu's assistant. Madam Xu gave her the floor to explain her theory. The class had a huge number of students—essentially every upper-year familiar who hadn't found a second shift yet. Rosy did her best not to stumble over her words as she laid out her theory. Step one was figuring out what it was that had drawn the familiar to their first shift. What aspect of their animal voice called to them most. Then, using that connection, step two was finding an animal that fulfilled a similar role. Once the prep work was done, if the familiar was still unable to shift, then they could draw upon the magic of the cursed lands that would help push the shift through.

"But doesn't that mean we can't do anything here?" Froya asked, frowning at Rosy from the front row of logs. Toketie, sitting next to her, nodded along with Froya's comment. "If we have to be on the Frozen Mountain to find our second shift, what is the point of this workshop?"

"It would be easier for you if you were on the Mountain, but it's also possible to find your second voice off of it," Rosy clarified.

After she'd had her conversation with Madam Xu, she'd asked every student from last term's Advanced Shapeshifting workshop where they were when they found their second shift. As she'd suspected, a good three-fourths of them had been in the land associated with their magic. Oluk had found his rattlesnake during the school trip to the Desert last summer, Charles while on a ride in the Forest, Kwaddis while swimming in the Lake, and so forth. But some hadn't. Lei had been nowhere near the Lake when she'd found her second shift, but upon prodding, she'd admitted that she had been thinking about the hermit crab she'd accidentally stepped on last time she'd visited Multah for Beltane and how it had pinched her toe in retaliation. And those with a third shift were even less likely to need the magical lands. A good half of the Advanced Shapeshifting group had found a third or fourth shift while at school last term.

"The key is to remember all the animals you've encountered there," Rosy continued. "Every one of you has taken school trips to the source of your magic. So think about those trips. What animals did you see? What were they doing? Once you've established your connection to your first shift, you can begin figuring out what draws you to the other animals you've encountered. And if that doesn't work, then you'll know what to look for the next time you visit that land."

Madam Xu took over, instructing the class to take out paper and write down their reflections. Once the class got started, Madam Xu pulled Rosy aside to discuss a lesson plan for the rest of the term.

"It's a start," Madam Xu said once they were done. "If your theory holds true, Miss Rosamund, it will be a huge leap forward. I hope you are proud of yourself and your accomplishments."

Rosy shrugged. She'd be proud after it worked.

She walked with Toketie to lunch after Madam Xu released the workshop. Rosy had everyone's reflections stuffed into her bag to look over. Luckily, she had a free period after lunch. Apparently there was no remedial workshop to put her in on Friday afternoons, which was a relief.

"Froya—" Toketie said, then stopped.

"I'm not Froya," Rosy said, rolling her eyes. "If you want to go sit with your friends today, you can. You don't need to be with us every meal." Last term, Rosy had alternated between sitting just with Oluk or sitting with Shaw's entourage. It was different now that Einar was courting Oluk, but sometimes she missed those quiet lunches.

"No, it's not that. It's just, while you and Madam Xu were talking, Froya asked me about your wolf shift. Emma jumped in before I could say anything, telling everyone about what you did at Samhain. Not that most hadn't heard the story already."

Emma Chambers was one of the senior bone familiars. Rosy had made a point of finally learning all their names, after she'd stubbornly refused to last term. Emma was a large girl with a disproportionately small dog shift—one of those little hunting dogs that chased prey up trees and yapped at them until the hunter caught up. She was boisterous and one of the few bone familiars who dared to tease Charles despite his prickly nature. Rosy hadn't spent much time with her, but the moments she had were enjoyable. She thought that she and Emma might have become fast friends if Rosy had come to Witch Hall after the first time she'd shifted, instead of hiding her wolf and training with Gran in the Bone Forest.

"I am sorry I never told you about my wolf," Rosy said. She didn't feel bad about concealing it from the rest of the school, but hiding that part of herself from her family had always hurt. Rosy's gaze was drawn to Toketie's scars—the raised scrapes that ran from her chin down her shoulder and her arm. "I was worried," she admitted. "Gran made me promise not to tell anyone, but I think I would have told you eventually. Except, I was worried you'd be scared of me too."

Toketie stopped and pulled Rosy under the awning of one of the longhouses, out of the way of the rest of the students headed to lunch. "I was never scared of Gran," she murmured. "Not like you're thinking. I avoided her because I knew it hurt her to be near me. I just didn't know why, not until the princess told us what Pops said."

Rosy frowned. "What do you mean?"

"What do I smell like to you? When you shift, what scent do I carry the strongest?"

Toketie always smelled like winter. Even when she was human, she carried around the distinct smell of frost on the air, like most strong ice familiars did.

Rosy thought about what that would mean to Gran, to smell ice magic on her granddaughter. "Oh."

Toketie nodded. "Now that I know the truth about what the Witch King did to Pops, I can't blame her for it. You know they've done studies on familiars who panic-shift? It wouldn't have happened if the swan wasn't already there, just under the surface. I was a late bloomer, so it was always going to take something to force my body to make that first change, but I think the smell of the shift must have begun nestling in my skin beforehand."

Rosy finished for her. "And when Gran smelled it, all she could remember was Pops and the Mountain and the supposed avalanche."

"I never blamed her," Toketie repeated. "But it's nice to finally have an explanation."

Maybe Toketie didn't blame Gran, but Rosy could still see the grief she carried in the tenseness of her shoulders and the way she had her arms wrapped around her middle. For the first time in years, Rosy remembered that Gran had always been Toketie's favorite, growing up. Over Pops. Over her brother or her parents. When Rosy and Toketie were finished playing and Rosy had gone to beg Pops for a story, Toketie had always headed straight to Gran. A hot pang of grief filled Rosy's throat, making it hard to breathe.

"Gran loved you," Rosy choked out, then swallowed harshly to clear it. "She always asked how you were doing, every time I went to visit. I'm not a good bone familiar, Tokey, not in this. I could guess what message she wanted me to give Mama and Uncle Inge and Solemie, but I don't know what to say to you. Just—she did love you. And she missed you. She never blamed you for staying away."

Toketie sniffed and rubbed at her eyes. "Not a good bone familiar, you say. Shut up and go to lunch, Rosy, before you make me cry."

At lunch, Shaw stayed unusually quiet as the rest of the table talked about some large exercise they'd be doing in Army Training. Rosy kept glancing over at her, wondering what she was thinking about. She wanted to ask, but when she opened her mouth to do so, Shaw very deliberately turned her shoulders away. Taking the hint, Rosy went back to her food.

That afternoon, after Shaw and the entourage headed off to

Army Training, Rosy began to comb through the reflections. Shaw needed a partner. That was what she'd said on Samhain, hadn't she? Rosy couldn't be that person for her, but surely someone could? Who among the bone familiars would be a good partner for the future Witch Queen? Who would be willing to press Shaw when she got lost in her own thoughts? Not Charles, that was for sure. He was far too interested in pleasing Shaw to ever push her on anything.

Frustrated, Rosy set the papers aside and checked the position of the sun. It was barely half an hour into the four-hour workshop block. She contemplated heading to the stable to exercise one of the horses, then discarded the idea. She missed those afternoons she used to spend with Guanyu and Shantie. All the experimental potions she'd drunk trying to find an aid to prevent feral rages, and all those hours talking Guanyu through trying to find his second shift. She would have loved tutoring him on all the advanced shapeshifting tricks she'd learned.

Shantie never returned to school. Rosy had looked for her all week, though she only shared one class with the senior flower witches. She'd even asked Yuyan if she knew where Shantie was, but Yuyan hadn't heard anything from her over the entire fall break.

"Her family lives in a little town house along Multah's western docks," Yuyan had said. "I wish they would move. I don't think it'll be easy for Shantie to recover in the same city where Guanyu was killed."

Rosy agreed. Guanyu hadn't wanted his witch to waste away in his death. She didn't know exactly what his final message meant, but surely that was the point of it.

All Rosy's uncertainty, that underlying layer of anxiety she'd been wrestling with since Samhain and everything that had come after, twisted into a sudden determination. She hadn't been able to save Guanyu, but she could at least deliver his dying message to Shantie.

Students weren't supposed to leave Witch Hall without permission during the school term, but Rosy couldn't care less. She headed to the stable just in case anyone was watching her. Once she was out of sight behind the corral, she shifted into a squirrel to hop the treetops until she was a good distance from campus. From there, she shifted into her horse and set a nice pace to Multah.

It took about two hours to get to the city as a horse. Rosy skirted past the section that had burned in the Market Day fire, not yet ready to face what remained of that nightmare. She wasn't sure if the lingering call of the dead was all in her imagination or if she could really feel it. Bone familiars were more sensitive to the energies of death, but surely the Samhain rituals had calmed all the remaining ghosts here?

Rosy found it ironic how Gran had made her promise to avoid war so that Rosy wouldn't end up as traumatized as her—and in the end, Rosy's own trauma had pushed her to pursue it. She expected those little moments of remembered panic would only worsen once the war with Vinland truly began, but at least she was taking agency over it. Sometimes it felt like having a plan was the only thing that kept her sane these days.

Rosy shifted back to human to walk down the main streets of Multah, stopping several times to ask directions. As she walked northwest, the houses grew steadily less fancy and more clustered. The tiny alleys made wind tunnels that whipped at her with warnings of a coming cold front. Rosy regretted not bringing her cloak. The school uniform was nicer quality than most of her own clothes, but it wasn't thick enough to block the wind's bite.

Finally, Rosy arrived in what looked to be an older district of workhouses and townhomes. Yuyan hadn't said which house was Shantie's, but someone would know. Nothing for it but to ask. Rosy spotted a man watering a plant on his crooked front step. She stepped up to him. "Excuse me, sir? Could you direct me to the Cosho house?"

The man looked up, squinting against the afternoon sun. "They're away."

"Away?"

He shrugged. "Headed off a couple weeks ago, after the army finally dropped off the boy's bones. Their daughter was married, or close enough to, but he died in the fire. They left with the boy's family to bury him in Waiming."

Rosy's heart sank. "When will they be back?" she asked.

"How should I know?" He slipped inside, closing the door to prevent Rosy from asking any more questions.

Dejected, Rosy shifted into her horse form to begin the long walk back to school. Could she write Shantie a letter? She wasn't crass enough to put Guanyu's final words in writing, but she could let her know that Rosy wanted to talk when Shantie returned from the Waiming Territories. Would Shantie even accept a letter from her, or would she be too angry at Rosy for having failed to save her familiar?

Rosy didn't feel like winding her way back through the city, so she trotted along the river instead. It wasn't the easiest route, but whenever her path was blocked, she shifted to a squirrel to climb over the cliff or cluster of trees in her way. A few times, she considered trying to pull up her otter and diving into the river itself—but she hadn't heard the otter's voice since that afternoon spent exploring Lake Bloom with Guanyu and she was afraid to reach for it now.

She was so lost in her own spiraling sadness that she nearly didn't notice the boats until she was right on top of them. It was only luck that she'd shifted into a squirrel to cross over a dense cluster of white oaks—her squirrel form blending in perfectly with the browns and oranges of its autumn leaves.

There, below her, half a dozen Vinish longboats had been pulled ashore. The largest of the longboats, she was horrified to note, bore the flag of a rampant bear. The symbol of the Empire of Vinland.

No, Rosy thought. Hadn't the entourage been talking about some exercise off campus with the Royal Company today?

She hadn't done anything when the Vinlanders killed Guanyu. Never again. If more Vinlanders had come, she wouldn't hesitate to kill if it meant saving her friends from Guanyu's fate.

From the distance, Rosy heard the call of what might have been a hunting horn.

The wolf in her heart howled. Rosy leaped from the tree, shifting into her wolf halfway to the ground. She was running as soon as her paws touched the ground, a flurry of leaves cascading down in her wake.

Chapter 6

SHAW

It was a warm day for November, and the sunlight was bright. I hoped everyone had eaten well at lunch because it was a long way by foot from Witch Hall to Goose Point, a cliff overlooking the river halfway to Multah where migrating geese gathered by the thousands each spring. Our assignment was to march in company formation to the small encampment made on the cliff top, then await new orders there. I'd been given the role of general for the makeshift company and had split the hundred or so students in Army Training into five platoons, each under the command of one of my entourage.

In the front was Einar's platoon, those trained to be part of the shield wall and the familiars with strong combat-oriented shifts. Behind Einar was Oluk's platoon, the secondary line of defense. Those were the archers and others with ranged abilities, alongside the familiars with smaller but still-deadly shifts.

Aklemin's platoon was in the middle. I'd put Aklemin in charge of intelligence gathering—both with the other ice witches good at scrying and the familiars with small shifts who'd been training in scouting. I marched next to them so that I could get the full picture of what was happening and deliver orders to the rest of the company.

Taking the rear were Yuyan's and Toketie's platoons—healing and logistics respectively. In a real march, Toketie's platoon would be in charge of wagons full of equipment and Yuyan's would be transporting both medical supplies and any injured soldiers. As this was just practice, General Tepeh had provided the two small platoons with some handcarts to pull.

I knew to expect something more than just a simple march to Goose Point and back. With all four thanes and the general spread out among the group observing, the pressure to succeed was high. General Tepeh might hope to surprise me, but I had spent my life under scrutiny and tended to assume most things were tests.

We were two hours in, and I estimated still an hour away. And that didn't account for the march back. Had the general cleared this exercise with Madam Kawak? At the current rate, we were liable to miss dinner. Perhaps General Tepeh planned to have us ferried back to campus by the river once we passed whatever test they'd orchestrated. Or perhaps the test was to push on until nightfall and see how we reacted. As a subordinate of General Tepeh, I was to listen to their orders, but I was also a student of Witch Hall and we had our own rules to follow. Whose rules was I supposed to prioritize?

The thanes and their general had not spoken on the trek, but I knew they were all observing closely. Several times, I called out specific students for stepping out of formation. It was happening more and more now, as the long march began to sap everyone's energy. General Tepeh appeared unruffled despite the harsh rays of the late-afternoon sun. I hoped I didn't look as sweaty as I felt.

My black witch's uniform was certainly not helping. I was trying to stay calm and collected, but the beginnings of irritation bubbled up in my chest. I wanted the real test to start so that I could properly plan how to solve it without going in endless circles in my own head. I hated uncertainty.

As if they'd heard my thoughts, General Tepeh called for the company to halt. I looked sharply at them, unsure whether I was supposed to reprimand the general for ordering my company around when they were meant to only observe. Before I could decide whether to say something, I spotted the ice sparrow darting over our heads. It dove for the ground a few feet in front of Thane Anders, three lines ahead of us, and shifted to land neatly on two feet.

The woman bowed to Thane Anders. She was dressed in a soldier's brown uniform, including the white stripe of a familiar down her pants and the crest of the Royal Company above her right breast. On the edge of the crest was a small symbol matching the one embroidered on Thane Anders's red thane sash, marking her as a member of his platoon. "Sir, we've discovered something by the river that requires your immediate attention," she said.

Thane Anders turned to look at the general. The sparrow familiar followed his gaze and bowed again, lower this time. "Sir!"

"We're in the middle of training students," General Tepeh said sternly. "Can the squad leaders report to Thane Anders later?"

"It's urgent, sir."

"Might be best if we all go, General," Thane Anders said. "If this is about that one matter . . ."

General Tepeh ran a hand through their hair, dislodging a few strands from the tie at the base of their neck. "Very well. Thanes, we're needed!"

Thanes Beck, Huang, and Olhiyu broke from their sections of

the march to join Thane Anders and the sparrow familiar. Aklemin looked over to catch my gaze, frowning deeply. I very deliberately said nothing. This was so obviously the start of a test that I wasn't sure if I was even supposed to feel tricked about it.

"Princess, you are to lead your company the rest of the way to the encampment," General Tepeh commanded. "We will meet you there once we've handled the platoon's concerns."

"Yes, sir," I said.

The general and their thanes were gone moments later, following after the soldier's sparrow shift. I waited until they were out of sight before turning to my fellow students.

"If you haven't taken advantage of this break to drink water, do so now. We resume our march in two minutes!"

I didn't look to see if they complied, focusing instead on Aklemin. The ice witch was already ahead of me though. They'd poured some of their water into a small bowl, head bowed as they stared intently into it.

"Resume march!" I called a couple minutes later. I waited for Aklemin to pull away from the bowl and report what they'd seen, but they didn't. Instead, they stepped back into line and began walking with their head still craned over the bowl.

We walked for another half an hour before Aklemin finally leaned over, whispering my name.

"What do you see?" I asked, just as softly. It wouldn't stop the nearby lines from overhearing, especially the familiars, but it was better than shouting our concerns to the entire makeshift company.

"Nothing," Aklemin said. "That's the issue."

"What do you mean?"

"Goose Point is empty. I see the encampment, but there's no one outside. I watched for as long as I could, but there's no movement in the tents." Aklemin held up the bowl of water as if to prove their story, even though I wouldn't be able to see what they could.

Was this the test, then? Were we meant to show up to an abandoned encampment and figure out what to do from there? Or was there more to it?

"Can you see what General Tepeh is doing?" I asked.

Aklemin glanced down at the bowl. They swirled the water inside a few times, somehow not spilling any of it despite the brutal walking pace we were maintaining.

"They've met up with what looks to be an entire platoon at the shore of the river," Aklemin said after a few seconds studying the water. "A squad leader is explaining something to them. There's a lot of arm gestures, but she's too blurry for me to read more than that."

Considering Aklemin had never met anyone in Thane Anders's platoon before, that wasn't surprising to me. I was more surprised they could see as much as they did. They had to be better at scrying than I'd thought.

I wondered if the sparrow familiar's report had been real after all and the general had merely used it as an excuse to take the thanes and leave. What would their original excuse have been in that case? Or had they planned to stay with us and just fade into the background while I dealt with whatever was going on with the abandoned encampment?

Was this even the test after all? It sounded like the entire platoon was at the river. Most of the Royal Company was stationed at Witch Hall. I doubted this encampment had more than the single platoon stationed here. Farther west, the border would be watched by Multah's Company, so Goose Point was the outermost edge of the Royal Company's current patrol area.

Perhaps the squad leader was explaining some hiccup that had prevented them from setting up whatever test General Tepeh and Thane Anders had planned for us.

"I don't like this, Shaw," Aklemin murmured, dropping their voice even lower. "There was too much red in the sunrise this morning."

My heart began to beat heavily at Aklemin's warning. They were so rarely serious that I couldn't help but take them at their word.

I turned, marching backward so that I could see the lines behind us. "Toketie, come here," I called.

Toketie hurriedly handed over the cart she'd been pulling to another student in the logistics section and trotted through the lines to get to me.

"Aklemin, show her where the general is," I said. As an ice familiar, Toketie should be able to see what was in the scrying bowl with Aklemin's help.

Aklemin did, and I waited a few moments for Toketie to carefully study the scene before saying, "If something goes wrong, I need you to shift into your swan and go get the general. Demand the entire platoon come if it's serious enough."

"Wouldn't one of the scouts be a better choice?" Toketie argued. "My swan is really visible."

It was, but swans were also among the strongest fliers of the animal world. "We'll be up on Goose Point. Take a dive off the cliff and use the momentum to get away. You'll have a better view of the shoreline than any of the songbird familiars, and I can't afford to send one of the hunting birds if there's going to be a fight. Find the general as quickly as possible and make a ruckus until they take you seriously. I'll deal with any repercussions later."

Toketie nodded. "When should I—"

"Stay with me, I'll tell you when to go." I paused, then turned back around to the rear of the company. "Yuyan! You've got command of Toketie's platoon as well."

"Understood!" Yuyan called back.

Toketie took General Tepeh's place between Aklemin and me in the line, and we continued marching. Thirty minutes later, we arrived at the encampment. It was indeed deserted. I ordered the students to stay in formation as we pushed into the center of the small camp and asked Aklemin to send their scouts out in every direction. We waited in silence until the first scouts began to return. One by one they brought back their reports to Aklemin and me. Nothing. Nothing. Nothing.

Finally we were down to a single missing scout. It was Zhihao, one of the twins who ruled the year under mine. His half brother, Mengjiao, stood in the front with Einar. If Mengjiao was worried about his brother, I couldn't tell from here. Mengjiao was a glass witch, but Zhihao was a familiar with a small snake shift. Of all the scouts, I'd been least concerned for him. Where Mengjiao was the son of Mister and Madam Xu, Zhihao was the son of Mister Xu and Madam Bai. He had more training than any of the scouts here, so what was taking him so long?

I'd barely finished the thought when a rustle in the leaf litter alerted me to the snake's return. Zhihao shifted at the outer edges of our formation. "Princess!" he cried. "It's Vinlanders! They're coming this way."

Vinlanders? My heart sank. This was no mere test. It couldn't be. By the kingdom's laws, only those actively enlisted in the army were allowed to own a metal sword, so we'd been issued wooden practice swords during Army Training. The witches in Einar's squad had been given enchanted shields to hold alongside their practice swords and the layer behind had dulled spears. Those trained in archery each had a quiver of padded arrows to go alongside their bows and a wooden ax at their hips in case of close-range combat. But that was all just for training. Our wooden weapons would do nothing in a real fight.

There was no time to raid the encampment for real weapons. "Form ranks!" I called, even as a dozen adults burst through the trees at the southwestern end of Goose Point.

They were, indeed, dressed in the typical fashion of Vinland. Fur coats and leather helmets. In the center of the group was a woman with blond hair and a smattering of freckles. She raised her chin at the sight of our small company.

"Look what we've found," the woman said, brandishing a gleaming metal sword. "Lost little lambs far from home."

"Hold!" I said before anyone could attack. After that sudden spike of anxiety, I was more than a little disappointed with this whole farce. "Are we meant to believe you're actual Vinlanders, ma'am?"

The leader's smirk fell away. "A lack of belief won't save you," she growled.

I raised an eyebrow, wondering if she thought me a child. "If you really wanted to sell it, you'd be using double-edged swords with crossguards. Single-edged sabers are standard issue for the Cursed Kingdom's army."

Next to me, Toketie let out a nervous giggle. In front, I could see Einar and the students in the shield wall relaxing.

The disguised soldier kept her scowl for another couple seconds before she too relaxed. "Ah, Princess, you are a sharp one! Mimie Moolocks, at your service, and this here's my squad."

"A pleasure, Squad Leader Moolocks," I said politely. "Are we meant to wait here for General Tepeh to return, then?"

"Oh, I think they'll be upset if they come back to find we've just been sitting around," Squad Leader Moolocks said. "Giving the game away doesn't mean you don't have to play it. I've got my orders after all."

"It seems risky, Squad Leader," I said, because I could see out of the corner of my eye that Aklemin was one of the few who hadn't relaxed. "Several of the familiars here are deadly, and your swords look real enough. Without knowing we're allies, someone could have been seriously injured."

"These swords are dulled enough to prevent any real damage," Squad Leader Moolocks said. "And we've got a flower witch on standby to deal with any venom. Have more faith in your army, Princess, we're hardier than you think."

It seemed we weren't going to get out of this. I glanced sideways at Aklemin, but they weren't looking back at me. They were staring at something over the squad's heads. At the sun, I realized. It was starting to set now, turning the edges of the horizon a soft shade of orange.

"Well, then I suppose we'd best get started before we lose all light," I said finally. "Should I let you make your grand entrance again? I promise to act appropriately this time."

"Might as well," Squad Leader Moolocks said. "You heard the princess, troops, back to the woods."

Her squad grumbled good-naturedly but marched down the shallow incline to the trees beyond Goose Point.

I was pleased she'd listened to me. It gave me enough time to rearrange the company. "Einar's group, take the space between those tents and form up. Yuyan, we need those handcarts as barricades! Oluk's platoon, spread out. Familiars, take cover and wait for the opportune moment to strike. Those with long-range attacks, get behind the handcarts."

The students scrambled to obey. I stayed in the center of the small camp, watching them work. "Pretend this is a real fight! Take them seriously, but don't be stubborn." I didn't want General Tepeh to have any excuse to call my classmates childish or point out our inexperience. "If you get hit, fall to the ground and let one of Toketie's platoon rescue you. Yuyan, do you have a place to set up for the injured?"

"We're good!" Yuyan said, waving at several of the logistics students to move some supply crates away from the space in between the last tent and the edge of the cliff. It was the most protected area of the entire camp. The cliff was too tall for there to be any attacks from that side, outside of a few errant ice familiars.

"Should we keep to less dangerous shifts?" Charles asked from his place behind the shield wall.

I considered it for just a second before saying, "No, but keep it friendly. No venom for those who can control it and no claws to faces. Don't hold back otherwise. I know we outnumber them, but they are experienced. Don't underestimate them."

Charles nodded and shifted into his bobcat form. Froya shifted into her eagle and found a perch on top of the tent poles. The other familiars with larger bird shifts joined her. Oluk and the others with snake and lizard forms took the chance to disappear into the autumn leaves.

I counted my breaths as we waited. How long would it take Squad Leader Moolocks to return? I reached a hundred and stopped counting. She was trying to unnerve us. We had to be patient.

A hunting horn rang out from the distant woods.

"What was that?" Einar asked, turning to look back at me.

"Eyes forward!" I called. "Keep formation! They're just trying to scare us."

The clarion call of the hunting horn sounded again. I pulled my wooden sword from my belt, then reached out with my bone magic for a better weapon. I was looking for half-decomposed animals or a scattered skeleton, so I almost didn't notice when something much stronger reached back for me.

"Shaw," Emma said from her place in the secondary line of fighters. Her little dog shift was more distracting than dangerous, but she'd been determined to join her cousin in the combat group, even though I thought she'd have done better with the scouts. As if to prove my point, she had her nose raised high, obviously relying on her dog's advanced sense of smell to catch something on the wind. "There's blood in the air. A lot of it."

I finally realized what my own senses were telling me. There were ghosts. Half a dozen at least, wailing at the edge of my reach. Recently killed, and violently at that. I called the nearest one, and it came flying through the woods and over the heads of the shield wall.

Chao swore, which made Jingyi-the-fox yelp. "Isn't that—" he began.

It was Squad Leader Moolocks. She was in monochrome now, and a few years younger than she'd been when living, as ghosts liked to do, but it was easy to recognize her all the same. "Princess, run," she yelled, tendrils like smoke flickering at the edges of her form. "This isn't a game anymore. Run!"

"Toketie, go!" I shouted.

I didn't have time to watch as the ice familiar darted through the camp to the edge of the cliff. A whole hoard of figures were climbing the slope to the encampment. Unlike the fake Vinlander outfits Squad Leader Moolocks and her squad had worn, these figures were dressed far more authentically. Einar called for the shield wall to hold strong as half a dozen, then a dozen, then two dozen Vinlanders poured out of the trees and into the entrance of the camp.

"Oh?" one of the Vinlanders said, stopping a good distance from our group. He was an archer, with a traditional Vinland war bow already primed. "And here I thought there would be more soldiers. Not a bunch of kids."

I felt another person die somewhere in the woods. Squad Leader Moolocks was still wailing for us to run. The other bone witches were visibly wincing, and Jingyi, one of the few bonded bone familiars of our group, had her ears pinned flat.

"We have no quarrel with you," I said, though I'd never told a worse lie. "Please let us pass."

The archer raised an eyebrow. "Pass to where? What's a group of kids doing so far from the city?"

So this man wasn't magical, not that I was surprised by that. I expected any magicals living in Vinland had already fled to the Cursed Kingdom after the sudden rise in anti-magical bigotry. It was a boon to us. The enchanted wards protecting the school would keep Vinlanders from noticing its existence. They were a much larger form of the eavesdropping runes Einar had etched into our table at school. If they stumbled past the wards, they'd see it, but then the secondary line of defensive magic would kick in.

Not that Witch Hall's wards would save us now, three hours' march from campus.

"We're on a school trip," I said honestly. My goal was to get my fellow students away to safety. We hadn't been attacked yet. Perhaps we'd be able to defeat these two dozen Vinlanders, but with only wooden swords and padded arrows, I worried for how many of my classmates would die. I couldn't let that happen. I had to stall, to give Toketie time to find General Tepeh and Thane Anders's platoon.

Unless the platoon was already dead. The Vinlanders had slaughtered Moolocks's squad. Could they have taken the rest of the platoon by surprise too?

Another twenty or so Vinlanders came into the encampment. The odds were getting worse. They fanned out, keeping their distance but blocking our escape route. I cast about wildly for a plan to save my classmates. Only, I couldn't see a way out of this without fighting.

My father had promised the war wouldn't start until after my graduation. Had he truly not foreseen this attack?

A shuffle occurred behind the archer. He stepped aside, letting another man come to the front. This one held a two-handed broadsword, and his metal helmet had a horn mounted to the center of it—a boar tusk that pointed out and up. The tip was painted bright red, like the bear on Vinland's royal crest. Where most of the Vinlanders were older, this one looked closer to my age. He had broad shoulders, but he was lean like he was still growing into his chest. His arms made up for it. His biceps swelled as he held the broadsword aloft. His dark blue eyes were fixed on my school uniform.

"You dress like a witch," the new Vinlander spat.

I made a show of dropping my wooden sword and holding my hands up in the universal sign that I was unarmed. I was far from it. I reached with my bone magic for the bodies of those recently killed.

Necromancy is a different beast on the battlefield, Shaw, Aklemin had told me once. They were right. It was easy to grab the corpses. They were fresh—muscles not yet stiffened, bones not yet rotted. Better yet, pieces of their spiritual essence still clung to the bodies.

"We're just students," I said as I worked. "Let us return to Multah. We've no quarrel with you."

The Vinlander raised an eyebrow in obvious disbelief. "No quarrel? Your king burns down our lands, kills our people, and you say you have no quarrel?"

His words were enough to make me lose grip on the corpses. My mind raced, trying to figure out a way to interpret his words besides the obvious. I couldn't. "I'm sorry for your people's suffering, but the Cursed Kingdom had no hand in the fires that besieged your villages," I tried.

"Maybe you are children," the Vinlander sneered. "Ignorant fools. You think three whole villages would burn down, on their own, months apart? What about Vingate? Half the city was destroyed in your king's last attack! Thousands lay dead. And you won't even let us grieve in peace."

My heart raced in my chest. I'd been so sure that General Holt was wrong when he'd told me that my father and General Tepeh had planned to burn down those villages. It couldn't be true, could it? Why would my father dare anger our strongest neighbor? There had to be some other explanation.

My classmates began murmuring among themselves at the Vinlander's proclamation. I had no time to worry what that might mean. Even though everything within me refused to believe the Vinlander's accusation, I had a duty as heir to the kingdom. I'd been raised from childhood to listen impartially to my people when they brought their grievances. I called upon that training now. I said, as calmly as I could manage, "If the Witch King has incited violence against Vinland without just cause, then he will be tried as a traitor like any citizen of our kingdom would be. Do you have evidence that I could bring before the jarls' council?"

The Vinlander's face turned red with rage. "Evidence? You asked for evidence? What more evidence do you need? We ran out of graves months ago. Should I start sending bodies across the river for you to corrupt with your dark magic?"

"My liege," the archer murmured.

"You can't negotiate with them," the ghost of Squad Leader Moolocks pleaded. "We've paid our dues, but you don't need to. Run, Princess! Cut a hole through their force and get out of here."

"Who are you?" the Vinlander said, talking over Squad Leader Moolocks's last words.

"Shaw—" Aklemin warned.

"Princess—" the ghost screeched.

The Vinlander grew even more red in the face. "I *have* seen your face before. Princess Shaw Colchuck. The latest of a long line of monsters."

"My liege," the archer tried again, obviously not convinced.

But the angry Vinlander had already raised his sword. "Death to the witches! Let none with magic live to corrupt more of our own!"

The other Vinlanders rallied around him, their own weapons raised high. A chant rose. "For the prince! For the prince!"

Prince? I hadn't memorized the portraits of the emperor of Vinland's many children, but judging by his age, he would be something like the fifth or sixth son. Just the kind of person the emperor might send to lead an attack against his enemies.

"Die!" the prince roared.

I had just enough time to shout "Defend yourselves!" before the Vinlanders were on us.

Chapter 7

It was chaos immediately. I reached for the corpses again, grabbing at the ghosts that had been left behind when the soldiers were killed. It wasn't hard to give them the push they needed to repossess their own bodies, then nudge them to the encampment. It left just three corpses whose owners hadn't left behind ghosts. I pushed my magic into the lingering essence of those owners' spirits and used it to puppet the bodies.

"Chao!" I called, holding out a hand for my fellow necromancer. "Take one!"

Chao reached over to touch my outstretched fingers. I used the touch to transfer control of one of the corpses, and he took it effortlessly.

The first of the possessed bodies reached the outer layer of Vinlanders and began to attack. It was enough to distract some, but the rest were too focused on pounding on the shield wall. An arrow flew past my head. One of the students behind me cried out in pain. I didn't have the time to look back, but I hoped that Yuyan or one of the other flower witches could get to them in time.

The Vinlander prince roared in anger. His warriors struck with swords and axes at the shield wall. With each blow, the enchantments on the shields grew stronger, creating a barrier that prevented any of the other Vinlanders from getting too close. Several of the smaller familiars darted underneath the shields to bite at the ankles of the Vinlanders before retreating again. Our own archers pelted the Vinlanders with padded arrows, but it didn't do much more than annoy them.

"Aklemin, get the arrows they're firing at us to our own archers!" I called. I pushed the two corpses I was controlling to walk faster. I wished I could just rip the skeletons out of their bodies—I had an easier time with bare bones.

A flash of red caught my attention. There was another ghost lingering on the edge of the battlefield, this one halfway corrupted to a spirit already. Red anger swirled inside her translucent form. I spent a second contemplating whether to push her all the way over. Unlike the lingering traces of spirit left on dead bodies or the more common spiritual imprints made by dead animals, fully-fledged spirits were powerful weapons to bone witches strong enough to control them. But with the dozen possessed bodies and two puppet corpses I was already managing, I worried I'd let her slip—and corrupted spirits almost always targeted bone witches first. So instead, I sent enough soothing magic her way to cleanse her fully back to a rational ghost, then pulled her into one of the empty bodies. There was no time to figure out which one was hers—she'd have to make do with the closest.

A loud growl caught my attention. I looked up in time to see a bone wolf barrel through the woods and into the ranks of Vinlanders. One of the warriors turned to confront it and ended up on the ground with a chunk out of her shoulder.

Rosamund. I didn't have time to wonder how she'd found us. Her presence was a welcome relief. Bone wolves were over four feet tall and nearly two hundred pounds. There was a reason my grandmother had made a weapon out of Ylva the Red Wolf. Rosamund ripped through the Vinlanders, neatly dodging their attacks by shifting from wolf to mouse and back again.

"Die!" the Vinlander prince shouted, sounding nearly animalistic himself.

He swiped at the shields, once, twice, three times. His attacks seemed to speed up with each blow. The enchantments began to falter. With a rallying cry, the other Vinlanders doubled their own attacks. The barrier flickered.

"Brace yourselves!" Einar yelled just as the prince cleaved at the shields with a massive swing of his broadsword.

The students in the shield wall went flying back, knocking into those standing behind them. The other Vinlanders cried out in victory, rushing forward into the open space. Charles led a group of familiars into the fray to keep the warriors away from our fallen classmates. I glimpsed a rattlesnake dart between the legs of one of the bodies, biting down on one of the Vinlanders before turning into a smaller garter snake and retreating. Oluk and the other venomous familiars were doing what they could, but it took time for their venom to work and it would only take a single good hit for any one of them to fall to a Vinlander blade.

There was no time for hesitation. I commanded the possessed bodies to abandon their current targets, pushing through the ranks of Vinlanders until they stood in front like a line of human shields.

Several of the Vinlanders had made it through before I could turn the corpses into another barrier. Mengjiao cried out as one of the Vinlanders slashed him across the leg. I pulled the corpse I was puppeting back to attack the Vinlander before he could do more.

"Shaw!" Einar yelled. Someone rammed me from behind, and I fell to the ground. I scrambled to my knees in time to see Einar trying to ward off the Vinlander prince. I'd lost hold of the corpses in my fall. Half had collapsed back to the ground while the others had lost their will to fight, standing there as the Vinlanders slashed at them.

I grabbed the closest possessed body and directed it to get between Einar and the Vinlander prince. Einar backed away as the dead soldier half attacked, half fell on the prince.

The prince roared, "Monster! You dishonor even your own dead!"

"Quickly," Einar said, helping me to my feet. I barely noticed, concentrating on the other corpses. Vinlanders were spilling over the gaps between corpses, aiming for the students beyond the undead wall. I had to keep them safe. I wouldn't, couldn't, allow any of my classmates to die here.

"Enough of this!" the prince shouted. With another great swing of his broadsword, he sliced the corpse in two. I stared as the torso hit the ground first, and then the legs collapsed sideway. I'd never seen a human body completely bisected. The ghost flew out of the body, no longer able to maintain a hold over it.

"How—" But I couldn't finish the question. The prince had turned on us.

He swung his sword. I dodged out of the way, only to realize that Einar hadn't followed. He raised his own wooden sword in an instinctive attempt to block. The wood shattered, but it had at least managed to deflect the blow wide. The prince pulled back, then raised his broadsword high, like he wanted to slice Einar from head to foot.

"No!" I cried. I pulled at the bones of the bisected corpse, ripping them from flesh.

The sword drew up past the prince's shoulder, then came

swinging back down. Einar turned to duck out of the way. I watched—my vision distorted as if I was seeing the scene through muddy water—as the prince switched his grip halfway through the arched descent and forced the sword sideways.

"No," I said, but this time it was barely more than a whisper.

The prince's blade caught Einar along the lower back.

Flesh split with a spray of blood. All I could see in my mind's eye were the two halves of the soldier's body. Any second now, I expected Einar's torso to separate from his legs. But instead, Einar let out a guttural grunt of pain.

A ferocious growl ripped through the air. Rosamund-the-wolf had thrown herself at the prince. He pulled his broadsword back with a squelch and another spray of blood, just barely getting it up in time to stop Rosamund from tearing out his throat.

Without the prince's sword holding him up, Einar let out a horrible choking sound and fell to his knees. I collapsed next to him, trying desperately to put pressure on his wounds, but his entire lower back had been splayed open. I saw with dismay that chunks of vertebrae had been cut free from his spine.

"Yuyan!" I called, unable to keep the raw desperation out of my voice. "Yuyan, quickly!"

I didn't even know if she'd be able to hear me in the chaos. Shouts poured out from the woods. General Tepeh and the platoon had finally arrived.

I kept pressure on Einar's wound, though my hands were soaked with blood. People were dying all around us. I couldn't concentrate enough to feel if they were students or Vinlanders or the newly arrived soldiers.

"Here, I'm here!" Yuyan said, nearly knocking me over in her haste to get her hands on Einar. "Hold on, Einar, I have you."

I stumbled away, leaving Yuyan to work. Another fierce growl cut through the throng. I looked up to see the Vinlander prince and Rosamund circling each other, each looking for an opening. Rosamund's mouth was drawn back in a snarl and her eyes practically glowed with anger.

She'd gone feral.

"Rosamund, I need you!" I called, still desperate. Still terrified. A feral familiar was a fierce fighter, but not a smart one. She would be killed.

The prince struck out, the tip of his sword catching on the exposed bone on Rosamund's shoulder. I didn't wait for him to try another strike. I lunged forward to get my hands on Rosamund's flank. I poured my magic into her, hoping against everything that it would be enough.

Rosamund shifted from wolf to squirrel, dodging the prince's next strike. I held out a hand to her, more grateful than ever that our unusual connection was enough to break her out of her feral rage even without a bond. Rosamund went mouse to scurry into my palm, and I pulled her up to my chest.

I drew on the comforting swell of her magic and used it to grab hold of all the dead. There were more now. I didn't try to figure out who they were, couldn't let myself be distracted by the thought of those who might have died. I grabbed hold of every corpse I could and pulled them into the fight. Ghosts got flung into whatever bodies were nearest. I channeled all my panic into the rest, holding more corpses than I'd thought myself capable of and making them frantically flail at the enemy. I would have the dead beat the Vinlanders back with their bare fists.

The prince swung his blood-soaked sword at me. I threw myself out of the way even as Rosamund launched herself from my hand. She shifted badger and got her teeth in the prince's wrist. Mid-bite, she shifted wolf. With a vicious growl, she tore his leather bracer off and must have caught at least some skin, for even more blood sprayed the air. The prince threw his head back in pain.

"Protect the prince!" someone yelled.

The prince wasn't paying attention to his own people. He surged forward to attack again. Rosamund went horse to block the blow with the exposed bone on her chest, only to let out a high-pitched whinny as the force of it was enough to shatter a whole chunk of the bone.

My terror was giving way to fury. I couldn't do anything about Einar, but I could throw all my energy into the dead. The ghosts I'd captured wailed through the open mouths of their possessed bodies. Out of the corner of my eye, I saw one corpse wildly bludgeoning a Vinlander with what remained of their hands. Their bloodied fingers had been sliced off, and with a little tendril of magic, I grabbed hold of the finger bones to throw like darts at a different Vinlander.

The tide of the battle turned. Where the Vinlanders had been on the offensive, now they were being attacked from all sides.

"Retreat!" the archer from earlier called. He ran up, shooting an arrow at Rosamund to get her to back off so he could go to the prince's side. "My liege, we must retreat!"

The prince roared in fury, but the other Vinlanders were unperturbed. Three stepped in front of their prince, covering him as they pushed for a retreat.

"After them!" General Tepeh yelled. The soldiers surged to follow. Within seconds, the fight left the encampment, draining away into the woods.

My tenuous hold over the dead collapsed. I let the ghosts drift away, suddenly exhausted. Rosamund came close, pressing against my side as if to hold me up. I held on to her, and we both turned to look at Einar.

Oluk was already there, holding his witch's limp hand as Yuyan worked. Blood soaked the ground under Oluk's knees. I stumbled a step closer, then fell. Fragments of bone dug into my legs. I wasn't sure if they were from Rosamund's horse shift or Einar's shattered spine.

On Einar's other side, several feet behind Yuyan, Aklemin was crying. A flap of wings signaled the arrival of Toketie. She landed next to Aklemin, but they didn't acknowledge her, too fixed upon watching Yuyan work.

Above our heads, the sunset had turned the sky a deep blood-red.

IT TOOK SOME TWENTY HOURS before Yuyan emerged from Witch Hall's infirmary. The cheery morning sunlight felt like it was mocking us.

"Madam Tukwilla told me to rest," Yuyan murmured as she approached our somber huddle.

Rosamund, Aklemin, Toketie, and I stood in a loose circle. Oluk was the only one who'd been let into the infirmary while the flower witches worked.

"Is he—" I found I couldn't finish the question.

"He's still breathing," Yuyan said. "More than that, we can't know yet. It's too close." She took a shuddering breath. "It's far too close, Shaw."

I closed my eyes and turned away. I was still furious, but it was a numb sort of anger. I didn't understand how everything had devolved so quickly. Without Aklemin's warning, we'd have been left entirely unprepared. It was only luck that had saved most of our classmates. Einar was the only serious injury. Rosamund and Charles had both been given some potions to help with losing pieces of exposed bone, but that could have just as easily happened in class. Mengjiao had been in and out of the infirmary, the deep cut on his leg healed in a handful of hours, just like the few others who'd been struck by Vinlander sword or arrow.

I would be glad for how lucky we'd been, if only Einar made it through. I couldn't imagine a world where he died here. My glass witch. My trusted companion. My friend. The war hadn't even started and I might already have lost him.

"We paid our dues," I mumbled.

Rosamund turned to me. "What?"

"That's what Squad Leader Moolocks said when the Vinlander prince attacked." I rubbed the exhaustion and crusted tears from my eyes. I needed answers, and I would not rest before I got them. "Come with me," I told what remained of my entourage. "Quickly."

I ran from the infirmary in the direction of the school stable. Judging by the footsteps behind me, they all followed.

The stable master, Mister Jostein, was a bone witch. Though he didn't use his magic day-to-day, I knew he kept a little ritual room set up in the corner of the barn. I knocked on the door once and opened it without waiting for an answer. Luckily there was no one around to watch as we crammed into the small space.

Mister Jostein had been in there that morning to light a candle for the dead. I noted the hanging herbs, the kind meant to attract nearby ghosts and spirits. There was a spirit jar in the center of the room to capture any that might wander onto campus and be a danger to the young bone witch students. We bone witches could control the dead, but for the consequence of being especially vulnerable to possession. I closed the top of the container and used the nearby bowl of mountain ash to make a circle in the center of the room instead.

"Rosamund, can you anchor me?" I asked. "I don't need the wolf, something smaller is fine."

Rosamund shifted into her mouse in reply. I leaned down with my palm out so she could scurry into my hand, then up my arm to my shoulders. The wolf would have been a better anchor, but I didn't want her to strain her body while she was still recovering from losing some of her exposed bone. Familiars who shifted into smaller creatures had an easier time with nutrient distribution. That was one of the reasons those with large shifts, like Rosamund and Charles, ate significantly more than those like Oluk with exclusively smaller forms.

Luckily, we were close enough that it shouldn't take too much power for me to pull the ghosts of the soldiers to me. I just wished I'd thought of this sooner. I'd spent all night and the entire morning in a haze, waiting for any news of Einar, but in that time General Tepeh may have already thought to get some of the bone witches among their soldiers to force the ghosts to move on. I just had to hope they'd been distracted with their own injured.

The rest of my entourage stayed quiet as I reached for my sixth sense. I'd touched the ghosts of the soldiers before, so I used that memory to cast a net. I imagined it like fog, billowing out from the barn, across the campus, and into the woods on either side. I didn't know if the ghosts had left to hover around their loved ones or stayed haunting those woods. Some had likely already dissipated into the afterlife. But violent death tended to keep a ghost around longer than peaceful death.

There. I felt a tug like I'd hooked a fish on a line. I reeled it in.

There was a gasp. Toketie, I thought. Because of the setup of the ritual room, even those without bone magic would be able to see whatever ghost I'd trapped. When I opened my eyes, Squad Leader Moolocks floated in the center of the circle. She looked around the room, from the herbs to the ash to the spirit jar, then turned her attention to me.

"Does anyone have paper?" I asked.

"I do," Toketie volunteered.

"Take notes."

"You just keep surprising me, Princess," the ghost said as Toketie pulled out a notebook and graphite stick.

"Squad Leader Moolocks," I greeted her. "I have questions for you."

"What can she tell you that you didn't witness yourself?" Yuyan asked. She sounded tired. For however little sleep I'd gotten, I knew Yuyan had gotten even less. She was Madam Tukwilla's prized student, better than even the other flower witch teachers at healing. The fact that Einar was still fighting for life was entirely down to Yuyan's power.

I answered Yuyan with a question for Squad Leader Moolocks instead. "When the Vinlander prince arrived, you told me to run. And then you said something else. Repeat it for us."

Ghosts couldn't lie to bone witches, but they could misdirect. I was ready to press the question in a different way, but the ghost didn't even try to hide the truth. "I told you we'd paid our dues, but you shouldn't have to. Course, I didn't even think about the fact that you could raise our bodies to fight back. Foolish of me. You are Death's Heir."

Despite her clear admiration, I couldn't help but flinch. What did my power matter when I couldn't even save one of my own entourage?

Squad Leader Moolocks snorted, as if responding to my sudden doubt. "Don't chicken out now. I know the question you're dying to ask. Your father didn't tell you anything, did he?"

My throat felt suddenly dry. "What should he have told me?"

"Well, that's a broad question. You sure you've done this before?" Moolocks shook her head. "Ah, don't give me that look, I'll answer. You deserve to know, in my humble opinion. It's your prophecy, isn't it? I was only on one of the missions myself. Didn't have the stomach for it, I'm afraid. War's messy, there's no doubt, but it never feels right hurting simple folk. Could've been my own ma whose house I burned."

"Explain." I knew my voice was cold, but I didn't bother softening it. The dead could take my anger.

"I wasn't part of Anders's platoon originally. The Royal Company took me on when I enlisted, but they transferred me from logistics to Anders's group later. It took a couple months for me to realize everyone in that platoon was like me."

"What do you mean?"

"No family left. No outside ties at all, really. It was easy to become loyal to each other, with no one else in the way. And then Anders showed us the writ. The king himself signed those orders, Princess. We had to weaken Vinland first, or they'd overrun us. That's why we burned the towns."

"You said yourself the towns held just commonfolk," I argued. My neck ached. My body had only grown stiffer the more the ghost talked. "How would that weaken the empire's army?"

"It's about the magic. I'm a flower familiar, but I never could afford Witch Hall, so I don't know much. General Tepeh made it clear that it was important. Burn it down to leave room for the magic."

"That's not how magic works! It doesn't just fill any empty space," Yuyan protested.

"What do you need to leave room for?" I pressed.

"For you, Princess," the ghost said.

I remembered the prince's accusation. *Was* my father deliberately creating mass graves across the border that I could use as an army of the dead?

"Should've known it would get me killed," Squad Leader Moolocks continued. "None of my squad were willing to participate in another raid after that first one. Thought it was weird that Thane Anders volunteered us to test you, but it all makes sense now."

"What do you mean?"

"We've no one left to mourn us," Squad Leader Moolocks said.

What did that have to do with them being chosen for the test, before the real Vinlanders arrived to send everything into chaos? I asked as much to the ghost. Only, Squad Leader Moolocks rolled her eyes.

"Isn't it obvious? Can we be done with questions now, Princess? I've said my piece. You'll have to ask the Witch King for anything more. Let me rest."

"No," I said, frustrated and tired and numb to the bone. The trap that the ghost floated in made it impossible for her to fade. For all that I sympathized with her weary tone, I could not let her rest. Not yet.

In my hand, Rosamund-the-mouse let out a series of high-pitched squeaks. I ignored her, reaching instead for the spirit jar. With the toe of my boot, I broke the line of ash. The ghost flickered red in anger, but the jar was already doing its job. She flew inside it, and I closed the lid to trap her there.

"What does this mean?" Toketie asked into the silence that filled the little ritual room after that.

Rosamund shifted back to human, forcing me to drop her to the ground. She straightened up, crossing her arms. "It means Pops was right. The Witch King did cause this war with Vinland deliberately."

I very carefully set the jar down so it wouldn't crack. My hands trembled. I wanted to argue with Rosamund, but I didn't know how. "He said it was inevitable," I tried, but my words sounded weak even to my own ears.

Aklemin stepped forward, skirting around the broken line of ash until they could meet my eyes. "Was it always inevitable, or only because he made it so?"

I felt like I should have been the one to ask them that. They knew more about ice magic than I did. "Why Vinland?" I asked instead. "If he wanted to control the kingdom we'd go to war with, to fulfill the prophecy, then why our strongest neighbor? It makes no sense."

Aklemin said nothing. I searched their face for answers, but as always, I couldn't read anything from their placid expression.

"*Is* it inevitable?" I asked then. "No declarations of war have been written. The emperor may have sent one of his sons to test our defenses, but it seems we burned their villages first. What happens if we send reparations? If we prove that the culprit of those attacks was acting without the will of our governing council?"

"Were they?" Yuyan asked. "Can you be sure the jarls didn't know?"

I couldn't, not truly, but I also couldn't believe they did know. "Jarl Tenas would never have allowed the Market Day fire to happen if he'd known it was coming. Maybe some of the jarls are complicit, but not everyone. If we present evidence—"

"If we present evidence, and the jarls believe you, then your father will be tried for treason," Toketie said quietly. Like her cousin and her grandfather, she seemed to believe softening her tone would make the words hurt less.

I closed my eyes. Against the dark on the inside of my eyelids, I saw images of people burning. Of the Vinlander prince's rage. Of Einar, bleeding out before me.

"My father told me that the war would not begin until after graduation. He didn't warn Multah of the fire, but he made me believe he would tell me if another attack like that was going to occur. He said he would trust me." I opened my eyes. "He lied."

"Most of the platoon was away from the encampment. Only a small squad was there to test us," Yuyan said slowly. "We outnumbered them by a lot. We would have easily won that fight. Wouldn't it have made more sense to test us against Thane Anders's entire platoon?"

It was all starting to make sense, my tired mind finally putting together the pieces. "Squad Leader Moolocks seemed to believe they wanted her squad dead," I said. "Which means General Tepeh and Thane Anders knew. They planned it."

"None of them are ice witches. It would have been the Witch King who told them when the attack would occur," Aklemin said.

"But why?" Rosamund cried out. "You all could have died!"

"What would you have done if half our classmates had been slaughtered?" Aklemin asked me.

I thought of Guanyu's final request. "I would have wanted to bring them justice."

"And if some of those classmates were heirs to the jarls? What would the council have done?" Aklemin pressed.

They would have shouted for war. Would have sent the declaration as soon as they heard the news. Especially if Charles or Froya or Kwaddis had been among those killed. The three strongest jarls had heirs in my grade, and all three had been in real danger yesterday.

"You're saying our classmates dying was the point," Yuyan said. "If everything went according to the king's plan, it wouldn't be just Einar in the infirmary."

"An ice witch's visions are only as good as the people they know," Aklemin said. "The Witch King has never met Rosy. He's made a point of meeting the rest of our year. At the assembly last spring, remember? But Rosy joined more recently. He had no way of knowing she'd be strong enough to fend off so many Vinlanders until the platoon arrived."

"If they wanted more dead, why would General Tepeh follow me at all?" Toketie asked.

"Well, the king couldn't let his own heir die, could he?" Aklemin said. "A delicate balance—let enough be slain for Shaw to be overtaken by a desire for vengeance, but not so many as to risk her life in the process."

"But I would have died," I murmured. The numbness had spread throughout my whole body. I couldn't feel my fingers anymore. My vision was blurry. "If Einar hadn't pushed me out of the way . . ."

A hand touched the center of my back. I nearly jumped as the familiar tickle of Yuyan's flower magic flowed into me.

"We all need to sleep," Yuyan said. "You're on the verge of collapsing, Shaw. Drink some water and go to bed. We can discuss this more in the morning."

"But—"

"She's right," Rosamund said, appearing at my side. She got her shoulder under my arm, helping to support me. In comparison to the cold tickle of Yuyan's magic, Rosamund's touch was shockingly warm. "Tokey, grab the jar. We'll hide it in Shaw's room."

I barely remembered the walk back to my suite. My mind was stuck on my father's betrayal. I kept revisiting the conversation I'd had with him. *War requires sacrifices,* he'd said.

I fell asleep to the memory of pieces of bone floating in a puddle of Einar's blood.

Chapter 8

Monday arrived far too quickly. My first class of the day felt strangely colorless without Einar at my side. I went through the motions and took notes I knew I wouldn't remember later. I was caught in indecision and didn't know how to overcome it. I despised uncertainty.

Einar was alive, but he had yet to awaken and I knew that wasn't a good sign. Yuyan had been given special permission to miss Monday's classes to continue helping Madam Tukwilla with his recovery.

Except, at lunch, she burst into the dining hall and ran to our table. My heart was in my throat until she said, breathless from the run and beaming with joy, "He's up!"

Oluk wasted no time. He bolted out of his chair. One of the teachers yelled out a reprimand, but none of us cared to listen. I followed in Oluk's wake along with the rest of my entourage.

Inside the infirmary, Einar was talking with Madam Tukwilla. He cut off as we tumbled through the doors.

"Sorry, Madam Tukwilla," Yuyan said, even as Oluk crossed the final distance to his witch's side, whole body shaking.

"I'll be back later," Madam Tukwilla said. "Make sure he drinks plenty of water and those potions I left. You can help me this afternoon, Yuyan, then it's back to your regular class schedule tomorrow."

I was relieved to hear the flower witch's instructions. If she was releasing Yuyan, that meant Einar was no longer in active danger. I walked around the other side of his bed and collapsed into the seat next to it, studying Einar's face. The glass witch was fully focused on his sobbing familiar. He was undeniably pale and couldn't seem to lift his arms to hold Oluk properly, but he was propped up against the bed's headboard. He'd been healed enough to be on his back, which was already a massive improvement.

Madam Tukwilla closed the infirmary door, leaving us to our reunion. Rosamund and Toketie took a seat on the other, empty infirmary bed while Aklemin leaned against the foot of Einar's. Yuyan bustled about, collecting the potions Madam Tukwilla had mentioned and pouring a glass of water from a large pitcher.

"Here," Yuyan said, handing the water to Oluk. "Help him drink."

Having a task to do seemed to help. Oluk's sobs died down. He didn't bother wiping his face, but he did pull away from Einar enough to grab the water. Einar didn't complain as Oluk held it to his lips. I wondered how weak he must feel.

"I'm sorry," I said.

I hadn't intended to speak, but the words were already out. Einar turned his head to look at me, brow furrowing.

"It was not your fault, Shaw," he said. His tone was frail, but his words were sure. "None of us knew we'd be attacked."

"My father did," I said. "He must have known, and he did nothing to prevent it." I stood, unable to stay seated any longer. Aklemin moved out of my way as I began to pace along the length of the infirmary. "If I'd just listened to General Holt. If we'd been more prepared. I nearly got you killed because of my arrogance—"

"Shaw," Rosamund snapped. She reached out to grab my arm.

I stopped. Rosamund gestured back at Einar's bed. I looked and nearly winced. Einar was even paler now. Yuyan quickly handed Oluk the potions to give to him.

"Will you explain what you mean?" Einar asked slowly once he'd drunk the last of the potions.

Rosamund's grip on my arm tightened. I glanced at her. She had her head cocked to one side, listening.

"There's no one nearby," she said finally. "But the walls aren't soundproof."

I nodded, and she let go of me. I walked back to the empty chair and sat. In a quiet voice, I explained about Squad Leader Moolocks and what we'd determined about the so-called test. About my father's culpability in it all. I'd forgotten Oluk hadn't been with us until I saw him pale nearly as much as his witch.

"I still don't understand why," I concluded. "We've just as much chance of losing to Vinland as winning against them. My father has never been a risk-taker."

"The why doesn't matter as much as the what," Rosamund argued. "He created this situation. The Witch King is a monster."

"Rosy!" Toketie reprimanded her.

Rosamund was correct. My father had done a monstrous thing in sparking this war. He'd knowingly allowed hundreds of our own people to be slaughtered for his own gain. I didn't know what gain that was, but the truth remained nonetheless.

"Our people deserve justice." I looked to Einar, but it was Guanyu's ghost I saw in that bed. "Will you be angry if I worked to stop this war, instead of finishing it? If I convince the jarls' council to offer Vinland reparations for the people we've killed, even if we receive no reparations of our own?"

"Hate begets hate," Einar said, and the image of Guanyu's ghost faded away. "The Vinlanders killed in revenge. If we kill them to enact our own, we merely perpetuate the cycle. It is far more noble to prevent further deaths, Shaw."

I straightened, turning to meet the eyes of my entire entourage—Rosamund included. "Then that's what we'll do."

The plan was simple, primarily because I could not be deeply involved in it. My father knew me too well. If I began to make real plans to send him to trial, he would begin to foresee it. Our trump card was Rosamund. As Aklemin had said, Rosamund was the only one of us whom the Witch King hadn't met.

"But why didn't he make a point of meeting you during fall break?" Yuyan asked. "You were in Gravestown at the same time, weren't you?"

"He attempted to," I said. "The second day of court, he called up everyone who fought at Samhain to reward us for our bravery. But Rosamund had already left by that point."

"He also tried to meet me the next day," Rosamund added. "Jingyi told me later that he requested I join him for breakfast. But Mama and Papa and I had gone back to the cottage to pack everything. And after, we dropped by Woodside to give the news to Uncle Inge and Uncle Chetwoot and Solemie. Then we had to settle the herd into one of Jarl Almstedt's breeding pastures. Point is, we didn't return to Gravestown until the day Shaw and the rest were heading back to Witch Hall."

So the first step was to keep Rosamund well away from my father. Any and all plans we made had to involve her completely, to muddy the Witch King's readings. I set Rosamund in charge of collecting more evidence. Squad Leader Moolocks's testimony would help, but I knew better than to rely on a single ghost. There was no way to force her to speak when I brought her before the jarls. Better to have some physical proof, then use her testimony as supporting evidence. Something like the map that General Holt had found before he'd been murdered would help immensely.

Since Toketie was working with the Royal Company's quartermaster, she would look for places in the encampment that might hide secrets and relay those to Rosamund. Rosamund mentioned that she could use her free period on Friday afternoons to sneak into the camp.

"You should use every afternoon," I said. "General Tepeh and their thanes will be distracted by Army Training. It's the best time."

"But I'm in class Monday through Thursday," Rosamund argued.

"Remedial classes," Oluk said. "You were just complaining how boring they were. Can't you skip some of them?"

"No, don't miss class," I said. "The teachers may complain about it, and you know that General Tepeh has been taking most of their meals with the headmistress. Instead, make sure to do all your work perfectly and efficiently. Finish before any of the younger students, then ask to go to the bathroom. The teachers won't be suspicious if you take extra long to return if they know you've already finished your assignments for the day."

Rosamund nodded. "I can do that."

"What shall we do?" Einar asked.

"Focus on recovering your strength," I told Einar. "The rest of us will build better relations with the heirs. We need the jarls on our side, and that means getting their heirs' support."

"There *are* a lot of heirs in our year, aren't there?" Rosamund mused.

That had been purposeful. Once the Familiar Queen, my mother, had announced her pregnancy, many of the jarls had done their best to make sure to copy her. They'd wanted their heirs to be at school with the future queen. I had a suspicion that Froya was actually a year older than the rest of us, but I couldn't prove that she'd been held back to enter Witch Hall at the same time as me and Aklemin. Jarl Falk was clever like that.

"Toketie, Aklemin, I need you both to work on Froya. You have my permission to tell her just enough to get her on our side, if you can be sure she won't go run to Jarl Falk about it immediately. Or, that if she does, it won't be enough to give away our plans to my father."

Toketie glanced at Aklemin, then nodded. "We can do that."

"Yuyan, spend more time with Kwaddis. Make Jarl Tenas think you're on the verge of courting him."

"I don't want to be dishonest," Yuyan protested. "Not like that."

"Then don't. Tell Kwaddis honestly that you don't want to bond with him, but that you're still considering him as your partner in the entourage." I paused. "Unless you're not?"

"Oh, no, it'll be him or Lei. I've just been waiting to see what hole we need filled."

Ah, but of course. She'd been waiting to see if I'd bond with Charles after all. Charles and Kwaddis hated each other, raised as they were by Jarl Almstedt and Jarl Tenas. Having both in my entourage would lead to more infighting than unity.

"Don't promise him anything," I said, which was as close as I was going to come to saying aloud that I hadn't completely ruled out Charles as my future familiar.

Yuyan glanced from me to Rosamund and back, obviously confused. I still hadn't explained my complicated relationship with Rosamund to my entourage. I didn't want to. Yuyan had the option to select someone for the entourage she'd never bond with, but I couldn't choose my consort that way. The Familiar King or Queen or Consort needed to be my bonded familiar or my people would never trust them to lead if anything happened to me.

My father had been able to act as the ruler of the Cursed Kingdom since my mother's death because of their bond. The reason witches went catatonic and familiars went feral upon a bond breaking was because they absorbed the majority of their partner's power when that partner died. Sometimes, it was enough to kill the one remaining. My father had been strong enough to learn to control it, and had remained the most powerful ice witch in the kingdom since.

"I'll work on Chao," I said. Though, as he was a child of my father's entourage, I wasn't sure it would be wise to trust him at all. "As for Charles—"

"I'll take him," Rosamund said.

I paused, looking at her. "You will?"

Rosamund shrugged. "My parents work for Jarl Almstedt now, so I have a reason to talk with him about her."

The logic was sound, though the thought of Rosamund and Charles talking disquieted me. I said nothing. I'd been the one to choose this. I'd known keeping Rosamund close would be an implicit rejection of Charles and all the other bone familiars. Several had started courting or being courted by my fellow bone witches. When this was over, my pool of candidates would be significantly smaller.

I couldn't bring myself to care. My choice of familiar was far less important than stopping the coming war.

The most important heirs done, we moved on to the children of the other jarls. Oluk promised to talk with Shugh Esalth, one of the glass familiars in our year and a grandson of the jarl of Desertmouth, and I said I would take Kalitan. We divvied up the heirs in the younger years as well, but it was the seniors who would matter most in the end.

It would be a delicate dance, gathering what we needed to successfully bring my father's crimes to light. I could only hope that the emperor of Vinland would be open to our reparations—and that his son would not risk any more attacks in the meantime.

"We have until Candlemas," I said, referring to the holiday over winter break. "That will be the only time the jarls meet before our graduation—and we can't afford to wait that long. We must act now if we've any hope of stopping this war."

"We'll do it, Shaw," Rosamund said, fierce and unbowed. "We won't let the Witch King hurt anyone else."

There were nine weeks left of winter term. Barely over two months to gather evidence and get the heirs on our side, without letting on to my father or his entourage that we knew the truth.

"Tell me this is possible," I said to Aklemin. "Tell me we have a chance of stopping this war."

Aklemin walked over to the pitcher of water and looked into it. Their mouth began to tremble, their usual mask lowered for just a moment. "Yes," Aklemin said, hoarse and shaky and so very relieved. "Yes, we have a chance."

It was enough.

A LETTER ARRIVED FROM MY father the next Saturday morning—not quite a week after we'd made our plan. I took it from the young student with mail duty and made sure to show none of my worry on my face as I thanked her.

Einar was still in the infirmary, so there was no one to activate the privacy runes on our table. I tucked the letter into my bag without opening it. "I think I'll go for a ride after breakfast," I said.

"I'll join you," Rosamund quickly volunteered.

I didn't argue. The rest of my entourage turned back to their food, knowing we'd share the contents of the letter when it was safe to do so.

Last term, Rosamund had taken to riding one of the horses in the stable every Saturday morning. I'd joined her a few times before our courtship fell apart. I cherished those memories, even the one where we'd had to chase after an escaped herd. That had been the first time she'd admitted she trusted me. Those mornings together had given me hope in our relationship.

Everything was different now. I had no choice but to rely on Rosamund, but keeping her close wasn't helping me move on from her rejection. She made it all too easy to dream of things I would never be allowed.

A weapon, not a partner, I reminded myself, but the words

felt hollow. I reached under the table to touch the outlines of the moonstone bones in my pocket.

We finished eating and put our dishes in the bucket before heading to the stable. My duty during the school year was caring for the tack and exercising the horses. I chose Madam Xu's black gelding, Banye, to ride that morning. I wasn't surprised to see Rosamund bring out Pyre.

"What has Mister Jostein said about her?" I asked, nodding to the sorrel bone mare.

Rosamund shook her head. "Madam Dyer had no family, at least none she talked about, and they couldn't find a will. If Pyre was a draft, Mister Jostein said he would have kept her, but he has no reason to stable a bone horse for the school. She'll be sold as soon as he can find a buyer."

I watched the way Rosamund carefully checked Pyre's hooves, deftly avoiding the horse's attempt at biting her. Bone horses were vicious. Like all magical animals, they were a third larger than their counterparts. There was exposed bone along Pyre's long neck and across her ankles. Her sorrel-red coat had caused Madam Dyer to name her after the death she'd run from when she immigrated from the Colonies to the Cursed Kingdom. It was uncomfortable to realize this horse was the only family Madam Dyer had left behind.

"Would your family buy her?" I asked. Rosamund's family bred bone horses, and Pyre was a fine one.

Rosamund hesitated. I could tell she wanted to say yes, but instead she shook her head. "You never asked why my parents were working for Jarl Almstedt now."

I hadn't. I might have, if I hadn't been determined to ignore Rosamund for most of our journey from Gravestown back to school. "Why?" I asked now.

"Jarl Snass took our ranch the week before Samhain," Rosamund explained, her voice barely above a whisper.

I accidentally clipped Banye's teeth with the bit in my surprise. Apologizing with a hand on his neck, I asked, "What reason would he have to do that?"

"Your fa—the Witch King demanded it. Apparently every jarl had to give up some portion of land for army purposes, in preparation for the war. Since we're so far from the border, Jarl Snass decided to take the ranch as a supply post."

I'd always thought of my father as a good king. I knew his politics were heavy-handed, but he gave good reasons when I pressed him on them. Tax this group to give relief to these people who needed it. Recruit new soldiers here to give jobs to those without. It wasn't until Rosamund had come into my life that I'd started to question some of those policies. I didn't disagree with them all, but I thought there might be a better way. She'd been so adamant about giving people options. It made me reconsider some of those laws and taxes and political strategies. Was there a kinder way to rule, without leaving the kingdom vulnerable in the process?

"That's why you want me to gift you land," I realized.

"I want it in writing that it can't be taken from my descendants," Rosamund said. "Not all of it, anyway. A portion if there's a need, but the house should be assured. If Jarl Snass needed land, he could have taken half our pastures and some of the surrounding fields from our neighbors. It wouldn't have been comfortable for our village, but we'd have made it work."

I grimaced. "Instead, he saw the opportunity to fulfill the quota with a family whose reputation was already damaged, never mind the profits your family's horses brought to his holdings. And he stole your home doing it."

"Yes, well"—Rosamund shrugged—"at least Charles's mother is reasonable. She gave my parents a job in her own stables and put them in charge of training the horses for Gravestown's Company. I guarantee they'll have the best steeds in the entire army before the year is through."

"But it doesn't give your family the income to buy another mare," I finished, understanding the issue.

"They can barely keep the ones we have left. The rest of our herd has already been sold."

"And your uncles?" I had met Rosamund's family in Forest's Edge just before the incident with the moose that had led me to invite her to come to Witch Hall. It had felt homey, her ranch. A large family, seated on charmingly mismatched furniture.

"My cousin, Toketie's brother, is getting married over winter break to a shoemaker in Woodside. Uncle Inge and Uncle Chetwoot are staying with Uncle Chetwoot's sister, who lives in Woodside too, while they help prepare for the wedding. I think they plan to join Ma and Papa in Gravestown after, though they might want to stay closer to Solemie. Especially if his new wife gets pregnant fast." Rosamund shook her head, obviously upset at the reminder of what her family was going through. She led Pyre to the nearest mounting block without another word.

I dropped the subject, instead making a mental note to talk with Mister Jostein. Pyre was a beautiful mare, and I knew she got along well with Cow, which was always a toss-up with bone horses. She didn't deserve to lose her home because of her rider's death. I could afford to pay the school to board her, at least for now.

I wished I could gift her to Rosamund. It would have made a wonderful third courtship present. The first, to prove my power, had come in the form of a red cloak. She'd tried to return it to me once we'd settled back into Witch Hall, but I'd refused. It suited her. I was pleased to see that, as the weather had dipped further toward true winter, she'd begun to wear it again.

The second courtship gift had been a terrible idea in retrospect. I'd given her a contract. Not the same one the rest of us had signed but the one General Tepeh had given to me to sign—which guaranteed a place as a thane in the Royal Company. When General Thane had handed me the contract before that fateful assembly, I'd tucked it away and signed the generic one instead.

I'd been sure of Rosamund's power even then. Sure that she could lead a platoon in the war with Vinland and achieve victory. She was so protective of her friends. Her command style inspired loyalty, even though she didn't seem to see it like the rest of us did. But that was the point of the second gift. To show how I perceived her. I'd handed her the contract and waited for her to read it. I had been ready to explain, ready to prove to her that I knew she could do it. First a thane, then my fellow queen. She had so much potential as a ruler, if only she would see it.

Instead, Rosamund had ripped up the contract. She'd torn off my courtship necklace and left me in tatters, alongside those pieces of paper and scattered moonstone bones.

"Coming, Shaw?" Rosamund asked.

I quickly mounted Banye and nudged him to follow Pyre out of the barn. Rosamund clicked Pyre into a trot and set off. Banye followed without me having to ask. Nonmagical horses usually went where bone horses led.

The third and final courtship gift was to prove I understood Rosamund's desires. I obviously hadn't last term, not really. I'd always compared Rosamund to a bone horse, back when I'd thought the horse her first shift. I'd thought I could bridle her, like Cow or

Banye or any other steed. I'd thought I could ride out her bucks and earn her respect.

I knew better now. Rosamund was a bone wolf. She could not be trapped or tamed or broken in.

If I were still courting her, I'd give Pyre to Rosamund. Gift that beautiful bone horse and ten acres of land to house her on. A home big enough for her whole family to live comfortably. A place for Rosamund to visit when she needed a break from court politics—from ruling with me on the Frozen Mountain. But bone wolves choose their pack. I had been so busy trying to make her part of mine that I had failed to become part of hers.

All I could do now was live with that failure. I'd buy Pyre for the school, and pay for her boarding. I'd tell Mister Jostein that she could be lent out to bone witches and familiars in need of a horse to ride during school trips to the Bone Forest. Or maybe, once I graduated, I'd take Pyre home with me and let Cow have her as a companion. I wouldn't allow either horse to suffer just because I'd failed in courting my ideal partner.

We rode out by the river, far enough from the nearest buildings that I determined our chance of being overheard was small. I ripped open my father's letter. Rosamund kept watch while I carefully read the contents.

My dear,

I turned to this letter as soon as I received the news. I must apologize for the grievous injury suffered upon a member of your entourage. I know you must be angry, with me as much as with the Vinlanders who attacked you. Please be aware that I did not foresee the attack until the morning before it occurred. By then it was far too late to get a warning to Kiwa, even using our fastest courier.

None of this excuses the injustice. The jarls argue that it is still too soon to send a declaration of war, but if you believe it time, I will lend my voice to your decision. There are rumors that the Vinlander invaders were led by one of the emperor's own children. If this is true, it will be a grave sign. Write to me and we will confer about the best path forward.

Your loving father,
David Colchuck
Witch King of the Cursed Kingdom

"He's still lying to me," I said. I felt like I could breathe frost with how cold I was. "He claims he didn't know about the attack until the morning of."

Rosamund reached over to touch the back of my hand. Her fingers were warm and her magic warmer. "We'll stop him, Shaw."

I folded the letter away. I wasn't sure if it would count as evidence, but better to keep it just in case. "He's trying to manipulate me into starting the war early. He'd only do that if he's begun seeing versions of the future where the war has been stopped, even if he doesn't yet know why or how."

"Then it's working," Rosamund said. "We can do this."

We could do this. We had to do this. "Have you tried sneaking into the camp?" I asked.

Rosamund nodded. "I keep getting lost though," she admitted.

That, at least, was a problem I could solve. Rosamund and I kept the horses to a slow walk as we talked over what I knew of the layout of the Royal Company's encampment.

"Ask Toketie where the supply tents are," I said. "See if you can find anything that might have been used to set fire to the villages.

An excess of oil or torches perhaps." We needed the evidence, or it would simply be my word against my father's. I knew who the jarls' council would believe in the end.

"I'll find something," Rosamund promised.

"We need to ask what the heirs told their parents about the Vinlander prince," I continued. "I don't know if General Tepeh was close enough to hear the Vinlanders calling him that. We may be able to get away with claiming it was just another group of terrorists instead of an organized force, so long as we can convince the seniors who heard it not to share."

"None of us want the war to start, especially not before we graduate," Rosamund said. "We can probably use that."

Once again, Rosamund proved she had a better understanding of politics than she believed of herself. I ignored the twist of bitterness, focusing instead on my anger over my father's attempts at manipulation. Had he always been like that, or was it merely worse because he was so close to starting this war, only to feel it slipping away again? I hated that I couldn't trust my own memory of him. I'd always thought of people as predictable, but in my arrogance, I'd fallen into the same trap.

I'd consult with Aklemin before writing a reply. Of all my entourage, Aklemin knew the Witch King best. Together, we'd figure out what to say to make him believe that I was still his willing pawn, without giving him enough to push the council into declaring war early.

"Let's go," I said, turning Banye back toward the stable. "We have work to do."

Chapter 9

I tried to be patient about Einar's healing process, but even though he soon transitioned to solid food and could begin catching up on his schoolwork, he was still too weak to leave the infirmary bed. Without our glass witch there to keep our table's conversations private, it was difficult to make plans. At least every Saturday, at the most secluded part of our morning ride, Rosamund could report on what area of the camp she'd managed to search. She'd yet to find anything of worth in the supply tents, though with such short windows she hadn't been able to search through everything.

We'd made some progress on the heirs. Most were rattled by the attack and had agreed that we shouldn't rush into war with Vinland. More than a few outright stated they would follow where I led. Apparently, many attributed the fact that none of our classmates had died to my skill at necromancy. I was gratified by their trust in me, and just as angry at the circumstances that had caused it.

The week of midterms arrived before I was prepared to face it. I'd normally be glad to see half the term complete, but I felt our dwindling time like a candle drowning in what was left of its own wax.

"I think it's time we put our theories to practice," Mister Xu said on Monday morning during our Experimental Wards class. "For our midterm, I must ask each of you to prepare a small proof of concept. You'll split into pairs, one glass witch and one bone witch, to create a simple spell, ritual, or rune sequence that successfully combines both glass and bone magic. You'll have the next three class periods to work on this project. We'll present on Thursday for your midterm grade."

Chao frowned from his seat to my left, glancing at me. I knew what he was waiting for. The rest of the witches in the class waited for the same thing—for me to choose which glass witch I would work with for the midterm. I took a deep breath and then released it out slowly to try to calm my anger at their assumptions.

I didn't want to choose a different partner. Einar was the first witch who'd officially joined my entourage. I'd asked Aklemin before him, but they'd put me off for an entire year before finally agreeing to it. I'd chosen Einar during my fourth year at Witch Hall, when Aklemin and I had been fighting every other week over their refusal to actually try in school and their indecision about being part of my entourage. Einar's calming nature had been a boon. Yuyan had joined us about six months after Aklemin had finally settled down and I'd spent these last two years as one of four, but I would never forget the long months it had been just Einar at my side.

I stood and walked the few feet to Mister Xu's desk. "I'd like to partner with Einar," I said. "We can work out of the infirmary. So long as I have your permission to present our midterm for the both of us on Thursday."

Mister Xu visibly softened at my words. "Yes, of course you may. If the notes he turned in last week are any indication, he's more than caught up with the rest of his classmates on theory. Get Madam Tukwilla's permission before he does any active spellwork, but if he's not ready I'm happy to step in and perform his side of whatever sequence you two develop."

"Thank you, Mister Xu," I said, and walked back to my desk.

"I should have guessed you'd be too loyal to choose anyone else," Chao murmured ruefully as I gathered up my things.

I paused in the act of sliding my notebook into my bag. "I've always done my best to reward loyalty with loyalty," I said. The statement came out a little sharper than I'd intended.

I still didn't know where Chao's loyalties lay. Though his parents were part of my father's entourage, I hadn't grown up with him. He'd stayed in the town his mother ruled even when his parents traveled to court. We hadn't really started interacting until we both came to Witch Hall, but we'd been quick to find each other once here.

I'd always considered Chao my closest friend outside of my entourage, which made me all the more wary of trusting him. Though he'd agreed not to share anything about the Vinlander prince until I had a chance to tell the jarls' council about it in person, part of me wondered if he'd already written to his mother. I hadn't forgotten the way he'd shared my courtship of Rosamund with her, and through her, my father, before I was ready last term.

Looking back, I could tell that my father's letter on the subject had been motivated partially by fear. My father didn't know Rosamund and thus had not been able to easily predict her effect on my life. Ice witches could often see vague connections between people even when they'd not met the other end of that connection—enough to give love fortunes and things like that—but for my father to successfully control the course of my destiny, he needed more clarity. He'd met Charles many times and had always supported Jarl Almstedt's plan to see us bonded, though he'd never overtly pushed me to court the stag familiar. That was his way, I'd come to realize. Subtle manipulations—enough to make me or the jarls believe we'd come up with the ideas ourselves when really he'd been the one pulling the strings.

Perhaps Chao's parents had manipulated their son just the same. That didn't mean Chao would take their side in the end. Jingyi had put her support behind Rosamund last term before any of the rest of the seniors—Oluk excluded. Perhaps Chao and his familiar would be loyal to me over my father when the truth became public. I could only hope, and plan for contingencies.

I touched Chao's shoulder as I passed him and leaned down to say, "Let me know if any of our classmates need help with their projects."

"Will do," Chao replied, shoulders thrown back like he was proud to have been given the responsibility. Had he noticed my hesitance in interacting with him lately? I needed to be more careful about what my own actions were revealing. I made a mental note to talk with Chao about less important topics, just to get back into our old routine.

Einar was asleep when I arrived at the infirmary. I sat down at his bedside and took out a notebook to get to work drafting ideas for our project.

The glass witch stirred awake after twenty minutes or so. "Oluk?" he mumbled.

"It's me," I said. "Water?"

Einar croaked what was probably an agreement. I grabbed the pitcher at his bedside and poured him a glass, then helped him sit up just enough to drink it.

"Thanks, Shaw," he said, setting the glass aside. He blinked a few times until he looked more aware. "What time is it?"

"Early. The first morning block just started," I said. "Want to hear about our midterm assignment?"

"For Mister Xu's class?" Einar struggled to sit up further. I rearranged his pillows for him.

"We're working together on this one," I said. "See if you like any of these ideas."

And then we were off. It was heartening to see Einar closer to his old self as he listened to my thoughts and asked the right questions to poke holes in them. By the end of the first morning block, we were down to one workable idea and a dozen potential starting points for it.

"I'll show it to Mister Xu tomorrow to get his thoughts," I said.

"I wish I could be there," Einar remarked, more morose than I'd ever seen him before the injury. He collapsed back against his pillows, staring up at the ceiling. He was sweating from the pain again. "I hate this, Shaw."

"I know," I replied, caught between awkward and sympathetic.

I'm not sure what I would have done if I'd been stuck in bed for an entire month, but it wouldn't have been pretty. I knew Yuyan had done her best to mitigate bed sores and activate Einar's muscles so he'd still be able to move once they figured out how to get him out of bed, but for now he wasn't even able to sit up of his own accord and that would be a nightmare for almost anyone.

I waited for Einar to fall asleep before I collected our notes and left, even though it made me late for Madam Kawak's class. The ice witch didn't remark on it as I walked to my usual log and I knew she must have foreseen my tardiness, and the reason for it. All the teachers had been remarkably patient about Einar's injury and my entourage's reaction to it, even the notoriously strict ones.

General Tepeh was a different story.

"On Friday, I will proctor a midterm test for Army Training," the general told me that afternoon. We were in the command tent in the center of the encampment, as usual. "I believe we can both agree that you and yours need more experience in large-scale combat situations after what happened on the company march."

"I hope you're not suggesting to send us out to Goose Point again, General Tepeh," I said. Would my father truly dare to repeat the exercise in an attempt to actually kill more of my classmates?

"No, of course not," General Tepeh said. "We will stay on campus. I will not put students in unnecessary danger and the Vinlanders are obviously ravenous for blood, even with the coming snowstorm. Winter will put them off for a while but not forever. We must use whatever reprieve the snow gives us to make sure you are ready to face them."

More manipulations. I was at least grateful I wouldn't have to argue against another off-campus exercise. "What do you envision for the midterm, or am I meant to be surprised?"

"We will split the group into two companies. Two of my thanes will lead each group in the place of generals. You and your entourage may act as thanes under the command of those generals so that you may experience leading not just your own classmates but also the soldiers who will be spread among the various squads and platoons of each group."

I took a few seconds to breathe and think through my reply to that proposal. General Tepeh had already turned back to the map in the center of the command tent, putting out a group of army markers so they could teach me some new strategy.

"Do you believe I failed, General?" I asked finally.

General Tepeh's head whipped up at that. "Princess?"

"On the company march. You allowed me to lead my classmates to prove that I could. To prove that the jarls' proposal to split them up among the companies of the Cursed Kingdom was flawed and they would be better served under my command in the Royal Company upon graduation. Yet you would have us split now, and take command from your thanes. You must believe that I am not fit to lead them."

"Shaw," General Tepeh said, breaking formality in favor of a pandering tone. "You are young. I never would have left you alone if I'd known what would happen. You nearly lost a member of your entourage in that disaster. Would it not be better to learn under more experienced leaders so that you are better prepared to face the coming conflicts?"

Everything about the general's words were meant to make me feel like a failure so that I would believe it was my fault Einar had been injured. I couldn't deny the guilt lingered in me. I had rehashed the attack in my head over and over again, wondering what I could have done differently to save Einar the pain he was now in. But I was not at fault for the *disaster,* as General Tepeh had called it. I'd done everything I could to save my classmates and they had been saved. Perhaps I'd have been easier to manipulate if any of the students had died, but I would not let myself fall to my father's schemes any longer. I had already decided my course.

I understood the general's angle with this midterm. They wished to discredit my leadership. It wasn't even a good test—how would they grade how much my fellow students had learned when all they'd be doing was following along with the soldiers? No, I could see my father's hands all over this. He may not have perfectly foreseen our plans to take him to trial, but he must have seen enough to be wary.

I still didn't know why my father wanted to go to war with Vinland, but I was beginning to wonder if he even intended for me to lead the army. Was my destiny to be a figurehead puppeted by General Tepeh and the Witch King? Did he plan to guide me along a path of destruction, using my ability to summon the dead as a weapon for his own purposes?

I wished I could take Cow and ride up to the Frozen Mountain to confront him. I wanted to understand *why*. I'd spent my entire life so certain of my future, and now everything was crumbling around me. I would not let General Tepeh take away the little control I'd worked to recover.

"I will learn best by being given my own command," I said. "Allow me to lead my classmates as a company again. Pit us against your thanes and see how we do. You will have an easier time grading our progress under those circumstances, wouldn't you agree, General?"

General Tepeh frowned, obviously unhappy with my suggestion. "Do you not believe your classmates will be upset to be reminded of the trauma they recently faced?"

As if they cared about my classmates' trauma. "Better to work through our trauma now, under safer circumstances, than in actual war," I countered.

General Tepeh's nostrils flared, but finally they nodded in agreement. "Very well, Princess, we shall do it your way. On Friday, you will lead your classmates in battle against my thanes. I expect you to be prepared."

I carefully hid the shiver that ran down my spine at the dark promise in General Tepeh's words.

ON WEDNESDAY, DURING MISTER XU'S class, I brought Einar a collection of small bones I'd fetched from the woods to the west of Witch Hall's campus. He spent a painstaking hour carefully carving runes into each one.

"Ready?" I asked once he was finished.

Einar couldn't lean very far, so I'd placed the engraved bones on his bedside table. He reached over and put his finger on one of the runes. The rest lit up in an array of color as his magic spread across the circle.

"Try it," Einar said.

I hated how pale he looked. Even just that little bit of magic was enough to exhaust him. I said nothing though, knowing he would hate for me to fuss over him after all the work we'd done to get Madam Tukwilla to approve him using magic.

I took out a small jar with a grasshopper I'd caught just before breakfast that morning. Carefully, I opened the lid and tipped the grasshopper into the center of the circle.

The runes flared again. The grasshopper tried to jump off the table and slammed into an invisible barrier right before the circle of bone. It fell back. I held my breath, waiting, but it took barely a second before the grasshopper was back up and trying to jump away once more. Again, it was repelled by the ward we'd created.

Einar whooped, and I wanted to do the same. It had been a

risk. Because the runes were being powered from bone magic, there'd been a real chance they'd suck the life out of a living prisoner. Mister Xu had told several horror stories from Daming to that same effect. Luckily, it seemed our work had paid off. We'd designed it to be a prison—and one that could contain anyone. Not even a glass witch would be able to affect the ward once inside the circle. It could only be activated or deactivated from the outside, and only by a glass and bone witch working together. While not practical for most prisons, it was a real proof of concept for the ability to combine bone and glass magic. My mind raced with possibilities—what about combining glass magic with flower to make for stronger healing? Could we combine bone and ice, despite being polar opposite types of magic?

"Good work," I said as Einar pulled his power back from the runes. I collected the inscribed bones to show to Mister Xu tomorrow. The grasshopper had already made its bid for freedom, but it wouldn't be difficult to catch another small test subject before the midterm demonstration.

"You look tired," Einar said. "I know I can't do much right now, but I would like to help. If I can."

I paused in the middle of packing up. That was new. Einar had never been the type to push, waiting for others to seek out his support first. It had worked for us, as I didn't like to share my troubles until I was sure of their cause. He wasn't wrong, however. I *was* tired. My nightmares had grown more detailed as of late.

"It's not something you can help with. At least, not now. I just . . . Einar, what if some of the jarls . . . What if some of the jarls really have been working with my father on this plot? Or if they agree with what he's done? I truly don't believe Jarl Tenas or Jarl Esalth will, but only because their lands would be in the initial line of fire. What if the other jarls are less concerned about the casualties and care more for the potential rewards? Whatever my father's true motivations, you can be sure he'll share it while on trial if there is a chance it will save him from being deposed. And whatever he shares, the jarls will believe. He is an ice witch. If he says we can defeat Vinland and earn a thousand years of peace for doing so, would they take that deal?"

"Would you?" Einar asked, steady even in the aftermath of my increasingly panicked ruminations. "If that is truly the reason?"

No, but only because I didn't believe it possible. My father was a powerful ice witch, but even he couldn't really promise a thousand years of peace. "You said it yourself. Hate begets hate. I don't believe that warring with Vinland will do anything but light the spark for more anti-magical bigotry. We saw how it was with the Colonies. They only got worse as the Crusades dragged on."

"What is your real concern, then?"

I took a second to think it through. What was I really worried about? War, of course. I'd already decided to try to stop it, but what if I couldn't? What if my war truly was inevitable?

"What if . . ." I began aloud. "What if it's a mistake to fight against this? What if our attempts to stop the war with Vinland sparks civil war among our own people instead?"

"Ah." Einar looked down at his own hands, shaking minutely against his lap. "I'm not the one to ask. Aklemin may have a better idea if such a future is at risk. But, Shaw"—at that, he looked up to meet my eyes—"you are doing the right thing, attempting to prevent this war. It is criminal to slaughter innocent civilians, no matter the reason. Your father should be brought to justice, along with all who followed the orders to burn those Vinland villages."

As always, Einar knew just what to say to rebuild my confidence.

"You're right. Thank you, Einar. We should all strive to your level of honor."

Einar blushed slightly at my praise, and as I left the infirmary, I felt satisfied that I'd at least managed to distract him from his current circumstances, even if I only felt worse about my own.

In Madam Kawak's class, I considered Aklemin. Would they let me know if there was a chance our plan would spark civil war? I wanted to say yes, but they had always played their cards close to their chest. I resolved to ask them directly, as soon as I found a private place to do so.

Madam Kawak called for our attention, and I looked back to her. "Tomorrow, you will each write me an essay for your midterm on any topic we have discussed thus far this term. I would encourage you to do some research in the library tonight to make sure you are adequately prepared to speak to your topic of choice. For today, we will finish our unit on ritual magics."

I pulled out my notebook and graphite stick to begin taking notes as Madam Kawak continued. "We have already discussed the most known rituals. Those which take place upon our four cardinal holidays: Candlemas, Beltane, Lammas, and Samhain. Now, let us widen our view to discuss the act of ritual magic as a whole, and what purposes other rituals may serve. Can someone share with class the three categories of ritual?"

I glanced around, but none of the seniors had their hand raised. Rituals weren't a common subject in our classes at Witch Hall, but the uncertainty on my classmates' faces still surprised me. I raised my hand, and Madam Kawak called on me to answer.

"The most common type of rituals are about strengthening our innate magic, often for a singular purpose," I began. "We see this on Samhain, when bone magic is strengthened to allow a greater number of the dead to be calmed. Or on Candlemas, where ice witches can use the ritual to access more detailed visions of the future. The next most common type of ritual draws upon magic to enhance a particular trait or effect, such as Beltane's ritual to bring love and protection to a community or Lammas's to bring luck and prosperity. The final type is rarer. These rituals are about change—turning one thing into another. Sometimes physically and other times less tangibly. They are more similar to curses than the other two rituals, as they often require some kind of payment to work."

"Very good, Princess," Madam Kawak said. There was a glimmer of surprise in her voice, as if she hadn't expected me to give such a thorough answer.

I'd always been fascinated by rituals. It was something my father and I had explored together, back when I was a child. I'd been allowed to observe my first Samhain ritual at the age of nine—not long after my bone magic had begun to manifest. I'd become obsessed with the idea of rituals after and frustrated that my tutors hadn't known more than the basic information. My father had taken time from his own duties to help me research them, and we'd spent several glorious months learning all we could together. When I'd gone off to Witch Hall the next year, I'd looked back upon those months each time I felt homesick.

The memory tasted sour now. It was hard to reconcile my loving father with the warmongering king he'd somehow become.

"As we have covered strengthening rituals and effecting rituals in the lectures on the cardinal holidays, let us now turn our attention to transmuting rituals. The ones which change one thing into another," Madam Kawak was saying. "As was so succinctly explained, transmuting rituals always have a cost. This cost can be lessened, however, by making sure the thing you are attempting to change is similar to what you wish it to become. For instance, turning water to wine is easier than turning lead to gold."

I was surprised to see Aklemin taking real notes as Madam Kawak began to explain transmuting rituals in detail. "Do you intend to write about rituals for your midterm?" I whispered.

Aklemin hummed instead of answering. I turned back to my own notes with a shrug. Far be it from me to complain about Aklemin actually putting effort into their schoolwork. It might have taken years, but they had seemed more focused these past few terms.

Madam Kawak finished her explanation and bid us split into pairs to theorize a simple transmuting ritual. I expected she'd have some volunteers share their ritual ideas and then move on to discussing the likely cost of such a ritual. In all my research, the payments needed for these rituals were almost never worth the benefits—hence why they were so rare.

"You seem to know a lot about this," Rosamund said. Aklemin had already turned to pair up with Toketie, so it was no surprise that Rosamund assumed we would be partners. A few weeks ago, that assumption would have hurt, but I had grown numb to our unnamed partnership and the bitterness that never quite left me because of it.

"Rituals are fascinating," I said, because I didn't want to get into the story of my childhood with Rosamund. Not anymore. Not when it wouldn't mean anything for our relationship to make myself vulnerable to her. "Let's say we wanted arable land where once there was only untenable desert. We could use a transmuting ritual to change the land."

"That sounds too good to be true," Rosamund said. "Why don't more people do these rituals, then?"

"Because of the cost," I said. "To make the land farmable, you'd need to change the composition of the soil. But it's more than that. Depending on the power of the ritual, you may also be attempting to change the weather patterns so there's more frequent rain or divert a nearby river so there's irrigation. How much do you think it would cost to physically alter the landscape like that?"

"I don't know," Rosamund said.

"Too much," I said. "It'd be less expensive to merely move to where there is fertile soil. That is the problem with transmuting rituals."

Madam Kawak called for volunteers to share their rituals before I could go into it further, but I'd made my point. Some things weren't worth the cost, no matter how good the final outcome might be.

Chapter 10

ROSY

ROSY WAS THE FIRST TO TURN IN HER MIDTERM EXAM during her second afternoon class on Thursday. All that extra studying had paid off, it seemed, though she didn't think it was that great to boast about being the best in the class when all the other students were several years younger than her.

She opened her mouth to ask Mister Abramsen, the flower familiar in charge of the class, if she could go to the bathroom, but he waved a hand to cut her off.

"Get out of here, Miss Rosamund. Enjoy your afternoon," he said.

"Thank you, sir," Rosy murmured.

That wasn't what she'd been looking for. According to Shaw's plan, it was best if Rosy had the excuse of being in class when she snuck into the army's camp. She just hoped that Mister Abramsen would have no reason to tell General Tepeh he'd let her out early that day.

The class was in the eastern longhouse. Instead of risking being seen leaving the building, Rosy cracked open one of the side doors, called up the voice of her mouse, and shifted. The first snow of the year had fallen the previous weekend, and she used the now-dirty snowdrifts to blend in as she darted away from Witch Hall's campus toward the army's camp. She'd done this enough times now to know exactly which tree to make for on this side of the waterfall's creek. A quick shift to her squirrel and she was up the trunk and onto the branches. One jump to a tree on the other side, and then she was hopping branches all the way to the camp.

The army had cleared out a whole section of the eastern woods to set up their encampment, so Rosy was forced to shift back into her mouse once she was at the border of the camp. She slowed down considerably for this last part. The snow had begun icing over and the cold was uncomfortable on her paws, but she did her best to burrow her way through the drifts or find the gaps at the edges of the tent walls.

She'd checked the supply tents already, and though part of her thought to go back for a more thorough search now that she had the time, she figured she may as well try something different. So, she headed to the very center of the camp, where Shaw had said the command tent was located. Rosy found it easily enough. It was a perfectly round pavilion with a flag hanging from the top depicting the crest of the royal family—the three-eyed raven on its dark blue backdrop.

The tent wasn't empty. Rosy could hear the sound of conversation coming from inside. She crept close. Field mice were tiny, but as a bone mouse, she was large enough to be clearly visible against the woven mat of the command tent's floor. She hesitated just outside the tent flap, camouflaged by her white fur against the snow. Should she attempt to chew her way into the back of the tent, or creep through the shadows along the tent walls?

"—beside the point, General," Shaw was saying.

Rosy paused in her dithering, curious.

"Then I fail to see the point entirely," General Tepeh responded.

"If my classmates cannot trust me to lead them to victory, how will the kingdom?"

"You cannot be blamed for your age and lack of experience, Princess," General Tepeh said soothingly. Poisonously. "This war comes sooner than I'd hoped, but your father believes you nearly ready for it. It is my job to make sure of that. Let me help you and you can be sure all your people will look to you for leadership."

Was General Tepeh trying to make Shaw believe her classmates *didn't* trust her? Rosy wanted to shift back so she could run into the tent and shout at them both. Of course Shaw's classmates trusted her. She just needed to remember Samhain to see that. When things got bad, they'd all turned to Shaw to lead them. Whether that was fair was a completely different question—but Shaw hadn't failed any of them yet. It was Rosy who had failed, when she'd run instead of saving Guanyu. She wondered if he'd have survived if Shaw had been there that fateful market day.

Now she was the one being unfair. She shouldn't have needed Shaw to be there for her to have done the right thing.

"What would you suggest, then, General?" Shaw asked.

"You need to learn to see the larger picture. You focus too much on the strongest weapons in your armory instead of the power that comes from large numbers of disposable pieces."

Shaw's voice turned frosty as she asked, "What do you mean?"

"I've looked into your victories. The Combat midterm. Samhain night. Even the Vinland ambush, if you can call surviving a victory." General Tepeh paced across the tent as they talked. Rosy drew away as they neared the front of the tent, but they didn't go through. The strong smell of their shoe polish lingered even as they paced back toward Shaw. "Can you tell me what stands in common among all three? What you used as a lynchpin to win?"

Shaw did not answer.

"Rosamund Holt. A bone wolf familiar. In the same way your grandmother used Ylva the Red Wolf to tear holes in the ranks of the Crusaders. But Ylva did not win the war alone. She was merely a single weapon, and she was not even paramount to your grandmother's victory in the final battle."

Rosy thumped her long tail against the ground, upset for reasons she couldn't name. Was it being compared to her grandmother? She'd spent most her life trying to avoid Gran's fate—and yet here she was. When Pops had died and Gran lost the comfort of their bond, she'd lost her ability to control her wolf. What if Rosy never got a handle on her own feral rages? Would the council lock her away too once her use was done?

"You've made your point, General," Shaw said stiffly. "I have no wolf to fight with me in tomorrow's midterm, but do not mistake me for being unarmed. I know very well that even the most unlikely of people can change the game entirely."

"I suppose we'll see," General Tepeh said noncommittally.

Their conversation turned to strategy, and Rosy left to go search a different area of the encampment. Thirty minutes later, she was forced to give up and head for stable duty—once more unsuccessful.

Rosy was contemplating where in the encampment she could possibly search next when she walked into the stable and heard the sound of muffled crying. She rushed to the feed room to find Oluk on the ground, kneeling in a mess of spilled grain.

"What happened?" Rosy asked, worry making her tone sharp. She cast an eye across Oluk, but there wasn't any visible sign of injury.

Oluk shook his head, still crying.

Rosy kneeled down and ignored the way the spilled grain cut into her knees. "Are you hurt?" she asked, softer this time.

Once again, Oluk shook his head.

Rosy pulled Oluk into an awkward hug. "We'll fix it," she said. "Don't worry, we'll clean this up. It'll be fine."

"It's not the grain," Oluk said against her shoulder. "I don't care about the grain." But even as he said it, he sobbed harder. "I don't—I don't know what to do, Rosy," Oluk said between great gasping breaths.

"I'll help. Just tell me what's going on," Rosy promised.

Oluk rubbed his face harshly against her shoulder. "You can't. No one can. That's the problem."

Of course. Rosy should have realized what this was all about. Einar. Still stuck in the infirmary and in need of constant care by flower witches to numb the pain. She could only imagine how helpless Oluk must feel about the situation. She was equally helpless to do anything. Oluk was right—if Yuyan and Madam Tukwilla hadn't been able to do more, what could she and Oluk do?

"It'll be okay," Rosy said again, though the words felt empty. "We'll figure it out. He's doing better, isn't he? He can stay awake nearly all day now. His teachers are helping him get through their lessons even from bed. He just needs time to recover, that's all."

Oluk pulled away to put his head in his hands, still crying. Rosy stopped filling the space with platitudes. After a time, she pulled back to begin cleaning up the grain.

"Sorry," Oluk said once his sobs had died down. He still hadn't risen from the ground, even as Rosy swept up the last of the spilled grain.

"Why don't you join Einar for dinner, just the two of you?" Rosy suggested. "If that would help?"

Oluk hesitated, then nodded.

"I'll finish the chores up. Go on."

Oluk wiped at his face. "Thanks, Rosy."

Rosy shook her head. She didn't feel like she did much of anything. "You've covered for me before. It's fine. I'll grab you a tray from the dining hall after I'm done and drop it off, okay?"

The silence that stretched through the barn after Oluk left was uncomfortable. Rosy pushed through it, hating the way her gut squirmed with feelings she couldn't even parse through. What had Mister Sorensen's tarot reading said, last term? He'd predicted the pain that would come, but he'd also said Einar and his familiar would make it through to the other side of that pain.

Thinking of Einar's injury and Oluk's pain made her think of Shantie. She still hadn't received a return letter yet. How long did it take to travel to the Waiming Territories and back? It had been a month since she'd sent that letter. Surely the Cosho family had returned by now?

She didn't understand how the Witch King could be so cruel as to see his own people being cut down and still say it was the right path. War was never the answer—Rosy was sure of that. But if she couldn't find any evidence of the Witch King's culpability in it, would they have any choice?

Rosy hadn't been able to get General Tepeh's words out of her head. They mingled with the echoes of Oluk's sobs. She was still hearing it as she collected midterm essays at the end of Intermediate Shapeshifting on Friday.

She hadn't been able to do much during last night's assembly since she'd spent the whole time in page duty—punishment for sneaking off campus that first week. Shaw had attempted to argue the headmistress out of it, since Rosy's presence had kept the Vinlanders at bay, but Madam Kawak was a stickler for the rules. It hadn't been that bad in the end. The seniors had protected her while she was in the enchanted tabard by giving her simple tasks all night and keeping her far away from either visitors or younger students who might be less kind. Rosy had wanted to laugh at the irony of Charles herding her away from one of the jarls when he'd been the worst of her tormentors during her first page duty.

The next day, Madam Xu had charged her with watching over the students in Intermediate Shapeshifting while they wrote out their midterm essays. It had given her time to think. To mull over General Tepeh's words. *Was* Shaw too reliant on her? What Shaw needed was the support of a familiar, like how Shaw's grandfather had kept her grandmother alive while the Witch Queen did what was necessary to claim victory in that final battle of the great war. If Rosy and Shaw were destined to follow in the footsteps of their grandmothers, then Rosy at least wanted to find Shaw someone like her grandfather to stand at her side.

Rosy's eyes lingered on the bone familiars working on their midterms. Who was Shaw's ideal partner? No, the better question was: Who would be ideal to rule the kingdom at Shaw's side? Someone with a broad perspective on the issues facing people in the kingdom. Not just the nobility, but also the commonfolk. She knew

Charles would be a terrible Familiar King in that regard. He had no perspective to offer Shaw that she didn't already have herself.

Shaw would need a strong familiar though. If it couldn't be Charles, it would have to be someone else capable of fighting for her. Capable of giving Shaw enough power through their bond that she could do what was needed to keep the kingdom safe. And they would need to be decisive in the defense of both Shaw and her people. Rosy knew that was where she'd failed herself. If only she'd been quick enough to throw away the trappings of fear, Guanyu would be alive. Shaw would need a familiar who wouldn't hesitate, as she had.

Someone inspirational too. There hadn't been a Familiar King or Queen or Consort in eighteen years. The familiars of the kingdom deserved to have a monarch that they could look up to. Someone with the same kind of honor that Rosy so admired in Shaw. The kind that meant, no matter their flaws, they wanted to do best by their people. Someone who could learn from their mistakes and rule with inherent nobility—not inherited nobility. They would need enough knowledge of kingdom politics to help in court though. Rosy's head still spun whenever she tried to figure out all the different potential sides in this conflict with the Witch King.

She swept her gaze back and forth over the bone familiars in the Intermediate Workshop. She would have chosen Jingyi in an instant if the fox familiar weren't already bonded. Then there was Powish Sandelie, who was in the year below theirs. His wolverine shift was impressive, but Rosy hadn't seen him lording over his classmates with less powerful shifts. After the conversation about heirs, Rosy knew now that he was heir to the jarl of Solberg—a large town at the southwestern edge of the kingdom.

So Powish would be a great choice, if not for the fact that, a week ago, he'd presented a beautiful diamond necklace to offer courtship to a bone witch named Lin Ruan—a boy so pretty that he made even Shaw look plain. From the commotion Rosy had overheard, Lin had officially accepted the courtship at last night's assembly. So, Rosy turned her contemplation to her suitemates instead. A couple had committed to courtships of their own. Two of her suitemates, Goran and Illahie, had even begun courting each other. But there were two more in Intermediate Shapeshifting who were still looking for witches.

Ragna Strand was a wisp of a girl with thin blond hair and a strong nose. She had a weasel shift—an ermine to be precise. It wasn't a particularly powerful animal, but Rosy had learned over the course of last term that Ragna was one of the more talented bone familiars at sensing the magic of the dead. Just like how Toketie's talent at dream interpretation belied her simple swan shift, Rosy wouldn't be surprised if Ragna unlocked a much stronger second shift.

But Ragna was quiet, seeming to prefer to fade into the background of groups. Rosy wasn't sure that behavior would make for an inspiring Familiar Queen. Judging by how studious she was in class, she would undoubtedly be better at political strategy than Rosy, but would she be able to command the council? Would she need to? Perhaps she could leave that to Shaw and support from the shadows. She wasn't from a powerful family, Rosy didn't think. She'd heard something about Ragna's parents being tailors. A lack of her own political power, then, but perhaps she'd have the perspective to help Shaw rule more than just the nobility.

Then there was Emma Chambers. In direct contrast to Ragna, Emma was a large, curvy girl with luscious hair and loud voice. Judging by her late-night stories around the fire at their suite, she certainly knew how to hold people's attention. Her dog form was small, but all dogs were considered fairly powerful on the scale of bone animals. Since most familiars tended to find another form similar to their first, there was a good chance her next shift would be another type of canine. Even just a larger dog breed would make her a more threatening figure in a fight.

Emma was also one of the ones that Shaw had mentioned when they talked about the jarls' families. She was apparently Charles's cousin on his mother's side. If she and Shaw bonded, it would practically ensure the cooperation of Jarl Almstedt despite Shaw passing up Charles himself. Except, it was exactly because of her being from such a family that Rosy worried about her ability to speak for all familiars—rich and poor. She had no evidence to say that Emma was as spoiled as Charles was, but no evidence that she wasn't either.

Both Ragna and Emma were strong choices. Neither perfect, but Rosy thought both could learn to fulfill the duties of Familiar Queen better than Rosy herself ever could. She rushed through lunch, itching to read their midterm essays to see what she could glean from their reflections on their first shifts.

Rosy spent the afternoon reading through the essays. Even as she worked, she knew that Shaw and the rest of her classmates were doing the Army midterm. Part of her wanted to go watch—to assure herself that it was all safe. But the battle was happening in the woods to the east of campus, just north of the Army encampment. She'd hear it if another Vinlander invasion was happening.

Rosy threw herself into the midterm essays to distract her anxious voices. Emma's essay about her connection to her dog shift was sweet. Apparently, though her mother was the sister of Jarl

Almstedt, her father had come from more humble beginnings as a small-game hunter. To this day, he raised dogs to sell to hunters in Gravestown. When Emma was young, before coming to Witch Hall, she'd helped him with training. One litter had a runt that wasn't predicted to last the night. Emma had bottle-fed the runt herself. It never grew as large as its siblings, but it had become one of the best trackers they'd ever trained. Her shift had come from her connection to that dog and so she always associated it with the perseverance to push beyond people's expectations and achieve greatness.

Ragna's answer was less endearing than Emma's, but easy to see potential in. Her weasel shift represented intelligence. Ermines were brown in the summer and grew a white winter coat as the snow fell. They were clever and curious creatures. It made sense that quiet Ragna who liked to fade into the background saw herself in that. Rosy could imagine a number of other bone animals Ragna might find clever enough to claim her second shift.

Rosy's own connection to her wolf was because of her grandmother. Because she'd wanted Gran not to feel alone after Pops's death. Her wolf meant pack. Her horse meant herd. And every animal after had come to her based off its relationship with its colony or family or mate. Emma would have a harder time. Rosy had no idea what other animal would give Emma the same story that runt had. She'd need to figure out a broader definition of perseverance in order to find more shifts.

She resolved to offer extra tutoring to both Ragna and Emma outside of class to help them find a second shift. Depending on who did, and what that second shift was, she'd do her best to nudge Shaw in their direction.

She still had a good hour left of her free block when she finished reading the essays, and with everyone else doing the Army Training midterm, she was left with nothing to occupy her time.

"Shaw wouldn't want me going now," she murmured. It was risky to sneak into the encampment when she didn't have an alibi . . . but they were running out of time. The term was already more than halfway over, and all they had was a single ghost trapped in a jar to prove anything.

Decided, Rosy put the essays away and shifted. She stayed well clear of the area where she could hear the shouts of the Army Training midterm and crossed into the encampment.

Most of the camp was empty, with a huge portion of the soldiers being roped into helping with the midterm. It gave Rosy the space to take her time. She sniffed around, hoping to smell anything that might lead her to some sort of evidence.

She caught the scent outside one of the tents. A jar of General Tepeh's distinctive shoe polish was inside.

The tent wasn't visibly unique. All the thanes had their own, while the soldiers slept three or four to an even more nondescript tent. There would be no indicator that this tent was the general's if not for the strength of their leather polish.

Carefully, Rosy crept through the partially open tent flap. Once inside, she almost shifted human to begin her search but stopped at the last second. There was a chance a passing soldier would see her shadow through the tent walls. She went raccoon instead, because it was both small enough to be more easily missed and had the maneuverability to sort through the general's things.

The first place she looked was the chest at the end of the bed, but there was nothing there except General Tepeh's uniforms and a few pairs of casual robes. She went to the small writing table next.

There wasn't much on top of it aside from a few blank pieces of parchment and a bottle of ink. However, there was a locked chest half hidden behind the table. There was no key in sight, but she wouldn't have expected there to be. General Tepeh was too cautious to keep a key just lying around. It was probably hanging from a necklace or buried deep in one of their pockets. Rosy didn't need a key though. Raccoons were one of the few animals who had both the intelligence and the physical capability for picking locks. Rosy herself only vaguely understood the theory behind lockpicking, but the voice of the raccoon was strong enough that she could pull from its experience to jam her claws into the lock and jostle about until she heard a click.

Inside the locked chest was a jumble of papers and rolled-up scrolls. She began sorting through them, conscious that, at any minute, someone could come into General Tepeh's tent. How much longer did she have before the afternoon block was over? Would General Tepeh come to change before dinner? Would they send a soldier to fetch something from their tent beforehand? There were so many ways this could go horribly wrong.

Rosy kept her ears peeled for any sound outside while she read through paper after paper. Many were written orders for various platoons and squads, but try as she might, she didn't see anything that referenced the writ Thane Anders had shown his platoon. All the orders signed by the Witch King were far more generic.

Rosy moved on to the larger scrolls. One looked older than the rest. Aged in the way paper did by time and wear—yellowing and softer to the touch. She carefully spread it out over the woven mat of the floor.

It was a map. Rosy took a second to figure out exactly what she was looking at. The neatly drawn lines stretched from the northern half of the Cursed Kingdom to the southwestern extent of the Empire of Vinland. It was *the* map. The one Pops had died for. Her raccoon claws nearly tore a hole into the map as she clutched it tight. She didn't have great color vision as a raccoon—the world was in shades of gray and yellow. What Pops had described as red marks showing the towns the army planned to burn down were instead dark brown.

General Tepeh had compared her to Gran, but she had not been forced into this war the way Gran had been conscripted into the Witch Queen's. Rosy had made herself into a weapon. She had killed in defense of Shaw and Einar when the Vinlander prince attacked. She could still remember the taste of blood gushing into her mouth when she'd ripped into Vinlander flesh. Just like Gran had ripped out Madam Dyer's throat. But she hadn't been feral then—hadn't grown feral until after the prince had stabbed Einar through and gone after Shaw next.

Staring at this map now, Rosy realized how foolish she'd been. Not for choosing to fight, but for believing that this war was Shaw's first and foremost. It may have been Shaw's father who'd instigated it and Shaw's father who they needed to thwart, but it was also Shaw's father who'd killed Pops. Shaw's father who very likely encouraged the jarls' council to lock Gran away in the Forest so she wouldn't have the freedom to dig into her husband's death. He was no longer simply a faceless enemy, some shadowy figure behind the curtain. The Witch King was *her* enemy, and Rosy had a duty to her grandparents to see him defeated. To her grandparents and to Einar and Guanyu and everyone else hurt or killed by the Witch King's plot.

Rosy rolled the map again and set it aside. She did her best to put the rest of the papers back as she'd found them, trying to leave no trace of her presence in the tent. With luck, General Tepeh would have no reason to look for this old map again—not now that the campaign to burn down Vinland was well underway.

She couldn't carry the map out as a mouse, so she had to settle for creeping away as the raccoon. She did her best to hold the map above the snow so it wouldn't be ruined. A few times she had to tuck the map against the side of a tent and shift into her mouse to avoid being seen by passing soldiers, but no one caught her.

She made it all the way back to her dormitory room with the map Pops had died over. With trembling hands, she hid it deep in her chest. She'd give it to Shaw the next morning, during their usual ride.

For now, she sat heavily on her bed and stared at the closed wooden trunk. She wished Pops's ghost were still around. She wanted him to drift close, to feel his pride envelop her. Without it, all she felt was a deep sadness at the reminder that she'd lost both her grandparents to the machinations of a warmonger.

Chapter 11

SHAW

I WOULD HAVE LIKED MORE TIME TO PREPARE FOR THE Army Training midterm. Perhaps that was why General Tepeh had waited until the week of the test to explain it to me. I knew I should be grateful that they were willing to allow me to change the parameters, but gratitude was far from my mind.

With the benefit of sleep and time to think, I was suspicious of how easily General Tepeh acquiesced to my request. If I was right in believing my father was beginning to see inklings of our plan, then one of the counters would be to discredit me before my classmates. Without significant evidence, I needed to have the steady ground to tread upon. I needed to be seen as a leader coming to the council with a genuine concern, not a scared child trying to find any way out of fighting her prophesied war.

In order to have any chance of stopping the coming war, I needed to win this midterm, and win it well.

At our usual classroom clearing, General Tepeh announced the rules of the midterm. I'd learned from my entourage that I was the only one who'd been given a forewarning about the nature of the test. I'd made them promise to keep it secret, so as not to encourage General Tepeh to change it at the last minute.

General Tepeh stuck to their word. I would be leading my classmates in a mock battle against squads that were each composed of a hundred soldiers picked from Thane Anders's, Beck's, Olhiyu's, and Huang's respective platoons. Thane Anders would lead the soldiers, with General Tepeh and the other three thanes observing to determine each individual student's midterm score. The battle would take place in the woods west of campus. The encampment would serve as the northern boundary, and the waterfall's creek the western. The massive cliff that created the waterfall and blocked off any passage east of campus served as the southern and eastern edges of our battlefield.

The goal was simple. The first to kill the enemy commander won. Which meant Thane Anders was our target, and I was our weak point.

"Listen closely," I said to the amassed group of students. "Instead of five larger platoons, today we will fight within specialized squads."

We'd gathered just outside the waterfall's small cave. Hopefully the waterfall itself would prevent any of Thane Anders's scouts from listening in from a safe distance. Any who tried creeping closer would then get caught by our border of guards.

I'd decided on the squad assignments after discarding another attempt at rearranging the platoons without Einar, but I thought it might work out better regardless. Smaller squads meant more maneuverability in the dense crop of woods here at the eastern edge of campus.

"Charles, you'll be in charge of one of the combat squads," I continued.

Charles looked surprised to have been chosen as a squad leader, though his shocked expression quickly turned smug. I gestured him to one side of the clearing and called out the names of the other familiars with more combat-oriented shifts to join his group. I then announced Chao as the leader of the other combat squad, the long-range attackers under his command and a couple close-ranged support to keep them safe. Chao didn't outwardly react, but Jingyi grinned as he joined his witch—obviously happy that Chao had been publicly recognized.

I assigned Froya the third combat squad composed of ice familiars with hunting bird shifts and a few of the small but deadly bone and glass familiars. Aklemin was given a squad of ice and glass witches while Oluk got a select combination of familiars trained in scouting. There was a great deal of murmuring as I assigned Toketie to go with Oluk's group, but Toketie merely nodded. No one was surprised when I assigned Yuyan the squad of healers—primarily flower witches but also those familiars in Thane Beck's section whom Yuyan had told me stood out during medic training. Kwaddis got the final squad, which included all those left over from the logistics group.

I drew the squad leaders, plus Toketie, into the cave to discuss our plan while the students in Kwaddis's and Aklemin's groups were tasked with equipping everyone with weapons and enchantments.

"Are you sure this will work?" Chao asked once I'd finished relaying my idea.

Half of leadership was projecting confidence. I raised my chin. "Do you trust me?"

Charles looked at Chao like he was prepared to snap at the bone witch if he gave the wrong answer. Chao didn't seem to even notice, huffing out a laugh.

"Of course I do," my fellow bone witch said, easy as that.

"Let's do this!" Kwaddis declared, bouncing on his heels. Froya nodded her agreement.

My own entourage said nothing, but I didn't need them to. I already knew I had their support—even if this did end in abject failure. Right now, it was the four powerful heirs here with us who mattered the most.

"Here," I said, handing my cloak to Toketie. She gave me her own cloak in return, a much simpler piece of hemmed wool. I put it on because it was too cold not to, but made a mental note to ask Rosamund when Toketie's birthday was so I could gift her a nicer-quality one.

"Charles, you're with me," I said as I turned to leave the cave.

Charles shifted into his bobcat and loped to my side. I did my best not to compare him with Rosamund's wolf. General Tepeh had said I relied too much on my most powerful weapon. Today, I would prove them wrong.

One of the bone familiars in the year below mine had a massive elk shift. I did my best to hide behind him, letting Charles and the rest of his squad spread out around me. Out of the corner of my eye, I saw Oluk beckon his squad, Toketie included, to follow him into the underbrush.

We made it nearly an hour without seeing anyone. The bone familiars around me had excellent hearing, and Charles steered his squad well away from the conflict. The only thing I hated about the current plan was that I was in the dark about how the rest of the fight was proceeding. How many of my classmates had come across Thane Anders's soldiers?

Charles yowled and leaped forward to grab something. I drew against the nearest tree, protecting my back. Whatever Charles had seen was evading him, but a few seconds later Powish-the-wolverine snapped forward to catch something.

The small lizard Powish had caught shifted into one of the soldiers. She stared at me.

"Why are you here?" she asked incredulously. "Who are your people reporting to in that clearing?"

"You'll never know, seeing as you're dead," I said.

The lizard familiar sighed at that but nodded in acknowledgment. She scurried away to go to the area the dead were meant to gather. I let out a long breath.

"That was too close. If she'd been an ice familiar, we may not have caught her," I said.

Charles shifted so he could talk. "Maybe we should go back to the cave. It'll be more secure, with only the one entrance."

Toketie flew in before I could reply. The swan familiar landed on the large branch of a nearby red oak, legs dangling as she shifted atop it and leaned over. "The trap's sprung."

"Let's move!" I called. "Toketie, get Froya's and Chao's squads to meet us there."

Toketie shifted and took off. The bone familiars in Charles's squad re-formed around me, and we set off.

The clearing I'd chosen for the plan was tucked up against the cliffs on the eastern border. Kwaddis's squad had done their job—I could feel the bones piled up nearby. Inside the clearing, several of Thane Anders's soldiers had been caught in traps set by Aklemin's squad. Shugh was the lone familiar left standing in the clearing, guarding a cloaked figure with her back turned to the soldiers.

"I won't let you!" Shugh was saying as we snuck up.

"You've lost," Thane Anders snarled. "There's no point in brave heroics here."

One of the soldiers swore. Thane Anders looked over, scowling.

"The rattlesnake got me, sir," the soldier said.

So Oluk was still alive, then. Good. He wasn't injecting venom, but in this mock combat General Tepeh had set a blanket two minutes for anyone bitten by a venomous familiar. Unfortunately, Thane Anders was too well surrounded by his own soldiers for Oluk to sneak up and bite him.

"Dead!" one of the soldiers shouted, wooden sword pointed at something in the brush.

Oluk shifted, hands raised. I grimaced. Shugh was the only one left. I spun around as a soft crackle of leaves alerted me to someone behind us, but it was just Jingyi-the-fox. I nodded sharply. We needed to move now. Jingyi darted away.

Three, two, one . . . Charles and his squad burst into the northern end of the clearing while Chao's squad took the south and Froya's the west. Within seconds, my classmates had Thane Anders and his soldiers surrounded.

I kept myself tucked behind a tree, but I reached a hand out to grab the bones. Half of them fought me, and I let them go so Chao could have his share for the fight. My decoy in the cloak lifted an arm, and I sent a couple bones her way to control. It wouldn't do to give the game away until we'd won it.

It didn't take long. The rush of a coordinated attack overwhelmed Thane Anders's soldiers. They went down one after the other.

Thane Anders lunged forward, pulling away from the dwindling protection of his soldiers to get at the cloaked figure. Shugh got in his way and received a nasty smack to the side with Thane Anders's wooden sword for his trouble. Froya screeched and swooped down to distract Thane Anders, but he merely dodged out of the way of her talons, still unerringly set upon his target.

I stepped around the tree. "Thane Anders!" I called. "Looking for me?"

The thane spun around, nearly purple in the face, but it was too late. One of the bones I'd been controlling tapped him on the forehead.

"That's a kill," I said. "We win."

Behind Thane Anders, Kalitan drew back the hood of my cloak to reveal herself. My fellow bone witch twirled her fingers mockingly in Thane Anders's direction.

We all walked together back to the outdoor classroom. I headed straight for where Oluk and the other glass familiars in his squad stood among the group of dead.

"You were the lynchpin," I told him. "We couldn't have won without you."

Oluk turned pink at the praise. "It was your plan," he protested.

"You and your squad had the hardest job, and you did it perfectly," I said, making sure to encompass Shugh in the acknowledgment. The other snake familiar grinned. He'd always been a dramatic one, and it seemed he'd loved playing the part of desperation.

"An excellent trap, Princess," General Tepeh said from the front of the classroom clearing. "I think it's safe to say that you passed this test."

I pulled away from Oluk and his squad to walk up to them. "Thank you, sir."

The thanes called over their usual sections of Army Training to discuss the performances in the midterm. I headed with General Tepeh to the command tent. The general had me explain my plan in detail. I did so as concisely as I could, trying to project the same confidence and leadership I'd shown my classmates earlier.

Oluk and his scouts had spent the entire first hour of the test reporting on the movements of Thane Anders's soldiers to Kalitan, hidden in my cloak. To sell the story, I'd had Aklemin's ice and glass witches set as many traps as they could think of around the clearing. Furthermore, Froya's and Chao's squads were in charge of drawing any soldiers away from it. Once they were out of the way, Aklemin's, Kwaddis's, and Yuyan's squads took over distracting them while Froya's and Chao's circled back around.

With most of Thane Anders's soldiers stuck on the other side of the battlefield, he'd been drawn to the clearing himself. Oluk's squad was meant to sound out the alarm at that, using themselves as the final line of defense to buy time for me and the combat squads to get in position. Thane Anders had fallen for the trap, just as I'd hoped he would.

"I am impressed, Princess," General Tepeh said. "It seems you have learned something after all."

"Sir?"

"Thane Anders did not believe you willing to sacrifice your classmates, even in a mock combat like this. He underestimated you, and that became your triumph. That was well done indeed."

Sacrifice.

"Kalitan wasn't killed," I said. We had managed to stop Thane Anders before he struck at her.

"That is true," General Tepeh acknowledged. "But your glass familiar was, wasn't he? Alongside his entire squad."

I'd known it was unlikely that Oluk's squad would be able to make it out of the clearing once they'd met the soldiers there, but I hadn't thought of it as sacrificing them.

Or had I? When I'd been developing strategies, I'd considered using Charles's squad as the decoy instead. I'd dismissed the thought, even though it would have been easier to execute, solely because of Charles's mother. If I was going to convince her to listen to me, I needed to show her that I respected her son. Sacrificing him as a pawn would have gotten back to her.

I would have never sacrificed Oluk in a real battle though. I imagined having to walk into the infirmary to tell Einar the news. Imagined the gaping hole that would leave in my own entourage. Oluk may not be from a prestigious family, but he was just as worthy of life as Charles or the other jarls' heirs.

I hadn't just lost Oluk either, but all the scouts I'd sent with him. Shugh wasn't an heir, but as the grandson of the jarl of Desertmouth, he was still politically important. And what of the students in other squads killed during the prolonged combat? Even though it had only been a mock battle, I shouldn't ever have seen it as a game. Not a single one of my classmates were sacrificeable. No one should be.

"Do not take it as a reprimand," General Tepeh said, obviously reading something of my disquiet on my face. "You saved the lives of most of your classmates by sacrificing a few scouts. It was an admirable plan."

My father's words echoed in my ears once more. *War requires sacrifices.*

"Thank you, sir," I said stiffly. "I still have much to learn."

"As do we all," General Tepeh said. They were in good cheer, and I hated that I could understand why. I'd proven myself capable of war in their eyes. Except, I did not want to have the capacity to triumph if triumphing meant becoming the kind of ruler who would willingly sacrifice my own.

Rosamund was shivering like an overly excited puppy as I tacked up Cow for our Saturday-morning ride. My own mare was equally as excited—I'd been so focused on exercising the other horses that I hadn't ridden her enough lately.

I understood the reason for Rosamund's excitement as soon as we arrived at the secluded section of the riverbank where she normally shared her latest progress. From behind the folds of her red cloak, Rosamund pulled out a rolled-up tube of fabric. She handed it to me.

"What is this?" I asked, turning the package over. It looked like one of Rosamund's spare blouses.

"Unwrap it," Rosamund whispered. She had her eyes fixed upon the rest of campus, obviously watching for any eavesdroppers.

I found the edge of the blouse and pulled it back. There was something wrapped inside it. A piece of parchment.

"No," I hissed, in disbelief more than despair. "Did you really—"

"It's the map, Shaw," Rosamund cut in, obviously too excited to stay quiet any longer. "It was in General Tepeh's tent, in a locked chest."

I carefully unrolled the parchment to stare at the map. It was exactly as General Holt had described. With how old the parchment looked and felt, I knew my father wouldn't be able to pass this off as a recent map, made after the fires. He might be able to argue that he'd merely predicted the events, as he'd implied to me when I'd asked, but between this and Squad Leader Moolocks's testimony, we had real evidence to present.

"I need to know which heirs were close enough to actually hear what the Vinlander prince said about the fires," I said even as I carefully rerolled the map and hid it inside Rosamund's spare shirt. "And which of them would be willing to testify before the jarls about what they heard."

"Charles was," Rosamund said. "He mentioned it when I talked to him about keeping the prince's presence a secret. If you tell him that you want to share it with the jarls at Candlemas, I'm sure he'd be willing."

"Perfect." It'd be even better if Froya and Kwaddis could corroborate Charles's story. I'd talk with Aklemin and Yuyan about it as soon as I had the chance.

Rosamund and I finished our ride. Rosamund took Cow's reins from me after I dismounted. "I'll take care of her," she said with a significant look.

I nodded. I needed to find a place to hide the map, in case General Tepeh realized it had been stolen. I hoped desperately that they wouldn't. That would be undeniable proof that someone was attempting to uncover the truth behind the coming war—even if they couldn't be sure that someone was me.

As I left the stable, I kept my arm tucked under my cloak, map nestled in the crook of my elbow. I began to head back to my own room, then thought better of it. I turned instead to the flower witches' dormitory and, specifically, the seniors' suite.

When I ducked inside, I unintentionally startled a few of the senior flower witches. The group of them were standing around a sad little fire in the center of the room. One of them, a boy named Birger Berg—Big B to his friends—saw my confused look and grimaced. "We were just arguing over who had to go out and get more wood from the stockpile."

"Best decide soon," I said, and couldn't help my wry tone. "That fire doesn't have much left in it."

Birger flushed pink in embarrassment, and one of the other flower familiars laughed before heading back to her room presumably to get her cloak and boots.

I left them to it and knocked on the door to Yuyan's room. She never was one to sleep in, so I was surprised to hear her sound groggy when she said, "Come in."

Yuyan was sitting cross-legged on her bed as I opened the door. There was a pile of books in front of her and several pages of scribbled notes.

"Midterms finished yesterday, Yuyan," I said, closing the door behind me.

"I know," Yuyan said, half distracted by some passage in one of the multiple open books spread across her crumpled bedsheets. "I didn't have time last week to work on this because of studying, and I felt awful about it."

I moved closer and sat gingerly on the corner of Yuyan's bed so I could look over the books with her. "What is it?"

Yuyan glanced up to meet my eyes. There were dark circles under hers. I hadn't seen her so visibly restless since the weekend she'd spent healing Rosamund after the Market Day fire.

"He's not getting better, Shaw," Yuyan murmured.

My breath caught in my throat. All my elation at having the map drained away in an instant. "But he has—"

Yuyan shook her head. "The blade chopped through his spinal cord. It takes daily care to keep him from screaming in pain. The only way we've found to manage it is to numb practically everything. He can move a little now, yes, but he can't feel much of anything below the neck. Even if we could figure out a way to get him out of that bed, it'd be dangerous. Pain exists for a reason. Without it . . ." She trailed off, obviously unwilling to continue.

I understood regardless. I remembered Einar's slow care as he'd sketched the runes in the bones for our midterm project. How he'd fumbled a few so badly, I'd had to collect more bones so he could redo them entirely. I swallowed around my dry throat and tapped at the nearest book. "What's this, then?"

Yuyan grimaced. "I don't even know. I thought maybe Duchane's texts would have something to help, but it was another dead end. People don't normally survive that kind of wound. Magic kept him alive, but for what? Madam Tukwilla's not one for experimental treatments, and I'm afraid that if I start mucking about without a solid theory, I'll just make it worse."

My chest felt heavy with the pain. If Yuyan was out of ideas, what chance did the rest of us have? I had only a passing knowledge of anatomy, and bone magic was useless when it came to healing physical wounds.

Yuyan let out a disgruntled sound and slapped her hand down on the page she'd been reading. "I need a break. What time is it anyway?"

"Almost noon," I said. "How long have you been up?"

Yuyan gave me a sour look. "Apparently, I never went to bed." She rubbed at her temples. "Are you here to fetch me for lunch, then? That's not like you."

I cast a glance at Yuyan's door and lowered my voice. "No. I'm here because Rosamund found this."

I pulled the map out from under my dress skirts and unrolled it over Yuyan's pile of books. Yuyan stared at it uncomprehendingly for a few seconds, and then her eyes cleared. She too gave her door a look, as if worried one of her suitemates might have their ear pressed to it.

"My room's the first place the general will look if they notice it missing," I whispered as soft as I could.

"They'll check all of ours if it's not in yours," Yuyan replied. She hesitated. "Here, follow me."

I rolled the map up and hid it back under my cloak.

Apparently the flower witches had gone to lunch because all that was left in the central area of the suite was a pile of wood and a hearty fire. I expected Yuyan to lead us out of the suite, but instead she went to one of the other doors and opened it without knocking.

The inside was barren. Just a mattress covered in a single sheet and an empty shelf hanging over it.

"This was Shantie's room," Yuyan said. Even though the suite seemed empty, she still whispered. Or maybe it was this room, this dusty forgotten space, that made her lower her voice like a mourner.

I walked into the room. Yuyan helped me lift up the mattress. I tucked the map all the way into the corner and placed the mattress back on top of it. Hopefully that hiding space would keep it safe for this last month of term.

I cast around for something to say. The heaviness in the room made it hard to breathe. It was easy with the mundanity of school to forget about why we were doing this. But Yuyan had never forgotten. She'd walked past this empty room every day. Spent hours trying to find a way to help Einar recover without even mentioning it to any of us. I rarely felt as humbled as I was then, standing before the realization that my entourage was far stronger than I'd even thought possible.

My eyes landed on Shantie's empty bed. "Can I ask you something?"

There was silence. When I turned to look at Yuyan, she was giving me a strange look. "Since when have you needed my permission to ask me a question?" she asked.

"When the question is insensitive."

Yuyan let out a loud sigh. She sat down heavily on Shantie's bed. "Oh, go ahead. I'm not sure I can feel any worse than I do now."

I sat down next to her. "You were in love with Shantie—"

"Am."

"Sorry?"

"I'm still in love with Shantie," Yuyan said. She didn't bother looking surprised that I knew. "Doesn't matter that she's not here. I won't stop loving her just because she's gone home."

"How did you do it?" I murmured. "Be near her every day knowing she wasn't ever going to be yours? How do you do it now, when she's gone and you can't even be there to comfort her? I just . . . I can't deal with it sometimes, Yuyan. Why does longing have to feel so much like pain?"

Yuyan met my eyes, and I resisted the urge to drop mine like a chastised child. "Are you finally ready to tell me? About what happened with Rosamund?"

All my reasons for holding back felt so thin in that moment. I was carrying around so many weights, it felt good to finally relieve the burden of this one.

"She rejected me," I said. "And I don't know if I wish she were gone, or if I'm glad she's still close. All I know is that I still lo—I still care for her."

"You can say you love her. If that's how you feel."

Did I love her? I'd thought I did, back before she tore off my courtship necklace and ran away. The betrayal I'd felt was so deep, I'd assumed it was because I'd loved her. But the fondness I felt seemed to only have grown since then. The fondness—and the pain of her rejection.

"She acts the same as she did when you were courting her," Yuyan noted.

That was an accurate assessment, but the implication wasn't what Yuyan meant. I'd never told Yuyan that the courtship was fake. From the outside, it would seem like Rosamund still wanted me. At least, as much as she'd supposedly wanted me when she'd accepted my courtship. And I knew a part of her did. Our magical compatibility mixed with the partnership we were building was a heady combination.

There were times when I almost wanted to offer Rosamund a courtship necklace again, just to see what she'd say. Just to see it on her face if she was tempted to say yes—to see if I still had a chance to win her over. But I knew the truth. If I did offer her courtship, Rosamund would pull away. She'd made herself clear, and she had no reason to believe I wasn't doing my part to work through my feelings and move on. If I gave her any indication, this fragile partnership would crumble. Even if Rosamund still fought at my side, I'd lose the rest. The companionship, the comfort.

It was painful. I knew I was just delaying the inevitable. Running a knife over a scab again and again so the wound wouldn't have time to heal.

"She said no," I said firmly. "How do I— How did you deal with it?"

"It's different," Yuyan admitted. "I never told Shantie how I felt. A part of me was always able to hope, you know?" She grimaced. "It feels awful to say that now. As if I'd have a chance just because her familiar was killed. You asked how I feel about her being gone, and the truth is, I feel terrible. I wish she were here. I know I can't ever tell her how I feel now, not without it sounding manipulative. But I'd still be happy to have her close, to know that I could be there if she needed me."

The pain in Yuyan's voice touched something deep within me. A few times since the term had started, I'd uncharitably wished that Rosamund had stayed behind at Gravestown with her parents. Now I wondered if it would have actually felt worse.

I rubbed my face and stood. "Come on, let's go to lunch. Then you need to sleep. At least for a few hours."

Yuyan snorted. "You're not my mother."

"Would you rather I get Aklemin to nag you?"

Yuyan rolled her eyes. "No need to threaten me, I'll do as I'm told."

I made it halfway to the door to Shantie's room when Yuyan stopped me with a quiet "Shaw."

I turned back, raising an eyebrow. "I'm not joking about getting Aklemin."

But despite my teasing tone, Yuyan's expression was serious. "You *are* allowed to love her. Even if she doesn't want you, that doesn't make your feelings wrong. It would be wrong to push your feelings on her, but it's also wrong for her to string you along. You can set boundaries with her if she's making it worse for you."

Was she? Would it help if I asked Rosamund to be a bit more formal? To keep a little more distance?

General Tepeh had told me I relied on Rosamund's wolf too much, but I knew the truth was that I relied on Rosamund-the-human far more. Somewhere in the last five months since we'd met, she'd become integral to my life. The thought of putting distance between us was hard to contemplate.

I tried my best to give it real thought as Yuyan and I walked to lunch, but it was difficult to quantify what I needed. I wanted Rosamund, of course, but in the face of Rosamund's rejection and her continued friendship, I didn't know if I needed her or if I was just clinging on.

We passed the infirmary, and I cleared my throat. "This afternoon, will you let me help you read through the medical texts?"

Yuyan softened at that. "Of course. I probably should ask Oluk to help too. I know he's been worrying himself sick."

I expected having something productive to work at would do him good. "We'll all help. Everyone wants Einar to recover."

"I know," Yuyan said. "It's enough that he's alive and well. It means we have time to figure out a solution. And we will, Shaw. I promise."

"I have never doubted you, not for a single second," I said honestly.

If anyone were to ask why Yuyan's eyes looked suspiciously wet as we entered the dining hall, I would have blamed it on the sunlight reflecting off the snow. No one did, too focused on their own silent reflections to even spare her a second glance. I realized then that each of us had grown too used to suffering silently under the hushed weight of grief and pain and fear. I resolved to be more aware of my entourage's struggles. My own drama with Rosamund meant little compared to what my friends and our kingdom were going through because of my father's machinations. If we could stand together under this weight, then maybe we could work as one to lift our kingdom out of the shadows it had fallen into.

Chapter 12

Rosamund found me on Wednesday cleaning the horse tack before dinner. She thrust a small square of folded paper in my face. I almost thought it was another piece of evidence, and was about to reprimand her for being so blatant, even if we were seemingly alone in the stable, but when I opened the paper, I found a letter instead.

"What is this?" I asked.

The letter was addressed to Rosamund and said simply:

We thank you for your concern. Though we have returned home, our daughter is not prepared to receive any visitors at this time.

"Shantie's parents," Rosamund said. "I don't think I ever told you the reason I was off campus that Friday when you were attacked. I tried going to Multah to visit Shantie. I wanted to give her Guanyu's final message. But she wasn't there and her neighbor said they'd gone to the Waiming Territories for Guanyu's funeral. So I wrote her a letter, to ask if I could visit when they got back. And I finally got this reply."

She'd said all that in one breath. I had to take a second to parse out the individual words near the end.

"Ah," I said finally, taking another look at the letter. The writing was a touch sloppy, as if written by a shaking hand.

"It's not right, Shaw," Rosamund said. "Shantie deserves to know the truth about why Guanyu was killed. At the very least, she needs to hear Guanyu's message."

Rosamund was correct. Shantie did deserve to know the truth. It would be undeniably risky to tell her now, on the precipice of exposing the whole plot to the jarls' council. Except, I couldn't help but think of Yuyan's words. Of the pain on her face.

We hadn't found a cure for Einar and I hadn't figured out how to get over Rosamund, but I could at least do this.

"The winter solstice is tomorrow," I said. "There will be a feast. Traditionally, seniors are allowed alcohol for the solstice, since most of us are of age. The teachers deliberately ignore any partying that occurs. If we can sneak away amid the chaos, we can go to Multah. The Coshos won't turn me away, especially not if I say we've been charged with delivering Guanyu's final message."

"Really?" Rosamund said, eyes lighting up. Then she frowned. "But you're not an ordinary student. Won't people notice if you go missing?"

If Rosamund and I were still fake courting, it would be easy to fool them. I'd make a public show of wooing her and pull her away toward the suites. Even when the students didn't see us in our beds, the bone familiars would assume that Rosamund was with me and the bone witches would assume that I was with Rosamund. So long as we were back by morning, they'd have no reason to do anything except gossip about our relationship.

Maybe it was best that I couldn't use that ploy. I tried to imagine how it would feel to have the other seniors teasing me about spending the night with Rosamund when the truth was so much more painful.

"We'll sneak away after the feast," I said instead. "Everyone should be too distracted to notice."

I DIDN'T TELL MY ENTOURAGE much, partially because I didn't want to hurt Yuyan by mentioning Shantie until I came back with hopefully good news to share about Shantie's recovery process. Also, because I wanted them to honestly be able to say they knew nothing if Rosamund and I were discovered missing in the night.

Rosamund and I both made a point of saying we were tired several times over the feast, until Aklemin finally suggested we should go to bed early. I wouldn't be surprised if they, at least, knew something of our plan.

That done, we snuck out to the stable where we'd hidden our cloaks and bags full of provisions, in case we needed to stay the night in Multah. The winter solstice was the longest night of the year, and the coldest thus far. I'd dressed in one of my thicker long-sleeved tunics, but it was a relief to throw on my cloak too. I swung the bag over my shoulder and turned to Rosamund. She looked gorgeous, dressed in one of her nicer wool dresses, her brassy hair held back in a neat plait, and the bright red cloak draped like power over her shoulders.

I grabbed Rosamund's bag for her. Unlike the clothes she was wearing, cloak included, the bag wouldn't shift with her. She shifted into her horse, and I used the nearby mounting block to get on her back.

It wasn't comfortable riding bareback for the couple hours it took to get to the city, but I didn't complain. It wouldn't have made sense to bring Cow or Pyre. Their absence would have been far more noticeable than ours, especially if Mister Jostein checked the stable before bed like he often did.

We were lucky. It was a dark night—only a sliver of a waning moon. We dodged around one group of soldiers patrolling the river's edge, but the path to Multah was mostly clear. The sounds of drunken revelry filled the air as we began passing the houses and meeting halls that sprawled along the outskirts of the city.

I dismounted Rosamund once we'd reached the more populated part of the city and let her shift back to human. It would be less noticeable for us to walk through the city streets than for me to ride a bone horse through them, even if it would have been faster.

The road from Witch Hall into the city passed near Lake Bloom. The center of all flower magic in the kingdom was a perfectly still body of water. During the day, Lake Bloom was a gorgeous blue-green, but tonight it almost looked purple under the starlight.

Rosamund saw where I was looking and let out a long breath. "One of the last things Guanyu ever did was play with me inside the Lake," Rosamund murmured. "We killed a flower lamprey together. Shantie needed the spines for her potion. But when we surfaced and smelled the fire, we left the lamprey's body behind. And then, well, you know what happened in the market."

I hadn't known that Rosamund had actually dove into the Lake. "You must be one of the few non-flower familiars to have survived a venture in Lake Bloom," I said, impressed despite myself.

Rosamund's smile was small. "Guanyu thought I was being ridiculous, but I'm glad we did it. I'm glad I have that memory to hold on to." She turned away from the Lake. "Come on, let's go find his witch."

The Shantie Cosho I'd known was a cheerful girl with glowing skin and a gorgeous laugh. The Shantie Cosho who opened the door to the little house off Multah's docks was a different being altogether.

Shantie had lost so much weight since the last time I'd seen her, I worried a stiff breeze could pick her up and take her away. She didn't smile or greet us once she saw who we were. She merely stood there, waiting for us to state our business.

"Shantie," Rosamund whispered, then obviously couldn't think of what else to say.

I took over. "May we come in?"

Silently, Shantie stepped away from the door and inside the house, leaving space for us to join her. I let Rosamund go first so that I could close the door behind us.

Shantie led us to the kitchen. I'd stayed in this house last spring break while doing an army recruitment tour. We'd made a stop in Multah just after Beltane, and Yuyan had insisted we visit Shantie. I remembered how homey it had been, how cheerful and comfortable. There was nothing of that cheer here now.

The flower witch gestured for us to take a seat at the table and then left to pour us both glasses of water. Unlike larger houses, this dockyard town house had the dining table set up in front of the kitchen hearth. There was a fire lit to warm the cramped room, but a huge black grate had been installed over the front of the hearth to block the flames from view.

I took the water with murmured thanks and set it down on the table without drinking it. I'd contemplated what I would say the entire ride to Multah. How much would I, could I, reveal to Shantie?

Looking at the flower witch now, I knew gentleness wouldn't work. Some bonded witches never recovered from losing their familiars. They simply faded away, too focused on trying to grasp the lingering remnants of their familiar's magic that they forget to take in the rest of the world. I worried that Shantie was doing exactly that.

I was not a reckless person at heart, but I doubted anything except recklessness would spark a reaction from the witch who sat down across from us.

"Rosamund and I talked with Guanyu on Samhain," I said.

Rosamund shot me a startled look. Shantie, meanwhile, flinched so violently that she spilled half her water down her front.

"Shaw," Rosamund hissed, obviously angry at how insensitive I'd been.

But I had Shantie's attention now. I couldn't stop. I gathered up whatever bravery I had and said, "Guanyu asked me to give him vengeance, only the person ultimately at fault for his death is not who we thought. My father is the reason those men set fire to the market that day. He sent our soldiers across the border first. Sent them to burn down simple fishing villages and set fire to Vingate's own market a week before the Vinlanders did the same to ours."

Shantie's hands trembled as she set her glass of water back on the table.

"At the beginning of term, General Tepeh sent us off campus for an exercise," I said. "We were attacked by a prince of Vinland and his men. He said outright that he was here for revenge."

I took a deep breath. It felt terrifying to be saying this all aloud, without any guarantee of privacy. No guarantee that the person in front of me might not share what I said with anyone who'd listen. This could ruin everything. All our plans, our careful maneuvering, the evidence we'd gathered . . . everything.

But Shantie deserved to know the truth.

I pressed on. "We have evidence of the Witch King's crimes. At the next council meeting, I'll present our case. I will see my father face justice and convince the jarls that we must offer reparations to Vinland. I will stop this cycle of violence before our nations fall into full-scale war. Shantie, I promise you that I will avenge Guanyu. His death mattered. It still matters. I will make sure the person ultimately responsible pays for it, even if he is my own father."

Shantie let out a hitched gasp. Rosamund reached forward and took Shantie's hands in hers.

"Guanyu gave me a message for you," Rosamund murmured. "If you're ready to hear it."

Shantie's gasping turned into tiny little sobs. She opened her mouth several times before, finally, she croaked a soft "Please."

Rosamund was crying now too. If she wasn't already holding Shantie's hands across the table, I would have reached out to take her hand myself. But Shantie's knuckles were white from how tight she held on to Rosamund.

"He told me to tell you to swim upstream," Rosamund said, only just barely getting the words out.

I took over, speaking as gently as I knew how. "He said that he loves you. That he hopes you will respect his last wish and do as he says."

All bone witches and familiars took classes on how to talk with those the dead left behind. I'd had an entire class my fourth year on the different types of grief and how to share final messages with loved ones. It felt different now, doing it for someone I considered a friend.

"Swim upstream, Shantie," Rosamund said, and the gentle command in her voice—something so reminiscent of Guanyu's own tone—was exactly what Shantie needed to hear. I could see it on the flower witch's face and in the way she clung to Rosamund. Rosamund didn't seem to have needed a class to know how to fulfill this duty of those of us with bone magic.

"How dare he ask that of me?" Shantie cried. "That brat. That utter brat."

Rosamund stood so she could go around the table and pull Shantie into a hug. I looked away. I'd known Guanyu, of course, but not well. I'd rarely spent any time with familiars before Rosamund came into my life. I considered Shantie as close to a friend as I considered anyone outside my entourage, simply because she and Yuyan had been so close that I'd spent enough time with her to warrant it. Somehow, in a single term Rosamund had become an even closer friend to Shantie and Guanyu both. All I could do was give the two a moment of privacy to share in their grief.

It was only because I'd looked away that I saw her. An older woman I recognized as Shantie's mother standing in the entrance of the kitchen. How long had she been there? Had she heard what I'd said about the Witch King? She had her hand to her mouth, visible tears in her eyes.

"Madam Cosho—" I began, worried over her reaction.

Madam Cosho shook her head, stopping me from continuing. She beckoned me closer. I stood and took the two steps across the kitchen to be at her side.

Madam Cosho wrapped me up in a tight hug before I could react. Her breath ghosted over my ear as she fervently whispered, "She hasn't said a single word since Guanyu's funeral. Thank you, Princess. Thank you so much."

It was nearly midnight by the time we left Shantie's house. Shantie hadn't agreed to come back to Witch Hall, though I'd encouraged her to consider it. It would help, settling back into the routine of school. Learning to use her magic again, now that it had changed with Guanyu's death.

Both her parents had joined us at the table, obviously overjoyed she was talking again. I wondered if Shantie would ever be as bright a presence as she had been before her familiar's death, but she wasn't a shallow reflection of herself anymore. It was enough to make her parents beam with joy, and tears were shed by all of us before the end.

Rosamund let out a massive yawn that turned into a chattering of teeth as we stepped out into the winter wind.

"Are you sure you can carry me all the way back?" I asked her. "We can wait until morning." The Coshos had offered us their bed for the night if we wanted to sleep before returning to school.

"Not worth it," Rosamund said. "Let's just—"

Rosamund didn't finish her sentence, attention caught on something happening at the docks. Her shoulders had straightened, head perked to the side like a predator who'd caught the trail of their prey.

"What is it?" I asked, suddenly tense and wary. My thoughts immediately jumped to the prince's attack, that first Friday of the term. Were the Vinlanders attempting another raid on Multah?

"I thought I smelled . . . Hold on, I'll be right back."

Rosamund dropped her bag and shifted into her mouse form. Within seconds, she was swallowed by the night.

I hesitated outside Shantie's house. I hadn't thought to bring a weapon, and that now felt like a massive mistake. I couldn't let Multah be attacked again. We were so close to winter break. Let the Market Day fire be a one-time tragedy. Let my father pay for the horrendous crime that he had instigated. Let me keep my promise to Guanyu and Shantie. Let me stop this war before anyone else had to die.

A scurry of tiny scratches—sharp claws over cobblestone—alerted me to Rosamund's return. She shifted a few feet from me. "Shaw, come quick," she whispered, even as she swooped down to grab her pack. She didn't wait for me to agree, just set back off in the direction she'd come.

I followed after her. Rosamund kept to the deep shadows, and the secrecy made me all the more wary. I tried to ask her what she'd seen, but she shushed me. She led us through the dockyard to the edge of one of the far piers.

"What is it?" I whispered as we crouched behind a stack of timber for the nearby dry dock. I couldn't make a plan if I didn't have any information.

Rosamund put one hand to my mouth. My lips tingled under

her touch, but my attention was swiftly caught by her other hand—pointing to something ahead of us.

There was a group of people loading into a set of long canoes. They all wore dark clothing and carried no torches or lanterns. With the moon a sliver, there was only dim starlight to see by. I squinted, trying to make them out.

And then one figure turned his head just so, and I recognized the close-cropped blond beard. Thane Anders and at least two squads of his platoon were obviously about to take another run at Vinland. They must have used the cover of winter solstice celebrations, as Rosamund and I had, to sneak away from campus.

I could stop them. I could walk up and demand to know what they were doing. I could raise a fuss, so that the people sleeping in the dockyard houses nearby might peek out their windows and doors to check what the commotion was.

Except, if I made a fuss now, Thane Anders would take it to General Tepeh. Who would in turn take it to my father. I wouldn't have the element of surprise for the Candlemas council meeting anymore.

I hesitated. Was it worth the risk? It was possible I didn't even have the surprise at all. My father was an ice witch. Even if his visions of me were cloudier than they used to be—before Rosamund entered my life—he was still strong enough to be able to foresee something happening in the upcoming council meeting. Shouldn't I value the lives of the Vinlanders the soldiers might kill over the uncertain potential that we'd actually managed to hide things from my father?

Rosamund removed her hand from my mouth. I'd hesitated too long. All of Thane Anders's soldiers were loaded onto the boats.

They'd be swallowed by the darkness over Wimahl River any second.

"What now?" Rosamund asked in a soft whisper.

It was a night for recklessness. I took a breath and let it out slowly, before saying, "If I ask you to walk into danger with me, Rosamund Holt, will you do it?"

Rosamund scowled. "Do you even need to ask?"

I couldn't help but smile at that. Perhaps I did rely on Rosamund too much, but she made it all too easy. "No, I suppose not. Here's to hoping I'm not about to get us both killed."

There were dozens of boats in the dock. The larger ones were all padlocked to the pier, but the people of Multah didn't bother locking up the tiny rowboats. They were typically only used to ferry people to the larger ships that had to anchor out in the middle of the river and had very little monetary worth to a port city otherwise. I headed to the nearest rowboat, Rosamund right at my heel. At least we'd packed provisions, just in case. If we rationed, we could make it a few days off what was in our packs.

"What's the plan?" Rosamund asked as I began to row us away from the pier and after Thane Anders's canoes.

"We figure out what town they plan to burn tonight," I said. "And we find a witness."

I could present the map and Squad Leader Moolocks's testimony, and when my father attempted to sway the council, I would bring in our witness. My father's actions across the river had only worked because no Vinlander would think to go to the jarls when they had every reason to believe the attacks were planned by the Cursed Kingdom. But I had faith that most of the council would be on my side once I had the evidence to prove my accusations.

"We can't let the soldiers see us," I whispered to Rosamund. "I know it will be difficult, but if we can sneak a witness away before any of the soldiers notice us, then we'll have a much better chance of actually stopping my father."

"I don't like the thought of sacrificing everyone else, just to avoid being seen," Rosamund retorted.

There it was again. *Sacrifice.* I winced. "If you can keep out of sight, save as many as you can," I said, because Rosamund was right. It would make me no better than my father if I deemed it right to sacrifice a village, even if my reasoning was stopping a war instead of starting one.

"I'll do my best," Rosamund agreed, though she obviously wasn't happy about it.

"We both will," I promised, because I wouldn't stand by if my own powers could be used to save innocent citizens—Vinlanders or not.

Chapter 13

We hid the rowboat behind some bushes on the other side of Wimahl River. Rosamund shifted into her wolf and used its superior nose to track whatever she'd smelled on Thane Anders or his soldiers back at the docks.

All my own exhaustion had faded away in light of the nervous energy that now thrummed through my body. I had no idea what kind of violence we were heading toward. Did the soldiers slaughter everyone in the village before setting it on fire? During? Or did they just set the buildings ablaze and kill those who tried to run to safety?

There obviously weren't many fishing villages left to burn in this region of Vinland, because the trail took us inland. I worried for several minutes that Thane Anders was aiming for the city of Vingate again. It was the burning of Vingate's northern district that had sparked the revenge fire in Multah after all. But Rosamund's nose led us away from the large river port.

The woods on Vinland's side of the river were nearly identical to those on the Cursed Kingdom's side. This deep into winter, the evergreens were encrusted with ice and the ground was covered by a thick layer of snow. We had to stick to the animal trails until we found our way to a human-made road. And even then, it felt eerily disconcerting, walking across ground I knew to be an entirely different nation but that looked so similar to my own.

I half expected the soldiers to circle around Vingate and head toward the ocean and all the port cities and fishing villages out that way. Instead, their trail led us east, up the steep slopes of the river gorge.

It was several hours before Rosamund finally stopped. I pulled her waterskin out of her pack to hand over. I'd already drunk half of my own water on our walk, but she hadn't stopped once the entire trek. Rosamund shifted to human and accepted the waterskin.

"I don't hear or smell a village nearby," Rosamund whispered. "Maybe they're camping out for the night?"

"How far are they?" I asked while Rosamund took several large gulps of water.

Rosamund waved for me to follow her, still drinking. She slid around a few large red cedars, then stored her waterskin so she could pick her way up the side of a large incline. This area of Vinland, just like the Cursed Kingdom, was littered with basalt cliffs. I knew Rosamund could have shifted into one of her animal forms better at climbing, but she stayed human. I carefully watched for the crevices where she put her hands and feet so I could climb up after her.

Luckily, it was only about ten feet to the top. Rosamund kept herself crouched low and scooted forward. I regretted giving her such an eye-catchingly red cloak now, no matter how good it looked on her. My own dark blue cloak blended better against the rocks. Rosamund was a more experienced hunter than I was though, and she tucked herself neatly behind a large boulder. She left just enough room for me to join her. I did so, then peered around the edge of the rock.

There, in the valley below the small cliff we'd climbed, were Thane Anders and his soldiers. They stood around the base of a gorgeous waterfall. It wasn't as tall as Witch Hall's waterfall, but it had three separate layers that cascaded down to a small pool. A stream curved away from the pool, through the low points in the gorge.

Maybe Rosamund was right. It was a fairly defensible spot to camp for the night. The only entrance to the little valley was following the path of the stream. And any of the familiars in the group, Thane Anders included, would hear people coming that direction from a ways out.

But it didn't look like the soldiers were setting up a camp. A group of six had their hands linked in a semicircle, facing the waterfall. A few of the other soldiers had lit torches and held them up. It was enough light for me to clearly make out the soldiers in the circle. They all were witches and familiars, judging by the stripes on their uniforms. And they stood in a mix—one familiar, then one witch, then one familiar, and so on. The one on the end nearest to me was recognizable—the ice familiar with the sparrow shift who'd come to take General Tepeh and the thanes that day of our company march.

They were doing some sort of ritual. I glanced around to try to figure out why, and that's when I noticed it.

The waterfall was completely frozen. But not in the way waterfalls normally froze for winter. Each layer had frozen independently into massive icicles the size of tree trunks. And yet, the icicles continued to move. I tracked one as it formed at the top of the cliff and slowly grew until it reached the second layer. Then it detached from the top and continued moving down to the bottom layer. Like a snake gliding down stairs, if the snake were stiffened like a stick.

There was only one explanation for it. Ice magic. I'd grown up on the Frozen Mountain. There were no frozen waterfalls up at Falconridge, but I'd seen enough moving ice to recognize it. The same way I recognized the skeletal limbs of the bone pines in the Forest.

I tugged Rosamund away. This wasn't what I'd been expecting at all, and I didn't know what to do.

Rosamund seemed to understand me even without words. We slowly climbed down the cliff together. I let Rosamund lead us safely away from the soldiers. Far enough away that she could be sure we wouldn't be overheard. We finally stopped at the base of an even larger cliff. I leaned back against the rocks and moss and ferns and stared up at the stars glittering across the sky.

"I don't understand," Rosamund said. "What are they doing?"

"They're cursing the waterfall," I said. "Like Mesachie cursed the Mountain, and the Forest, and the Lake, and the Desert."

"Who?"

"Mesachie. The first Witch Queen." Sometimes I forgot that Rosamund hadn't been at Witch Hall with us all these years, then other times I was distinctly reminded of her small-town upbringing. "I'll tell you the story later. The important part is that my father must have discovered the secret to deliberately creating new magical wells."

"But why? It's not connected to the Mountain. It won't affect his own power, right?"

"Not back home," I agreed. The witches and familiars of the Cursed Kingdom had gotten stronger with every passing year since Mesachie's curse—because every passing year, the magical lands she'd created had continued growing. "But what if having a well of ice magic in Vinland allows him to make more accurate predictions about the Vinlanders and their army?"

Rosamund slowly nodded. "But then . . . what can we do about it? Will the council see it as evidence of your father's guilt?"

No, they wouldn't. The jarls would see no issue with my father adding a well of ice magic to Vinland. Even if it was just part of his plan to make the Vinlanders hate us, in the jarls' minds they'd see it as a necessary precaution against the escalation of a conflict that had already begun.

"The soldiers will go back to school soon. We have class tomorrow." Today, really. It was already well past midnight.

Rosamund nodded slowly, obviously still confused. "I can lead us back."

As soon as we'd crawled down the cliff, she shifted wolf. I kept my eyes on her, breathing in and out, trying to keep myself calm. It was difficult. I didn't dare say it aloud, but I feared that, no matter our evidence, we might be too late to stop this war after all. My father had physically cursed Vinland's lands. I knew of no way to reverse that process. What reparations could we offer in the face of such disrespect?

Rosamund took us directly west. We'd followed Thane Anders for hours, and it took several more for us to weave our way back over the cliffs and valleys to a main road that had been cleared of snow, with large banks piled up on either side. Unlike the packed dirt roads of the Cursed Kingdom, this road was made of cut stone and lined in brick. I wondered what it had cost them to pave their roads and whether it would be worth it to implement something similar in the Cursed Kingdom.

The sky was only just beginning to lighten. I didn't want

to contemplate having to go to class in another few hours. We'd be cutting it close as it was—there would be no time for a nap beforehand.

I was so tired that I almost missed the prickle of cold seeping down my spine. At least, until Rosamund stopped dead in the center of the road, ears perked up. The creeping shiver came over me then, and I spun in a full circle, trying to make out anything distinct in the predawn light.

There, at a small crossroads up ahead, standing in the shadows of a snow-encrusted cedar, was a ghost.

I put a hand in Rosamund's scruff, anchoring myself. With access to Rosamund's magic, it would take barely any effort to subdue a single ghost should it suddenly devolve into a spirit. And this one wanted to—it kept flickering between the translucence of a ghost and the red of an angry spirit. Assured of my control over the situation, I walked a few paces closer with Rosamund in step beside me.

There was something about the ghost that I recognized, but it took me a few seconds to place from where. "You were there," I said aloud for Rosamund's benefit. "When we fought the Vinlanders."

The young woman flickered with a much deeper and more vibrant shade of red. I sent a touch of magic her way to calm her. I was sure of it now. She'd been the ghost who'd hovered on the edge of the battlefield. I'd thrown her into a random body in the middle of the fight. Somehow, afterward, she must have detached from the body and drifted away.

How had she followed us? Ghosts didn't usually leave where they'd died. Strong pulls of bone magic, like from rituals or the Bone Forest itself, could summon ghosts. More often they haunted loved ones or, rarely, the people who'd killed them—at least until they saw their lingering regrets appeased and faded, or were overwhelmed by emotion and devolved into spirits.

"Prince Vetle," the ghost said, as if answering a question we hadn't actually asked. "Prince Vetle, fifth of his name. Vetle, my—" She cut herself off with a wail and the red returned.

"You know him?" I magically brushed her anger away so I could look closer at her appearance. I'd thought her one of the soldiers, but perhaps she was one of the Vinland warriors instead. Surely Squad Leader Moolocks's crew had managed to kill at least a few before being slaughtered.

The ghost didn't reply, but she did move. She floated down the smaller path that turned north from the crossroads we stood at. After getting about fifty feet away, she stopped and looked back at us, making it clear she expected us to follow.

I felt a ripple under my fingers and pulled my hand away as Rosamund shifted human.

"What do you think?" I asked.

"I don't like it," Rosamund said immediately.

"It could be a trap," I agreed. Though a trap for who? For what? "Let's go."

Rosamund let out a surprised laugh as I walked after the ghost. "I think I need to check you for possession."

"You're a bone familiar, you'd already be able to tell if I was."

"It was a joke, Shaw. You're not acting like you."

No, I supposed I wasn't. I was being reckless—there was no doubt. But up against such insurmountable foes, recklessness felt appropriate. And I had faith that Rosamund would stop me if I went too far. She'd never been afraid of sharing her opinion.

We followed the road as it wound northeast. The evergreens on either side were weighed down by snow and ice. I observed the icicles carefully, but unlike those at the waterfall, I could find no hint that they had been formed by magic.

It took about twenty minutes before we saw the first obvious sign that something had happened. The healthy evergreens began to give way to the husks of trees. First a few, then the entire forest. Dead trees, all burned to ashy shells.

Rosamund reached out to grip my hand. I squeezed back. We kept walking.

It wasn't much longer before the ghost stopped at the crest of a steep hill. Whoever had shoveled the snow off the main road hadn't come all the way out here. I slipped and skidded backward several times before Rosamund shifted into her badger, dug her claws in, and practically pulled me up the road. I could feel my cheeks burn with mortification by the time we reached the crest.

Rosamund shifted back, giving me an amused look that instantly vanished as she turned to look at the sight below. Just as quickly, any embarrassment I felt was overshadowed as I turned my own gaze upon it.

"Oh," Rosamund said, distress coloring that single word.

My heart mimicked it. The town below us was larger than I'd expected. Perhaps the size of Falconridge or Desertmouth. But instead of bustling with people, it lay completely deserted. A huge sign had been mounted in the center of the road that led into the town square.

ENTRY FORBIDDEN BY ORDER OF THE PRINCE

The ghost let out a long, mournful cry. She floated down the hill, through the sign, and into the town itself.

I exchanged a look with Rosamund. Without having to say a word, we both headed down the hill after her. I gave up on dignity and slid the last few feet on my butt. What did it matter? We were alone, outside of the dead.

The buildings on either side of us were nothing more than frames. Half-burned timbers, the charred remains of personal belongings. One house had been burned down to the foundation. Another still remained, except for what must have been a thatched roof gone up in smoke.

My ears popped and I stumbled. The visible damage was horrifying, but I could barely focus on it. The true horror was in the bones. The dead screamed from their shallow graves. The bodies had been thrown into pits together, and they were so very angry.

Rosamund caught my elbow. "Are you okay?"

The dead called to me. Hundreds of corpses rattling in the remains of their homes. The bone witches in the Royal Company had to have done a ritual to cleanse the dead here since Rosamund and I weren't beset by ghosts and spirits, but they hadn't given the dead proper burials. The physical and metaphysical stench of death was pungent. I could barely move, overtaken by the power of it.

Rosamund still held my elbow. I twisted out of her grip, then caught her hand in mine. I needed skin-to-skin contact.

As soon as our hands touched, the pressure lifted. I straightened my shoulders. Gorging on Rosamund's magic, I gathered myself. Pulled the combined weight of our power like a cloak around me.

Suddenly, I wasn't scared anymore. The call of the dead was intoxicating. A hundred corpses so disgraced they wanted revenge. It would be easy to make them rise and set them loose. I could summon the dead to rampage, and they would not care if they attacked friend or foe. It was pure temptation. Why shouldn't I set them upon the Vinlanders? They wished to attack us. Prince

Vetle had injured a member of my entourage so severely he might never leave the infirmary. Didn't I deserve revenge?

"Shaw," Rosamund snapped. It was obvious by her tone that she'd called to me several times.

I breathed out and let go of the power. I was dizzy. I realized I was crushing Rosamund's fingers between my own. I released her, and the call of the dead subsided as if someone had smothered it beneath a thick blanket.

"I don't—I'm not sure what came over me," I told her.

Rosamund's gaze darted over my face, searching for something. Finally, she nodded. "I can feel it too, you know. The death here."

"It's overwhelming," I murmured. "It's no surprise they had a sign to keep people out. There must have been so many spirits before they were cleansed."

Rosamund frowned. "Were they cleansed?"

What kind of question was that? I knew Rosamund had come to Witch Hall late, but surely even she understood the concept of ghosts and spirits after the disaster that was last Samhain.

Except—it wasn't Rosamund who'd made the incorrect assumption. I had been so overwhelmed by the call of corpses that I hadn't noticed, but there *was* a larger presence here. Just like the Lake Bloom or the Frozen Mountain or the Obsidian Desert. This town had become something more than just a husk of buildings and graves. The ghosts and spirits hadn't been cleansed at all. They'd coalesced into something more.

"It's like the Bone Forest," Rosamund said. She had her free hand pressed to her chest. Over her heart. "I can feel it."

A Bone Town. No, that didn't sound right. A Ghost Town. As far as I knew, Vinland's first and only well of bone magic.

"Do you think they did it on purpose?" I asked. "Like with the waterfall?"

"Finally opened your eyes, have you?"

I spun around, heart in my throat. I recognized that voice. I would never forget it. It had haunted my nightmares for weeks after Einar's injury.

Prince Vetle stood at the crest of the same hill we'd crossed to enter the town. The ghost who'd led us to the Ghost Town was at the base of the hill, looking up at him. She continued flickering red.

"Prince Vetle, if we could talk—" I began, hoping we might be able to negotiate now that I knew the truth.

"You salted the earth," the prince said. If the ghost's red spoke to anger, his voice spoke to unadulterated rage. "Salted the earth and planted your own ashes."

"I will see my father tried for the crimes he's committed," I attempted.

"Do you think I care?" Prince Vetle shouted. "Don't you see, Princess Shaw? It's already too late!" He gestured broadly at the destroyed trees and the Ghost Town behind us.

I didn't flinch, but I wanted to. I'd been thinking the same thing. There was a reason that no one lived inside the Bone Forest or the Obsidian Desert. There was a reason that only flower familiars safely dove into Lake Bloom. A reason that the only town still standing on the Frozen Mountain was Falconridge—a town protected by the royal palace and the power of my ancestors.

This Ghost Town had every chance of growing and encroaching upon the surrounding areas of Vinland, just like the Bone Forest had. And without witches and familiars, the Vinlanders would have no way to work within it and find uses for the resources such magical lands could give. In their eyes, the Witch King had scorched their land so thoroughly, it would never be rebuilt. My father had turned the very thing that had made our kingdom a magical sanctuary into a weapon against theirs.

"The Cursed Kingdom will offer reparations," I said, because that was all I could say. "I will make this right."

Prince Vetle stared at me. The ghost flickered red and stayed there. Screeching, she swooped up the hill, heading toward the prince.

I didn't hesitate. I raised a hand in the newly turned spirit's direction and magically tugged her away from the prince. She turned on me, successfully distracted. The prince let out a yell, as if he thought I'd put my hand up to attack him instead of the spirit.

"Wait—" I tried, but it was too late. Only bone witches and familiars could see ghosts and spirits outside rituals, and I'd used my hand to raise corpses the first time the prince had attacked us.

Vetle lifted an engraved hunting horn to his lips and blew. I recognized the sound from that day his band of warriors had attacked us at Goose Point. A loud, clear tone that rang across the desolate land we stood upon.

I could kill the prince. Before his warriors arrived, I could kill him and take Rosamund and flee. No one would be any wiser about who had done it. It would be so easy. Between the angry spirit and the corpses at our back, I had a plethora of choices. But if I killed a prince of Vinland, there would be no stopping further conflict. Even if I did it here, on Vinland soil, and left no witnesses, it would incite the emperor into war. He would have every reason to believe this cursed land had been his son's downfall—and in a way, he'd be correct.

"Shaw," Rosamund said. "I hear them."

The prince's warriors couldn't have been far. It wasn't long before the first helmet appeared at the crest of the hill to stand next to the prince. Vetle unsheathed his massive broadsword. The group blocked the path that led back to the main road. If we had to flee, we'd need to risk cutting through the burned forest.

But we didn't need to run. The corpses would not take much more than a thought to lift to their feet.

I still had hold of the angry spirit. I concentrated on her, instead of on the siren's call of the Ghost Town's dead, and drained the anger away until she settled back into a ghost once more. If we had time, I would have forced her to move on, but I saw the prince lift his sword to ready the charge and knew we didn't.

"We can't kill any of them," I said. "Not without ruining our chance at peace."

"I think . . ." Rosamund paused. She had a hand pressed to her chest, head cocked to the side like she was listening to something. "Yes, I can do it. Shaw, are you able to feed me power too?"

Could I? In theory, a witch-familiar bond went two ways. Familiars were more likely to unlock second shifts after bonding, or unlock stronger shifts if they'd already found their second. Of course, Rosamund and I didn't have a bond, but with how compatible our magic was, we'd already proven that we didn't need one for me to take her magic.

I held out my hand for Rosamund to hold. Just like how I'd pushed the anger away from the spirit, I tried to push some of my power into Rosamund.

Rosamund gasped and let go of my hand. "Too much!"

"We're out of time," I said. We'd already be under attack if the prince had ordered his archers to shoot, but he seemed to want to kill us himself. With a cry like a wounded bear, he sprinted down the hill toward us. He didn't seem to care about the snow and ice—nor did it seem to slow him down like I thought it should. For every skid of his boots, he simply held his balance and kept going.

"I've got it," Rosamund said, as if to herself.

A fog began to roll through the burned trees all around us. A fog that moved unnaturally low. Familiarly so.

"How?"

"The Bone Forest," Rosamund murmured. "It's trying to help, but we're so far away. And this Town has its own wishes."

"But—"

"Later, let me focus."

There was no time at all. I scooped a palm up toward the sky, using the move to help visualize my power as I grabbed the nearest corpse and made it rise. It ambled between us and the Vinlanders just as Prince Vetle burst through the fog. I used the corpse to block the swing of his sword.

Just like the first time he'd attacked us, Vetle cut the body cleanly in two. I tore the spine out of the corpse's rotting flesh and wrapped it tight around the prince's throat. He snarled, using one hand to rip the vertebrae apart and throw them off him.

"Rosamund!" I cried even as the other warriors began to charge through the fog toward us.

Rosamund shifted wolf. She slammed herself bodily into the nearest warrior, knocking him over, then headed straight toward me.

Even though we hadn't discussed it beforehand, I knew what she meant to do. As she got close, she slowed down just enough that I could throw my leg over her and pull myself onto her back. Rosamund's wolf form was four feet tall and some seven and a half feet in length, but wolves were not meant to be ridden and

I could feel the strain of Rosamund's muscles as she carried me a few steps.

It didn't matter. For all the power of a bone wolf, Rosamund's true strength was that she wasn't contained to one form. I took care to keep my knees from digging into her sides as Rosamund shifted underneath me into her horse. I nearly fell off as I twisted around to send pieces of vertebrae flying at the faces of the nearest warriors. It wouldn't be enough to kill them, but everyone flinched back when something hit them in the face. It was gave us the room to flee.

Rosamund didn't stop once we were on the main road. She thundered over the stone bricks, dodging around the travelers and merchants in our way. I kept myself low to her neck, letting her run. My pack bounced uncomfortably against my spine. I did my best to ignore it. We passed a few guards, but we were going fast enough that by the time anyone could react we were far ahead.

We made it to the river shore without any more issues. I dismounted into the mud and tried not to think about the state of my boots. It wasn't important. Rosamund shifted. I watched her put her hands on her knees, breathing hard. After a second, she swore.

"What?" I asked, alert for danger. "Are you injured?"

"No, I'm fine. One of the men caught some fur, but . . ." She showed me a slice in the side of her sleeve. "It's just, I left my pack behind when I shifted into the wolf."

There was no reason to laugh at that, but I found myself doing so anyway. It was the sudden swell of relief, maybe, that we had survived. Rosamund looked at me like I had lost my mind.

I waved a hand in front of my face and tried to calm down. "We'll figure it out back home. Let's just get out of this forsaken land."

"You don't need to tell me twice," Rosamund muttered.

The issue, of course, was getting across the river. Looking downstream, I saw that we'd somehow ended up east of the gorge. It didn't make sense to double back for our little boat and row to Multah. If we could make it across the river on this side, we wouldn't be far from Desertmouth, the second-largest port in the Cursed Kingdom.

"We'll have to swim," I said. I opened up my pack and grabbed the last of the food—a couple pieces of dried meat and half a loaf of almost-stale bread. The only other thing in my pack was a change of clothes and a small coin purse. It would be fine to get wet. Even though it was freezing, I stuffed my cloak in the bag as well. It would drag less that way.

Rosamund took the bread and one of the slices of jerky. I ate the rest of the meat as quickly as I could.

"If I shift into the horse, I can help drag you across," Rosamund said.

"The temperature will make it dangerous," I warned.

Rosamund gave me a long look. "Push your magic into me and I'll be warm enough."

Did my magic feel as warm to Rosamund as hers did to me? I wasn't even sure that warmth translated to real heat, but I agreed, if only because I didn't have a better plan.

The water was so cold that I went stiff and nearly didn't remember how to swim until Rosamund-the-horse splashed up next to me. I grabbed hold of her mane and tried to push my magic to her, but my fingers were so chilled that I kept losing grip. It felt like the river had grabbed my legs and was trying to drag me down into the dark depths. I wrapped myself up in Rosamund's mane as best I could and tried to stay afloat.

It wasn't until Rosamund was bodily pulling me onto shore that I realized we'd reached the other side.

"Let go!" Rosamund shouted, jolting me awake. I had no idea how long it had been. My whole body was numb. Rosamund's fingers were scratching at my legs, untangling some kind of vine that had somehow gotten wrapped around my ankles.

"Come on, stand up. You can do it, Shaw."

Rosamund helped me stumble away from the river and farther onto land. The landscape flashed around us. First mud and reeds. Then trees. Then houses. I tried to figure out how we'd gotten from the river to wherever we were now, but it was hard to concentrate.

"Please, can you help?"

I opened my eyes. When had I closed them? Someone needed help. That was Rosamund. Why was Rosamund calling for help?

I went to move toward her and stumbled as something pulled me back at the shoulder.

"Oh dear, what happened?"

"She fell in the river. Please, can we sit by your fire?"

"Come in, quickly, quickly."

My head was spinning. My skin began to tingle, and then the tingles became knives stabbing into my arms.

"You're okay, I've got you," Rosamund said.

"Got you too," I said, but my words didn't come out right. I tried to say it again, but Rosamund shushed me.

Someone with a squeaky sort of voice said something, but I no longer had any energy to figure out what. I leaned sideways into the blazing warmth that was Rosamund and let myself slip away from everything.

Chapter 14

I WOKE TO A VISION OF RED. THE VINLANDER GHOST stared at me. She flashed red again, like the fire reflected behind her translucent form.

"Who are you?" I asked.

"I miss you, my love," the ghost said, low and mournful.

Even as she warbled the final word, she turned red and stayed that way. A true angry spirit, drawn as only spirits were to the siren song of death all bone witches unintentionally exuded.

"Wait!" I cried out, throwing out a hand.

It was too late. Though I had calmed hundreds of spirits, I'd never been so close to one. Close enough to touch. The spirit grabbed my outstretched hand and sank under my skin. I scrambled backward, but the red mist followed me, crawling through my skin like a thousand ants seeking food inside my soul.

Fire erupted in my lungs. I felt like I was choking on flames. I coughed wildly, gasping for breath that wouldn't come. Smoke filled my vision, the scent of burning hair in my nose, screams in my ears.

"Shaw!" someone shouted. Then a two-hundred-pound wolf was on top of me. I grabbed Rosamund's fur, desperately siphoning her magic into myself.

The spirit yelled with my own mouth as it was forced out of my body. The magic of bone familiars was the antithesis of possession. There was no room for it inside me with Rosamund's magic taking space. The fury of the spirit's fire settled into a more soothing warmth as it fled in response to Rosamund's presence.

We lay there for few seconds while I caught my breath. At least until the weight of Rosamund's wolf grew too heavy and I pushed at her in a silent request to be let up. Rosamund pulled away and shifted.

"What was that?" she asked, looking me up and down as if the evidence of the possession would be clear on my physical body.

"An angry spirit," I said. "Bone witches as strong as I am normally sleep behind protective enchantments."

Rosamund's face twisted into something between anger and apology. I hadn't meant it as a complaint. She'd obviously saved my life twice over—first in the river, and then again just now.

A flicker of red caught my attention, and I spun around. But it was just the fire, confined to a stone firepit in the center of what looked to be a one-room house.

Rosamund touched my shoulder in silent support, and the warm trickle of her magic that flowed into me soothed the lingering panic. I put my hand over hers, pulling it up to rest against my cheek. Only after I felt Rosamund tense did I realize what I was doing.

I let go and made a point of looking around. "Where are we?" I asked.

We were, apparently, at the outskirts of Desertmouth. An elderly weaver by the name of Arud had offered us use of their house and I'd slept straight through morning into the afternoon. Luckily, I still had my bag, including the small coin purse. I gave Arud a few coins despite their protests. They insisted on making us a meal in exchange for the money. It was simple fare but utterly filling. Rosamund thanked them again for sheltering us for the night while I hid another coin under one of the empty bowls.

We headed into the center of Desertmouth. Though not as large as Multah, it had multiple piers on the river and a large town square with a dozen different brick-and-mortar stores alongside the typical market square booths. Despite its name, Desertmouth wasn't in the high desert—it was too close to the river for that—but for most of the small villages that lived at the edge of the Obsidian Desert, Desertmouth was the main supplier of all the necessities to survive the dry, freezing winters and the even drier, blazing-hot summers.

I used what was left of my coin to buy provisions in the market for the trip back to Witch Hall. Rosamund's waterskin had been with her bag and was therefore lost to Vinland, so I bought her a new one and a simple linen dress she could use to switch out with her current attire. I'd changed into my spare tunic and breeches before leaving Arud's house. Despite getting soaked by our foray into the river, they'd dried well in front of Arud's fire and were certainly cleaner than the outfit I'd worn from Multah into Vinland.

Rosamund ducked into one of the inns ringing the market square and returned with her new dress on and her old clothing neatly folded. I stuffed them into the bottom of my bag alongside my own dirtied clothes, using it as an excuse to look away. I'd bought a pale green dress for Rosamund without thinking, and now I was regretting it. The way it brought out the green flecks in her eyes was dangerous to my already-bruised heart.

"How do we get back to school?" Rosamund asked as I closed up my bag. "It should be straight west, right?" She was looking at the steep cliffs that jutted up along the riverside. On the other side of the massive gorge before us was Witch Hall, but there was no easy route through those cliffs.

"We'll need to take a ferry," I said. "Otherwise, we have to take the road south of Desertmouth that winds toward the Frozen Mountain. It eventually meets up with the road we took from Gravestown."

Rosamund made a face, realizing as I did how long that route would take us. A couple days at least. The ferry would get us back to school before dinner.

A glimmer of red caught my attention. This time, when I spun around to look, I saw her. The ghost from earlier, flickering to the red of an angry spirit again. Her eyes were fixed upon something in the distance.

"Shaw," Rosamund said, sharp enough to pull my attention to where she pointed. The same direction the ghost had been looking.

Prince Vetle stood at the end of the nearest pier, just barely visible amid the dockhands and traders bustling about the docks. He hadn't drawn his sword yet, but his eyes were fixed on us. He grabbed his hunting horn with his left hand and raised it to his lips.

I acted instinctively, reaching out for any bones I could feel. I was shocked when the hunting horn jerked toward me in answer. It had to be made of some type of bone—though the polish and craft had dulled the lingering spiritual energy to almost nothing. It was enough, now that I knew, for me to grab hold of it. Vetle got out only the start of a note before the horn flew through the air and clattered somewhere over the awning of one of the market stalls.

"We need to lead him away from the town," I told Rosamund. "Quickly." No one seemed to have realized Vetle was anything more than a typical visitor, but that would change if he drew his sword.

Rosamund took my hand and ran through the market. I wasn't sure if I imagined the roar that followed us, or if Vetle truly had yelled.

We didn't stop until we were far away from the market and nearing the southern outskirts of Desertmouth. Only then did Rosamund let me go so she could shift into a horse. I climbed atop the nearest boulder to get on her back.

Rosamund's ears flicked somewhere behind us. I turned to look. Vetle had found us—and he was gaining ground fast.

"Go," I told Rosamund. "Veer south. We'll lose him in the Desert."

Rosamund took off. I clamped my thighs and lowered myself over her mane. With any luck, Vetle would give up once we hit the Desert itself and go back to his people. I doubted he'd risk a full-scale assault on Desertmouth, not in the middle of winter. He seemed to have fixated on me, and though that didn't give me any hope for peace between us, at least it meant he wasn't killing any of my people.

It was sudden, the change from red cedar and high desert pines to black dust and obsidian dunes. I tugged at Rosamund's mane and leaned back as far as I dared without a saddle. We'd gained some ground between us and the prince. It was too dangerous now to race through the Desert, especially without a glass witch or familiar like Einar and Oluk to guide us.

"Let's skirt the outside as much as we can," I told Rosamund.

She slowed to a trot. My thighs ached from the pain of riding bareback for so long. Once we returned to Witch Hall, I would request a break from riding duty. My legs needed time to recover.

I looked around to distract myself. The Desert had changed the landscape around us completely. I'd only ever been on the outskirts of it before, and I feared we might have crossed farther inside than was safe. In the distance, giant mounds of black sand slowly crawled across the horizon. Unlike dunes at the beach whose top layers shifted by the ocean breeze, these obsidian dunes moved on their own. I watched one of the massive sand hills envelop a hunk of obsidian. The solid obsidian cracked and groaned, shattering into sand and joining the moving dune.

"We need to leave," I whispered. The dunes were approaching us. "Head west."

Rosamund turned and picked up a canter. I used the opportunity to glance back for any sign of Vetle. I didn't see him, but what I did see was enough to make my stomach drop. Where I expected to have a view of the path we'd taken, now all I saw were more glittering black sand dunes.

"Wait, slow down," I said, heart pounding.

Rosamund slowed to a walk, her ears flicking back and forth in obvious discomfort.

The dunes had encroached far quicker than I'd thought possible. There was no longer a clear path forward through the Desert. I did my best to ignore those towering mounds of black sand and obsidian glass, focusing on Rosamund.

"We need to head due west. Don't trust the position of the sun. The Desert likes to play with sunlight as much as the Forest plays with fog."

Even as I spoke, I could feel the sunbeams glaring off the obsidian glass. It was still winter, but it was starting to get unbearably hot under my cloak. I didn't take it off. The cloak was a layer of protection against the sharp shards of glass around us.

"Head toward the Mountain," I said, but instead Rosamund stopped, throwing her head in obvious protest.

I winced. There was nowhere for us to go. The obsidian dunes had surrounded us. They were taller now and still growing. The light clinks of glass rubbing against glass grew into a loud, crunching sound. I dismounted and Rosamund immediately shifted human. She turned to face me, grabbing on to the front of my cloak like she could keep us both safe by pulling me close.

"We mean no disrespect," I told the dune at Rosamund's back. "Please, let us pass."

The wind rose, carrying small flecks of obsidian glass. They hit my face, stinging my cheeks like a reprimand.

I drew myself up as tall as I could. "I am Princess Shaw Colchuck, heir to the Cursed Throne. It was my ancestor who gave you life. I ask you to honor her and what she sacrificed to let us through."

The nearest dune rumbled ominously. Obsidian sand began to ripple down toward us like a miniature waterfall. I quickly pressed even closer to Rosamund, not wanting to be in the way if the whole dune decided to collapse. Her hands trembled and she ducked her face against my chest to avoid the stinging shards of sand whipping around us.

I tried again. "There is a man following us, an enemy of magic. He would kill us for being a witch and familiar. We came to you for protection."

The Desert stilled. I cupped the back of Rosamund's head, pulling her as close as I could. I was furious at myself for thinking that it would be safe to go this way. I'd never gone close to the Desert without a glass witch around before. My mistake might see both Rosamund and me killed.

"Please," Rosamund added, her voice muffled by my chest. She didn't pull back, but she did turn her head toward the nearest dune. "Help us escape."

Nothing moved for what felt like minutes, though it might have been mere seconds. Even the wind had stopped, settling all the obsidian sand back onto the dunes instead of swirling around our faces.

Finally, the dunes pulled away. First the tips of them trickled down the back sides. Then, with growing speed, entire mounds fell backward, re-formed, and fell again. Within minutes, they were fifty feet away and still fading.

Rosamund and I didn't move as we watched the dunes retreat. I couldn't tell if I was shaking or she was. Perhaps both of us.

We didn't have time to bask in our survival long. I was still facing the way we'd come, and with the dunes retreating, I had a clear sight of Prince Vetle charging along the road toward us.

"Shit," I said.

Farther ahead, huge obsidian chunks covered the ground. The boulders had become misshapen hills. At some angles, the obsidian chunks looked like plain black rocks. At other angles, you could see sheer slabs of reflective black glass. I grabbed Rosamund's arm and tugged her with me to higher ground.

"Watch out, the edges are sharp," I told her, then failed to listen to my own advice as I slipped over a sheer side of glass and cut my palm against the edge of another rock. At least the cut looked shallow. I did my best to ignore the slow drip of blood onto the obsidian and focused on climbing.

We reached the top of the little hill just as Vetle arrived at the ravine below us.

"Killing me won't help your people, Vetle," I called to him. "It will only give mine a reason to do far worse."

"Don't think to threaten me, *Shaw*," Vetle hissed. "My people have already seen your worst and we are not afraid."

There was a wild look in his eyes, an almost painful intensity that I didn't understand. Why had he dared follow us all the way into the Cursed Kingdom? His single-minded obsession with revenge felt personal—more so even than just a prince hurting for the death of his people. I should know. I wanted revenge for Multah. For Guanyu. For Einar. But I knew better than to put revenge above the rest of my people. Vetle seemed not to care for the political consequences.

Then again, I was raised to rule a small kingdom and Vetle was a prince of the Empire of Vinland. Perhaps that was enough of a difference.

This was not the location for a fight. Even if the prince didn't realize the danger, Rosamund and I did. I knew how strong the prince was, how easy it would be for him to swing that enormous broadsword and knock me off balance. If I hit my head against the wrong edge of one of the obsidian boulders, that would be it.

"This is no place for those without magic," I told him. "You stand in the Obsidian Desert. It has never taken kindly to trespassers. Turn back now, or you'll be killed."

Vetle seemed unfazed by my warning. "You'd like that, wouldn't you? I'm no coward."

Screeching interrupted my response. The wind had picked up again, bringing with it little flecks of obsidian glass. They scraped through the sides of the hills.

"Neither am I," I said, looking past Vetle to the horizon. "But it's not cowardly to run when faced with that."

Rosamund began to swear. I nudged her to climb down from the hill. We didn't have much time. Vetle finally gave in to temptation and turned to look behind him. I didn't wait to see his reaction, scrambling down after Rosamund instead.

Rosamund had already shifted into her horse form. I jumped from the last layer of rocks onto her back and wrapped my fingers in her mane. "Don't stop," I said as she began to run. My heart pounded in fear. I squeezed my legs tighter, urging her on.

Rosamund threw herself into a gallop. I leaned down over her neck and held on as tight as I could. Behind us, a black cloud billowed across the horizon—a massive obsidian sandstorm racing toward us with unnatural speed.

Taking a tumble anywhere in the Desert was liable to get you injured, but the true danger was in the sand. Obsidian did not naturally erode down like that, or at least not in the quantities that existed in the Desert. But then, pine trees did not naturally have skeletal limbs that moved by the whims of the Bone Forest. The issue with the obsidian sand of the Desert was that it retained the sharp edges of shattered glass, no matter how small the piece.

The obsidian sandstorm was too fast to outrun. Already, the wind whipped black sand around us. I felt it slice into my cheeks. I dared to untangle one hand from Rosamund's mane so I could pull the hood of my cloak tight over my face.

We should have taken our chances with Vetle in the hills and hunkered down in the shelter the large chunks of obsidian provided. It was too late now. Turning back toward the storm would get us killed. We needed to find a place to wait it out, and quickly.

As soon as I'd thought it, I noticed the edge of what looked to be a massive chasm up ahead. "Look there!" I yelled.

The chasm widened as we approached. It was no canyon—it was a quarry. An old obsidian quarry, back before the Desert swallowed this section of the land and pushed the miners farther north.

"Slow down, you'll break a leg jumping into it."

But Rosamund did not slow down. She skirted around the edge

of the quarry instead and kept going. I tugged at her mane as hard as I could, trying to lean back. "Rosamund, stop!"

When that didn't work, I pulled to the right and dug in with my left knee. With a harsh whinny, Rosamund veered right, circling back around the quarry. From this angle, I could see the whites of her eyes. She'd gone feral.

I let go of her mane so that I could bend down and hug her neck. It was a much more dangerous position. All she needed to do was toss her head and I would be thrown off her back. It didn't matter. I needed to touch her skin so that I could push my magic toward her.

"I'm here. Calm down. I'm with you, Rosamund," I chanted as I did.

It didn't take much more than that. Rosamund shifted under me without warning, and I tumbled toward the ground. I landed hard, though luckily not hard enough to break anything. Next to me, Rosamund shuddered out several uneven breaths.

I wanted to give her time to recover, but the wind carried enough glass now to take out an eye. I kept my face turned away from it, though I wished I could see how close the body of the sandstorm was.

"Hurry," I said, tugging Rosamund up by the arm. "We have to go."

There was an ancient set of wooden stairs leading down into the quarry. It hardly looked stable, but what choice did we have? I didn't give Rosamund a chance to protest. Keeping hold of her arm, I walked down confidently.

The wood groaned and swayed in a horrifying way. I ignored it. There was no time to worry. Over our heads, the wind howled.

Near the bottom, Rosamund's foot broke through one of the steps. She spooked like an animal, and I let her go out of instinct.

She leaped down to the ground, shifting squirrel, and scurried away.

Shit. If she'd gone feral again, I wasn't sure how I was going to catch her in that form. I jogged down the last few steps and hurried after her. Except, as I got close, Rosamund-the-squirrel spun around to face me and within seconds grew into Rosamund-the-wolf.

I froze. The wolf growled at me, reminiscent of Rosamund's grandmother in her own feral state. It hadn't been like this when she'd gone feral during Vetle's first ambush. But then she'd had an enemy to focus on. This was different. There was just me and her and a life-threatening storm spiraling down into the quarry with us.

On the other side of the quarry, I could see what looked to be the entrance to an old mine shaft. If I could just get Rosamund inside, we'd hopefully be safe from the worst of the sandstorm. There was nothing for it. I gathered every ounce of courage and approached her. The wolf continued to growl, but it didn't attack, even when I was in range. I let that bolster me and reached out toward its head.

I almost expected to lose my hand like Madam Dyer had in the Forest on Samhain night, but Rosamund stopped growling. My fingers rested lightly on the fur between her ears. I stroked her head once, but I didn't have time for more than that. "Come on," I said, hoping the wolf would follow me even if Rosamund hadn't regained control yet.

Whether it was Rosamund or her wolf, she loped at my side as I ran toward the old mine. The wind was so strong now that my cloak attempted to choke me. I ducked inside, using one hand to trace the wall.

It was dark inside the mine shaft. The ground sloped gently

downward. I shuffled forward, unable to wait until my eyes had adjusted.

It was only after I heard Rosamund ask "Do you think this is far enough?" that I realized she had shifted back to human.

I forced my shoulders to relax. The danger, it seemed, had passed. "It should be," I replied.

I took off my cloak and tried my best to shake the shards of obsidian sand from it. When that didn't work, I folded it inside out and used it as a cushion to sit on. As soon as I sat, I felt Rosamund join me. It was still too dark for me to make out much beyond a vague idea of her shape, but I expected her vision was better in the dark than mine.

Now that the fear was fading, my body felt strangely shaky. The cold didn't help. I knew it would only get colder as night fell. Winters in the Desert were almost as bad as winters on the Mountain.

"When did you go feral?" I asked into the darkness.

I felt Rosamund shuffle. Our arms touched briefly, and then she pulled back. The silence stretched on long enough that I thought she wasn't going to answer.

"I'm not sure," she said finally. "There was the prince, then the sandstorm, and you sounded so scared when you told me to run. I think it set my horse off." She paused, then said, "I'm sorry. I nearly got us both killed."

I shook my head, though I wasn't sure if Rosamund would be able to see it. "You snapped out of it eventually."

Rosamund said nothing. In the darkness, I couldn't hide from my thoughts. Faintly, I heard the wind howling across the opening of the mine shaft. We were safe here—or as safe as was possible. The prince wouldn't be able to find us through the storm outside, if he even survived it.

I couldn't think about the prince dying inside the Obsidian Desert. Not now. Even the idea of it was enough to double the shaking I couldn't seem to stop.

"You followed me while feral," I said, though I hadn't meant to. I hadn't thought it through before speaking. I'd just wanted the silence to end. I was fairly sure of the truth of my words though. The wolf had still been at the forefront when Rosamund followed me into the mine.

"I guess I did."

The silence returned. The sound of my own breathing was obnoxious. I tried to slow it down, even it out.

Rosamund shuffled again. I felt her press her arm to mine, and then her head to my shoulder. I took the implicit permission to move my arm out of the way, curl my hand around her opposite shoulder, and pull her close. Her cheek moved to my neck, her breaths tickling the hollow of my throat.

"Rosamund . . ." I trailed off, unsure what I'd wanted to say.

"You can call me Rosy, you know."

My fingers tightened over her shoulder. Had I known that? She'd never mentioned it before. Oluk and Toketie did. As did Aklemin, though Rosamund used to complain about it. Not recently though. Not for some months. Had she just given up, or had she come to see my entourage as true friends in a way she had refused to do before?

Was I only allowed to call her Rosy because of the clear boundary between us? Her friends could call her Rosy, and that was all we were. All we were ever going to be. Friends.

I told myself I was happy with that title. I was. I'd rather have Rosamund as a friend than not. Rather have her here than away.

I just wanted. Horribly. Madly. Wanted so badly it choked me.

"I'll stick with Rosamund," I murmured.

Rosamund's shoulders stiffened.

"Unless you'd rather I didn't?"

Rosamund pulled away just slightly. I could tell she was looking at me, though it had grown even darker in the mine shaft. I couldn't make out the features of her face at all, but I wouldn't be surprised if she could see mine. I wondered what I was revealing in my expression. The shaking had subsided into shivers, but I still couldn't seem to control my body.

"No, it's fine," Rosamund said finally. "I like the way you say my name. It's not clunky in your mouth."

"It's a beautiful name," I told her honestly. "A fitting one."

Rosamund laid her head back down against the flat of my shoulder. My shivers finally eased.

"How long is the storm going to last?" she asked after a while.

"I don't know. A while. We should try to sleep."

She nodded, cheek rubbing up and down against my tunic as she did. Her magic felt so warm, more than just the natural heat of her proximity. The storm outside had already blocked out the sun, but night would fall soon enough. The mine shaft would protect us from the worst of it, but I wasn't looking forward to feeling my breath freeze as soon as it left my lips.

"We need to share heat," I whispered. "Do you mind?"

"It's fine," Rosamund whispered in return.

I rearranged us, and she let me. We curled up together on top of my cloak with hers as a blanket over us. I put my back flat to the ground and pulled Rosamund to lie half on top of me. I would take the pain of sleeping on the ground to have more of her warmth covering my body. It was as comfortable as it could be.

It was also torture. We'd hugged plenty of times. Her head had always found a home in the crook of my neck, my arm around her shoulders. This was different. Every time she twitched, I felt it down the length of my body. Desire stirred, hotter than it had ever stirred outside of the solace of my own room.

I breathed in the smell of her hair and tried to think of other things.

"I thought your wolf might attack me while feral," I said. "But you didn't. Not this time, and not the time before."

Rosamund said nothing. I realized I was rubbing circles in her back. I forced myself to stop. Her shoulder blades twitched, as if protesting the lack of petting.

I thought about the issue further. "You were able to bring your grandmother out of her feral rages. It's obvious from the way you two interacted, and compared to the rest of your family. Toketie's scars . . . that's why she was a late bloomer. She panic-shifted after your grandmother attacked her, is that it?"

Rosamund still didn't respond.

"So, there must have been a reason your grandmother didn't attack you the same way. Something to do with your wolf shift. As if . . . as if she saw you as her pack." I paused. Rosamund pressed her forehead against my shoulder and didn't make a sound. "Am I your pack, Rosamund?"

The only answer was the steady rhythm of Rosamund's breathing.

I closed my eyes. She hadn't been deliberately ignoring me. She hadn't even heard my murmured deductions. She'd fallen asleep.

I knew I wouldn't ask again. Under the light of day, the question would bury itself into the depths of my heart and fester there along with all the other wounds that had formed since Rosamund tore off my courtship necklace and ran away. I already knew the answer.

Somehow, Rosamund's shifts had come to see me as pack. That was the only logical explanation for my ability to calm her out of those feral rages. But Rosamund-the-human refused to acknowledge what that meant, just as she turned her back on our magical compatibility. No matter what I did, she wouldn't give a future with me any more consideration, and that hurt worse than it would have otherwise.

I let myself lean into the comfort offered by Rosamund's presence, by the steadiness of her breathing, the warmth of her touch. It wasn't hard to fall into the exhaustion that had dodged my steps since we crossed the river to Vinland.

In that old abandoned mine shaft, with an obsidian sandstorm raging outside, I finally slept.

Chapter 15

ROSY

ROSY WOKE UP TO THE SIGHT OF SHAW'S FACE. SHE STARED for a second, enthralled by it. Shaw always held herself so composed, so dignified, and yet in sleep her mouth hung open ever so slightly and her chin was tucked toward her chest in what looked like a horribly awkward angle.

It made Rosy's chest squeeze to see her like this. To know that she was one of the few people who would ever see the princess of the Cursed Kingdom relaxed in sleep. Perhaps the first to ever be so close to her upon waking. Their legs were tangled together in the kind of casual intimacy that made Rosy blush.

Despite everything, she wanted to press even closer to Shaw. She wanted to lean down those scant few inches and press her lips to Shaw's open ones. She wanted to watch Shaw wake up, feel her smile as she realized who was kissing her. She wanted Shaw to twist a hand through her hair and hold her as she deepened the kiss. She wanted Shaw to roll them around, press Rosy into the ground with the weight of her body. She wanted. She wanted. She—

She wasn't allowed to want this. Wanting Shaw meant wanting the crown. Meant wanting a life of politics and inter-kingdom relations. The court would tear Rosy apart. All she had to do was remind herself about what had happened during fall term, when she first came to Witch Hall. Even with Shaw by her side, Rosy worried. How long would it take before the bond began to feel like a cage? It'd be a different kind of prison than the one Gran had lived, but it'd be a prison nonetheless.

Was Shaw pack? She'd pretended to be asleep instead of answering Shaw's question, but the truth was, she didn't know. She didn't *want* to know. It didn't matter. It couldn't matter.

Shaw let out a little groan as she drifted into wakefulness. Rosy pulled back—lifting herself up and away. It had warmed up in the mine shaft, though it hadn't brightened much. By the howling of wind outside, the sandstorm still raged. She didn't know how long it had been, but she felt rested enough that it had to have been many hours already.

"Rosamund?" Shaw asked groggily.

"I'm here," Rosy said. "We should eat. We didn't have anything before falling asleep."

It was lucky they'd gotten more provisions in Desertmouth, because she had no idea how long they'd be trapped here. She helped Shaw find food and water in the darkness, and they ate to the melody of obsidian sand scratching at the walls of the quarry just outside.

"You were going to tell me about that woman you mentioned," Rosy said after some time. "Your ancestor?"

Shaw paused in the middle of stretching. She settled back down onto the cloak where they'd been sitting. "What would you like to know?"

"I remember learning about the first Witch Queen," Rosy said. "But it was a long time ago, and I don't remember much."

Shaw nodded. "Her name was Mesachie. The Wicked One, they called her after. She wasn't a queen originally. It was her son who was crowned our first ruler, but he labeled her the founder of our kingdom."

"I know more about the first Familiar King," Rosy admitted. He'd been the one who'd organized most of the structure of the Cursed Kingdom's government and the public celebrations of Samhain, Candlemas, Beltane, and Lammas. He'd been an ice raven familiar, an anchor to the infant Frozen Mountain, and was the reason that the folklore figure of the three-eyed raven became the crest of the royal family.

"Before him the Cursed Kingdom didn't exist as a singular government," Shaw explained. "We lived as separate villages. There was trade and the occasional intermarrying, but each community otherwise kept to its own. Mesachie lived in one of the smaller villages on the Mountain. It's called Falconridge today. According to the accounts I read, she was described as an odd girl, but as the daughter of the village's leader, she was left to her oddities."

"What do you mean, odd?"

"There are debates, but my tutors believed it had to do with her intrinsic magic," Shaw said. "Before the curse, the magic that permeated the land was simpler. It lived in every rock and tree and creek. Wild magic, without purpose or direction. The rare human was born with sparks inside them—the ability to shift into an owl or the power to speak with the dead. Mesachie was like that. Today we'd call her an ice witch, but they didn't have a structured understanding of magic then or education on controlling it. From a young age, she was beset with prophetic dreams so strong she woke screaming night after night."

"Screaming?" Rosy frowned. She knew Aklemin often had prophetic dreams, but as far as she was aware, they never woke up screaming because of it. How bad had those dreams been?

"No one knew what Mesachie saw in her dreams. She never wrote it down," Shaw continued. "The firsthand accounts I read described how she was haunted by them from childhood. How she grew gaunt and frail, with dark circles under her eyes that never seemed to fade. She lived her life anyway. Her father married her to a traveling merchant who was gone so often that he wouldn't much mind his wife's nightmares. They had a son together, and for a time, things seemed to be peaceful."

"Did the dreams go away?"

"No, I don't think so, but they were so normal by then that no one thought anything of them. Until one winter day when her son was six years of age. She gave him a basket of biscuits to take to his grandfather on the other side of the village. As soon as he'd gone, she climbed to the very peak of what would become the Frozen Mountain. There, she threw her arms to the sky and she cried out, a cry so loud they say it echoed in every corner of our kingdom. Just as the cry began to fade, a great column of smoke rose from the top of the Mountain."

"I thought the Frozen Mountain couldn't spew fire," Rosamund protested. Most of the other mountains in the nations north and south were volcanoes, but she'd been taught that, because of the ice magic, they were safe from the Frozen Mountain ever erupting.

"Not anymore," Shaw agreed. "But it could then. The eruption covered the sky in darkness. The people who dared to venture from their ash-coated homes in the days after witnessed the birth of the Cursed Kingdom. At the center of the storm stood the Mountain, now covered with everlasting ice. To its northwest, the largest lake bloomed with sentient flowers. To the east, an ancient obsidian flow had crumbled into sand. And to the south, the old pines began to rattle with the voices of the dead."

"What happened to Mesachie?"

Shaw leaned her head back against the shaft wall. "When her father dared to venture up the Mountain, he found nothing. Not even a body. What we can guess is that, in the moment of the eruption, the moment of her death, whether intentionally or not, Mesachie cast a curse upon this land. In her death, it turned into a powerful blood curse that coalesced the wild magic. It created the magical wells we have today, the Forest and Lake and Mountain and Desert."

"And that's how we became the only land with all four magic types so close together?" Rosy asked.

She'd learned about that from her papa. How magical wells existed elsewhere, like the massive whirlpool surrounded by the western islands where flower magic bloomed. Or how Daming has several burial sites that had grown strong enough to become wells of bone magic and, even more fascinating, a massive bamboo forest made entirely of glass. But so far as everyone knew, the Cursed Kingdom was unique by the proximity of all four types of magic.

"Yes," Shaw agreed. "And that's why my father must face justice. I still don't understand why he would deliberately foster anti-magical bigotry in our neighbors. Cursing Vinland like he did . . . I don't believe Mesachie would approve. She cursed this land to save everyone from the volcanic eruption. The Cursed Kingdom was *always* meant to be a sanctuary. Whatever prize my father believes may come from a war with Vinland, it's not worth the cost."

Rosy agreed with that wholeheartedly.

THE SANDSTORM LASTED FOR TWO full days. Throughout it all, the temperature dropped colder and colder. Nights in the desert were often chilly, and the sandstorm blocked the sunlight from leaving much ambient heat even during the day. When they were awake, they did their best to move around. After that first night, Rosy shifted into her wolf to curl up against Shaw's side to sleep.

On the third morning, Rosy woke to find Shaw rifling through her bag. "We're low on food and on water," she said as Rosy padded over.

Rosy twitched her ears in the direction of the mine shaft entrance. She'd become so used to the howling wind and scraping sand that the patter outside almost didn't register.

Shifting to human, Rosy grabbed Shaw by the arm and began to tug her. "Shaw, it's raining!"

They rushed out to the entrance of the mine shaft. It was early morning, and a soft drizzle was coming down from light gray clouds. A new layer of obsidian sand rested at the bottom of the quarry, and the rain dripped through it. A small stream began to run into the entrance of the mine shaft as Rosy and Shaw watched.

"I didn't realize it could rain in the Desert," Rosy said.

"It's rare, but it does happen," Shaw said. "Come on, we should refill our canteens while we have the chance."

They did so, then ate the last of their food. No point in rationing now. They'd either make it out of the Desert or they wouldn't. Then they threw on their cloaks, packed their bags, and headed out into the quarry.

"Let's hope the wind didn't damage it further," Shaw said as they stood at the base of the already-rickety staircase they'd used to get down into the quarry.

Rosy hadn't even considered that. What would they do if they couldn't get out? Rosy's squirrel might be able to climb up, but she wouldn't abandon Shaw.

Shaw must have seen her concern, because she reached forward and squeezed Rosy's hand. "It'll be fine. Come on."

Shaw went first, just as she had on their way down. She walked slower this time, testing each step before putting her weight on it. Rosy made sure to track the route so she could follow it exactly. The steps creaked and groaned and the columns holding them to the edge swayed, but miraculously it held. Rosy didn't dare breathe until her feet were safely on flat ground again.

"Well," Shaw said, and there were a thousand unspoken things hidden in that one word. "Let's get back to school."

"Here." Rosy undid the clasp of her cloak. She folded it and handed it to Shaw. "You can use it as a saddle blanket." She should have thought of it earlier. It couldn't have been comfortable for Shaw to ride bareback this whole time, especially with the speed Rosy had been going.

Shaw thanked her. Rosy shifted into her horse and waited for Shaw to settle the cloak over her back. Shaw used a nearby chunk of obsidian to climb on top. The cloak slid down a bit and Rosy suddenly understood then why some horses got antsy if their saddles weren't in the right place. She stomped her foot to express her displeasure at the strange sensation, and Shaw, being as attuned with horses as she was, fixed the position of the cloak.

The rain felt nice after being stuck in the mine shaft for days, but Rosy knew they wouldn't have long before they were soaked through and freezing. She picked up a canter, aiming for the distant Mountain. She hoped the Desert would let them out without a fight.

Shaw motioned for her to slow down once the landscape started to change. The black sand gave way to dirt, the obsidian hills to basalt cliffs. They'd reached the normal high desert, where rain was still rare but there was enough ice melt from the Frozen Mountain to create rivers and streams that flowed toward Wimahl River and kept a steady supply of vegetation that ensured the desert villages' survival.

They stopped at one of those small villages, where a rancher was generous enough to share a meal and let them refill their waterskins. The next morning, they set off again. It took another two days for them to reach the northern watchtower, where they'd stopped some five months prior on Rosy's first journey to Witch Hall.

There was a massive commotion as they approached the watchtower. Rosy vaguely recognized the thane in charge as he rushed out to greet them. He'd been Shaw's escort for her recruitment tour when she'd come to Forest's Edge all those months ago.

Shaw dismounted from Rosy's back as the thane stopped in front of them. "Your father will be most glad to see you safe, Princess!" he said. "You've been missing for nearly a week. Are you injured? Do you need assistance?"

"We're fine, Thane Hagen," Shaw said. "We merely hope to get a meal before we journey the rest of the way back to Witch Hall."

Rosy shifted and used the opportunity to stretch. Even as a bone horse, carrying a passenger for so many days wasn't easy. As she pulled up from an attempt at a backbend, she saw that another man was walking out of the watchtower toward them. His clothes were fine, made of silks and velvets, and his skin was lined more from stress than age. His hair was a medium brown, the sides pressed down by a silver circlet. A jarl, she assumed, though she didn't know which. This watchtower was officially part of Jarl Tenas's territory, right? Was Kwaddis's father coming to greet them?

The man got close enough for Rosy to make out the sharp line of his chin. The shape of his eyes. The expression he wore, still as an untouched pond and just as hard to read. Suddenly, she recognized that circlet not as a fashion statement, but as a simple silver crown.

Shaw moved in front of Rosy, as if attempting to block her from view. It was too late. Rosy had already met the man's dark gray gaze.

Pops had said something that evening Rosy and Gran summoned him for the Samhain ritual. Before he was pulled deeper into the Forest and Gran went feral and Madam Dyer cursed her and everything that came after that.

It's hard to counteract a man who can see every possible future any time he wishes.

This was the man who ordered her grandfather's assassination and her grandmother's imprisonment. The man who plotted to start a war with the Empire of Vinland. The man who wasn't supposed to ever see her, because as soon as he did, he'd be able to foresee the plot she and Shaw were working on to stop him.

This man, this monster, met her gaze and smiled that same amused smile Shaw wore whenever a plan came together.

"You must be Miss Rosamund Holt," the Witch King said. "It is truly a pleasure to meet you at last."

THEY COULDN'T GET OUT OF eating with the Witch King. Shaw tried to make some excuse about wanting to get back to school, but the Witch King simply sent one of the soldiers to Witch Hall to let the headmistress and General Tepeh know they were safe and would be returning that evening.

Thane Hagen led them to a small room at the top of the watchtower to eat away from the peering eyes of curious soldiers. Rosy stayed quiet as a mouse as Shaw talked with her father over the meal, but she doubted it helped. Every time she looked up from her plate, the man's eyes were on her.

Rosy wasn't sure that the Witch King was buying Shaw's story, though she was spinning an excellent one. As close to the truth as was possible without sharing anything dangerous. How Rosy and Shaw had gone to Multah to visit Shantie, then decided to take one of the rowboats back to school so they could return before they were found missing. Only, in the darkness, they missed Witch Hall's small dock and ended up crashing against the cliffs of the gorge farther east. Rosy dragged them both ashore, and they were forced to rest in a small fishing village. Rosy admired how Shaw carefully didn't say how long they were in the fishing village, but clearly implied it was for several days.

Shaw then explained how they didn't want to risk taking another boat after their experience with the first, so decided to ride back instead. Only, they drifted too close to the Desert and were caught in a sandstorm. They hid out in the quarry for several days before finally making it to the watchtower.

"We were foolish, Father," Shaw concluded. "We didn't stop to think about what we were doing, leaving school without permission, or how risky it would be to try to row back without enough light to see."

"Yes, it was risky," the Witch King said.

Rosy couldn't resist the urge to glance up again. For once, the man was watching his daughter instead of her. She still couldn't read his expression, but she got the feeling that he was talking about more than Shaw's story.

Shaw put down her fork. She'd eaten just enough to make it look good, but not as much as Rosy was sure she should have eaten after their long days of rationing. "We must return to school. We have much work to catch up on. I promise that I will submit myself to Madam Kawak for punishment for breaking school rules and apologize to General Tepeh for any panic I caused."

"I do not doubt your honor, my dear," Shaw's father said. "All foolishness aside, I do hope you enjoy your last month of term."

Rosy was still trying to parse out whether that was a threat when the Witch King turned to look at her. "And you, Miss Holt, do you plan to travel with my daughter to Falconridge for Candlemas?"

He *definitely* knew of their plan to present the evidence. Rosy chewed on her bottom lip for a second, wondering what to say. "I don't know yet," she settled on.

"You are more than welcome," he said, and Rosy reflected that Shaw's own formal tone came straight from her father. He stood and nodded to them both. "I should get back to the Mountain. There is much to prepare."

Shaw stood too, and Rosy scrambled to follow. "Father," Shaw said respectfully.

"I am glad you are safe, my dear," the Witch King said, and it sounded sincere, even to Rosy's ears. "I will see you soon."

"Yes, Father. Safe travels."

"You as well."

The Witch King left, and Rosy stared after him. That was it? Not even a hug goodbye? For all he knew, Shaw had been dead the past week, and he'd barely reacted to finding out she was safe!

Then again, he was an ice witch. He probably would have known if she'd died.

"He used the excuse of our absence to come here," Shaw murmured. "He must have scried us and figured out we would be coming this way."

"Now what?" Rosy asked. She felt wrung out. She almost could believe that, any second, she'd wake up and find out this had all been some drawn-out nightmare.

Shaw ran a hand through her hair, obviously aggravated. "Let's get back to school."

Thane Hagen insisted on escorting them to Witch Hall. The commotion when they passed the four columns and the gate onto campus was near instantaneous. Rosy jumped down from the cart to a flurry of hugs from Toketie and Oluk.

"We were so worried!" Toketie cried, squeezing her as if Rosy was going to run off again.

"Rosy, did you really—" Oluk began.

"Where have you been?" Yuyan demanded, even as she pulled Shaw into a hug.

"Not here," Shaw murmured.

Aklemin dodged around a few soldiers to make their way over. "Not here," they agreed with a sideways look at where the headmistress and General Tepeh were striding toward their little group with matching expressions of anger on their faces.

Rosy scowled. She'd never been a troublemaker growing up, but at Witch Hall, she couldn't seem to stay out of it.

Later, after Rosy had sat through Madam Kawak's lecture and General Tepeh's own questioning—of which Shaw had given the same story she'd given her father—they snuck into the infirmary to meet up with the entourage.

Einar had apparently carved runes into his infirmary bed while they were gone that worked to prevent eavesdropping just the same as the ones on their usual table in the dining hall. The entourage had needed a place to talk safely while Rosy and Shaw were missing, not that it had helped them figure out where the two had gone. Rosy winced at the obvious worry they'd put their friends through.

For the third time that day, Shaw explained where they'd been. But this time, she told the truth.

"It was kind of you to talk with Shantie, but why couldn't you have waited until the end of term?" Yuyan lamented.

"Then we wouldn't have discovered Thane Anders taking his platoon across the river," Shaw countered. "I won't lie to you. Things are much more dire than we assumed."

Rosy closed her eyes as Shaw began to describe the frozen waterfall they'd found and the Ghost Town after. Toketie gasped when Shaw explained how the prince had attacked them, and how they'd ended up fleeing through Desertmouth and into the Obsidian Desert.

"You were lucky to survive," Einar chided, once Shaw had finally finished.

"The Desert is always calmest in the winter," Oluk murmured. "It would have thrown far worse than a sandstorm at you in the summer."

Rosy opened her eyes in time to see Shaw close hers. Neither of them was looking forward to sharing the remaining piece of their story.

"There's more," Rosy said, because Shaw had taken the brunt of it and it was time for her to be the one to share the bad news. "The Witch King was at the watchtower when we arrived."

"Wait, but that means—" Toketie began, eyes wide.

"Yes," Shaw confirmed. "He's met Rosamund now."

"We've our own news to share," Aklemin said. By the grim expressions that came over the entourage's faces, it wasn't any better than Rosy and Shaw's.

"What?" Rosy demanded of Aklemin, then Toketie when they didn't answer quickly enough. "What happened?"

"Shaw, they searched your room," Einar said. "Supposedly for hints as to where you may have gone, but . . ."

Rosy's stomach sank as Shaw swore. "The jar with Squad Leader Moolocks's ghost, is it—"

"It's gone," Yuyan said. "I checked after. They took it."

Shaw scowled at Aklemin. "Was there really no way to sneak the jar away before they found it?"

"They did it while we were still in our Friday morning workshops," Toketie said defensively. "We had no way of knowing, not until the headmistress questioned us at lunch."

"Did she say anything about the jar?" Rosy asked. Was Madam Kawak in on the plot to instigate the war?

"No. She just mentioned the soldiers searching both your rooms and asked us if we knew the reason you'd leave," Oluk murmured.

"General Tepeh would have found a bone witch to force Squad Leader Moolocks to fade by now," Shaw said. "She's gone."

"The map's still where we put it," Yuyan said. "I snuck out in the middle of the night to make sure, so no one would see me going into Shantie's room. And Toketie still has the notes she took, when you questioned that ghost."

That was something, but was it enough? "Does it even matter?" Rosy asked. "The Witch King has to know about our plan by now."

Her stomach was in knots. She felt like this was all her fault. If she hadn't encouraged Shaw to come visit Shantie with her, none of this would have happened.

"It was foolish to think we could hide this from him even before that," Shaw said. She buried her face in her hands. "He could have been spying on us the entire time. He wouldn't have been able to see our conversation with Squad Leader Moolocks's ghost, but he may well have seen me hide that jar in my room."

That was a terrifying prospect. The voices in Rosy's heart began to speak up, their squeaks and growls demanding that Rosy do *something*. "Do the runes prevent scrying?" Rosy asked Einar.

"They do," Einar said. "But with my injury . . ."

Rosy grimaced. They'd done a lot of their plotting out from under the protection of Einar's runes. She wondered if the Witch King had planned for that. If he'd known that Einar was the most likely to die or be injured in Vetle's first attack and had wished for it, to better be able to keep an eye on Shaw.

Shaw lifted her face and looked at Aklemin. "Should we commit ourselves to preparing for this war? I won't make an enemy of my father unless I need to, Aklemin. Never mind ruining my reputation for the council, we also need him if there's to be war with Vinland. Taking what evidence we have to the jarls is pointless unless we can be sure we'll convince the council to try for peace, and if we can be sure peace is even achievable. There's every chance Prince Vetle died in the Desert."

Despair flooded Rosy like snowmelt down the Mountain. "You can't give up now, Shaw. Even if it's difficult, we have to try. For Guanyu's sake, if nothing else."

"It's exactly because of deaths like Guanyu's that I have to be practical," Shaw responded. "I've told you before, Rosamund, I will not let my people die when I can do something to prevent it. If that means stopping this war, then I will do so, but if that means doing everything I can to prepare for war so I can defend them, I will turn my attention to that."

Anger began to overwhelm her despair. "If Vinlanders come across our border again, we'll fight them," Rosy said. "But this war with Vinland is much more than simply defending our borders. Your father is a warmonger. He's been the most powerful man in this kingdom long enough to let it go to his head. He's too focused on the bigger picture to realize the pain he's bringing upon the commonfolk. It's not right."

Aklemin stepped in between them before Shaw could reply. They put a hand on Shaw's shoulder, and she shook them off angrily.

"There is still hope for peace, Shaw," Aklemin said, unperturbed. "That path hasn't collapsed yet. There is a chance, so long as you're willing to tread it."

Shaw dug the heel of her palm into the bridge of her nose, as if trying to ward off tears. Rosy's anger drained away at Shaw's obvious frustration. She sat back in her seat, fighting the urge to scowl. She didn't know what to do, and she hated it.

Finally, Shaw let loose a loud sigh and straightened to face them all. "Very well. There isn't much time left until Candlemas. We no longer have strength in evidence, so we must have strength in support instead. We have the rest of the term to shore up our position with the heirs. It's time to be honest, at least with some of them."

"Are you sure that's wise?" Yuyan asked.

"My father will know our plan," Shaw said. "He will focus on convincing the jarls to ignore what evidence we still have. If we've any chance to circumvent that, we must use their children. It may be our only chance, but so long as that chance exists, we must try for it."

The wolf in Rosy's heart let out a soft huff. Rosy agreed with it. It was at times like these that keeping her distance from Shaw felt so hard, because she was so beautifully admirable that Rosy wanted nothing more than to bask in her presence. To thank her for listening, even when she had every reason to turn her back on the right choice in favor of the easier road. It made her feel simultaneously flushed and guilty.

The feeling only grew as Shaw turned to Rosy and added, a touch softer, "You're right to argue with me. We've come too far to turn our backs now. The Cursed Kingdom deserves peace."

Rosy said nothing, because she knew she would regret anything that came out of her mouth. Luckily Shaw was already moving on before the feelings bubbling up inside her had the chance to break free.

Chapter 16

SHAW

We spent the next two weeks—in between catching up on our missed assignments—determining what exactly we should share, and with which heirs. Eventually we decided on just Charles, Froya, and Kwaddis. Though it might cause sour feelings from the heirs we left out, it was better to keep it to the ones who would have the largest impact.

There were several reasons I decided to tell them during the final full moon assembly of the winter term. The first was timing—the assembly was taking place just a week before the end of term. If the conversation went poorly, the heirs wouldn't have much time to write a letter to their parents before we were all traveling together to the Frozen Mountain for Candlemas. Or at least, the letter wouldn't arrive before I had a chance for damage control.

The second reason was because Rosamund and I had both been assigned page duty as punishment for leaving campus the night of the solstice. It was my first page duty, which was novel, but I knew from the start that I would not have the typical experience.

"I hope there's not a maximum number of page duties allowed in a single year before you're kicked out or something," Rosamund muttered as we put on the tabards.

I glanced sideways at her. What number was she up to now? Three? Considering this was only her sixth full moon assembly since becoming a student at Witch Hall, that was impressive.

We'd barely made it a few feet from the teachers' tent, where Madam Kawak had given us the enchanted page-duty tabards when Froya strolled up. Aklemin must have already given her my request, because she didn't hesitate before commanding me to make her tea. I heard her ordering Rosamund to find Charles as I walked away. Rosamund had promised that Charles would behave, but a part of me wanted to turn around and follow her to the other side of the assembly regardless. I hadn't forgotten that scene I'd walked up on during Rosamund's first assembly—and her first time on page duty.

Nearly an hour later, I slid into the infirmary. Froya had done her job at publicly running me ragged, sending me on tasks in sight and earshot of as many teachers as we could find. By the time she sent me on an errand to fetch her gloves from her suite, no one blinked an eye.

I knew Charles was doing much the same to Rosamund. I'd only crossed paths with her twice, but she hadn't seemed too upset by it. Then again, I remembered how unbothered she'd been by my own attempts at page hazing. It took significant work to tear Rosamund down.

Froya and Charles already waited inside the infirmary. Toketie sat next to Froya, while Oluk sat on his usual chair next to Einar's bed. I handed Froya her gloves, mostly to keep up the story. I doubted she actually cared about them, since she was much more immune to the cold as an ice familiar. In direct contrast, Einar was bundled under a veritable mountain of blankets and Oluk wore both his cloak and Einar's over the top of it.

Rosamund arrived soon after me. Charles snickered as she threw something at him. "That was gross, Charles!" she exclaimed.

"You're the one who wanted it to be something no one would ask questions about," Charles retorted.

I resolutely did not ask as Charles tucked the small package into his pocket.

"Where are Yuyan and Kwaddis?" I asked the room at large.

"Here," Yuyan called from the infirmary doorway, followed by Kwaddis. Yuyan shut the door tight behind them. "Jarl Tenas was all too happy when I asked to steal Kwaddis for a bit," she said a touch sourly as she found a seat.

With this assembly so close to winter break—and therefore Candlemas and its associated council meeting—most jarls had elected not to come to campus. Jarl Tenas was one of the few who had, being so close to Witch Hall as he was. He'd pulled me aside early on in the assembly to ask if I needed rescuing from my over-zealous classmates. Apparently my desire to help one of the citizens of Multah recover from her grief had been enough to endear him to our escapade off campus. I'd told him that I wasn't afraid of facing the consequences of my own actions, but that I would tell Madam Kawak if it crossed the line. He'd seemed to approve of that and had waved me off to continue my task.

I nodded to Einar. He reached under the arm of the infirmary bed to touch the rune he'd carved there. A moment later, he nodded back at me.

"Thank you all for helping us make this meeting happen," I began. "And for being here. There's something I have to share with you. It may be difficult to accept, but it is the truth."

"Are you going to tell us the real reason you were gone for a week?" Froya asked. "Because we all know that story was horseshit."

Kwaddis nodded vigorously. Charles didn't, but he did sit forward in obvious interest.

"Yes," I said. "But first I need to tell you about Samhain, and one of the ghosts Rosamund and I talked with there."

In the end, my entourage and I had decided to share nearly everything with the three heirs. From General Holt's murder to my father's promise that the war would not begin until after graduation—and our belief that he'd wanted Prince Vetle's attack that first week of the term to go very differently. I talked about the evidence we'd found, what we'd lost, and finally of seeing Thane Anders on the night of the solstice and the frantic adventure that had sent Rosamund and me on.

Throughout my story, the three heirs kept glancing around my entourage as if hoping one of them would crack a smile or admit this was all some horrible joke. No one did. No one could.

Yuyan handed me a glass of water as I finished, which I took gladly but didn't drink immediately. Not until after I saw the reactions of the three heirs.

"Well," Kwaddis said after a beat of uncomfortable silence. "It wasn't like any of us really wanted to go to war, right?"

"Of course not," Froya said. "But we would have, if that's what was needed to keep our people safe. I can't believe the Witch King would deliberately instigate war with Vinland. It doesn't make any sense. You said that even he admitted there was a chance we'd lose!"

"He did," I agreed. Unless he'd been lying when he told me that Vinland might destroy us, but I didn't think so. Ice magic wasn't infallible. He might have done everything he could to prepare for this war, but there was always a chance we wouldn't win it.

"My dad is going to be pissed," Kwaddis said. Now that the shock had faded, he was beginning to look angry himself. "All those people who died . . . and for what? Some chance that *maybe* we'll beat the Empire of Vinland, after losing however many thousands of our own people to do it? This isn't right."

"Why tell us now?" Charles asked. "What do you need us to do?"

"I will present what evidence we do have to the jarls at the council meeting the day after Candlemas," I said. "I would like you three to corroborate what Prince Vetle said to us during the attack, if you were there to hear it."

"I heard it," Froya said.

"As did I," Charles agreed.

Kwaddis shook his head. "I was too far away."

I turned to Kwaddis. "Then I need you to talk with your father. Don't tell him everything I've said. Not yet. It's best if all the jarls hear the story from me, alongside the evidence."

"What should I tell him, then?"

"Ask him what he would do if he learned there was a traitor inside the Cursed Kingdom. Someone who knew the market would burn and did nothing."

Kwaddis's face twisted. "He won't be happy."

"Don't get yourself in trouble, but get him thinking about it, if you can." I drew a deep breath. "Froya, Charles, get your parents thinking about the practicalities of such a large-scale conflict. Of the cost, and the burden it will put on our resources."

"You want them to jump at the chance to stop this war," Froya observed.

"Yes," I said. "I'm sure my father has some ready-made reason as to why the war is good for the kingdom, or at least for its jarls. We need to preempt that by reminding them why war is never good."

"We can do that," Charles said.

"I don't usually go to Candlemas on the Mountain, but I'll convince my dad to bring me this year," Kwaddis added. "I'll mention it to him on the journey up."

"I can do the same," Charles said.

"I'll be traveling up the Mountain with the other ice students, but I'll talk with my bibi once they arrive at Falconridge a few days before Candlemas," Froya said.

I looked between the three of them, then at the rest of my entourage. Yuyan nodded. Oluk smiled. Einar inclined his head. Toketie clasped her hands together. Aklemin closed their eyes.

"We can do this," I said.

"Of course we can, and we will." Rosamund knocked her shoulder against mine. "We just have to make it through finals first."

No one was surprised when General Tepeh announced that our final for Army Training would be another mock combat. We all sat on our usual logs in the outdoor classroom, waiting for instructions to begin. It was early afternoon on the last Friday of the term, and I could tell that my classmates were eager to complete the test so that they could turn their attention to the coming winter break.

"The aim is simple," General Tepeh said. "You will be stationed at Witch Hall's dock. We will come by boat across the river. You must defend the dock by any means necessary."

I raised my hand and waited for General Tepeh to nod to me before asking, "*We*, sir?"

"Yes, Princess," General Tepeh said. "I will lead your opponents today. Furthermore, I will take charge of only half as many soldiers as you have classmates. The thanes will stand alongside you at the docks to observe but not interfere in either direction. Is that clear?"

It was. I had no doubt that my father had told the general of our plan to stop the war—whatever part of it he had foreseen. That was the point of all this. They wanted to humiliate me. To discredit me in front of my classmates, like they'd failed to do during the midterm. They would not trust the task to Thane Anders or any of the other thanes. Instead, they would take matters into their own hands.

"We'll be ready," I told General Tepeh.

Fifteen minutes later, my classmates and I were set up around Witch Hall's small dock. I had the flower familiars in the river and the ice familiars overhead. Half the bone familiars patrolled the dock itself, while the other half were stationed on the shore around it. Behind them, the bone and glass witches formed a line of defense, while the ice and flower witches took the far rear to give support.

The first of the ice familiars landed in front of me to report sightings of the longboats soon after. A few minutes later, a couple flower familiars, led by Lei Banks, came to give a more detailed report of the numbers in each boat. Strangely, General Tepeh wasn't visible in any of them.

"Archers, ready!" I called as the first of the longboats came into view. "Chao, Kalitan, together now."

Chao, Kalitan, and I all lifted our hands to guide our magic to a pile of bones we'd brought along. I hadn't been told about the specifics of the final, but I'd expected it to be a fight, so I'd prepared the bones in advance.

The soldiers in the two longboats cried out as they were pelted with padded arrows and dulled bones. At my signal, Kwaddis and a group of flower familiars capsized the next boat that came close. Charles led a group of large bone familiars to attack any soldiers who attempted to swim to shore.

The battle was going well, almost suspiciously so. I wasn't even surprised when Aklemin came rushing to my side. "Shaw," they said. "They're flanking us."

"Where?" I asked.

"To the west."

I turned, but there was no one west of the dock except the horses in the pasture that stretched from the stable to the edge of campus.

Then I heard the yells and looked back to the dock just in time to see a group of soldiers come out of nowhere to attack Charles's group from behind. One by one, the bone familiars went down.

"How—" I didn't have time to finish the question. Arrows shot across the side to rain down on us. I ducked away from the volley and watched as a third of my classmates went down.

"Re-form the line!" I called. "To me!"

It was too late. As if out of thin air, a group of soldiers appeared from the western shore.

"It's runes," Yuyan said from my other side.

Like those at the table, or on Einar's infirmary bed. Runes that misdirected our attention. They couldn't make the boat fully invisible, but even now it was hard to keep my eyes on it.

"To me!" I called again. A few of my classmates had listened and began to form a line, but far too many were distracted by the three boats that had made the frontal assault—ignoring the soldiers led by General Tepeh coming around their backs.

Without proper formation, it was a slaughter. I used the bones to hit those I could, but this new group of soldiers had enchanted shields that deflected my attacks. General Tepeh was a breathtaking fighter, dual-wielding two simple wooden swords. They slashed through the line in front of me. I threw up a wall of bones, and they batted them away. Yuyan and Aklemin both stepped in between us and were just as quickly smacked in the ribs and chest respectively.

I had nothing. I hadn't even armed myself with a sword, thinking I would stay back and use bones as a long-range attacker. I tried one more time to send a bone spear at the general, but they slipped around it and one of the soldiers following in their wake physically grabbed the bone before I could redirect it.

"You're dead," General Tepeh said, holding the wooden sword to my throat. "As is every student in this school, now that we have no more obstacles to our invasion. You've lost, Princess Shaw, and your kingdom has lost with you."

My body felt as though it was made of solid ice. Not only had we lost, but it had been a massacre. It took barely a minute for the rest of the students to be rounded up by the small squad of soldiers General Tepeh had led in that rune-hidden boat.

As I stood there at the far edge of the dock, still and silent and sullen, my classmates came to crowd around us. I felt my entourage line up at my back. I didn't dare look to see the disappointment I knew was on their faces. I stepped back into the hole between Yuyan and Aklemin, out of reach of the general's swords.

General Tepeh lowered both wooden swords and handed them off to one of the soldiers waiting at their shoulder. They lifted their chin to project their voice to the group of students crowded around us. "We will begin anew in the spring term. After the break, we will split you evenly among the squads of the Royal Company so that you can learn by example what it truly means to fight for this kingdom. Perhaps time to reflect upon this loss will give you the determination to put real effort in your training."

"Thank you for educating us, General," I said stiffly, because I needed to say something. Only, I wasn't sure what the right words truly were—what could salvage this situation. "We will all learn from this for next term."

"I should hope so," General Tepeh said. It was just to me, but my classmates were all close enough to hear the words. "Truly, I expected more of a fight."

To my surprise, Kwaddis stepped forward from the crowd, dislodging Birger Berg from his attempts at healing the massive bruise already forming on Kwaddis's temple. Fury was clear to see on his scowling face. "Well, if you'd allowed us more time to prepare, maybe we would have given you one!"

General Tepeh raised a single, thin eyebrow. "Do you think the Vinlanders will send notices in advance? War is not a game, Mister Tenas. Learning to think tactically instead of just strategically is a skill generals must master or they see their companies killed just as you would all have been killed today."

Froya stepped up next to Kwaddis and put a hand on his fist as if to stop him from punching someone. "You obviously had time to plan a strategic attack," she noted. "If we truly were stationed at this dock, then Shaw would have been able to plan her own defensive strategies in advance of any invasion occurring, and then decide tactically which best suited your style of attack."

"Besides, the Vinlanders won't be using magic to attack us!"

Charles added. "That was a completely unfair test, if the point is to be realistic."

"Enough," I said before the general could reprimand the three for insubordination. None of us were officially enlisted in the army yet, but General Tepeh was still taking the role of a teacher at Witch Hall. I had no doubt Madam Kawak would be on their side if they said students were disrespecting their authority. "I'm sure you all have packing left to do. Unless the general has more instructions to give us before break?"

General Tepeh pressed their lips into a thin line, obviously displeased, but they raised a hand in clear dismissal of the class.

I didn't move as my classmates funneled away from the dock, heading back to their suites. I hated that we were ending the term on such a horrible note when I knew the only reason for it was to target me. My entourage lingered around me. Aklemin and Toketie were both expressionless, but Oluk and Yuyan were easy to read. Oluk looked nearly in tears, and Yuyan was just as furious as Kwaddis had been. I shook my head at her. Whatever she was thinking of saying wasn't worth it.

"Come on," I murmured to them.

"One more thing, Princess," General Tepeh said as my entourage and I went to leave.

I didn't bother turning back around, but I did twist my head so that I could look at them.

The general watched me with cold eyes. None of the polite facade I'd seen growing up or pride they'd worn after the midterm. I wondered if this was the face they showed their enemies. If I weren't already made of ice, I might have shivered.

"Your father is eager to speak with you once you return home," they said. "I hope you still respect him enough to hear what he has to say."

I inclined my head but didn't reply. My entourage closed ranks around me as we left the dock and headed into the center of campus.

"Shaw!" Charles shouted.

I stopped, mostly out of surprise that Charles had called me by name. He'd always referred to my title before. Then again, hadn't Froya done the same? When had they decided to drop the formality that had chased at our heels all through our time at school?

The bone familiar jogged up to our group from where he'd, apparently, been waiting for us. "I know you're probably angry with how that went down," Charles said. He kept his voice low, but my entourage still spread out wide enough to block anyone from getting close enough to overhear. I mentally thanked them for protecting my privacy. I wasn't just angry, I was furious. Mostly with myself, for not having seen General Tepeh's ploy coming.

"I'll see you on the Mountain, Charles," I said, not in the mood to deal with him at the moment.

Charles grabbed my arm to stop me from leaving. His voice dropped into a whisper as he said, "It doesn't matter, what happened back there. Froya and Kwaddis and I are still with you. We know what needs to be done. You're the rightful ruler of the Cursed Kingdom, not your father. Not after all he's done. And if our parents don't agree, then we'll deal with that too."

The ice that had built up inside me cracked as if a massive weight had fallen on it. "I'm not doing this because of the throne," I said.

"Of course not," Charles said. "And that's exactly why it should be yours." He let go and pulled away. "Just remember that we support you. We'll see you at Candlemas."

I watched Charles walk away until Yuyan drifted close.

"Are you okay?" she asked.

"I need to finish packing," I said instead of answering. The truth was that I didn't know. Charles's words had reminded me of the question I'd asked Einar all those weeks ago. What if, in attempting to stop the war with Vinland, I sparked civil war instead? The thought of it made me nauseous. "We can talk later," I added when Yuyan didn't move away. I didn't have the capacity to answer her questions, not then.

Later never came, because the next day, I packed my things in a cart and got ready to begin the long journey up the Mountain with all the ice students and Rosamund. The ice students, of course, always traveled up the Frozen Mountain for winter break, and I typically joined them. I might have been able to convince Rosamund not to come if my father hadn't already met her, but since he had, she utterly refused to hear my reasons.

"If it ends up being dangerous, I want to be there," she said after my final attempt at argument. My heart twisted at her words. Why did all my classmates seem to believe the trial would end in a fight? Were they right to think so?

At least Yuyan had elected to stay at school with Einar and Oluk. She gave me a tight hug as we said goodbye.

"Whatever happens, you know we have your back," she murmured in my ear.

"I know," I replied, just as soft.

That was what I was afraid of.

Chapter 17

WE WERE BLESSED WITH BEAUTIFUL WEATHER THE ENTIRE journey to Falconridge. It was cold, but it only snowed once and that had been a gentle flurry. The road up the Frozen Mountain wound back and forth across the northern face, and it could be unforgiving in icy weather. But the Mountain was aware, just as the Forest and Desert and Lake were. It was never too difficult to travel up it in late January. It knew why we were visiting. Though it was well into winter now, the Mountain loved visitors for Candlemas. The more people to join in the ceremony, the stronger the ice magic was.

It was always much more dangerous to climb back down the Mountain in February, after Candlemas had passed.

Long winter nights meant it was fully dark by the time we arrived at Falconridge. But the Frozen Mountain had its own special magic, and Falconridge was called the Glowing City for a reason. Rosamund gasped as we turned one final, sharp corner and saw the edges of the city just ahead.

A large sign proclaimed WELCOME TO FALCONRIDGE. Draped from the base of the sign was a row of icicles. Each one glowed with a pale blue light, just bright enough that the sign's words were clearly visible despite the overarching darkness.

"Are they enchanted?" Rosamund asked me.

"Not that I'm aware," I said.

"They aren't," Toketie said. "It's ice magic, not glass. The Mountain always makes the icicles glow like this in winter."

"It's beautiful," Rosamund murmured.

She was right. Falconridge in winter was a hard place to live, but that didn't diminish its beauty. Stone houses coated in layers of ice and snow dotted the gentle slope. This part of the mountainside had been chosen for its natural shelf, allowing an entire city to build up between the steep edges of the eastern and western faces. The eaves of every single building held huge hanging icicles—and every one of those icicles glowed with that same pale blue light.

The caravan stopped at Jarl Alki's manor. The jarl's manor was the largest building in Falconridge outside the royal palace. Two massive icicles ran from the overhang above the door all the way to the ground—more like columns than anything else. The glow from them was bright enough to illuminate the entire entry courtyard of the manor.

Servants came to take the horses to the insulated stable. My father always opened rooms at the palace for the jarls of the kingdom, which meant there wasn't enough room for the ice witches and familiars coming from Witch Hall for the ceremony. The ice students stayed instead at Jarl Alki's manor, like they'd done every winter since Aklemin had become a student at Witch Hall. It relieved me that Rosamund could stay here with them. I wanted to keep as much distance between her and my father as I could. He had already met her, but more time spent with her would only make his visions clearer.

We'd arrived just in time for dinner. Jarl Alki came to greet our party and then ushered us inside for food. Ever the professional in front of others, he was overtly polite to me, though I noticed he barely greeted his own child. Aklemin said nothing, so neither did I.

Near the end of the meal, Aklemin leaned over to ask me, "Are you staying?"

"I can't."

Aklemin frowned but said nothing. They knew I couldn't stay the night, as much as I wanted to. My father would already know of my arrival in Falconridge.

"Take care of them," I said. Aklemin would know I meant Rosamund and Toketie. I wouldn't be able to spend much time with them in the week leading up to Candlemas.

"They'll be safe with me," Aklemin murmured. "And I will be safe with them, when the time comes for it."

I paused with my fork halfway to my mouth. Aklemin went back to eating their dessert like nothing had happened. I wanted to press them to explain, but when I darted a look across the table, I found Jarl Alki watching us. I took the bite left hanging instead.

"Walk me to the palace?" I asked once we'd finished our food.

Aklemin reached for their water glass and swirled it a few times, staring at the half-full cup.

"Aklemin," I hissed, annoyed that they hadn't immediately agreed.

It was a tradition for us to walk each other home after spending time in the other's residence. The walk from the jarl's manor to the royal palace was barely fifteen minutes, and the weather was still lovely, even this late at night. They had no reason to refuse.

I couldn't let them refuse. Not when I needed to ask them something before meeting with my father.

Aklemin nodded but said nothing. I didn't let their reluctance bother me. We said good night to Rosamund and Toketie. Rosamund promised to stick by her cousin until I had need of her. I hoped that I wouldn't. I hoped that Aklemin would tell me all my unease the last few days had been for naught.

The soldiers who'd escorted us up the Mountain had already taken my things to the palace, so I didn't have anything to carry as Aklemin and I left the manor and began to tread the winding road up. Neither Falconridge nor the royal palace was anywhere near the peak of the Mountain, but they were at a much higher elevation than anywhere else in the kingdom. I breathed in the crisp air and let it bolster me.

"Am I leading us to civil war, Aklemin?" I asked softly. We'd left Falconridge itself, and there were no more houses on either side of the road leading to the palace. The Colchucks had always kept ourselves separate from the people of Falconridge, ever since Mesachie's curse had altered the land so completely. At least that distance kept our chances of being overheard small.

Aklemin didn't answer. I couldn't tell if that meant that I was right or if they simply didn't know.

"I'm prophesied to lead this kingdom into war," I tried again. "What if we stop the war with Vinland, but only by creating a schism so vast within our own people that it leads to real internal conflict? Charles wants to see me take my father's throne. I know I may need to. If my father is found guilty of inciting war with Vinland, the jarls will see him deposed. They'll have no choice but to crown me. But what if half the council doesn't agree? What if there are more jarls who helped my father plan this war than just his entourage?"

Still Aklemin said nothing. I wanted to shake them.

"Tell me before it's too late!" I snapped. "I would rather fight Vinland than lead my people into civil war."

Aklemin made a sharp turn, leaving the road and heading into the wilds of the Mountain. I scrambled after them, feeling a bit like I had as a child, all those times Aklemin had abruptly decided they no longer wanted to play games with me and left without even saying goodbye.

Unlike how they had as a child, though Aklemin didn't turn to tell me off for following after them. They led me in silence away from the palace and to a small cave we'd explored as children. It was almost too tiny to fit both of us now, but when Aklemin squeezed inside, so did I.

We sat on the ground because the cave was too small for us to stand. Aklemin stared at the softly glowing ice crystals shimmering on the wall in front of us. I stared at them. I'd never been as unnerved by that carefully blank expression as I was then.

"I know you always wondered why I hid what I could do," Aklemin said, their tone flat, emotion dead. "The truth is, I had to. I knew young that if the Witch King ever discovered the depth of my abilities, he would order my father to kill me. My father would have needed little prompting."

I wondered if I would ever truly grasp the horrors that Aklemin had been through growing up in Jarl Alki's manor. Looking back, was that the real reason Aklemin had spent so much time begging for sleepovers at the palace? For a good five or six years of our childhood, I'd been convinced Aklemin hated me, but they'd come over to play every day and I'd tell myself I was being silly.

"Why would my father want you dead?" I asked.

"Because if he looked hard enough, he would know I saw the

same things he did." Aklemin finally turned to look at me. The fractal reflections of the glowing ice crystals created strange shadows on their face. "No, Shaw, you will not lead the kingdom to civil war. If you stop this war with Vinland, that will be it. There will be no war at all."

"There will be, someday," I argued. "I'm prophesied—"

"There is no prophecy," Aklemin interrupted. "War has always been a choice. It has always been *your* choice."

The cold of the ice-encrusted ground was beginning to seep through my clothing. I didn't know what to think. "That can't be true. Every ice witch I've ever met has called it prophecy."

"Do you know what prophecies are?" Aklemin shook their head, as if disappointed. "Destiny is merely the most probable future. If vision after vision shows the same thing, then the idea is that thing must be set. That nothing can change it. In the past, those who tried merely made it happen through their attempts at stopping it."

"Self-fulfilling prophecies," I said.

"Yes. But your war is not that. It's merely the machinations of a man who saw, as I did, what would come of it. A man powerful enough to make that war happen, and in doing so caused every other ice witch to see its coming as prophecy."

"I don't understand what you're saying, Aklemin."

Aklemin's eyes were so very dark against the glow of the ice magic all around us. "Even good intentions do not withstand the weight of expectation. The cost of power. You have the strength to slaughter hunters before they touch a single strand of familiar fur. The strength to burn anti-magical terrorists on the same pyres they would have burned you on."

"For once in your life, speak plainly."

Aklemin smiled at that, but it wasn't a nice one. "You have the power to conquer the continent, Shaw. That is what your father wants. To see you rule not just the Cursed Kingdom, but everyone who could ever think to threaten us."

I was so taken aback by the absurdity of such a claim that my mind bounced off it. I came back to the first thing Aklemin said, just to buy myself time. "Why would my father have killed you for being a strong ice witch?"

Aklemin straightened, lowering their shoulders and lifting their chin. I recognized the motion. I did the same thing when I needed to put on an air of confidence. Had Aklemin learned it from me, or had I learned it from Aklemin?

"He would have seen what I am capable of," they said.

"Aklemin, please."

"I betray you," they said plainly. "In every future where you walk the road of the warlord, there will come a moment when you stop being the girl I trust and start being a woman I hate. Your father would never stand to allow an ice witch as strong as me be in the position to turn treason upon your throne of corpses."

I let out a laugh, because what else could I do? This had started to feel like a strange dream. "Why would you tell me that? Aklemin, why in the world would you—"

"Einar never betrays you, even when he should," Aklemin continued, as if I hadn't spoken. "Yuyan leaves usually. Retreats to Waiming, to prepare her childhood home for your eventual arrival. Because of her, you annex them peacefully. But she never returns to your court and you never ask her to. Whatever familiars any of us manage to bond with are usually dead by that point. War is harder on familiars than on witches. It's easier to see them as expendable when they look like animals."

Was that why they'd refused to court Toketie? But no, that was ridiculous. I would never sacrifice her, even if the picture Aklemin painted was true.

But you did sacrifice Oluk, a voice in my mind whispered. *You passed General Tepeh's midterm because of it. If you'd thought to sacrifice another group of familiars, would you have won the final?*

"This isn't funny, Aklemin," I said.

Aklemin chuckled, as if this really was all a joke, but then they said, "When your father sent his soldiers to Vinland last summer, I was desperate. I knew it was coming, and I could see no way to stop it. No way to save the Shaw I knew, without killing her to stop a monster from forming in her place. But that was never the answer either. Even if I could manage to stab you in the back, I would just doom us to a different kind of terror. Without you, the Cursed Kingdom falls. To Prince Vetle or what comes after him, always, inevitably."

What comes after him? I knew it would not stop there. Even if I brokered peace with Vinland, there would always be those who hated us. I'd just hoped to buy time—time to prepare before my war cast its heavy shadow over my people.

But hadn't Aklemin said that my war wasn't prophesied after all?

"What choice did I have?" Aklemin continued, and there was a trace of bitterness now in their voice. "Let the rest of the continent suffer, to save one small piece of it? I tried everything I could to find a solution. Then, one day, as we were planning the route for your recruitment tour across the southern towns, I threw some stones across the map. Do you remember?"

I did. Aklemin liked to pretend they weren't good at lithomancy, but they'd always pretended they weren't good at anything except dream magic—which was one of the least accurate forms of foresight. At the time, I'd thought they were just fooling around when they stared at the pebble that had landed on a small town along the southern border. A town nearly engulfed by the Bone Forest.

"You were the one to suggest Rosamund's village," I remembered. "Even though it was tiny and out of our way."

"I didn't know what we would find there. All I knew was something in Forest's Edge that had the potential to change all of our fates. When I laid eyes on Rosamund Holt for the first time, I saw your father's carefully plotted future fracture."

All the energy that had been building in me since the start of Aklemin's strange story erupted. I stood and nearly hit my head on the roof of the small cave. "Rosamund rejected me. She won't be part of my future."

"Perhaps, perhaps not," Aklemin said. They didn't bother standing with me, turning back to staring at the ice crystals on the cave wall. "There are still choices left to make, for both of you."

Aklemin said nothing more after that. After a few frustrating minutes demanding answers, I stalked away, head pounding. I felt a bit like I'd owned a dog my entire life, only to have been told it was a cat the whole time. What was the point of all that? What did Aklemin mean by telling me such a strange tale? How was I supposed to believe it, when the whole thing started with their promise of betrayal? I was confused and angry and confused as to why I was angry.

But a part of me couldn't help but wonder. I'd spent my entire life trusting Aklemin. Even when they'd pretended to be the weakest ice witch in our grade, I'd always known their predictions to be accurate. If what they said about my father's reasons was true . . . but how could it be? Conquer Vinland? Conquer the *continent*? That was absurd.

I slowed down as I neared the entrance of the palace, staring up at the massive structure, trying to divine some meaning from it. The royal palace had been built initially by the third Familiar Queen of the Cursed Kingdom and expanded some hundred years later by the fifth Witch King. Outside of occasionally swapping the furniture and curtains, it had not changed much since. The palace stone was made of andesite from the lava flows that had formed the Mountain long ago. The dark gray rock was speckled with white crystals that shone under the light of the massive icicles that hung from the eaves. Several were taller than I was and so thick in the center that I doubted they would ever melt, even if the Mountain lost its magic one day.

There were no outward-facing windows in the palace, to protect against the chill of long nights. I walked through the main gate and ended up in the central courtyard, where huge two-paned windows covered every wall. Since it was winter, curtains were drawn in each one. In the summer, those courtyard windows allowed in the palace's only source of natural light.

I wasn't surprised to see my father waiting for me in the center of the courtyard. I wasn't upset by it either. It saved me from having to track him down.

"My dear," he said. "Welcome home."

"Father," I said, striding up to him. I didn't bother to smooth out my expression. The time for secrecy had passed. "No more lying or obscuring or avoiding. I want answers. Why did you curse Vinland? What is the real reason you sought to start this war?"

The Witch King stilled, as if I'd surprised him. I wondered what vision had come over him at my words. After a few seconds, he nodded. "Very well. I see you are ready to hear the truth. Follow me, my dear, and I will tell you everything you wish to know."

As we walked inside the palace, I began to shake. It could have been from the cold that had seeped into me from the Mountain's winter chill, but I thought it was because of a different kind of cold. Ice swelled in my veins. Cold like brutality. Practicality. A grim willingness to persevere. An expectation that victory was necessary, no matter the cost.

Aklemin had said they would betray me. I needed to know why.

My father led me to his office in the far depths of the royal wing of the palace. Not even the guards were allowed this far inside. There were no windows, no entry outside of the wing's main corridor. It was as safe and private as one could possibly be. I sat in one of the armchairs before my father could prompt me. He followed suit, settling onto his preferred reading couch.

"Every parent wishes to see their child succeed," my father began. "I am blessed in that I have always known just how. You are destined for greatness, my dear. You know of the vision I had at your mother's funeral. The strength of it caused me to collapse. I wasn't yet used to the combined weight of our magic. Hers, now nestled with mine forever. I would give almost anything to have her back with us. I know how proud she would have been to see the future you'll lead us to."

"What future?" I pressed. "What is this war with Vinland really about, Father?"

"I think someone has been confusing you," the Witch King said. "How muddled you seem. Calm yourself, my dear. You are more than capable of dealing with what's to come."

I felt plenty calm. Or perhaps focused was a better adjective. I'd homed in on my father like a hunter on its prey. I would not rest until I was satisfied. "You promised me answers, Father."

"I know you fear war with Vinland, but it will not be what you think," the Witch King said. "You see, the empire has declared war on the Colonies. Even now, they send armies to fight along the eastern edge of the continent."

"What? Why? When?" I didn't know which question I wanted to hear answered first. "Surely news of that war should have reached us by now?"

"It will soon enough. Winter slows down trade, and few merchants travel from Vinland to the Cursed Kingdom nowadays. That matters little. What should concern you is what it means for us. We have an opportunity. Prince Vetle attempts to sway his father to bring war upon the Cursed Kingdom, but the emperor refuses to fight a war on two fronts. He will not react until it's too late. Upon your graduation, I will have you lead an army into Vinland. You will have conquered half the nation by the time the emperor sees fit to worry, or respond in kind. But by then, it will be too late. You'll have raised an army of twenty thousand undead to fight alongside you, and not even a hundred thousand living soldiers would be a match against that."

"I'm not strong enough to do that! No bone witch is," I protested.

"You will be," my father responded. "You asked why we cursed Vinland. This is why. We will grow the Cursed Kingdom, and in doing so, you, who are heir to this land, will never want for power. You may leave your entourage at home if you wish. Keep everyone you care for far away from the conflict. You won't need them. You can face down all of Vinland alone. I've seen it, Shaw."

Something about the gleam in my father's eyes made me uncomfortable, but I didn't dare look away. "But why, Father? Just because we can beat Vinland doesn't mean we should."

"Ah, but of course we should. What if I told you that I've seen a future where there are no more witch burnings or familiar hunts?

A future where the Crusaders who call us heathens for being born with magic are the ones no longer being born?"

"Beating Vinland won't stop others from hating us," I argued.

"You will not be *beating* Vinland like this is some mock combat with a winner and a loser," my father said, and I wanted to flinch at the reprimand in his tone. "You will conquer Vinland and claim that land for your own kingdom. And from there you will push into the Colonies. They will already be weakened after months of warring with the empire."

I thought back to Aklemin's words. About Einar and Yuyan, and what they would do. "And after? Do you mean to have me conquer the entire continent?"

"You will unify it," the Witch King said. "With magic free to spread wheresoever it chooses. There will be no more bigotry when even bigots find their children born magical."

I'd never understood my father's permissive attitude toward Jarl Alki's treatment of his own child, but perhaps this was why. He seemed to believe no parent capable of harming their own flesh and blood. I thought I knew better, at least in this. The true bigots would rather burn their own children than destroy the pyres because magic had infiltrated their family.

There was no use arguing that, however. Not yet. "And how many will die for that future?" I asked, because all I could hear was Aklemin saying, *In every future where you walk the road of the warlord, there will come a moment when you stop being the girl I trust and start being a woman I hate.*

My father scoffed. "That bone familiar you pine for has made you soft. You never would have questioned this without her influence."

So Aklemin was right about that too. I closed my eyes. What

did that mean about me? Was I born to be the kind of monster who would conquer an entire continent without care for the consequences?

"And if I refuse?" I asked, opening my eyes to face down my father even though all I wanted to do was hide away until this horrible nightmare was over.

"It's too late, my dear," the Witch King said. Though his words were gentle, his tone was anything but. "Prince Vetle will drum up enough support to make a full army eventually. If you refuse to destroy him now, he will destroy us before next winter's snows."

"And if I kill him before he can do that, his father will declare war on us no matter their other conflict," I said, seeing the outline now of the trap my father had set months ago by his burning of Vinland's towns. I would have to fight. Would have to push forward and conquer. Without an army of the dead to fight with us, we had no hope of beating even a third of Vinland's active soldiers.

"You understand now." My father spread his arms. "Embrace your destiny, as you were always meant to. You will be great, Shaw. You will stand tall above all of us, before the end, and magic will thank you for it."

Chapter 18

PREPARATION FOR CANDLEMAS INVOLVED A LOT OF cleaning. Hearths were scrubbed, floors were mopped, and herbs like mint and thyme were hung from the rafters to bid welcome to the new year. I used those days before the ritual to think. Aklemin didn't come visit, not once, and they must have encouraged Toketie to keep Rosamund out of the way, because neither did she.

Not that I was alone. The jarls began to arrive, one by one, and most brought their heirs. Chao was the first. He tried to pull me aside to talk, but I distracted him by telling Jingyi that Rosamund was the jarl's manor and would surely love if the two of them visited. Jingyi pulled her witch away, giving me a wink behind Chao's shoulder that told me she knew I wanted to be alone and was happy to provide it. I got another day of peace from that, until Charles and Emma arrived with Jarl Almstedt's retinue. Kwaddis and his father came that same evening. I kept to the royal family's wing and avoided all of them.

The morning of Candlemas, I awoke with a terrible headache. There was nothing to do but push through it. The heir to the Cursed Kingdom could not simply skip out on the Candlemas ritual.

Samhain and Beltane were midnight rituals, but Lammas and Candlemas were for the light of day. In summer, that made the

Lammas games a kind of grueling challenge. For Candlemas, it was a relief. The Frozen Mountain was on its best behavior. The sky was full of fluffy white clouds, only a touch of gray hinting at the snow sitting heavily in them. Sunshine reflected off the glowing icicles that lined the central courtyard of the palace.

Each Candlemas circle was focused around one key point—one ice witch whose question was answered by a vision so complete, there could be no debate to its contents. Candlemas was about the coming of spring, and the bloom of possibility. It was the time when ice magic was strongest. Smaller Candlemas rituals were taking place all over the kingdom, but the center of ice magic was here on the Frozen Mountain. It was considered a great honor to help hold the Witch King's ritual circle during Candlemas.

As such, only the senior ice witches and familiars were allowed to be part of the ritual circle. The younger students and all of the Witch King's court were present to spectate the event and bear witness to the vision that came of it. Not that any of the audience would learn anything today. That information was always given to the jarls' council the next morning, after the Witch King had time to interpret it.

I would go to my father tonight and ask for early insight into the vision. I doubted he would lie to me, not after everything he'd shared. I needed to know more details about the coming conflict with Prince Vetle. About the effect of the curse my father had begun in Vinland, and what the emperor would do once he learned of it—even despite his war with the Colonies.

What I would do with that information, I didn't know. I still couldn't see any way out of the trap my father had set. I feared that there wasn't one. Already, I had begun to plan for how to make the future he'd foreseen tolerable. What policies could I put in place that would keep me from becoming a tyrannical warlord while still doing what was needed to keep the Cursed Kingdom safe?

The other students began to arrive. I'd already taken my seat, and Rosamund didn't hesitate before claiming the chair next to me, despite the fact that her social rank meant she should sit in the far back of the courtyard. From her spot several seats down my same row, Jarl Almstedt went to speak up, but Charles shushed his mother. She, in turn, redirected her outrage to him. On Charles's other side, Emma rolled her eyes and told her aunt to calm down.

I tried to ignore the drama, looking instead to Aklemin. They stood in the center of the courtyard, Toketie on one side, Froya on the other. Froya saw me and gave a nod. Aklemin didn't look my way, their eyes fixed upon the clouds in the sky.

There's still a choice left to make, they'd said, but I couldn't see it. What choice did I have, really? My father had planned out my future, and it was far too late to change it now. If I tried to stop it, I'd only doom my kingdom. I had to be practical, and practicality sometimes meant surrendering to inevitability.

My father entered the courtyard just as the last of the guests found their seats. I barely listened as he gave the typical speech about using Candlemas as an opportunity to lead the Cursed Kingdom to a brighter future. I felt like I was somehow living outside my own body. Rosamund brushed her arm against mine. A tingle of warmth drifted through me, but it faded all too quickly.

The ritual began. My father stood at the northern point of the circle of ice witches. Somehow, Aklemin had maneuvered themself to the southern point, even though that was typically claimed by one of the older ice witches in my father's circle. There was no time for anyone to change it. The ritual began with the ice witches clasping hands. All the ice familiars took to the sky, flying in their own circle overhead.

The ice witches chanted in unison. I couldn't feel ice magic the way I could feel bone magic, but I still felt something. Bone magic was about the past. Ice magic was the future. To bone witches and familiars, spectating a large ice ritual like this felt like someone had sucked away all the air until we were left suffocating. Rosamund made a small choking sound.

"Just breathe through it," Charles hissed to her.

I should have thought to tell Rosamund what would happen. That had been insensitive of me. She wasn't to blame for my future, no matter what Aklemin had said about lithomancy or my father about softness. I put my hand on top of hers. Her fingers were trembling. I worried, for a second, that it might be bad enough to make her go feral. But holding her hand seemed to help. Rosamund slowly relaxed at my side, steadying her breathing even as the ritual reached its crescendo.

All the ice witches broke hands. The Witch King stepped forward into the circle to receive the vision. Except, he wasn't the only one. From their place at the southern point, Aklemin also stepped into the circle.

Shocked gasps and murmurs rang through the crowd of spectators. My mind raced. What Aklemin was doing was foolish. With two witches in position to take the vision, the ice magic would choose the stronger one. There was no doubt that my father had that power. And then Aklemin would have broken protocol without anything to show for it. Why would they do that?

A lone snowflake, larger than any natural piece of snow, floated down from the clouds above. We all watched as it meandered its way toward the Witch King's outstretched hands. I began to plan out how to excuse Aklemin's reckless disrespect to the jarls' council.

Except, the snowflake was drifting. Slowly, almost too gradually to notice, its path veered south. I stood before I fully thought through how disruptive it would be. But I wasn't the only one. Most of the crowd had realized what was about to happen. Whispers were becoming shouts.

The Witch King opened his eyes. From where I stood, I had the perfect view of my father's face as he comprehended that the ritual was about to choose Aklemin instead.

The snowflake landed, oh so gently, in the center of Aklemin's palms. For a single second, we were all trapped there in the realization that the Witch King was no longer the strongest ice witch in the kingdom. In that moment, watching the fury even my father's typical mask couldn't contain, I was sure that Aklemin had been correct. If my father had known Aklemin was a more powerful ice witch than even him, he would have had them killed.

Then the Candlemas vision began, and Aklemin collapsed like a puppet whose strings had been cut.

Aklemin still hadn't surfaced from the vision by the time the council was to meet.

The winter jarls' council meeting always took place in the royal throne room. It was completely full for the first time in years. Aklemin had been laid on a sleeping pallet just in front of the first row of benches. The slow rise and fall of their chest was the only indication they still lived.

The Witch King strode down the long central aisle to his throne. As his heir, I followed just a step behind him, taking note of all the faces as I passed them. Every single jarl was in attendance, of course, but every jarl's heir over the age of fifteen was also in the crowd. I even saw a few of the younger heirs.

Jarls and heirs aside, the winter council meeting was also the only council meeting where every general in the Cursed Kingdom attended. From General Tepeh of the Royal Company to the generals of Multah's Company, Gravestown's Company, and so on. Once the Candlemas vision was announced, the generals typically left the jarls' council to go have their own meeting about the state of the army.

My father swept his heavy velvet robes up in his arms to take a seat on his throne. The robes lay artfully against his legs. I knew it was a practiced move because my father had taught me the trick of it when I was eight. The Witch King had come to the Cursed Kingdom as a refugee—all his courtly manners had been carefully curated. Including the deliberate way he sat, so casually confident, against the Witch Throne.

The back of the Witch Throne was carved and painted with an elaborate mural of the Cursed Kingdom. From Lake Bloom and its frog-covered lily pads over my father's left shoulder, to the Obsidian Desert and its black sand dunes over his right. Spread behind my father's head were the spindly bone pines of the Bone Forest. Past the top of his crown, reaching up toward the vaulted ceiling, the head of the throne was carved into a peak and painted the glowing ice-blue of the Frozen Mountain.

On the other side of the Witch Throne, the Familiar Throne sat empty. It was just as big as the Witch Throne and its mural was almost more impressive. Intertwined in painted engravings were a flower whale, glass python, ice raven, and bone wolf. I'd spent more than one sleepless night during the fall term imagining what Rosamund would look like sitting there. She'd be swallowed by it, but I knew she would make it look purposeful. Studying the throne now, I thought the bone wolf engraving would sit perfectly over her shoulders.

For the first time, I realized that Rosamund had been right to reject me. Aklemin had said it themself. Rosamund had promised to fight for me, but in a war that crossed the entire continent? How long would she last before she was killed?

And then there was the matter of what I'd have to become, to lead an army of twenty thousand dead as my father had foreseen. If there was a moment when even Aklemin saw fit to betray me, I was sure I'd cross Rosamund's line far sooner.

Once the Witch King had sat, everyone else was to sit. I settled into the Heir Throne, currently situated next to the Witch Throne to show my status as future Witch Queen. My own throne was half the size of the other two, but considering how elaborate and massive they were, that didn't mean much. The Heir Throne had a beautiful mural of Witch Hall, with its waterfall cascading from the tip of the throne down to engravings of the three historic longhouses.

I turned my attention back to the rest of court just in time to realize that, while all the jarls had sat after the Witch King had—just as I had—many of the heirs had not. All the seniors and more than a few of the younger years waited until I settled into my own throne before following. It wouldn't have been obvious, if not for the sheer number who did so in unison. Even Rosamund and Toketie, seated in the very back of the throne room. Near the front of the room, Charles looked smug enough that I figured it must have been him who'd organized that little bit of defiance.

I felt sick. What would they do when I failed to give the evidence, as I'd promised? There was no point to it now. No way to stop the coming war with Vinland, even if I managed to convince the jarls the true reason behind it.

"Shall we begin?" the Witch King asked.

Jarl Alki and Jarl Tenas both stood. The Witch King called on Jarl Alki, and Jarl Tenas sat to a few surprised murmurs. It was more blatant favoritism than my father would typically show. Jarls Tenas, Falk, and Almstedt were the three most powerful voices on the council. If one stood to propose a topic, they were always called to do so. To call upon Jarl Alki first was a direct snub. Jarl Tenas would never express his displeasure aloud though. Jarl Alki was nominally part of Jarl Almstedt's voting bloc, but everyone knew that he was really the Witch King's voice.

"I would like to propose a vote to change my legal heir," Jarl Alki said.

I'd been caught in my own head, trying to think around my persistent headache, but at Jarl Alki's words, I blinked awake. The colors of the scene returned, vibrant and nauseating.

Jarl Alki wanted to change his legal heir. Did that mean he wished to disown Aklemin? But he had no other children. Agalax and Aklemin were the last of the Alki line—there weren't even cousins who could take Aklemin's place. Though Aklemin had disagreed with their father many times before, Jarl Alki had never even threatened to replace them as heir.

Jarl Alki continued. "My child behaved dishonorably and, dare I say, traitorously during Candlemas. Their disrespect and disregard for our current situation may have cost this kingdom the coming war. I propose that the Witch King name a family to take over my seat, and a new heir for me to train to claim it. I trust in his visions to choose only the best to be jarl of Falconridge after my eventual passing."

The heated whispers this proclamation created were loud enough to echo off the vaulted ceilings and create a clamor in the hall. My head screamed at me. I pressed my thumbs to my temples, past the point of caring how weak it might look to the jarls present.

What was it that Aklemin had said? That if my father knew the truth about them, he would have Aklemin killed? *My father would have needed little prompting,* Aklemin had declared. Was this the first step to that? Or was this merely an attempt to discredit Aklemin before they woke from the vision and shared a path to undoing my father's plot—if one even existed.

In the back of the room, Rosamund had stood—unnoticed by anyone except Toketie and myself. She looked at me, her every emotion clear on her face. Anger. Determination. She was waiting for my signal. Waiting for me to tell her what to do. Nearer to the front of the throne room, Charles, Froya, and Kwaddis were all doing the same. Though their faces were calmer, none of us could completely hide our shock at Jarl Alki's proclamation.

Two warring voices pounded in my head. Aklemin's *I betray you* fighting with my father's *You will be great.*

A third voice joined the fray. Rosamund's, from when she'd yelled at me in the infirmary. *Your father is a warmonger,* she'd said. *He's been the most powerful man in this kingdom long enough to let it go to his head.*

War was always my choice. Isn't that what Aklemin had told me? There was no prophecy—only my own decision to make.

My headache faded, as if all I'd needed was to make that choice and everything would become clear.

In a different world, I might have pushed for war. In that other future, I would have conquered Vinland and the rest of the continent and called that my victory. In this world, all I could see were the echoes of Guanyu's ghost and Shantie's tears and Einar's blood.

I stood, and the cacophony of voices died down. "You called your child treasonous, Jarl Alki," I said, talking over the last of the chaos until it too quieted. "Treason is defined by betrayal of the kingdom, not betrayal of the king," I continued. "We are no absolute monarchy, and the king must follow the law as any other citizen. Am I wrong?"

Jarl Alki looked startled. Whatever my father had told him before the council meeting, it hadn't included this. Perhaps because I hadn't known that I would speak until that very moment.

In the back of the room, Rosamund shifted into some small creature and disappeared from my sight.

"Be that as it may," Jarl Alki spluttered, "the council decided upon the Witch King to center the Candlemas blessing at the last council meeting. To go against that—"

"Is not illegal," I said firmly. "Just as it was not illegal when I stepped in to finish the Samhain ritual upon Madam Dyer's death. The council may give suggestions, but it has always been the prerogative of the involved witches to determine the best focal points for our rituals. Aklemin did not interrupt the circle. They did not break the ritual. They merely determined themself a better fit to take the vision, and as it was, they were correct. The magic of Candlemas chose them. Your suggestion to remove Aklemin from your line of succession will only weaken the Cursed Kingdom's future rule. Why would the council agree to excommunicate so powerful an ice witch without proof of treason?"

"The princess speaks truthfully," Jarl Almstedt said. "Though the situation was unexpected, we should be celebrating the reveal of such a strong ice witch dedicated to helping our kingdom thrive."

"I'm deeply interested in the result of Aklemin's vision," Jarl Falk added.

"As am I," Jarl Tenas agreed.

"If I may, honored jarls, I have a topic related to Jarl Alki's proposal," I said. I didn't give my father time to approve my statement. Though he was officially in charge of what proposals would be heard next, I had to step over propriety for this one. "Prophecy is the backbone of our nation, ever since Queen Mesachie's vision led to the curse that created this haven of magic. There is indeed no good reason to excommunicate a strong ice witch from this council without proof of treason." I paused just long enough to be sure I had the attention of everyone in the throne room. "I do hold that proof."

The shouts for explanation that followed my words echoed so loudly that I couldn't make out a single thing, until finally Jarl Tenas stood and bellowed, "If this is a joke—?"

"I would never joke about such a topic," I said, holding up a hand to encourage the room to quiet.

Jarl Hu stood, looking ready to step in. My father might have signaled her to do so. I couldn't see him perfectly, as the Heir Throne was slightly farther forward on the raised dais. I knew I couldn't let him or anyone on his entourage interrupt me. I had to keep control of the council.

I stepped off the dais to stand in the stretch of room between the thrones and the benches. I pulled out the map I'd carefully hidden in the folds of my dress, just as I had every day since I'd retrieved it from Shantie's room at the end of term, and held the rolled-up parchment high for everyone to see.

General Tepeh stood too, eyes narrowed. I wondered if they could recognize the map from its exterior.

"I have evidence to present before the council," I said. "I'm sure many of you heard the reports that I went missing from school for a week at the end of December. I left campus for my own purposes the night of the solstice, but it meant I was in Multah, about to return to school, when my companion caught the scent of someone we recognized. Thane Anders of the Royal Company. He had a squad with him, and they were using the far-western pier of Multah's dock to sneak onto longboats."

Jarl Tenas abruptly sat at that. I'd obviously caught his attention. He was jarl of Multah, he knew how out of the way the far-west pier was from the main dockyard.

I kept my explanation as brief as I could to pull my audience through what I had seen in Vinland, specifically the cursed lands I'd named the Frozen Falls and the Ghost Town. I explained how we were attacked, and how Prince Vetle IV of Vinland confirmed that it was our soldiers who had wreaked such havoc on his lands.

"Was this a tactic determined by the general's council?" Jarl Almstedt asked, speaking to the general of Gravestown a few seats across from her. "We agreed last meeting not to engage in acts of war until spring."

Gravestown's general shook her head rapidly. "We certainly did not approve such actions."

"Jarl Almstedt, perhaps you would do us the honors of reading the transcript of this ghost's confession," I said. We may have lost the spirit jar, but I'd been pleasantly surprised by Toketie's detailed transcript of the interrogation.

Jarl Almstedt stood and crossed the room to take the proffered paper. She unrolled it. "Squad Leader Mimie Moolocks?"

"Of Thane Ander's platoon," I said. "I summoned her some three months ago, after she was killed by Vinlanders seeking revenge outside of Witch Hall. If you could please share her responses for the council."

I watched the faces of the crowd as Jarl Almstedt read from Toketie's meticulous notes. Only when Jarl Almstedt got to the part where Squad Leader Moolocks mentioned the Witch King's written order did I turn to look at my father.

He was hunched over in his throne, hands clasped to the sides of his temples like he was trying to ward off the same headache I'd been fighting. Except, for him, I was sure that headache was instead a vision. Most of my father's visions were small, quick things, but occasionally he had a vision that incapacitated him, like the one at my mother's funeral that knocked him unconscious for three days. Throughout my childhood, it hadn't been uncommon for him to collapse in his chair for minutes at a time as some unexpected event sparked a vision that completely overwhelmed his senses.

I had made my decision, and it was changing his carefully plotted future. Revealing this evidence was affecting his foresight so quickly that it was effectively keeping him imprisoned in his throne. It wouldn't last forever. I turned back to the crowd to see that, unlike the rest, Jarl Alki and Jarl Hu had their eyes firmly fixed upon the Witch King instead of on Jarl Almstedt. General Tepeh had left their seat and was making their way around the room to my father's side.

Jarl Almstedt finished reading from the interview and turned to me.

"General Tepeh, perhaps you can enlighten the council on this matter?" I asked. The general froze where they were. I held the rolled-up map in front of me like a taunt.

"You are making a grave mistake, Shaw," General Tepeh said, which wasn't an answer at all.

I would not let myself be intimidated. I unrolled the map. "Jarl Almstedt, if you can tell the room what this map shows?"

Jarl Almstedt took the map and studied it. "It's Vinland," she said. "Several towns are circled. Here, and here."

"This town, with the red cross over it, is the exact location that I discovered in December," I said. "The town that is now cursed with bone magic. Some three months ago, I told you all what had occurred during the Samhain ritual. I neglected to tell you of a ghost I talked with there. I wouldn't have dared bring this to you without evidence, but there is no denying the truth now."

I spoke then of General Otto Holt. Of the story he'd told me, of finding the map and being murdered for it.

"I questioned my father that night I arrived in Gravestown. Would you care to share with the jarls what you told me, Father?" I glanced at him, but the Witch King was too caught in his visions to speak, so I continued. "He confirmed it himself. General Holt was murdered to keep this information a secret. Just as my father attempted to murder the glass witch of my entourage and countless other classmates by hiding his knowledge of Prince Vetle's attack during our scheduled Army Training exercise last term."

All the jarls with heirs were visibly and verbally outraged at that. Froya stood even as her parent demanded answers.

"It's true," she said loudly. "There was no logical reason for our marching exercise to end with us alone at Goose Point, not without an ice witch's knowledge of the coming attack and their desire to see us ambushed there."

Kwaddis stood too. "We only survived because of Rosy, and she was given page duty for it!"

Charles raised his voice to be heard over the jarls. "The prince told us himself what the Witch King did. He attacked us for revenge because the Cursed Kingdom killed their people first."

"So you see, esteemed jarls," I said, and once again the room quieted to hear me, "our conflict with Vinland was deliberately cultivated. The Witch King used the Royal Company to spark literal flames to ignite war. It is our duty to bring him to justice, for the safety of both our nations."

"You!"

I'd been keeping my eye on General Tepeh, still inching closer to the throne, so it surprised me when Jarl Alki was the one to lunge forward. He was a flower witch, and I hadn't considered him much of a threat. He scrambled over the front bench, hands outstretched toward his target.

Toward Aklemin.

Jarl Alki got his hands around Aklemin's throat before any of us could act. His face went purple as he attempted to squeeze the life out of his only child.

"Jarl Alki!" Jarl Falk cried, visibly aghast by the sudden attack. They reached forward, trying unsuccessfully to tug Jarl Alki away by the back of his velvet robes.

"This is all your fault!" Jarl Alki yelled, his words echoing off the cavernous ceiling of the throne room. Even stuck in the vision coma, Aklemin began gasping for breath. "Treacherous beast. I should have killed you in the cradle. David warned me! I shouldn't have hesitated. I won't hesitate."

A sound like a trumpet rang out through the sudden pandemonium, and Toketie-the-swan flew forward to attack Jarl Alki's face. The jarl fell back with a cry. Toketie stood over Aklemin, huge wings flared wide to block anyone from coming after Aklemin again. I rushed to my friend's side, worried, but with Jarl Alki gone, the ice witch had begun breathing normally. They still had yet to wake. Not even the threat of death was enough to pull them out of the vision.

"Stop!" Jarl Tenas yelled.

I spun around to see General Tepeh reach for something inside their military coat, but before they could do anything, Rosamund was there. She shifted from mouse to wolf and jumped forward to tackle the general to the ground. General Tepeh's head hit the stone floor with an uncomfortable thud, and they lay unmoving.

Jarl Hu roared, the sound changing rapidly as she shifted into her only form—a clouded leopard. Several jarls and their heirs on either side of Jarl Hu screamed in fear and scrambled out of the way.

Before Jarl Hu could attempt to attack Rosamund, Chao stepped up in front of his mother. Jingyi had shifted into her fox and stood at Chao's heels, teeth bared in a threat. For a second, I worried that Jarl Hu would leap over her son, but she stopped just in front of him.

I turned from the standstill between mother and son to look at my father. The visions, it seemed, had finally died down. He straightened in his throne, breath visibly ragged. I had to wrap this up now, before he could reclaim control.

"It is treasonous to plot against our foreign neighbor without the approval of the jarls' council," I said. "Will you explain that, Father? Why you didn't share your reasoning with them six years ago, when you first began this plan? Unless you knew they would question it. Knew they would come to learn, as I have, that my *prophesied* war was a lie created for your own ambitions."

The Witch King looked up to meet my gaze, eyes cold as ice. "You've made a grave mistake, my dear," he said, soft and deadly.

The outrage in the room only grew louder as all the jarls demanded answers of the king.

"Perhaps," I said, only for his ears. "But it was my choice to make."

Chapter 19

THE TRIAL THAT FOLLOWED TOOK THE REST OF THE DAY. The council barely let my father or his entourage speak, not after Jarl Alki had attempted to kill his own child.

General Tepeh woke from being knocked unconscious about halfway through the proceedings. The blow to their head had made them overly sensitive to the light. They didn't seem to remember what they'd been doing. When the jarls questioned them about the map, they spoke in slightly slurred words about the necessity of starting the war with Vinland, for the empire was too strong to leave for last.

It wasn't the clearest of testimonies, but it was enough to finally convince the jarls of the truth. They eventually determined that my father and his entourage would be put under house arrest and guarded by a mix of soldiers from all the companies, excluding the Royal Company. I didn't believe it was enough to truly declaw him or his entourage, but it was the best concession I could get. The jarls refused to do any more for risk of our neighboring nations hearing about it.

"What if we need to tell them?" I argued, a good hour after my father, Jarl Alki, Jarl Hu, and General Tepeh had been escorted out of the throne room. "We still have a chance of stopping this war if we show Vinland that we have taken steps to repair our relations. To accept responsibility for the destruction my father wrought upon their land and people."

I saw several of my classmates nod along, but the jarls were silent, one and all. Finally, Jarl Falk sighed. "You have grown significantly, Princess. I can only speak for myself, but I do believe many of us greatly anticipate the queen you will be. And yet, I hope you will still acknowledge our greater experience on the matters of international relations. You said it yourself that Prince Vetle invaded our lands. Whether it was for revenge or not doesn't change our circumstances."

"The emperor does not fear us," Jarl Tenas added. "Perhaps there are Vinlanders who will be grateful that we have taken steps to apprehend the cause behind their suffering, but the emperor will only see opportunity. You're not yet of age. We cannot crown you now without assigning a regent to manage your rule, and that will make us appear weak."

"It is better to keep your father under a quiet house arrest," Jarl Almstedt added. "We'll crown you upon graduation and make it known that the former Witch King has graciously stepped into retirement. It will show a level of trust in you as our Witch Queen."

"But then Vinland will have no reason to accept our reparations. We will have no choice but to go to war," I protested.

"War is your destiny," Jarl Tenas said.

"This war is my destiny because my father wished it to be. We don't have to accept that."

Jarl Falk raised a single eyebrow. "Perhaps so. But you must consider your coming rule. Perhaps we don't need to go to war, but we do need to show a strong enough front to dissuade Vinland and our other neighbors from thinking to encroach upon us."

I hesitated. It wasn't so much the argument as it was the ubiquitous agreement. None of the jarls were protesting. Was that why my father hadn't spoken more to his own defense? Despite the choice I'd made, was it still too late to stop this war?

I glanced at Aklemin, still in a vision coma. The red marks Jarl Alki had left around their neck were already starting to darken into bruises. They had stolen the Candlemas vision for a reason, no matter the risk it posed to them. Once they woke, they would have a better idea of what we needed to do to stop this war for good.

"I understand," I told the council. "You said yourselves, honorable jarls, that we will send no declarations of war until the spring. Crown me upon graduation and, if that is what the council believes is the best path forward for our kingdom, I will abide by it."

The jarls began grumbling to themselves at that, as if affronted by my icy tone. I didn't care to listen to them. The trial was over, and Aklemin still lay vulnerable on a pallet on the floor of the throne room. I needed to get them away. Who knew what agents my father had on the Mountain. Jarl Alki had already attempted to kill his child once, and I would not give him room to do so again.

I moved to Aklemin's pallet. Toketie shifted from swan to human to help, but even with the two of us, it was hard to carry. I had only a second to wonder how we were going to get them out of the room when Chao and Jingyi stepped up to take the other corners.

Behind them, I noticed the heirs block the path between us and the jarls. Emma and Charles distracted Jarl Almstedt with a loud argument. Kwaddis was hugging his dad, whispering something into his ear. Shugh looked to be managing his grandfather, the jarl of Desertmouth, and several members of Jarl Tenas's voting bloc. Kalitan seemed to have prodded her brother into pulling Jarl Falk aside for a quiet word, with Froya nodding alongside with whatever the young jarl was saying.

Chao waited until we were out of the throne room. Rosamund-the-wolf prowled in front of us, keeping a watch for any potential threat.

"I understand why you didn't trust me," Chao said. "But I knew nothing of what my mother and the rest of the entourage had planned, Shaw, I promise you."

I looked at Chao. All term I'd questioned whether I could trust him, but he hadn't hesitated before standing in front of his mother, no matter how fierce her shift.

"I should have trusted you," I said, which was as close to an apology as I could give him. "Once Aklemin wakes up, I'll tell you everything. You and the rest of the seniors. You all deserve to know the future of this kingdom."

Chao inclined his head. "We'll be waiting."

We continued on through the halls of the palace, passing by harried servants and confused guards. I only saw her because I was looking for a servant to help us get Aklemin to my room. Thane Olhiyu, the woman in charge of the Royal Company's intelligence operations, was dressed as one of the palace servants. She turned away as soon as my eyes passed over her, so quickly that I might have thought it my imagination, if not for what had just happened in the throne room.

"We should get Aklemin to their own bed," I said as calmly as I could.

No one protested, despite the burden of having to carry Aklemin all the way to the jarl's manor on the other side of Falconridge.

Once we were there, I had Chao help me load Aklemin into a cart, instead of taking them up to their room like I'd said. I made him promise to explain what he could to the rest of the heirs so they could manage the jarls after my abrupt exit. Jingyi, I sent back to the palace to grab my things from my room. I hadn't truly unpacked, so it wouldn't be difficult for her to gather my travel bags and cloak. Rosamund volunteered to go raid the kitchen of Jarl Alki's manor for food while Toketie went inside to grab Aklemin's, Rosamund's, and her belongings. I fetched Cow from the stable, stowing her riding gear in the cart next to Aklemin and attaching her to the cart harness. With any other bone horses, it would be a disaster to try to get them to pull a cart, but Cow listened to me well enough to make it work.

Jingyi returned with my things. As she handed the bags to me, she leaned close enough to murmur, "We're being watched."

I said nothing, but I grabbed a set of travel clothes from my bag, glad I had an excuse to go inside. Chao and Jingyi stood guard over Aklemin. A part of me hesitated in leaving them, but I had promised to trust them. I just wished I didn't have to prove it in such dangerous circumstances.

I hurried inside. It didn't take long to find Toketie neatly packing Aklemin's bag.

"Here, don't forget this," I said, and pulled out Aklemin's heaviest traveling cloak from the depths of their massive armoire.

Toketie took the travel cloak from me, frowning slightly. I used the excuse of adjusting some things in Aklemin's bag to lean close to her and whisper a set of instructions. To her credit, the ice familiar barely reacted beyond a small widening of her eyes. When I pulled away, she gave me the tiniest of nods.

I changed quickly, grabbed the bags Toketie had packed, then headed back outside. Rosamund had returned with food and water, which Chao and Jingyi were helping to pack into the cart.

"Are you sure it's safe to return to campus without an escort?" Chao asked.

"It's safer than traveling with an escort I can't trust," I said. I knew we had to leave now, before the jarls got it in their heads to demand we stay until Aklemin woke up.

"We'll be fine," Rosamund added.

Chao looked like he wanted to argue more, but Jingyi placed a hand on his arm. The two looked at each other for a second before Chao gave a tight nod.

"We'll see you back at school," I said. As they left, I turned to Rosamund and said, "Toketie's gone to scout ahead in her swan shift. She'll meet us up the road."

Rosamund took my excuse without issue. We sat together in the front of the cart, and I took the reins. A few clicks and Cow was off. Though she had never been trained in pulling a cart, bone animals were smarter than their nonmagical cousins, and she got the hang of it quickly enough. It wasn't perfect, but it would do.

It took barely more than fifteen minutes to get to the fork in the road. Straight ahead, we could continue down increasingly lengthy switchbacks to get to the northern road that led back to Witch Hall. To the left, there was a longer road that sloped southward down the Mountain and headed toward Gravestown. I stopped the cart and sat back in the seat to wait.

I didn't know how long Toketie would need for the task I'd given her, so I took the chance to do something I'd been thinking about for a while. At least out here, I could be sure that no one could sneak up on us without Rosamund noticing them.

I still had the moonstone bones in my pocket. I'd transferred them to every new outfit I put on. It was habit by now, but when

I'd changed into travel clothes and held those smooth stones in between my fingers, I'd known it was time to let them go.

"Hold out your hands," I told Rosamund.

She turned to me, confused. "Why?"

"Please?"

Rosamund wrinkled her nose but did as I asked. I carefully deposited the moonstone bones into her palms. She stared down at them. "Shaw—"

"For your family," I said before she could refuse them. "The crown and its council have done poorly by you, Rosamund Holt. From the way the jarls dismissed your grandmother when she tried to tell them of your grandfather's murder, to the way your family was evicted from your home to aid a war that never should have existed. Moonstone sells well. I still plan to grant your family land once I'm crowned, but I hope this will pay for the house that you lost."

"More than," Rosamund murmured. "It's too much, Shaw."

It didn't feel like enough. Not even close to enough. "It's yours. I didn't give you my courtship necklace in good faith. It was only fair of you to tear it apart as you did. But I give you these in good faith now."

I couldn't imagine remaking the moonstone bone necklace. Even if I was forced to court another familiar one day, that necklace had been Rosamund's. Just like the red cloak with wolf pelt lining had become hers. She may not fit the vision of a familiar I'd once had, back when I'd commissioned both courtship pieces, but she was the only vision I had now.

Rosamund might not want to bond with me, and she'd probably been smart to refuse, but I could never regret having met her. She'd helped me reflect on things I'd never bothered caring about before. I wanted to be a better queen to live up to the trust she'd placed in me.

I looked away, blinking back the sudden tears that had welled up in my eyes without my say-so. I blamed it on the biting wind.

"I smell snow," Rosamund said, as if changing the subject would help me regain my dignity. Another gust of wind ripped between us, pulling at our hair.

I grimaced. "Let's hope we get off the Mountain before it hits."

Rosamund stood so abruptly, it half startled Cow from where she'd been nosing at the snow, looking for any frosty remains of grass.

"What is it?"

"It sounds like someone is dragging something?"

I relaxed. "Good. It's time, then."

Toketie came into view a minute later, pulling a large dog sled behind her.

"What *is* that?" Rosamund asked.

"They're meant to be pulled by a team of sled dogs, but I think your wolf can do it solo," I said. "Aklemin told me the night we arrived in Falconridge that I could trust you with their safety. Besides, I know you want to go to your brother's wedding, Toketie."

"If we need to miss it—" Toketie began.

I shook my head before she could offer to do so. "The opposite. I need you to go. And I need you to take Aklemin with you."

"Oh," Toketie said. "So you're . . ."

"Going to be a decoy, yes," I said.

"Shaw!" Rosamund protested. "By yourself?"

"I'll have Cow," I said, though we both knew that wouldn't be enough if I was attacked. "Look, right now, Aklemin is more vulnerable than I am. I don't believe my father would risk my life, even to try to kill Aklemin. He needs me to lead this war. To see his perfect future realized." At Rosamund's long look, I waved a hand. "I promise I'll explain everything when there's time. For now, the important thing is keeping Aklemin safe. They'll expect the three of us to take Aklemin north to Witch Hall. So take them south instead."

Rosamund and Toketie exchanged the kind of look siblings or old married couples gave each other. The kind that had a whole conversation with a single glance.

"I'm placing Aklemin's life, and my future, in your hands," I murmured. "Can I trust you to guard it?"

"We'll do it," Rosamund said. "But you'd better be right, Shaw. If we get back to Witch Hall and I find out you died, I'll call your ghost into a ritual circle and haunt you for the rest of my life."

"That doesn't make any sense, Rosy," Toketie muttered.

"I'll look forward to it," I said.

Rosamund huffed but didn't argue further.

We made quick work of moving Aklemin to the sled and covering them in the travel cloak. The sled was less insulated against the gusting wind and soft flurries that had begun to fall. I gave the cousins as much food and water as we could fit into the sled baskets around Aklemin. The sled came with ropes to tie everything down. We figured out how to get Rosamund's wolf attached to the harness. It took a bit of adjusting, but we managed to make it fit.

"I'll see you at school," I said.

Toketie waved a hand in goodbye, and I watched as Rosamund pulled the sled down the southern road until it was completely out of sight. I made quick work of brushing away the sled tracks and wolf prints, then hopped back onto the front seat of the cart.

"Just us, then," I told my horse. Cow flicked her ear back toward me. "Let's get to it. Hyah!"

The mare pointed her nose north, and we set off.

The cart was hard to maneuver along the curves of the switchback. I had to go slower than I wanted. It was truly snowing by the time night fell. I pushed on to the next rest area—a cleared patch by the road large enough to fit a small encampment of travelers. There was no one on the road with me, so I gave Cow the largest picket line I could manage and went to sleep inside the cart with my cloak as a bed and blanket both.

I woke from a dead sleep with my heart pounding in my chest and a ghost hovering only a foot from my face. For a brief moment, I thought the angry Vinlander spirit had found me again, but this was a different ghost.

"Quiet," the ghost said once she saw me awake. She was a gaunt-faced woman who looked maybe a few years older than me—though that, of course, said nothing about what age she'd been when she'd died.

"There's a group coming for you," the ghost said. "You've got maybe half a mark until they arrive. You'd best be gone before they do, or be prepared to fight."

Half a mark? This ghost was from before the age of clocks, which made her at least two hundred years old. If I remembered from my history lessons, one candle mark was typically half an hour. If the ghost was right—and she had to believe what she was telling me—then I had about fifteen minutes before I was ambushed.

Rosamund had packed the food in travel bags. I grabbed the largest one I could carry. I hoped there was a canteen of water inside, but if not, then I could always eat snow. The Frozen Mountain was not bereft of water the way the Obsidian Desert was.

I dithered for just a second over Cow's saddle and bridle. Fifteen minutes. If I'd have to ride Cow all the way back to Witch Hall, I'd want the bridle at least. I could ride bareback on Rosamund's horse form because Rosamund knew that I was, in fact, riding bareback. Cow was a true bone mare, and for all that she trusted me, she still had a temper.

Decided, I made quick work of placing Cow's bridle and saddle blanket over the saddle, then hoisted the pile up. I tried to keep quiet as I slipped out the back of the cart. It was still snowing, but not so badly that I was worried. I'd grown up on the Frozen Mountain—I was used to a steady winter snowfall.

Cow had been dozing at the far end of the picket line, but she lifted her head as I approached. I cinched her saddle on as tight as I could make it, then looped her halter around her neck to keep her in place while I bridled her. I wished I had time to pack the food into saddlebags to put on her. I didn't bother wasting time trying to tie the travel bag I carried onto her back.

There was no way I'd be able to heave myself onto Cow's back with the heavy bag of food, so I walked her over to the back of the cart and used that to mount. The ghost had floated away when I'd grabbed Cow's saddle, but I felt her approaching again before I saw her appear out of the gloom.

"Hurry!" she called. "They'll hear you leave if you don't go soon!"

I had to hope that none of them were bone witches, or the ghost's shout would have already given me away. I jabbed my finger northward down the slope, a silent question to the ghost if that way was safe.

"Go!" she urged. "There's no time."

Well, the ghost had woken me up to warn me. If I started heading directly into the ambush, presumably she'd let me know.

I kicked Cow into a trot. No matter the danger, I didn't dare canter down the Mountain. At least the fresh snow muffled the sound of hoof steps.

Despite straining my ears, I heard nothing as I fled. The ghost kept pace with me, flying through the air parallel to my bone horse. I could tell Cow knew something was there—all bone animals had an innate sense of death—but either she could also sense that the ghost was harmless or she was reading my body language enough to ignore her.

It was impossible to watch the sunrise in such a snow-coated sky, but eventually the gloom lightened enough that I could see more than two feet in front of me. It made the switchbacks easier to manage. I didn't dare stop, though exhaustion was beginning to set in. I didn't know how many hours of sleep I'd had, but it couldn't have been many.

Just as I was getting worried about needing to give Cow a break, the ghost called out again. "Here, this way!"

We'd made it to another of the rest areas set at the bend of a switchback. The ghost floated past it and farther around a gradual slope toward the eastern side of the Mountain.

"They'll see the tracks!" I called after her. By now, I had to hope we'd gained enough ground that I could at least talk to my dead helper.

"The Mountain will cover them," the ghost replied.

In response, the snow began to cascade like a curtain from the low-lying clouds. The ghost was right—it would take mere minutes for our tracks to completely disappear in this kind of weather.

"Thank you," I told the nearest snowdrift. I wasn't born with ice magic, but the Mountain had been my childhood home. I was touched by its protection. I would have thought it loyal to my father over me, but there was no malevolence that I could sense. Even the snowfall, while heavy, hadn't developed into a true blizzard the way I knew it could have.

I followed the ghost around the much narrower path eastward. It took maybe ten minutes before the path deposited us in something like a cave, though it had been made by two enormous boulders and a series of smaller rocks all piled up on each other.

Dismounting was painful. My thighs protested the relentless ride. I patted Cow for several minutes, thanking her for being so good for me. Luckily there were apples in the food pack I'd grabbed, and I was able to treat her with them. I'd have to find a place to let her graze once I made it off the Mountain, or rest at an inn with a stable and hay. That was, if I could do so without getting ambushed again.

"Who were the people you saw?" I asked the ghost, wondering if Thane Olhiyu had been the one pursuing me or someone else. "Can you describe them to me?"

The ghost snorted. "Why, goodness, there's no need to thank me for saving you! It was no trouble at all!"

Several hundred years old, but she was fluent in the language of sarcasm. I swallowed down my annoyance at her dodging my question because she was right—I was being rude. "Thank you, madam. I am truly in your debt."

"You are," the ghost replied. "And what is the name of my debtee?"

I supposed I shouldn't be surprised a ghost so ancient hadn't recognized me. I bowed low. "My name is Shaw Colchuck."

"Are you really?" The ghost's tone was wry enough that I straightened from my bow just to study her face. The ghost looked at the surface of the nearest boulder. "I suppose that's why the Mountain wanted me to help you," she murmured, as if to herself.

I looked with her and saw, upon closer inspection, that the rock was covered in a thin layer of ice. It glinted like it was wet, but when I touched it, I felt no dampness. And yet, when I went to take my fingers away, I found my glove stuck to the surface. I pulled unsuccessfully several times, before giving up and slipping my hand out of the glove. I really was tired—I should have known better.

The ghost watched me with a smile even wrier than her tone. "She's a temperamental beast, is she not? I thought I was snuffing her fire, but I merely changed its form."

"Pardon?" I asked.

"Colchuck. We weren't always called that, you know. It means ice. Yes, I see by your nodding that you knew that. But before we were Colchucks, we were just Tyees. Chiefs."

I studied the ghost again. She had no color to her, but there was something in the shape of her hairline and the curve of her eyes that looked familiar.

"Apologies, madam, what may I call you?" I asked slowly as a theory began to form.

"My people knew me as Mesachie," the ghost said. "But you may call me Grandmother, for I am that by many generations to you."

Chapter 20

ROSY

THE FIRST FEW STEPS WERE JARRING AS ROSY GOT USED to the push and pull of the sled. The harness was uncomfortably tight around her chest, but she could still run and that was all that mattered.

The southern road was a gentler incline than the tight switchbacks they'd climbed to get to Falconridge two weeks prior. It would have made pulling the sled more difficult, if not for the gentle snowfall padding their way. Every couple hundred feet, the road had a large switchback marked with a stone half wall. Rosy took those curves glacially slow so as not to catapult the sled off the side of the Mountain.

Toketie called for a break after a few hours. The cousins ate lunch together and forced water down Aklemin's throat. At least ice witches reflexively swallowed water or these long vision comas would be truly dangerous. By the time Rosy and Toketie had finished their food, the snow had begun coming down in faster flurries.

"Should we try to find shelter?" Rosy asked. Toketie knew the Mountain better than she did.

Toketie hesitated, then shook her head. "Solemie's wedding is only a couple days away. If we get snowed in near the summit, we'll never make it. The snow will be lighter the farther down we go."

"You're the expert," Rosy said. She didn't want to miss her cousin's wedding either.

Toketie helped fit the harness on over Rosy's wolf shift, faster now that they'd figured out the best way to do it, and they set off again. It was strange for her to be here, traveling down the same Mountain path her pops would have taken all those years ago, before the Witch King had him killed. Now the Witch King was trying to kill Aklemin too, for knowing too much. For daring to work against his plot. Rosy would not let that happen.

The snowfall picked up significantly within the first hour they were back on the road. The wind began to gust in ferocious bursts. Were they in the Bone Forest, Rosy would be doing her best to calm the land down. But she was a bone wolf, an anchor to bone magic, not ice. She had to rely on Toketie to understand the whims of ice magic—and she had no idea if the Mountain was as fond of her cousin as the Forest was of her.

Rosy tried to keep to the road, but it wasn't long before she lost the sense of its borders. The only clue to the curves were the stone half walls. Rosy wondered what kinds of drops lay on the other side of those barriers. She didn't try to look.

Her fur coat helped to insulate her, but the tip of her nose and the pads of her feet first stung, then grew numb. She looked for Toketie on the back of the sled every time she banked a corner and was relieved to see her cousin still holding on, hunched over in her cloak to ward off the bite of the wind.

Rosy was no stranger to hard work, but after another hour or so into their journey, she wasn't sure how safe it was to continue. The snow had only grown thicker—thick enough that she could barely make Toketie out anymore. The temperature continued to plummet as the afternoon sun dove for the horizon. It was already well below freezing, and nightfall would only make it worse.

Rosy began to slow down, thinking to convey her worries to her cousin. But Toketie shouted above the shriek of the wind, "Keep going! Don't stop, Rosy, we have to push through!"

The hard determination in Toketie's voice reminded Rosy of Shaw's fear as they fled the obsidian sandstorm. Rosy and Shaw had gotten lucky then, especially without a glass witch or familiar to guide them to safety. Was Toketie sensing something about the Mountain, about this snowstorm, that Rosy couldn't?

She pushed on. The snow continued to fall. The wind continued to bite. It was getting hard to pull the sled, even with the help of downward slopes.

"Stop!" Toketie screeched.

Rosy took a sharp left, seeing what Toketie had a step too late. The snowbank had piled high enough to completely cover the next stone half wall. Rosy skidded around it, but the force of her rotation pushed the sled up and over.

The sled dropped.

Rosy had just enough time to brace herself before the sled pulled her backward. She scrambled to keep her footing. Her claws dug into the snow, finding the top of the stone wall. She shifted into a deer. She wanted to go horse but feared the already-tight harness would break from the width of her horse's chest. Bone deer were large enough though, and she was able to plant her front legs against the wall and her back legs against the side of the cliff.

Rosy turned her head. She was balanced precariously. The sled hung down below her. The front rungs rested against the side of the cliff just past her back legs, but the rest of the sled was completely airborne. It swayed precariously. The harness dug into Rosy's chest. It wasn't designed for a deer's body. She worried it would slip off of her or, worse, snap completely.

Toketie had shifted into her swan form sometime during the fall. She flapped furiously in the air next to the sled, keeping herself aloft. As an ice swan, she had a wingspan of ten feet, and each flap blew another layer of snow over the limp body of Aklemin. It was lucky that Shaw had taken her time tying the ice witch down. Aklemin's head was bunched back against the packs by the angle of the sled, but they hadn't moved much past that.

Rosy had no idea how she would be able to pull the sled up. Any second now her legs were going to slip. Toketie was fine, and Rosy could probably survive by shifting into a squirrel. But Aklemin would plummet to their death.

Before Rosy could begin to panic, Toketie stretched her long neck through the handle of the sled. She twisted her body so that she could flap straight down, and with the force of each wingbeat, she pulled up.

Rosy spread her front legs as far apart as she could in this body and heaved. The front rungs of the sled scraped against the cliffside. Rosy shifted back into the wolf so she could claw her way forward. Inch by inch, she and Toketie pulled the sled up and over the stone wall, and safely onto the buried road on the other side.

Exhausted, Rosy shifted to human. She immediately regretted it as the cold penetrated through the clothes she wore. It didn't matter, because a second later Toketie had shifted next to her and the two were hugging.

"This is dangerous, Tokey," Rosy said. "We can't go to Solemie's wedding if we're dead. We need to find shelter."

"We can't," Toketie protested. "The Mountain's upset right now.

I don't know why. It's not about us, I don't think, but something is making it angry. There are no caves up here, and nothing else will keep us safe if it really starts to blizzard."

This wasn't already a blizzard? Rosy grimaced. "What do we do?"

"Keep going. That's all we can do." Toketie rubbed her face against Rosy's shoulders. "This is so ridiculous. I could lead us. I know the path. But I can't ride in the front of the sled and we didn't bring any reins or whatever they call the things they use to drive the dogs."

"You could fly in front of me?"

"Not as the swan. I'm too big to fly in a storm like this." Toketie pulled back, face screwed up in frustration and misery. "If only I had another shift! If I was less useless—"

"You are not useless," Rosy said fiercely.

"You spent an entire term trying to teach us how to find another voice," Toketie argued.

"You are not useless," Rosy repeated. "You are so incredibly brave, Tokey. You persevere when most people would flee. You make the best of every situation."

Toketie looked like she wanted to argue more, but Rosy was cold and the snowstorm was shrieking all around them and she had a better idea. Toketie might have struggled to find a voice during the winter term, but they were on the Frozen Mountain now. If her theory was right, there was no better place for Toketie to claim her second shift.

"Toketie," Rosy said sharply, catching her cousin's attention. "Tell me what bird would be better. When you picture one that can navigate a storm like this, what do you see?"

That question seemed to stump Toketie out of her frustrated anger. "I don't know. A snowy owl, maybe? Or a red crossbill?"

“Have you seen any of them fly in snow like this?” Rosy pressed.

Toketie stilled, obviously lost in thought. Finally, she nodded. “A couple winters ago, I saw a beautiful northern goshawk flush a squirrel out from its bolt-hole during a snowstorm.”

There, perfect. “Think about that goshawk,” Rosy said. “Can you picture it?”

Toketie was too smart not to realize what Rosy was doing. Rosy could see the second's indecision. Rosy had read Toketie's essays from the workshop—she knew Toketie dreamed of finding an eagle shift like Froya. But gaining a voice through the connection of another familiar was difficult, Rosy had experienced that herself with her badger shift. The goshawk would be easier for Toketie. The need, the feelings, and the image.

“Think about the bravery of it. Maybe even its casual recklessness,” Rosy continued. “Where most other birds were hunched in a tree waiting out the storm, that goshawk knew what it needed to do to feast. It didn't hesitate. It forged its own path.”

“But I'm just a swan,” Toketie whispered.

Rosy didn't remember the rankings enough to know how much further up a goshawk was to a swan, but it didn't matter. She knew Toketie could do this.

“You're never going to get an eagle shift if you can't claim a simple goshawk,” Rosy said, taking on the taunting tone she'd always used when challenging Toketie to whatever childish games they'd played growing up.

Toketie glanced at Aklemin. Rosy was close enough to see the way her eyes went steely as determination took dominion over anxiety.

That was all it took. Toketie spread her arms wide, and Rosy was delighted to see feathers begin to sprout. Seconds later, Toketie had shifted.

Rosy whooped in delight. Her cousin was a gorgeous bird. Half the size of the swan but still impressive. She had startling red eyes and a marbled black-and-white chest, frosted over with a layer of natural ice.

Toketie shifted back. "How was it that easy? Rosy, how in the world?"

"Because you felt it. You understood it. All you need is a second to open your heart to the essence of an animal, and the voice will come to you. And, well, we're at the home of ice magic in the Cursed Kingdom. Of course it was easy here."

Toketie laughed, an almost warbling sound like she still didn't really believe it. Rosy hugged her again.

Unfortunately, they had no time to really revel in Toketie's success. The two of them quickly checked Aklemin, making sure the ice witch was still secure in the sled and as bundled up as they could manage. Then Rosy shifted back into the wolf and Toketie refastened the harness around her. That done, Toketie took a few deep breaths. Rosy wondered if she was worried that she wouldn't be able to shift into the goshawk again.

Then Toketie was swooping in front of her on the goshawk's wings. Rosy howled in joy. Just like all the times swan and horse had raced across the pastures back home, now hawk and wolf soared down the Mountain.

Toketie's goshawk form was much more agile than her swan had been. She cut through the snow like a knife through butter, gliding left and right, up and down. She rode the wind, then flapped against it as needed. Rosy followed as close as she could manage. Toketie flew wide arcs along the curves of the road, helping Rosy keep the sled well clear of those sharp drops.

No matter their success, the Mountain still wasn't pleased. Night had truly fallen now. With human eyes, Rosy would have been lost in this blizzard. As the wolf, she just barely managed to keep track of Toketie.

The snow grew deep. Almost too deep. Normal sled dogs would be struggling. Only the size of Rosy's wolf was saving them, but even she would be unable to press forward soon.

Toketie let out an alarm call—a rapid series of high-pitched cries—then she swerved sharply right. Rosy followed, and her paws nearly slid out from under her as the sled tottered unsteadily on one set of rungs. It slammed back into the snow, and Rosy tried to ignore the way the harness dug into her shoulder as it twisted the wrong way.

Another cry, this one longer. What did that mean?

There! Ahead, there was a visible line of trees. The Frozen Mountain crept farther down from the peak each year, destroying pine trees and driving away all but the ice animals. The unnaturally straight line of pines and firs ahead was the clear divider between the Frozen Mountain and the nonmagical mountainside.

Toketie banked left, finding a gap in the trees large enough for the sled. Rosy followed her. She didn't slow until the end of the sled crossed that line, and then kept going a few feet more just for good measure. The trees were thin, this close to the year-round chill of ice magic, but the sparse clusters would thicken into a full forest soon enough. They'd need to find the road again to get the sled down safely.

Toketie shifted, landing on her feet in front of Rosy. She kneeled down and squeezed Rosy around the neck. Rosy licked her cheek, and a layer of frost came off.

"We made it," Toketie said, a touch too close and too loud for Rosy's sensitive wolf hearing. Rosy didn't care. She wagged her tail. Toketie laughed and said again, "Rosy, we made it."

ROSY AND TOKETIE FOUND AN inn just outside of Gravestown that didn't ask too many questions as they dragged Aklemin up to their room. The ice witch had stayed unconscious through the entire escape down the Mountain and hadn't stirred even after being physically dragged up two flights of stairs. Rosy supposed if their father's attempted murder hadn't pushed them from the vision, nothing would.

The familiars slept until well past noon. Aklemin still hadn't woken by the time they were ready to leave, so the cousins put them back on the sled and Rosy pulled it down the road all the way to Woodside. There was just enough snow on the ground to keep the sled from getting stuck in the mud, but not enough to stop regular horse-pulled carts from joining them on the road. They received more than a few strange looks from the other travelers. It wasn't every day you saw a bone wolf pulling a dog sled. Toketie had been smart enough to cover Aklemin completely with a blanket so at least no one would question the person sleeping in the cart.

It was late afternoon by the time they arrived in Woodside. Toketie's parents were staying with Uncle Chetwoot's sister, Itswoot. Aunt Itsy, Toketie called her. Rosy had only met her a few times before, but Aunt Itsy was all smiles when she opened her door just as Rosy pulled the sled up.

"Girls! Tokey, my darling. And dear Rosy, how fierce you look, I love it." Itsy hugged Toketie, kissing both cheeks, then did the same to Rosy's wolf. "Now, come. Let's get this sled stored, and we can have some tea. I just put the kettle on."

Ice witches always knew when guests were to arrive at their home, and Itsy was an ice witch, though not a strong one. She'd never been invited to, nor could she have afforded, Witch Hall. She made only a meager living telling fortunes for the hunters and farmers of Woodside. Her house had a single bedroom, but she insisted on helping them carry Aklemin to her bed to rest.

"I knew you'd be bringing another, but I had no idea about this," Aunt Itsy said, tucking Aklemin into her blankets. "A Candlemas vision, you say?"

Toketie nodded.

Aunt Itsy sighed. "We'll let the poor dear sleep and hope they wake in time for the wedding tomorrow. Now, the tea's about ready. And your parents will be here any second."

Aunt Itsy was right, of course. Just as the kettle whistled, Toketie's parents walked through the door. They weren't alone though. Rosy's parents were a step behind.

"Mama, Papa!" Rosy cried. She brushed past Toketie, who was greeting her own parents, and went to hug her parents tight.

They took the rest of the afternoon to catch up. Rosy didn't worry her family with any tales of the Vinland war or the trial, but she did explain how Aklemin had stolen the Candlemas vision from the Witch King and Shaw had asked them to get the ice witch away from the Mountain.

"Aklemin Alki?" Uncle Inge asked with a significant look to Toketie.

Toketie blushed, and Rosy remembered how the family had

teased her about her crush half a year ago. Before Rosy had gone to Witch Hall. Before Shaw and her entourage had invaded Rosy's life. Before the Market Day fire that had changed everything.

The conversation didn't go much further than that because Solemie arrived to join them for dinner and Toketie was able to redirect all the teasing to the soon-to-be groom.

It was snowing when they all woke up the next day to get ready for the wedding, as if the Mountain had tried to follow them after all. Aklemin was still unconscious, and Rosy was starting to get worried about it.

She wasn't the only one. Toketie hovered at Aklemin's bedside.

Aunt Itsy came to join them, still in the process of fixing her hair. "Don't you two fret. I always know when someone's coming to my house, even when I'm not home. I'll keep this witch of yours safe while they're in my charge."

"Thank you, Aunt Itsy," Toketie said, and the relief in her voice was enough for Rosy to trust that she could, for the first time in weeks, let herself relax.

Aunt Itsy smiled and patted Toketie's cheek. "Come now, it's your brother's big day."

Rosy forced some more water down Aklemin's throat and left them in Aunt Itsy's bed.

Solemie's bride, Sapolill, was undeniably beautiful. Her long dark hair was pinned up in an elaborate twist, the ends falling down her temples like miniature waterfalls. She was taller than Solemie by a good few inches, and he grinned besottedly up at her like she was the only thing he could see. Rosy felt her chest squeeze at the sight. Amid all the chaos and danger and uncertainty, it was nice to see her family like this. To see her cousin carving out his happiness, no matter everything standing in the way of it.

After the ceremony was a small feast. Compared to Witch Hall's feasts, it could barely be called that. But it was winter and Rosy had been raised on simpler fare. Half a year of luxury was not enough to spoil her. Then there was dancing and drinking and partying until well into the night.

By the time Rosy and Toketie stumbled back to Aunt Itsy's house to collapse into their bedrolls in the living room, Rosy felt nearly as worn out as she'd been on her venture into Vinland with Shaw. Maybe it was the fact that she and Toketie had fled down the Mountain only yesterday, but she fell into sleep the second her head touched the bedroll.

The next morning, Rosy's family joined Solemie's new one for breakfast. Rosy ended up sitting next to Solemie's wife while Sapolill's parents sat across from Uncle Inge and Uncle Chetwoot to trade funny stories from their kids' childhoods. Sapolill's two younger sisters, apparently a pair of troublemakers, protested loudly at the embarrassment. At the other end of the table, Rosy's parents sat with Aunt Itsy, talking in low tones. Meanwhile, Toketie and Solemie were having some half-legible sibling conversation across the table from Rosy and Sapolill.

"Rosamund, right?" Sapolill asked, bright and cheery despite how late she must have been up.

"You can call me Rosy."

"Then call me Lilly."

Lilly looked different outside the wedding dress. She wore a crafter's tunic and a leather half apron. Rosy asked about it, and Lilly slyly replied that she never went anywhere without her tools.

"The wedding was the only exception," she added with a laugh.

"So you make shoes too?" Rosy asked. She knew Lilly's family were shoemakers and that Solemie would be taking over their bookkeeping now that he'd become a Klahn instead of a Holt.

"Sure do. And some other things. I like working with leather. Trying to convince my folks that we could expand our wares a bit. Maybe get a wider customer base, you know?"

Rosy's hand migrated into her skirts, to her left pocket. She'd moved the moonstone bones from her bag to her pocket that morning, intent on presenting them. Shaw had said they were for Rosy's family, but Lilly was part of that family now. Rosy had to see it that way or she'd be admitting that Solemie wasn't anymore, and she refused to accept that. Her heart was big enough to bring Lilly and Lilly's family in—her many voices had proven that.

Rosy stood and cleared her throat to get everyone's attention. Mama and Papa, Uncle Inge and Uncle Chetwoot, Toketie and Solemie, Aunt Itsy and Lilly, all three of Lilly's parents, and her little sisters stopped their conversations to look at her. Rosy swallowed down any embarrassment. She hadn't been one of the ones making a speech at the wedding, but this wouldn't have been appropriate to do in such a public setting anyway.

"We all know that, four months ago, the land that the former Witch Queen granted to the Holt family was repossessed by Jarl Snass," Rosy began.

"Rosy, what are you—" Mama began.

Rosy silently apologized for interrupting her mother but pushed on louder. "Our family was given that land for service in the last war. Toketie and I have promised to fight in the conflict brewing with Vinland and everything associated with it."

Toketie gave Rosy a knowing glance for how she'd danced around what the actual conflict they were fighting was. Whether they ended up facing down Prince Vetle at Shaw's side or facing down the Witch King's own entourage, it didn't matter right now.

"Princess Shaw Colchuck gifted me something to give to my family as an apology for how ill-treated the Holt family has been since Pops's death." Rosy turned to Lilly's parents. "Even though we lost everything, you still agreed to honor the marriage between my cousin and your daughter. You agreed to welcome Solemie into your own family. In my eyes, that makes you my family too."

Rosy pulled out the moonstone bones. Aunt Itsy and Lilly's second father both gasped aloud. Rosy had done a quick count of the bones before putting them into her pocket, and so she knew she had enough when she walked around the table and handed each individual moonstone out. One for Lilly's parents, and then another one for them to hold on to for Lilly's little sisters.

Toketie got one. Solemie got another. Uncle Inge and Uncle Chetwoot got one. Her parents got the largest moonstone bone—the one that had been the centerpiece of the courtship necklace. Aunt Itsy, who'd been so kind in opening her one-bedroom home not just to Rosy and Toketie and Aklemin but also to Toketie's parents for months while they'd renegotiated the marriage contract, got her own.

Even though she'd given one to Solemie, Rosy gave Lilly one too, "As a wedding present," she said when Lilly tried to protest.

It left just two more bones, which Rosy palmed in her hands. She looked at Lilly. "You said you want to branch out into other types of leatherworking, right? Have you ever tried making necklaces?"

Lilly's whole face, which had slackened in shock at the gift, brightened. "I certainly have! I can show you my design sketches . . . that is, if you want?"

"Yes, please," Rosy said. She held up the final two bones. "I'd like to turn these two into bonding necklaces."

"Bonding?" Lilly oohed. "That's like a wedding for you familiars and witches, isn't it?"

Witches and familiars could get married the regular way too, but Rosy didn't care to explain. A witch-familiar bond was given the same protections marriage had in the kingdom's laws. "Yes. It's traditional for the necklaces to complement each other, and, well, anyway, I'd like to turn these into the centerpieces of two necklaces. If you think you'd have time the next couple days?" She grimaced, realizing that was a lot to ask of a woman who'd just gotten married. "If you don't, you can mail them to me at school!" she quickly amended.

"Oh, no, you've more than paid for my time," Lilly said, putting her own moonstone bone in her leather half apron. "So, who's the lucky witch?"

Rosy felt her face heat. "It's not for— I mean, it is— But not for me!"

Solemie snorted, a look of abject disbelief on his face. "At least give us a couple months before you upstage our wedding with your own, Rosy," he teased.

Rosy looked from one cousin to the other. Toketie had both eyebrows raised high. Unlike the rest of their family, Toketie knew exactly what those moonstone bones had represented, but she did Rosy the favor of staying silent.

Several hours later, after Rosy was able to escape her family's interrogation by going over Lilly's sketches and choosing two complementary designs she thought Shaw would like, Toketie managed to corner Rosy alone.

"What are you doing, Rosy?"

"Shaw needs to find a familiar, Tokey," Rosy murmured. "But

she refused to remake the courtship necklace, and I thought, well, I could give her these new ones."

Toketie crossed her arms. She didn't look happy at all, though Rosy wasn't quite sure why her cousin would be so upset.

"Look," Rosy said quickly. "I told Shaw I couldn't bond with her. I mean, she's about to be crowned queen! Imagine me on that other throne? You know me, Tokey, you know how bad an idea that would be. I'll help fight, of course, until Shaw can make peace official. Shaw's promised to give us land, after. But she needs to find a familiar to rule with her. She shouldn't have to do it alone."

Toketie huffed. "You're so oblivious sometimes, you know that?"

"I mean, I know it won't be that simple. I know we could die, or Shaw could, especially with the jarls not believing peace is even possible." Rosy was still bitter about that, but then, she'd never thought well of the jarls' council for what they'd done to her gran. "But I trust Shaw. She gave me the moonstone to help our family rebuild, didn't she?" Rosy paused. "Are you upset I gave some to the Klahns? I saw the house they're living in. Lilly and Solemie don't even have their own bedroom!"

"No, Rosy. I think it was sweet of you, doing that. Moonstone's worth a small fortune, if we find the right buyer." Toketie sighed heavily. "Just, before you give those necklaces back to Shaw, I need you to really think through how it'll feel to see some other familiar wearing one. That's all."

Rosy turned away. She knew how it would feel, and she didn't like being reminded of it. Her feelings weren't the thing at question here. She'd understood the trap she'd fallen into, watching Solemie and Lilly's wedding. She'd been able to imagine what it might look like if she were up there instead of her cousin. If there was a different dark-haired girl standing across from her.

Rosy hadn't planned to admit to herself that she wanted Shaw. That she'd wanted Shaw for nearly half a year now. But wanting someone wasn't, couldn't be, the only reason to marry them. From what she'd heard, a bond wouldn't even take if there was any sort of doubt in a witch or familiar's heart, and Rosy felt like she was drowning in it. Shaw deserved better. She deserved to be able to move on, to find a familiar who could give her their all. Rosy felt too much responsibility toward her family to be able to give Shaw anything more than she'd already given. There was no room left to feel any sort of responsibility for the Familiar Throne and the kingdom it came with after that.

Chapter 21

SHAW

MESACHIE. THE WICKED ONE. THE FIRST RULER OF THE Cursed Kingdom. The ice witch who'd cursed this land. My ancestor.

"Sit. Relax. The Mountain will not let them find you here," Mesachie said. "I have been sleeping for quite some time, I think, before the Mountain nudged me awake. Will you tell me what has happened to our people in recent years?"

"If you wish, Grandmother," I said dutifully. My mind was still reeling. Mesachie was right—I did need to drink water and eat something before I collapsed where I stood. I checked on Cow, who seemed content to catch some sleep in the shelter of the cave, then walked numbly back to where I'd dropped the travel bag and grabbed the first edible thing I could find. In between bites, I asked, "Will you tell me who was ruling when you last were awake?"

The monarch she named was my five times great-grandparent. Sleeping for a long time indeed. I'd theoretically known it was possible for ghosts to go dormant for long periods of time. It was one of the only ways the eldest ghosts stuck around without devolving into spirits. But still, it had been over six hundred years since Mesachie had died.

"You're not an ice witch or familiar," Mesachie observed.

"I'm a bone witch," I confirmed. I explained how the second grandson of the last ruler Mesachie had known had been born without any magic at all. He'd fallen in love with and married a bone familiar. No one had fussed about it, since he hadn't been in line for the throne, but then his elder brother had died without heirs. By the laws of the Cursed Kingdom, he couldn't be crowned without magic, but his wife had taken the Familiar Throne as regent for their children. Since then, bone and ice magic had both cropped up in the Colchuck line.

Mesachie pressed for more, and so, sitting in that cave-that-was-not-a-cave, on a volcano-that-was-no-longer-a-volcano, I told my grandmother-who-was-much-older-than-my-grandmother the story of her descendants. Talking through recent history with Mesachie was strangely liberating. It felt oddly like my ancestor had stepped forward to help lift a heavy weight from my shoulders. Disavowing my father meant disavowing the only family I had left, but Mesachie didn't blame me for the actions I'd taken. If anything, she commended them.

"You are my legacy, Shaw Colchuck. Not your father," she said once I'd finished my story, ending with the events that led to my flight down the Mountain. "I am proud of you for doing what needed to be done to see justice for our people and our neighbors."

I sucked in a deep breath, and it rattled in my chest. "Will you tell me your story, Grandmother?" I asked, a touch hesitant. Like I was five again and begging my great-uncle to tell me his tale of love and loss one more time.

"My story? It's not exciting. Not until the end. Ah, but perhaps that's the part you're asking for. Very well, but only for you, grandchild." Mesachie crossed her legs and settled down until she floated only about an inch off the ground in front of me. "Why don't you tell me what you think you know about my story?"

So I told her the story I'd given Rosamund, just as my tutors had once taught it to me. How Mesachie had likely been an ice witch, back when the magic of this land was wilder. How she'd had a vision, perhaps of the volcano erupting, and how she'd cursed the land to save what would become the Cursed Kingdom from its destruction. That curse had caused the Frozen Mountain, the Bone Forest, the Obsidian Desert, and Lake Bloom to manifest—and with them the ability for magic to stabilize so that more witches and familiars could awaken across the kingdom.

Mesachie nodded throughout my recollection of her history. "I'm impressed. History has not been completely lost, it seems, though altered, as it is wont to do."

"What was altered?" I didn't let her answer though, as a thought hit me with startling speed. "Can you tell me about what my father did in Vinland? How he cursed the Ghost Town and the Frozen Falls? If there's a way to reverse it—"

"There's no way to reverse a curse so entrenched in the land. I watched several of my grandchildren attempt it to no success. I couldn't even begin to fathom how you would go about it. Where would the magic go? Magical wells like the Mountain here act as a sinkhole for its magical type. Say you did find a way to destroy the well—all the magic it was containing would explode out, and who knows what that would do?"

My ancestor was right. Hadn't I thought the same thing when I'd seen the curse in Vinland? Once the process started, it was irreversible.

"I can't say for certain how your father or his soldiers created those wells," Mesachie continued. "But I can tell you how mine began, and perhaps that will tell you something. The truth is, I didn't intend them. The wells were merely a consequence of what my actual goal was."

"Your actual goal?" I pressed when Mesachie grew silent, looking off at the snow flurrying beyond the overhang the boulders had created. Despite the heavy wind, the snow wasn't swirling into the makeshift shelter, and I knew I had the Mountain to thank for that.

"To save my people, of course. Ah, but my people then are not our people now. We were just a single village." Mesachie waved a translucent hand in the air. "I was never much of a storyteller. Mountain, give me some aid, if you please?"

A swirl of wind careened into the shelter and made a spiral of snow in the air next to Mesachie.

"As you inferred, a volcanic eruption was imminent. I had visions of it. Of a massive landslide of smoke and ash coming for my village. We would have barely had warning before the landslide hit us. I don't think we would have even noticed dying, it would have happened so quickly. I tried all I could to warn my people. To get them to leave. The ground was shaking every day, and I knew we wouldn't have long. But my father refused. The snows were just beginning, and he knew that, if we left, we wouldn't make it back up to the village before winter was truly upon us. No matter my warning that there would be no village to come back to."

I'd seen illustrations of volcanic eruptions. About fifty years ago, while the Cursed Kingdom was busy fending off another wave of Crusades by the Colonies, one of the mountains farther north in Vinland had erupted so viciously, the entire cap of the mountain had vaporized. The Crusaders had blamed witches when the sky turned dark for days and ash rained down on the battlefield. It hadn't been our doing, but it had given my grandmother enough of an advantage to defeat that wave.

"I could have taken my son and fled, but the night before the eruption, I had a dream. A vision, I know now. I dreamed of magical ice coating the side of the mountain and saving my people. When I woke, I sent my son off to my father and traveled by foot as high as I could go. It took me many hours, but I barely felt them. I hadn't even told my son goodbye. I was haunted by my vision. I could think of nothing but that ice."

As Mesachie spoke, the snow drew pictures in the air. The outline of a woman—of Mesachie—climbing a steep slope. I could almost imagine I was there with her, aching and desperate and ready to do anything.

"I made it to the glacier," Mesachie murmured. "It wasn't so grand then. Now it's grown nearly to the top of the village, but it was far less in my time. It was only after I kneeled at the end of it that I realized I needed to sacrifice myself. I hadn't planned on it. I hadn't even brought a knife with me. It was . . . difficult. It was so difficult. To this day, I wish there had been another way."

Ghosts couldn't cry, but I felt myself wanting to cry for her. A deep blue began to flicker in the center of Mesachie's chest. Her sadness. I barely had to think before I was brushing it away so that Mesachie could continue her story without risk of turning into a spirit.

"I became like this once I was dead. The first thing I saw was the glacier spreading. The ice expanded rapidly, freezing the fresh snow as it went. It grew down the side of the Mountain—for it was the Mountain then. Oh, but, grandchild, I did not stop the volcano. I'm not sure I could have. The ice merely made it so our side of the Mountain was less vulnerable. When the eruption happened, it went south."

I stiffened. None of my tutors or history books had mentioned anything of the sort. As far as the Cursed Kingdom was aware, Mesachie's curse had halted the eruption entirely. I considered Mesachie's words. "Did you know it would?" I asked. "We weren't a kingdom then, and your priority was to your village. Do you know how many died in the eruption on the other side of the Mountain? Did you know how many you'd be sacrificing?"

"Oh, hundreds," Mesachie said. Despite her flippant tone, the blue of sadness was back in her chest. I soothed it away again. "There was a village there, at the southeastern base. They were farther away than my village. Just far enough to see their doom coming but too close to flee. So many died. The people, the animals, and the land. All that was left of the pines were skeletons of their former selves. I don't think I was surprised at all, the first time I saw them move."

"The Bone Forest," I murmured, watching the snow draw the picture of the eruption. Of villagers caught in its blast. Of the remains of pines left in its wake, skeletal forms remarkably familiar to me.

"Just so," Mesachie agreed. "Intentionally or not, it was by my hand that the Mountain and the Forest came to be. The others sparked, it seemed, only by proximity and circumstance. There was an enormous deposit of obsidian in the east, on the edge of the high desert. The village there would sell us tools whenever we needed. But the final quake, the one that immediately preceded the eruption, it shook the ground just so. The obsidian cracked and crumbled. Not into sand, not yet, but it was the start. The magic taught it how to fragment itself into smaller and smaller pieces."

I saw the pattern as the snow showed me the image of great boulders of obsidian slowly crumbling into sand. "How did Lake Bloom form, then?"

"There used to be a hot spring there. There was a large port village on Wimahl River just south of it. I hear it's grown even larger since. Their chief claimed the hot springs had healing properties. Visitors would come from all around to soak in it. I learned later that when the Mountain erupted, the hot springs collapsed in on itself. A massive sinkhole formed in the ground. Over time, it filled back up with water and became the Lake you know now."

Mesachie waved an incorporeal hand through the snow showing me a vision of Lake Bloom slowly filling. "I did not set out to curse the land, only to save my people. The land, it seems to me, cursed itself."

I ached, though whether it was physical or emotional, I couldn't tell. "You succeeded in your goal. Your people survived."

"They did," Mesachie agreed. "And grew. My son was not content with the solitary life my father led. He united all the people affected by my curse. He promised them strength in unity. It is not my legacy, Shaw Colchuck, that you carry. It is my son's. He made this kingdom. He named it. He promised to protect it. Can you hold to that duty, no matter how difficult the road may get?"

The snow had stopped showing me pictures, but I saw again that image of Mesachie at the foot of the glacier. I felt a new burden settle upon me. A mantle that I would wear for the rest of my life. It was heavy, but I was determined to carry it proudly. Determined to live up to my ancestor's trust. I put my right fist to my heart in the traditional salute of the Cursed Kingdom. "I will, Grandmother. I promise you."

THERE WERE ONLY A HANDFUL of students on campus when I arrived at Witch Hall—half my entourage among them. Oluk was in the stable helping Mister Jostein muck the stalls, and he stepped up immediately to help me take care of Cow.

"Where's Rosy? And Aklemin and Toketie?" Oluk asked, obviously worried that I was alone.

"They're fine," I said. I was surprised to find I believed it. I had no way of knowing that Rosamund and Toketie had escaped with Aklemin safely, but even without Aklemin's words, I trusted them. "I'll tell everyone together. Can you get Yuyan? I'll meet you in the infirmary."

"It's nearly dinnertime," Oluk pointed out. "We can use the table."

"But Einar—"

Oluk grinned then, bright enough that I stopped talking. Hope filled me.

"Is he—"

"You'll see," Oluk said, a touch sly. "At dinner."

Oluk helped me carry my things to my suite and walked with me to dinner after, a small bounce in his step. Had Einar finally been able to get out of that accursed infirmary bed? It felt unwise to hope, and yet I couldn't help but imagine it.

The only thing I could see when I entered the dining hall was Einar sitting at our usual table. My knees felt weak with relief. Only after I'd blinked away tears did I notice something odd about where he was sitting. Instead of being perched on the far-left corner of his usual bench, he was seated at the head of the table. But there was no seat there, normally. Why had they brought one up to the table? Was it for back support, to help his recovery?

Oluk sat in Einar's usual spot, putting him catty-corner to where Einar was now. Yuyan had slid down toward the middle of the bench, and on her right sat another witch I hadn't expected to see again. Shantie. She'd returned.

"Shaw," Yuyan said in greeting, pulling me into a hug. "Welcome back."

"Glad to be back," I said honestly.

Shantie hugged me too, and I hugged back instinctively, despite being startled at the gesture. I'd rarely considered any of my classmates friends outside my entourage, but in the past six months, I'd found myself opening up to the thought of it more and more. Besides, it was obvious now that Shantie had been able to help Einar recover enough that he could finally be free of his prison. I would forever be grateful for that.

Years ago, Yuyan had tried to convince me to accept Shantie into my entourage instead of her. She'd started by explaining how she didn't want to bond with a flower familiar, and when I'd insisted that I was okay with that, she'd changed tactics.

Shantie, Yuyan had said, *is a genius. A flower witch may innovate upon one or two potions in their life, if they're good at brewing. But Shantie's an inventor. None of us understand how she does it, but her experiments are their own type of magic. She'll invent the cure to half the ailments in the kingdom before she retires, I promise you.*

I let my relief show as I disengaged from Shantie's hug and turned to Einar.

"Shaw," he said, a touch softer than a true greeting would be. Almost hesitant. It was so unlike Einar that I paused, burgeoning hope already withering.

Oluk stood and grabbed the back of Einar's chair. He pulled it out, seemingly without any effort. Einar did not stand once he was free from the lip of the table. Oluk continued to push the chair around the side toward me.

"What—" I couldn't finish my question. I'd never seen anything like it.

What Einar sat in was a chair, yes, but it was also a small cart. Two large wheels were bolted to either side of the front and one smaller wheel protruded from the back. There was a small platform lifted just off the ground where his feet rested and the back of the chair was sloped slightly backward to keep him from tipping to the front.

"There was no way to save my legs," Einar explained as I took in the sight. "But Shantie helped Yuyan come up with a way to stop it from hurting so much."

"You do look better," I said, because it was true. He'd gained back most of the weight he'd lost. There was a vibrancy to his skin again and a brightness to his eyes. "What is it?"

"It's called a wheelchair," Shantie answered. "I'd seen mention of them in a few medical textbooks. They aren't as common this side of the continent, but they're used in the Colonies and the southern nations for transporting patients about their hospitals. Once I brought it up, Yuyan found a journal from an old clockmaker who'd lost both his legs and used a wheelchair with a crank to move himself around."

"Let me show you," Einar said.

Oluk let go of the back of the chair. I noticed then the two small cranks on each of the large wheels. Einar grabbed one in each hand and began cranking the wheels. The chair rolled across the floor remarkably quickly. Einar was even able to turn by cranking one wheel faster than the other.

"I'm still getting used to it," he said. "Yuyan keeps having to soothe my arms."

"Because you've been pushing yourself," Oluk scolded. "It'll be more natural over time."

I nodded. "It's brilliant. Shantie, Yuyan, this is amazing."

The flower witches exchanged a look I couldn't decipher.

"So you're not upset?" Yuyan asked.

I shook my head. Upset? I would probably always be upset that Einar was injured, but they'd obviously made the best of the situation. Compared to those months Einar was stuck in the infirmary bed, this truly was remarkable.

"I've been thinking of ways to improve the chair," Einar said. "Ways to enchant it so it can traverse unsteady ground more easily. Maybe a rune to help supplement my cranking, so it's not as difficult to get to speed quickly if I need to. I know I won't ever be able to fight like I used to, but now that the pain's manageable and I can get myself to classes, I can at least do my duties as your glass witch. I can still be useful to you, Shaw."

Ah. I understood everyone's hesitation, then. Taking a seat on the bench nearest to Einar's chair, I leaned forward so that he would focus entirely on me. "You don't need to be useful to be on my entourage. You don't need to be useful to be my friend. It was hard seeing you in that bed because you hated being there. And because it was difficult seeing you in so much pain. But I will always want you at my side, Einar, even if you're never able to enchant another rune, for as long as you want to be there."

Einar's hands shook as he wiped at his eyes. "Forever," he said. "I already promised, didn't I? You will always have my loyalty."

I thought then of Aklemin's words. *Einar never betrays you, even when he should.*

"For as long as you want to be there," I insisted. I turned back to Oluk and Yuyan and Shantie. Dropping my voice, I said, "I have to tell you all the truth about the war, and my place in it."

Everyone gathered back around the table. Einar activated the runes to prevent eavesdropping. Once he had, I explained everything to them. About Aklemin, the Candlemas vision, the council meeting, the trial, my pursuers, and Mesachie.

"I wonder if the Witch King sacrificed an ice witch to spark those Frozen Falls you found," Yuyan mused.

"He may have just figured out how to teach the lands to curse themselves, like Queen Mesachie said the Desert and the Lake did," Shantie said.

"Is that the most important thing to focus on?" I asked. My shoulders ached with tension. I hadn't had the chance to tell Rosamund and Toketie about Aklemin's words yet. The four sitting at this table were the first to learn about the truth of what I was capable of.

"I assume you wish to hear Aklemin's vision before we determine how to deal with the council and offer reparations to the Vinlanders," Einar said.

"Yes, but—" I didn't know how to continue. I breathed in and out. And then again. They waited for me. Oluk showed the most obvious concern, though Yuyan's forehead was crinkled and Einar's eyebrows furrowed. Even Shantie looked worried on my behalf.

"What kind of person is capable of conquering a continent?" I whispered finally. "What kind of monster would lead an army of twenty thousand undead warriors against nations that have never even thought to attack us? Vinland and the Colonies, perhaps I could justify that, but the rest? Aklemin said I would have even taken the Waiming Territories, if not for your help in annexing them. But Waiming is our ally!"

Shantie looked stunned. Maybe I should have waited to talk with Einar and Yuyan and Oluk when she wasn't around. This wasn't her burden to bear. Perhaps it wasn't even my entourage's. It was unfair of me to place the weight of that future on them when they'd done nothing but support me.

Maybe that's why I was. Aklemin had said there would come a point when they felt it necessary to betray me. Why hadn't Einar or Yuyan? I trusted them to advise me—how could I do that if I knew they would support even the worst of my decisions?

"You're not that person, Shaw." Shockingly, it was Oluk who spoke up. "Maybe you could have been, but you haven't been that person in a long time."

"You don't know that."

"I do," Oluk argued, fierce and undeterred. I'd never heard him sound angry before, but he was then. "Six months ago, you barely knew that I existed. You didn't care about any of your classmates, except as potential players on your game board. Pieces of entertainment to amuse you when you were bored."

"He's right," Yuyan said. "You claimed to trust us, but you never truly confided in us. Not until more recently."

Until Rosamund came to school and opened my eyes. I'd known the course of my future and never deviated from it. I'd believed people entirely predictable and treated them as such. But could the me of six months prior have predicted Charles's and Froya's and Kwaddis's support at the trial? What about Chao's? What had I truly known about Oluk, before he'd begun sitting at our table? I certainly hadn't expected that Shantie's first act upon returning to school would be to help Einar.

"I have always seen the good in you," Einar said then. "I think there must have been some of it, even in that future you fear, but it's so much easier to see now. You have grown into a softer ruler than you might have, Shaw, and I believe it's for the better."

Something dripped off my chin. I was crying. I blinked rapidly, dispelling the tears from my eyes.

"I don't think the Shaw I knew last year would have come to visit me in Multah, just to give me Guanyu's final message," Shantie said. "Maybe Rosy instigated that change, but you were the one who had to go through with it. That's what separates good rulers from tyrants—the willingness to change."

"Even if Aklemin comes back and tells us there's no way to stop this war after all, we won't let you go down that path, Shaw," Yuyan said. "Not anymore."

"We have all changed as well, and we are stronger for it," Einar agreed, looking at his familiar with the same besotted expression I once saw on General Holt's face as he'd looked at Ylva the Red Wolf. Oluk leaned over to bury his face in Einar's shoulder, though not quick enough to hide his pleased smile.

I patted my face dry, glad more than ever for Einar's runes. Even though most of school was still on break, there were enough students in the dining hall who'd be shocked to see their princess openly crying. Straightening up, I turned to Yuyan and Shantie, leaving the glass witch and familiar to their romantic moment.

"Tell me what Madam Kawak said of your return," I told Shantie. "Do I need to talk with her?"

Shantie shook her head. "I passed all my classes in the fall term since I was given an exemption for my finals, so even counting the winter term classes as failed, I'm on track to graduate if I pass everything this spring term."

"Good." I resolved to talk with Madam Kawak regardless, just to make sure Shantie wouldn't be punished for her grief.

Besides, there were some other changes that needed implementing before the start of the spring term.

Chapter 22

Rosamund and Toketie arrived in the dog sled three days before the start of term. They weren't the only students to arrive that day, which meant I heard the rumors before I even saw them.

Aklemin was still in a vision coma.

It had been a week since Candlemas. There was no record of a vision ever having gone on so long. As I stared down at Aklemin's body, now resting on one of the infirmary beds, I couldn't help but linger over the fresh gauntness of their face. Toketie was half in tears as she explained to me and the rest of the entourage how she and Rosamund had taken to forcing bone broth down their throat to keep them alive.

I wanted to rage at the unfairness of it all. We'd just gotten one member of the entourage out of this bed, and now Aklemin was taking his place.

Aklemin still had not woken by the time classes began for my final term of Witch Hall.

My first class of the day was Practice in Applicable Bone Magic, a course that had typically been taught by Madam Dyer. I'd been surprised to see it on my schedule, as Madam Kawak had yet to hire a bone witch instructor qualified to teach it. Somewhat more surprisingly, the classroom was listed as the library.

I walked with Rosamund, just slightly ahead of the rest of the senior bone witches and familiars. We reached the library as a group and headed inside. There were no traditional desks. Instead, there were a dozen or so low tables with pillows scattered around them. Mister Voll was ushering out a couple young students as we arrived.

"I know it's your free period, but I'm afraid I have to teach a class," Mister Voll was telling them. "Head to the teachers' cottages. They're expecting you. You'll have to study in the common areas there during your free period this term. You may also come back here to the library after dinner. I'll keep it open longer than I did last term, to give you time."

Mister Voll never usually taught. The library was meant to be open to students during the day, and Mister Voll's entire role was to help with homework and research. But I supposed the bone familiar was the only choice to teach this course now that Madam Dyer was dead. Though there were other bone witch and bone familiar instructors, they all taught the younger students. Mister Voll wasn't a powerful bone familiar, but as school librarian, he was at least aware of the subject matter intended for the upper-level courses.

Once we were all settled in on cushions around the low library tables, Mister Voll explained that the course would run as a kind of self-study—allowing small groups of three to choose a topic, work on it over the term, and present their findings to the class at midterms and finals.

I looked to Rosamund. A year ago, I would have partnered with Chao and Jingyi. Now I left it to Rosamund to choose our third member. Rosamund was scanning the other bone familiars, a deep look of concentration on her face.

Finally she called out, "Emma? Want to join us?"

Emma appeared startled, but she nodded quickly and gathered her stuff to come sit next to Rosamund, across the small table from me. Charles looked over at us, eyebrows raised, before joining Goran and Illahie, the two courting bone familiars. Chao and Jingyi took Kalitan as their group mate. From there, the rest of the senior bone witches and familiars sorted themselves out.

I spent half the class trying to figure out why Rosy had chosen Emma as our partner, only to give up. Even when I'd thought most people were predictable, I'd always struggled to understand Rosamund Holt.

Our second class was the Senior Seminar, something every graduating senior had to take to learn about finding jobs, negotiating contracts, and using magic as a profession. Mister Sorenson was the teacher for it this year, which both Rosamund and Oluk seemed disgruntled by. I paid attention to Mister Sorenson's lecture only because I always paid attention in class, not because I expected anything he said would be relevant to me personally. I would be crowned upon graduation and what happened after that was between the jarls' council and me.

Then Mister Sorenson began to talk about contracts, and I realized how wrong that expectation was.

"Now, I know that most of you"—Mister Sorenson paused to glance at Rosamund before continuing—"have already contracted with the army. I helped the headmistress negotiate on your behalf for the preliminary contract you all signed. It includes a clause that allows you to renegotiate upon successful graduation from Witch

Hall. For our first week of term, we will discuss what you can expect from such negotiations."

Mister Sorenson had copies of the basic contract we'd all signed, which he passed out. I stared down at it. With everything going on, I hadn't thought much about the contract. But if Aklemin woke to tell me that I had to go to war after all, I would do as my father had suggested—I would keep my classmates safe from the bloodshed to come. How could I do that if they were tied into a yearslong service to the army?

No. I'd been the one to convince the other students to sign this contract in the first place. I would not allow that one choice to harm them. Not if there was something I could do to stop it.

I went over the contract and my argument against it with my entourage while I ate a quick lunch. Toketie was the only one missing, as it was her turn to sit with Aklemin. We weren't taking any chances on their safety. Yuyan had badgered Madam Tukwilla for permission to sleep in the other infirmary bed. Meanwhile, the rest of us developed a rotation to ask to use the restroom every fifteen minutes during our classes so we could go check on them.

"We'll take care of your tray," Yuyan said as I stood with the army contract clutched tightly in hand.

"I think this should work," Oluk said. He turned to his witch. "Right?"

Einar nodded firmly in agreement.

"If it does works, get me added," Rosamund said.

I paused halfway off the bench. "Are you sure?"

Rosamund's eyes glinted in the light of the dining room's large windows. "Yes," she said, stubborn to a fault. "I'm sure, Shaw."

My heart stuttered. I couldn't deny that I wanted her at my side.

If there was to be a war, she would be invaluable. Except, my desire to have her close was entirely selfish. I trusted her with everything, even my own heart. No matter that I knew she would shatter it again as soon as it pleased her.

I glanced at Yuyan to see her frowning between the two of us. I knew her concern. For all my worry and distraction over the now-uncertain course of my destiny, I had been thinking more about my relationship with Rosamund. The journey back to Witch Hall alone, along with the absence of the moonstone bones in my pocket, had given me the space to really contemplate it.

I waited until Yuyan saw me looking at her, then nodded once. Yuyan looked away. I figured she'd corner me later to ask—something she never would have done a year ago. I wasn't sure how well I was adjusting to my entourage's new propensity to demand answers of me, but in light of all that I'd learned, I'd rather they be overzealous than complacent.

I walked over to the teachers' table at the other end of the dining hall and waited until Madam Kawak had paused her conversation with Mister Xu to acknowledge me.

"Are you here to ask about the progress of your demands?" the headmistress said. "The Royal Company moved their encampment to Goose Point. Thanes Beck and Huang will travel each day to Witch Hall to continue the afternoon Army Training, as the contract states, but they have agreed to bring no other soldiers with them. Thane Olhiyu will stay at the new encampment to lead the company in General Tepeh's absence."

After seeing Thane Olhiyu's disguise in the royal palace, I doubted Madam Kawak's request would truly stop her from sneaking into campus, but at least she couldn't waltz in as she pleased anymore. I knew from our conversation several days ago that Thane

Anders and his platoon had been summoned up the Mountain. Though Madam Kawak hadn't known why, I knew it was likely to face their own trials. Outside of the heirs, no one knew what had happened at the Candlemas council meeting. The heirs had all been sworn to secrecy, and from what I'd been able to discern, no one had broken that oath.

I was glad to leave the political nightmare of Thane Anders's trial to the jarls while I finished my schooling. There could be no denying his involvement, nor that of his platoon, but they had just been following orders. It would be a headache to figure out culpability and the proper response.

Unfortunately, Madam Kawak had insisted that the remaining thanes of the Royal Company would take over Army Training. I'd protested strongly and managed to negotiate her down to only Thanes Beck and Huang. Of course, I'd be shocked if they weren't also aware of my father's plot. They'd been there the day Prince Vetle had attacked us during the marching exercise, after all. Which was why I had to figure out a way to break the contract and protect my classmates from Army Training and everything that came with it.

I handed over the army contract, and Madam Kawak took it with a small frown. "I've circled the relevant section," I said.

Madam Kawak read the section, then put a finger up to stop me from speaking in order to read it over again.

"Gudmund," she called.

Mister Sorenson stood from the other teachers' table and walked over. Madam Kawak handed the contract to him. He took it and read the same circled section.

"What seems to be the problem, Headmistress?" he asked once he'd finished.

"The attack at Goose Point," I said. "Do you agree that it qualifies?"

Mister Sorenson's eyes widened. He quickly read the section again. When he finished, he handed the contract back to Madam Kawak with a tight nod. She traced a few words with one long finger.

"Yes," she said finally. "I do believe it does. You will have to get the jarls to agree, of course."

"They will," I said, because I knew Jarl Tenas, Almstedt, and Falk would happily see their heirs freed of this legal obligation. "I will write to them tonight."

"Very well," Madam Kawak said, giving the contract back to me. "What do you suggest might replace Army Training, Princess?"

"Given the current situation, I do think my classmates and I can benefit from more practice in combat," I said, just as my entourage and I had agreed. "But tell the thanes their services as instructors will no longer be necessary."

Madam Kawak's piercing blue eyes seemed to stare straight through me. "You grow more similar to your grandmother every day," she murmured. For some reason, her words weren't nearly as stifling as all the other times anyone had dared compare me to the former Witch Queen. I felt a strange surge of pride begin to fill me, as if I'd only just then lived up to expectations I hadn't even realized the headmistress had for me.

"Did she ever regret it?" I asked, even before realizing it was a question I needed answered. "My grandmother tried for years to broker peace with the Colonies, despite the many people they'd killed in their first Crusades. Did she ever wish she'd taken the fight to them instead?"

"Yes," Madam Kawak said. "And no. Your grandmother never

regretted trying for peace, but she regretted that peace was so unobtainable that her attempts were vilified by her own people. The jarls' council was especially vicious toward the end. None of us begrudged her though, even when half our entourage died in the attempt. We had over a decade of war, and perhaps we would not have if she'd been set upon destroying our enemy from the start, but perhaps too we could have found peace in the first few years and saved so many. On both sides."

"You have sympathy for the Crusaders?" I asked, shocked by it. I had some sympathy for the Vinlanders, since their anger was caused by my own father's machinations, but the Crusaders' hate was pure bigotry.

"Not as such. They are a people who wish to see everyone conform to their narrow views of the world. They slaughtered the tribes that once lived along the eastern coast, drove them from their ancestral homes. They've built a nation embroiled in hatred. But death is permanent. Your grandmother understood that. The dead cannot ever come to see the errors of their ways. Cannot learn and grow and change. There are good people in the Colonies, just as there are bad people in the Cursed Kingdom. I wonder, sometimes, what would become of that nation if they'd only were given a less-biased education. They are zealots because zealotry is all they were taught, not because it's an inherent part of their being."

I sat with Madam Kawak's words, nearly trembling under the force of them.

The headmistress turned to look at Mister Xu, as if to give me privacy. "Would you and Suzhen be amenable to giving up your free period to teach another course this term if I swear to give you both two free periods in the summer term to compensate?"

Mister Xu had been watching our conversation with interest.

Most of the other teachers had already left the table before I'd arrived to prepare for their afternoon classes, so it was just him and Madam Ipsoot there to pay privy. Given that Madam Ipsoot looked half-asleep in her soup, I wasn't sure she cared about the goings-on at the other end of the table.

"You know we would prefer not to teach our own children if it can be avoided," Mister Xu said, obviously having realized what students he would be taking on.

"You won't be," I told him. "Most of my classmates are of age, so I will give them a choice, but your children and the rest of their year should never have been asked to sign this contract in the first place. I will not allow them to throw their lives away because of my *destiny*." I couldn't help adding a bitter twist to the word, but at least the teachers didn't have the context to understand why.

Mister Xu leaned back in his chair. "Power is a heavy burden," he said. "I have always been impressed with how you've borne it. You must understand, I saw many young rulers turn rotten under that weight in the many domains of my homeland. But you've done your best to surround yourself with noble advisors, and that is the first step toward scraping away rot. It was well done of you, Princess."

"Well done indeed," Mister Sorenson added. "I admit to having my doubts about some you chose to trust, but if this is the result, then I shall lay my doubts to rest."

"The young always manage to surprise me," Madam Kawak said.

"It's the fresh eyes and that unending well of energy," Madam Ipsoot said. She still looked seconds from falling asleep, eyes closed and head resting on her hand, but her words were clear. "They still need tempering, mayhaps, but they aren't lacking for steel."

"Thank you," I said, bowing a little. "I will do my best to live up to your standards, for the betterment of all my people."

"We will do our best to support you. You are still our student, for these last ten weeks," Mister Xu said. "Suzhen and I will teach the class, Headmistress."

I was the last student to leave the dining hall, elation making my steps light. I arrived at the classroom clearing where we'd met for Army Training last term to find everyone already sitting on their typical logs. My entourage was in the front, as usual. Einar was in his wheelchair to the right of the log where Oluk sat, Yuyan and Shantie taking up the rest of that log.

Rosamund had been given a free period for the first half of the afternoon, so she'd gone to sit with Aklemin in the infirmary. A part of me was upset that she wouldn't be here to see me correct my mistakes—but I wasn't doing this because of her. At least, not entirely because of her. I walked up to the front of the clearing and took a second to look over all my classmates. The ones who'd listened and trusted and fought with me. I wondered how many would have died in the future I was determined to see unwritten.

I was doing this because of them.

"The headmistress and I have agreed that the Army contract we all signed was nullified by the gross negligence on the army's part. They were contractually obligated to keep us safe during the course of our training," I began. "The relevant clause is in section E, subsection fifteen. I will be writing to the jarls' council to get official notice of the contract's dissolution."

There were murmurs at that, but they quieted down quickly as my classmates waited to hear what else I had to tell them. I didn't know whether to be amused or not that these hundred or so students were more respectful than the jarls had been at the Candlemas council meeting.

I looked to Mengjiao and Zhihao. The seniors had continued their new trend of sitting in mixed groups, but they hadn't extended that to inviting the younger students on their benches. As a result, they were all clustered on the logs behind Mengjiao and Zhihao.

"Madam Kawak has found new classes to place you into," I told the younger students. "Tomorrow, you will be given fresh schedules for the term."

"What?" Zhihao squeaked.

"Why?" Mengjiao asked.

"None of you should have been asked to sign that contract in the first place. I take full responsibility for the danger you were placed in. It was wrong to ask you to fight when you still have a year until you graduate."

"The Vinlanders won't care if we're still students," Mengjiao said stubbornly. "They didn't care last time."

That wasn't entirely true. The Vinlanders hadn't attacked us immediately because of our age, not until Vetle had determined who I was. But it was true that, once he had, his warriors hadn't cared one bit who was an adult and who was still a student. Vetle certainly hadn't cared when he'd stabbed Einar.

"I care," I said. "I want you to be allowed to finish your education properly. If, upon your graduation, you wish to enlist in the army, that is your choice. But please know it's not one I expect from you. I want you to be prepared for whatever shape your future will form, not just the one you're being forced into."

Zhihao looked like he wanted to argue more, but Mengjiao stopped him with a small bump of shoulders. There was a look in his eyes like he'd heard more than I'd wanted to say. Mengjiao was smart—possibly one of the smartest students in school. Zhihao had more social grace, but it was Mengjiao's cleverness that let them keep hold over their grade even above the students with more political or magical power.

"There may come a time when you will need to fight despite your age," I added, because I didn't know if stopping the war was even possible. "If that happens, I'm happy to know that you'll be capable of it. That you've had this past term to prepare. But until that moment, you can leave the responsibility to the rest of us. I hope that we've proven ourselves enough that you can trust in us to handle it."

Zhihao scowled. "Of course you have. You're going to be our queen. Not just some ruler up on a distant throne. You're *ours*. You'll never stop fighting for us. We all know that."

Mengjiao nodded. Behind him, the rest of his grade—those who were old enough to join Army Training—did the same. It was humbling. I hadn't thought I'd put on a good show of leadership last term. I'd baited General Tepeh into being allowed to command us for the company march and nearly seen my classmates killed for it. I'd lost during the final and only won the midterm due to sacrificing Oluk's squad.

Objectively, there wasn't that large a gap between sixteen and seventeen versus seventeen and eighteen, but I felt every single one of those months standing before Mengjiao, Zhihao, and their classmates. My own classmates were always going to be involved by virtue of being *my* classmates. These ones didn't have to be. They could have a different future. There were ten weeks until my graduation. Another year after that until theirs. A lot could change in a year. Even if I were forced to take the army across Vinland and beyond, I would do everything in my power to carve out peace for the ones who followed in my footsteps.

Mengjiao stood and bowed low. His half brother and the rest of their classmates scrambled to follow. I wanted to bow back but forced myself to stand tall before the gesture instead. The twins led their classmates from the clearing, and I watched them go in silence.

Only after the last of the younger students had gone from sight did I turn to my fellow seniors.

I stood, as my ancestor once had, at the edge of something much greater than I. If war was inevitable, who would be sacrificed for that grand future? If my father's plan came to fruition, we would be forced to kill the Vinlanders before they came for us. We might have need to push into the Colonies, and beyond to the rest of the continent, just to keep from being slaughtered.

Was it possible for peace to come from conquering? This kingdom had not begun as a unified force, but now barely anyone remembered that. Would it be same in my father's future? In a couple generations, could we learn to forget we weren't always one united people? If I fell into my father's destiny and united the continent, would I find the world better or worse for it?

Mesachie had been titled the Wicked One. What name would they give me?

"I must thank you all for your faith in me," I said. I didn't need to speak loudly. I couldn't. All the uncertainty had stolen my voice, leaving me with barely more than a whisper. It was enough. All my fellow seniors were listening. "And I need to apologize. All of you have been caught up in something larger than you can even imagine. It's not fair. It never has been. No one should be obligated to fight, and you were solely because of the timing of your birth or the machinations of your parents."

I thought of Froya, placed in my year despite how I was sure she was older than all of us. I thought of Kwaddis, comforting his dad over the massacre at Multah's market. I thought of Charles, urged by his mother to make himself available to me so that I might deign to make him king.

I thought of Chao, standing between his mother and me, because somehow I'd won his trust even above familial loyalty.

"There is no prophecy," I said, and I'd regained enough of my voice to make it strong. "There is only choice. Know that if we do face Vinland in war, it will be because I have exhausted every possible avenue toward peace. I don't know if I can succeed. It may not be possible. The very land of Vinland has been cursed. Magic has been forced upon a people who did not ask for it, who have no understanding or experience in dealing with it. For that, the Cursed Kingdom *must* offer reparations. Should Vinland choose to reject them, war may be the only way to save our people from the consequences."

I took a deep breath. The silence in the clearing would have been unnerving, if not for my familiarity with my fellow seniors. They waited for me to tell them what to do. To command them, as I had done so many times before.

"We are the Accursed, but we are no blight nor plague nor affliction," I said. "We have a right to live in peace. To continue to use magic. To *be* magic. I promised to protect that right, and I will do so. If Vinland will not accept peace, then I will fight. I have always planned to do so, and I will not back down, even if destiny has no say after all. *That* is my choice."

There was a depth to the silence that hadn't existed before. A weight. I hadn't intended to spread the burden on my own shoulders with my classmates, and I quickly spoke to try to relieve it. "None of you are obligated by the army contract any longer. For those who wish, you may join our younger classmates in their classes. Madam Kawak has already agreed to find places for each of you."

"And if we wish to fight?" Charles asked. "Will you also insist that we're too young?"

There were two beasts warring within me. The one that so desperately wanted to have my classmates at my side. Who had gotten used to leading them over the past few months, the past few years. I trusted them more than I trusted any of the army's soldiers. I knew their capabilities, knew what we could do together.

The other yelled at me to keep my classmates safe. If Aklemin's vision spoke only of war, then I could take the burden of that alone. I could command soldiers without caring to learn their names, without letting myself see them as the people they were underneath that uniform. We would kill our way through Vinland until I could raise an army of dead composed of my people and theirs and use that to claim dominion over all.

But I had promised to listen to my entourage and they had all categorically refused to let me take this fight alone.

"I will not," I replied. "Just as I've made my choice, you all have the same power. For those who wish to fight, you may join me in a Combat class taught by Mister and Madam Xu. We will not learn army drills or the proper pattern to march, but we *will* learn how to win."

I did not want to be the kind of commander who had to sacrifice my own people to see victory. If my classmates were willing to fight with me, I would do everything I could to see their lives preserved.

"It's your choice," I said again. "I will not ask anyone to fight with me. Those who wish to must do so in acknowledgment of the danger. I promise that I will not be angry at those who choose otherwise. Unless you are absolutely sure that you are prepared to face down the might of Vinland, don't join us. You all have your own futures ahead of you, and I want nothing more than to see them fulfilled. That is the reason I will fight. So that all of you may yet live to see something better."

Chapter 23

"Tokey told me what you said to the seniors," Rosamund said.

It was the end of the first week of term, and we were in the stable, tacking up horses for our typical Saturday-morning ride. I'd chosen one of the bone horses to ride, wanting a challenge to help counteract my restless worry. Aklemin had been in a vision coma for two full weeks now, and still there was no sign of them waking. We'd done our best to stay vigilant at their bedside this first week of the term, but how much longer before one of us slipped up and my father's agents took advantage of it? All they needed to do was make it look like a natural effect of such a long vision—as though Aklemin had just slipped away.

I hadn't expected Rosamund to bring up my little speech from the first day of class. As she'd requested, I'd asked Madam Kawak to place her in the Advanced Combat course Mister and Madam Xu were now teaching in the second afternoon block. She'd taken her place among the other seniors who'd elected to take the course—including every single one of the heirs. It totaled about two thirds of the senior class, which was both more than I could have hoped for and more than I had wished to see. My classmates' desire to fight at my side was as encouraging as it was terrifying. Especially since I'd found our first week together less helpful than it could have been. Namely because we didn't yet know what we were fighting for. If only Aklemin would wake up and share the result of their Candlemas vision, then perhaps I could direct Mister and Madam Xu toward the kinds of lessons that would give me confidence in my ability to keep my classmates alive through the trials and tribulations of our collective future.

"You dissolved the army contracts," Rosamund said, and I realized I hadn't responded to her opening statement.

"You were right to rip apart the one I gave you," I said, dodging a lazy kick the bone horse gelding attempted to deliver as I came around his other side with a saddle. "I should never have encouraged my classmates to sign them. Indeed, General Tepeh should have never offered them. The legality of asking minors to enlist, even provisionally, was highly questionable."

"What's wrong, Shaw?"

I looked over at Rosamund then. She'd already finished tacking Pyre for the ride. The bone mare stood placidly at her side. Sometime over the past few months, Pyre had come to trust Rosamund. Maybe not quite as much as Cow trusted me, but certainly more than a typical bone horse trusted any rider.

As if to prove my point, the bone gelding tried to bite me as I worked his bridle on. I caught his teeth with the bit and had to spend a few seconds readjusting it so he wouldn't be uncomfortable on the ride.

"You should be well aware of my current concerns," I said finally, bridle secure.

"You're being extra formal. You only talk like that when you're hiding something," Rosamund accused.

Did I? I hadn't particularly noticed, but neither was I surprised.

I *was* hiding something. I'd spent all week planning it out, including a discussion with Yuyan to solidify the idea and a notice to the jarls' council tucked alongside my letter about dissolving the contracts.

"Let's ride," I said, instead of acknowledging it.

Rosamund scowled but didn't argue. We mounted the bone horses—Rosamund had to help me hold the gelding steady long enough for me to lift myself from the mounting block to the saddle—and then we set off on our usual route to the river.

I waited until we were riding through the secluded area of the riverbank where Rosamund had reported her progress to me last term. Then I slowed the bone gelding down to a walk. He huffed, trying to throw his head to loosen the reins, but eventually dropped out of his trot. Pyre followed suit as soon as Rosamund sat back in the saddle and lightly tugged at her reins.

"I need to offer you an apology," I said.

Rosamund directed Pyre to cut in front of my path. The bone gelding snapped at his fellow bone horse, but she pinned her ears back and he subsided. Cow and Pyre were the top of the horse hierarchy at the school's stable. I pulled the gelding to a halt, and Rosamund stopped Pyre close enough that we'd be able to touch if we reached for it.

"Shaw," Rosamund said firmly. "What is wrong?"

I couldn't resist smiling at that, bitter though it was. I couldn't remember ever making as large a mistake as the one I'd made with Rosamund. Even following my father's false prophecy without question was more understandable. Losing Rosamund was not. I'd let my own impatience over finding a partner ruin the best chance I'd ever had to claim one.

I reached into my pocket and pulled out the signed notice I had copied and sent to the jarls for official filing. It was slightly outside of my authority to grant, as I was still only the heir to the throne instead of its ruler, but if the jarls dared to argue with me, I would not hesitate to argue back. My father was imprisoned, and I would be crowned in a couple months.

Rosamund took the paper and read it over, first quickly, then another time slower. "What is this?" she asked, and her voice had dropped into an uncertain whisper.

"You told me you would fight at my side in exchange for land," I said. "But I promised all the seniors that they would be given the choice to fight. I don't want any debts to stand between us, Rosamund. That parcel of land is owned by the royal family and thus mine to grant in permanence. Any adults living upon it will be expected to pay the typical percentage of income to the royal coffers, as you would with any jarl, but it cannot be taken away except by proof that every single member of your family has committed treason."

I'd added a written clause that this proof must come after a full trial in front of the jarls' council, and that if there were any children at the time of such an unlikely event, they would be allowed to inherit the land upon coming of age. It was as close to assured as I could legally make it.

"This makes the Holt family vassals of the royal house!" Rosamund protested. "You can't give this to me, Shaw. This is much more than I asked for when I promised to fight. And besides, we don't even know if there's going to be war—"

"That's exactly why I've given it," I interrupted. "You should not be forced to fight with me just because Jarl Snass took your family's home. Your family should never have been punished for my father's schemes. It's only fair to right the wrongs of my house."

"You already gave me the moonstones," Rosamund said, still a protest, but not as strong. She hadn't taken her eyes off the paper, and the royal seal pressed to the bottom of it.

"There's a house on the property already," I continued, choosing to ignore Rosamund's words. "It may need some repairs, but it should be serviceable. Your family could move in tomorrow if they chose. There's ten acres, which should be enough to raise plenty of horses. It's farther from the Bone Forest than Forest's Edge, but only a day's ride from Gravestown." And a few days from Falconridge—but I didn't say that. What reason would Rosamund have to visit me on the Mountain once this was all over?

The house and the land it sat on had been my great-aunt and great-uncle's retreat during my grandmother's war. After my great-aunt and grandmother both died, my great-uncle had come to live in the royal palace with me and my father. Before his health had gotten too poor to travel, I'd gone with him several times a year to visit his old home.

I would miss that house and the beautiful rolling hills around it, but I didn't expect to ever regret giving the land to Rosamund and her family. Even if all our communications would eventually boil down to a yearly tax report, just the knowledge that Rosamund was living well would be enough. It had to be.

"There's one more thing," I said. "I know your family sold most of their herd. Pyre's still young enough, and she's an excellent bone mare."

"Shaw, no—"

"I've already given the money to the school to buy her, and Mister Jostein wrote an agreement of ownership in your name," I continued, talking over Rosamund's renewed protests. "We're just waiting for the headmistress to sign off on it, since Madam Dyer's employment contract stated all her possessions went back to the school, as she hadn't willed them to any other recipients."

"Shaw," Rosamund said again. "It's too much."

"She's yours, Rosamund. You don't have to breed her if you don't wish to, but she is yours."

Rosamund's grip on the notice was tight enough to mangle the corner of the parchment. I resisted the urge to reach over and save it from her grasp. While it would be smart of her to keep the official notice, it wasn't necessary. The one I'd sent to the jarls would be filed in the royal archives soon enough.

"These are gifts," I stated. I wanted to make that point clear. I'd meant it when I'd said there would be no more debts between us. "You have no obligation to fight with me."

Rosamund finally folded the notice and put it in her pocket. Pyre had picked up on her new owner's agitation and was beginning to get impatient. She stomped a hoof, ears flicking back and forth as if surveying for a threat.

"Do you not want me to?" Rosamund asked. If I'd thought her earlier whisper sounded uncertain, this one proved it had been far from that. She glanced at me and then away before I could be sure, but I thought there might have been the glimmer of tears in her eyes.

For months, I'd encased my heart in ice to push past the heartbreak this girl put me through. I hadn't been given proper time to grieve our lost relationship. I had too many responsibilities to give in to the temptation to rage like a child having a tantrum.

Yuyan had advised me to give Rosamund clear boundaries. She wasn't merely a weapon, because I would allow none of my classmates to be as expendable as that, but neither was she a true member of my entourage. I planned to wipe the debts remaining between us and, if Rosamund still wished to fight at my side, treat her as I would any of the other seniors who'd made that same choice.

And yet, at Rosamund's question—at the obvious hurt in her voice and on her face—I could no longer hold back the depths of lava-hot anger encased behind that cracking ice.

"You are not my familiar, Rosamund Holt. I admit to offering you courtship under false pretenses, but you knew exactly what I wanted by the end. I gave you sincerity and you threw it away. No, don't speak." I didn't care if she'd intended to apologize or protest. It no longer mattered. "We both behaved poorly, but that doesn't change the heart of the matter. You rejected my courtship, despite knowing that I would have gladly been your partner for the rest of our days. That is your right. What is not right is for you to prey upon my lingering feelings."

Rosamund jerked in her saddle so suddenly that Pyre pranced sideways in alarm. "Prey upon . . . When have I preyed upon your feelings?" she demanded.

The bone gelding I rode had begun to bunch up, as if all it would take for him to bolt would be one more shout. I took a long, steadying breath, and willed the ice to creep back over me. "I am not your witch," I said coldly. "You have no right to demand insight into my thoughts or emotions. If you wish to be my soldier, then I will command you as one, but I have no obligation to give you the why."

Rosamund's pale face had gone blotchy as angry red swatches colored her cheeks and forehead. I could tell that she was gearing up to yell. I held up a hand and was gratified to see her hesitate.

"I can't do this anymore, Rosamund," I said, and it was my turn to be gentle enough to hurt. Only, I thought it was hurting me more than it was her. I felt raw. Like I'd cracked the ice long enough to expose the beating heart underneath, and despite my best efforts, the frost I used as a shield wasn't quite enough to cover it all up again. "I can't keep relying on you as I have. All advantages aside, it's not good for me. I'll never move on properly if I don't demand space. You have your land, as I promised you. You are cleared of any remaining obligations. Fight beside me if you want, but do not attempt to support me as a partner when I know you will retract that partnership the second it suits you. I'm done relying on an empty promise."

And though it was cowardly to do, I clicked the gelding into a canter to escape any reply. I'd earned the right to run away from her this once, considering how she'd run away from me before.

I'd managed to remove all of the gelding's tack before Rosamund arrived back in the stable. She dismounted Pyre, and I waited for her to begin yelling, as she'd so obviously wanted to do earlier, but she stayed silent. When I dared to glance at her in the middle of brushing the horse down, she had her eyes firmly fixed on Pyre's coat. There were still unshed tears caught in her lower lashes, but the red had gone from her cheeks—leaving an almost unnatural paleness in its wake.

Someone banged open the door of the stable. The gelding reared up in surprise, and I just managed to avoid being trampled as he came back down.

"Rosy, Shaw!" Oluk yelled as I struggled to calm the startled bone horse. "Are you here?"

"We are!" I called when Rosamund didn't immediately answer.

Oluk rounded the corner of the stable and saw us. He rushed up, then stopped suddenly as he realized he was spooking the horses. "Sorry, sorry. It's just, finish quick. Yuyan said that Aklemin's finally coming out of the vision!"

AKLEMIN WAS ALREADY AWAKE WHEN I burst into the infirmary. They glanced at me only briefly, before refocusing on Toketie, who was crying into their chest.

"I knew you'd do well," they whispered, soft enough to make it clear that they were talking only to the ice familiar. "Thank you for taking care of me."

"Don't ever do that again," Toketie sobbed, voice partially muffled by Aklemin's thin sleep dress.

"I promise," Aklemin murmured. "Once was enough."

"Once was too much," Toketie said, but she was calming down. She pulled away and rubbed furiously at her face. "Drink your water," she snapped when Aklemin just watched her.

Aklemin obliged, draining the glass that Yuyan handed them. Shantie bustled about in the corner of the infirmary, mixing potions together into a tea. Einar helped her put the pot on a small fire to boil.

Rosamund slunk in behind me, closing the infirmary door. She glanced worriedly at me. It took me a moment to understand her hesitancy. Did she believe I would kick her out?

"You helped get them off the Mountain. You have just as much a right as anyone in this room to hear what they have to say," I told her. I'd aimed for a whisper, but the infirmary was too small for secrecy. Oluk glanced at us with a worried expression, obviously catching the tension.

"The runes, Einar," I said even as I walked up to Aklemin's bed and took one of the open seats next to it.

Einar rolled forward, awkwardly reaching around me until he could touch the runes inscribed into the infirmary bed. A second later, he nodded to show they'd activated correctly.

"Are you well enough to tell us what you saw in the vision?" I asked Aklemin.

Aklemin finally took their gaze off Toketie to look at me. For just a moment, all that existed in that infirmary was us. As it had been once, and may yet be again. A memory of the chill I felt that night atop the Frozen Mountain came over me. I did my best to hide the shiver that ran down my arms and legs.

"Do you trust everyone in this room to hear it?" Aklemin asked.

I raised an eyebrow to show how strange I felt the request was, but looked around the infirmary regardless. Yuyan and Einar had earned my trust too many times to count, especially recently. Oluk would have been given a modicum of trust by virtue of being Einar's familiar, but he had already earned more on his own merits. Shantie wasn't a member of my entourage, nor could she ever be, but she had saved Einar from a life of misery and spent the last ten days helping Yuyan keep Aklemin alive through their vision coma. Toketie was trustworthy for similar reasons—her obvious affection for Aklemin aside. And though I had to learn to stop relying on Rosamund as I would on my future familiar, I still trusted her.

I looked, at last, to Aklemin and studied their carefully blank expression. Their hair was recently braided—Toketie had taken to brushing it every day—but their face was gaunter than I'd ever seen it, and the infirmary gown did little to hide the thinness of their shoulders. For a second, all I could see in that bed was Aklemin's much younger self.

I betray you, they'd said, and they must have known what that might do to us. I'd never before been able to read past Aklemin's mask, but I thought I could see the real reason for their hesitancy now.

"I do," I said. "I trust every single person in this room."

Though the words had to mean something for everyone in the infirmary with us, I cared only for how they hit Aklemin. For the first time in our lives, I saw their expression crack, seemingly without their permission. Their chin quivered, and their eyes closed with repressed tears.

"Aklemin," I murmured. "Tell us, will we have peace, or war?"

Chapter 24

"There may yet be war," Aklemin began, voice soft enough to almost hide the way it cracked. "But it is not inevitable."

"How do we stop it?" I asked.

"You cannot. At least, not entirely," Aklemin said. "Prince Vetle must be the one to lay down his arms and agree to peace."

I glanced at Einar, sitting in his wheelchair beside me, but Einar didn't look nearly as affronted by the idea as I felt. When I'd envisioned giving reparations, it was to the emperor, not the prince. Considering what I now knew of their war with the Colonies, I figured the emperor was much more likely to accept the reparations and call for a truce. Then, even if the prince did continue to attack, it would be his father's duty to reel him back. But Vetle himself? He would sooner spit in the hand I offered instead of shaking it.

"Vetle will not negotiate with us," I argued. "He won't listen to reason."

"If Prince Vetle dies, there will be no path to take other than war," Aklemin said. "Your father will try to kill him, Shaw."

My father was supposed to be under guard, but I knew better than to believe him powerless. "How? When?"

"The vision showed me many branching paths. Endless variations, unraveling, then weaving, then unraveling again."

"I thought Candlemas visions were supposed to be clear!" Rosamund protested.

"It was," Aklemin replied. "As clear as if I was living each of those possibilities, but the vision could not show me a single truth, so it showed me thousands. That is the issue with going up against an ice witch like the Witch King. He knows how to adjust his plans constantly enough to twist even the fabric of destiny."

I'd never known Aklemin to show pain for any reason, even when they should, but there was a hollowness to their voice that spoke of nightmares I could only imagine. Toketie reached forward to claim one of Aklemin's hands. They looked startled by the gesture but seemed to find strength as she squeezed their fingers.

"What's the most likely?" I asked, because I needed the answer. If there was any chance for peace, real peace, I would fight for it.

"Beltane," Aklemin said immediately. "He intends to use the prince in a ritual. The curse is not yet complete. He's begun the process of creating magical wells inside Vinland, but there's something he intends to do with those wells. I've seen the start of a transmuting ritual. The prince, tied to a pole in the center of a circle. Your father and Bao Hu at opposite ends, with Jarl Alki and Jarl Hu standing watch."

"And General Tepeh?" I pressed. "Where are they?"

Aklemin shook their head. "I didn't see them, but that doesn't mean they weren't present. I caught only a glimpse of the ritual itself, but the vision was clear about the consequences of letting it be completed. It won't just be war. Your father wishes to see magic spread across the entire continent, but he is a witch. He thinks only of the power that can be drawn from such enormous wells of power—not the cost to anchor them. I don't believe it would even be appropriate to call them wells if the ritual is allowed to happen. Holes, perhaps. Large, ravenous things. Merciless to all except the powerful few."

I thought of the western islands and the enormous whirlpool said to exist in the center of them. No familiars in the world got as large as the flower whales that anchored that massive well of flower magic. What mammal or reptile or bird could possibly survive anchoring a hole that size of bone or glass or ice magic? What would it even look like? I imagined ice crawling down from the Frozen Mountain to envelop an entire nation. The shivers returned.

"Wait," Toketie said. "You said Bao Hu was there, helping with the ritual?"

"That's right."

Toketie glanced at me. "Jarl Hu's witch wasn't at the trial, was he?"

I swore. "No, he was not. I don't know if the jarls' council summoned him for a trial after."

They should have, as he was a member of my father's entourage, but many dismissed the quiet bone witch to focus on his more outspoken, powerful, and politically active wife. I had myself, until Toketie had reminded me, even with Aklemin's statement.

"Would he even go if they did?" Shantie pointed out. "He's probably on the run."

"I'll inform the jarls to double the guards watching my father and the rest of his entourage," I said. "So long as they don't escape, then all we have to contend with is one bone witch."

"And whatever supporters among the Royal Company who still walk free," Rosamund muttered.

I inclined my head, acknowledging the point. "Will you know if they're making a move on the prince, Aklemin?"

"I believe so," Aklemin said. "Last time I scried on him, Vetle was recovering from his foray into the Obsidian Desert at his manor in the center of Vingate. I don't believe they'd risk going for him there. They'll wait until he chooses to make another attack on the Cursed Kingdom."

I could get used to this version of Aklemin. They'd never been so up front about their visions before. "Is there any way for us to persuade him not to?"

Aklemin hesitated. "I can't be sure."

"We'll think of some options to attempt," I said, looking to Einar and Yuyan to make sure they both knew they were included in that *we*. "In the meantime, we'll train with the other seniors in Advanced Combat so that we can stop the ritual should Bao slip past us. We can work on negotiating for peace, so long as the prince is alive to hear it and the curse hasn't progressed enough to preclude it."

"At least Beltane's after graduation," Yuyan said. "We'll have plenty of time to enjoy being graduates of Witch Hall before we have to face down catastrophic doom."

For all her sarcasm, Yuyan was right. We were blessed with enough time to prepare. There were still nine weeks left until graduation, and then another ten days until Beltane.

My father had promised me the war wouldn't truly begin until I had a chance to graduate. Had he always planned on this ritual the Candlemas vision showed Aklemin? Was that how he'd envisioned me capable of commanding an army of so many corpses? I hadn't thought it possible—but if he somehow grew the well of bone magic into something even more deadly, that might explain it.

"What are our chances?" I asked Aklemin.

Aklemin said nothing, staring down at Toketie's fingers curled around theirs.

"Can we truly stop this?" I pressed. "Or should we also be preparing for war?"

"There is no guarantee," Aklemin said. "There are so many ways everything may yet fall apart around us. The prince dead, a martyr. You dead, our greatest failure. Your father dead, but in his death, victorious. The curse may spread despite our best intentions. We may succeed in stopping it but find Vetle impossible to sway. I don't know what will happen. But, Shaw"—and finally Aklemin looked up to meet my eyes—"if I don't know, neither does your father. And that, more than anything, gives us a chance."

THE SECOND WEEK OF MY last term at Witch Hall was a completely different beast from the first. I'd decided to be as honest as I could with my classmates in Advanced Combat, telling them that we had a chance to stop the war for good, but that there were those within the Cursed Kingdom who wanted to see it happen for their own gain.

"For peace to be assured, we may yet have to fight against our own people," I explained. "If you are uncomfortable with the idea, then it is not too late to join the other classes."

None of the seniors in the classroom clearing moved. Behind me, I heard Mister Xu cough—almost as if he were holding back a laugh.

Well then. Adding Rosamund, Aklemin, and myself, there were

fifty seniors in Advanced Combat. A proper platoon—and one who'd willingly placed themselves entirely under my command. I would endeavor to keep their trust. The first step of which was making sure we were all prepared to stop Bao and any deserters from the Royal Company who dared attempt the Beltane ritual in my father's stead.

I took my seat, and Mister and Madam Xu began to direct the class. Now that we had an idea what we might have to fight, our training could begin in earnest.

An hour later, I found myself in a small group with the other senior bone witches practicing necromancy. Madam Xu's idea had been for everyone to focus on the most practical applications of our magics. On Fridays, we'd then test those applications out in sparring matches and group melees.

Chao and I were the only bone witches who'd had great success in necromancy in Madam Dyer's previous classes, but Kalitan and the rest of our suitemates were determined to learn enough to be useful. Power-sharing rituals were less practical on the battlefield, even if it had worked well against the specter last Samhain.

I'd gathered a skeleton from the forest to bring into the clearing, and Chao was now talking the others through how to pull apart single bones to use as projectile weapons. Kalitan nodded along as the only other bone witch in our year who'd been able to manage that basic skill of necromancy. Several raised a hand to attempt to pull one of the bones toward themselves at Chao's instruction.

I left the group to their practice and wandered the clearing to observe how the others were doing. Even more than practicing my own combative magics, what I really needed to command my classmates was a solid grasp on everyone's capabilities. Mister Xu nodded to me as I crossed paths with him, but didn't comment on my wandering, so I assumed he agreed with me.

Rosamund presided over a group of familiars including Oluk, Toketie, and Emma. I lingered near long enough to figure out that everyone in the group had at least two shifts, but hadn't yet mastered the ability to shift directly between them without turning human in between. I knew Oluk's shifts and had been told of Toketie's new goshawk form, but Rosamund made a point of telling me that Emma had found the voice of an arctic bone fox over the winter break. I congratulated her for the success, and she grinned widely as she thanked me. When I turned to move on, I saw Rosamund give me a disgruntled look, though I couldn't begin to guess why.

The ice witches were crowding around Aklemin. The other ice witches had always respected Aklemin, to the surprise of many who'd perceived them as an underpowered witch whose only strength was in their position as heir to the jarl of Falconridge and their place on my entourage. Now though that respect had turned into fervent admiration. The other ice witches hung on to every word as Aklemin talked them through how to strengthen their scrying spells.

I moved on to where Einar was working with the other glass witches on designing traps and other enchantments that could be used on the battlefield. He seemed to have that well in hand, so I walked over to where Madam Xu was working with Charles, Jingyi, and several other familiars with more combat-oriented shifts. Madam Xu stopped me so she could point out where to bite or claw to sever the tendons in the arm that allowed people to lift swords. I let her use me as a living dummy for ten or so minutes, then left when it was time for everyone to begin practicing in earnest.

Like the bone and ice witches, those flower witches who'd never mastered direct healing were all listening carefully to Yuyan as she talked them through how to knit sliced muscles back together. Meanwhile, Shantie was explaining different potions to a mixed group of familiars. How to identify which was which by smell and look and how they could be handed out in the middle of battle to either save a life or give our side an edge.

I completed my circuit and came around to the back of the clearing, where the bone witches had moved on to discussing spiritual remnants. Just as I was about to join them, I noticed that Aklemin had stepped away from the other ice witches. They were watching Toketie start to shift from swan to goshawk, only to pop back into a human body in the middle. Face scrunched in determination, Toketie tried again, and again.

I took a couple steps toward Aklemin, only to pause as Froya beat me to it. She walked right up to Aklemin's side and pinched the sleeve of their robe to grab their attention.

"Are you going to stop being a coward?" she hissed. I was only just close enough to hear it, even against the chatter of the various groups practicing around the clearing.

"Froya . . ." Aklemin began.

"You watch her like she's the only water in the desert, but you haven't done anything about it," Froya snapped. "You'd better give that girl a necklace soon, Aklemin."

Aklemin looked away from Toketie toward Froya and, in doing so, caught sight of me dithering a dozen feet away. "It's more complicated than you know," they said softly.

"It's only as complicated as your twisted mind is making it,"

Froya said. "She has waited long enough. I've waited long enough. If you don't give her a necklace before graduation, I will. We both know she will accept it, even if you are her first choice. I'd win her heart eventually."

"You would," Aklemin acknowledged, and coming from an ice witch, it was practically prophecy.

Froya sniffed in contempt. "Too bad I love her enough to wish the best for her, even if that best is *you*."

"Am I the best for her?" Aklemin murmured, so soft I could only barely make out the words.

"You're what she wants. You should respect her enough to trust that at least."

Aklemin said nothing in reply. Froya spun on her heels, ready to storm off, only to falter as she saw me listening in. I gave her an apologetic smile because I hadn't meant to eavesdrop. She threw her shoulders back and turned up her nose, stalking away from both of us.

I crossed the final distance to Aklemin's side. Rosamund was looking toward us, frowning in a way that told me she too had overheard Froya's ultimatum. I glanced at Toketie, but it didn't seem like she had. Bone familiars had better hearing than ice familiars though, and we were far enough away that the other conversations in the clearing had probably drowned out Froya's words.

"Not here," Aklemin said before I could say anything.

"At the waterfall, before dinner," I commanded. I wouldn't let them put off a conversation any longer than that. Most of the other students would be distracted doing their predinner duties, but both Aklemin and I had more flexibility with our duty schedules and could afford to slip away from a talk.

Aklemin inclined their head. I returned to the bone witches with Froya's frustration still ringing in my ears.

AKLEMIN AND I WALKED TOGETHER from class to Witch Hall's waterfall in silence. Spring was creeping over campus like a rising tide. The ice had melted entirely from the edges of the waterfall and the shore of its little creek. There were still large banks of snow hiding in the shadows of buildings, but more dripped away each passing day.

"I want you to promise me something," I said as we stood at the base of the waterfall. It was still cold enough that the spray of water hitting my face left little prickles of pain. "Promise that if I begin to walk the path that leads to you betraying me, you'll tell me. Give me a chance to right my wrongs before it's too late for either of us."

"You've nearly destroyed that future," Aklemin said. "There may yet be war, but you are no tyrant."

"Yet you still won't give Toketie a necklace?"

Aklemin looked sideways at me. "Perhaps I simply don't want to."

I shook my head. Ever since their confession on the Mountain, I'd felt adrift in the sea of secrets that had stood between Aklemin and me. Now though I could see the person I'd claimed as my best friend, hidden under the fresh guardedness they were exuding. They wouldn't admit to liking Toketie, but their very reluctance made it obvious that they did.

"You told me on the Mountain that any familiars we bonded would be dead well before the end of the war," I said. "I will not sacrifice Toketie or Oluk or any other familiar, not anymore. I hate that some version of me would have."

Hated it, but understood it. Before Rosamund came into my life, I'd kept myself isolated, rarely interacting with anyone outside my entourage and a select few witch friends like Chao and Shantie. I hadn't even made an effort to befriend Charles or Froya or Kwaddis, despite them being the heirs of the three most powerful jarls of my kingdom. I could spend years reflecting on why. Was it the lack of familiars in my life growing up? Had a part of me dismissed them as beasts simply because of their ability to shift? Or had it started out of convenience, focusing on witches to choose my immediate entourage, and then settled into habit without my notice?

Regardless of the reason, I knew better now. I couldn't guarantee the lives of the forty-nine other seniors who'd chosen to fight with me, but I could at least guarantee that each and every one of them would be treated as worthy of living. They were not pawns on a board for me to debate strategy over—they were people. My people.

"What is the cost of anchoring those magical holes my father hopes to create?" I asked. "If we cannot stop this ritual. If we're forced to go to war simply to save ourselves. If we must find a way to control the magic my father wishes unleashed upon this continent . . . What will that do to the familiars?"

"Nothing good," Aklemin said darkly.

I contemplated it for a second, wondering at the cost of all that power. Witches who lost their bonded went catatonic as they struggled to process the increase in magic. Familiars went feral—the animal voices inside them too strong to control. I could picture Rosamund's wolf, enraged as it had been in the obsidian quarry.

Aklemin had said something about how expendable familiars seemed in the midst of war. What if my father's ritual turned them into mindless beasts, trapped inside feral rages they could never return from? I could see myself making the choice to send a feral bone wolf against my enemies, no matter the risk to the familiar in question, as much as it filled me with nausea.

"You said that our future is uncertain," I murmured, because I couldn't linger longer over that nightmarish thought. "Doesn't that mean you should claim what happiness can be found while there's still a chance?"

"And you, Shaw?" Aklemin asked.

Me? Aklemin should have known by now that my happiness was far from a priority. How could it be? "My happiness will come only after my people are safe and my friends have found theirs."

Aklemin stared up at the waterfall, and I stared at them. Finally, they closed their eyes. "I won't betray you," they whispered. "Not anymore. Not even if war claims dominion over us and you ride at the head of an army of the dead."

"I'd rather you betray me than live to see myself become a monster."

"We are all capable of monstrous things." They opened their eyes to look at me. "But you have never been and never will be a monster."

There were a million ways I could respond to that. I swallowed down the sudden lump in my throat. "Then neither are you," I said. "And if that is the reason you've been holding yourself back from offering courtship to a girl who we both know has wanted you for years, you should reconsider. We cannot let fear rule us, not anymore."

"I'll consider it," Aklemin replied. "So long as you do the same."

As if I hadn't already considered the myriad ways I could try to convince Rosamund to give courtship with me another chance. But I had asked for space and she had given it to me. She hadn't even eaten lunch with us today—spending time with Chao and Jingyi instead.

"Claim your happiness, Aklemin," I said. My own happiness might be far from reach, but I could at least be content to see that. To watch that too-guarded child who'd once begged me to sleep over, just for the chance to escape home for a single night, open themself up to partnership with a girl who'd never let them spend another night hurt and alone.

Chapter 25

ROSY

JUST AS ROSY AND OLUK WERE FINISHING THEIR NORMAL morning stable duty at the beginning of the third week of the term, Toketie ran up to the pasture fence calling for them. Rosy dropped the last grain bucket and rushed to her cousin, heart in her throat with worry, but Toketie didn't look upset when she got close enough to study her. If anything, she was glowing like it was her birthday and she'd just received the best present she could think of it.

"Oh, they finally asked!" Oluk exclaimed as he jogged up to the fence next to Rosy. "I caught Einar enchanting the necklace this weekend so it'll shift with you, but he swore me to secrecy."

Rosy finally noticed what Oluk had. Sitting in the hollow of Toketie's throat was a beautiful silver necklace. Three glimmering opals hung from the bottom, the ones on either side of the large centerpiece carved to look like wings.

"Aklemin asked to court you?" Rosy said, just to be sure.

"They did!" Toketie replied, practically squealing in excitement. "They caught me on the way to breakfast and pulled me to the dock so we'd have some privacy. Oh, Rosy, it was beautiful."

"How does it feel?" Oluk asked, seeming almost as excited as Rosy's cousin.

"Like a strong wind, carrying me high," Toketie said dreamily. "I never want to take it off. How did you deal with it? I don't want to wait a whole week before I can officially accept their courtship."

"I didn't want to wait either," Oluk said. "I actually, uh, well, I cornered Einar on the third day and tried to tell him yes, but he refused to hear it." Oluk blushed pink at the memory. "He didn't say anything, of course. But he cupped a hand over my cheek and kissed me on the forehead, and I just about died."

Toketie squealed again and reached over the fence to grab Oluk's hands as if she couldn't help herself. Rosy watched them, caught between feelings she couldn't even name. She'd spent the entire first week of Shaw's courtship request in a sulk, determined to reject the princess despite the warmth of Shaw's magic. She hadn't, of course, not then. Not until she'd run away like the coward she was trying not to be.

She still dreamed of the moonstone necklace and the magic Shaw had embedded in it. She missed the reassurance of that constant touch, especially now. She was trying to respect Shaw's request for space, but it was hard when every voice in her heart yearned to taste Shaw's magic one more time. She hated to think that she'd only ever feel that warmth again if they were forced to battle.

She'd told Shaw to use her like a weapon, but found the sheath stifling in its loneliness.

Toketie eventually left, shouting something about wanting to share the news with Froya and her suitemates. Rosy wandered over to the grain bucket she'd dropped, though of course the horses had already picked it clean. Oluk rambled excitedly as he and Rosy walked back to the grain room to return the buckets. He was in high spirits from Toketie's announcement and started telling Rosy about some new wheelchair enchantments Einar was nearly finished designing. With the enchantments, Einar wouldn't need to crank as hard to move even over rough terrain. As soon as he started moving, the runes he'd carve into the side of the wheels would help keep his momentum. There were other runes that stabilized him so his wheelchair wouldn't tip over while he was seated in it, which would make moving over uneven ground even easier.

"It's just brilliant," Oluk concluded. "The wheelchair was already brilliant, of course. It was an adjustment, but you saw how much happier he's been, being able to move around on his own. The teachers tried their best last term, but it's so much easier now that he's able to attend class. These runes will give him even more freedom."

"I'm glad it's working for him so well," Rosy said, and she meant it sincerely. "What's next?"

Oluk threw the grain bucket into the corner and wrote a couple notes on the feed chart for Mister Jostein to check later. "Everything else is a little more complicated, so Einar's decided to put it on hold. He wants to focus on helping Mister Xu and the others come up with enchantments for battle."

"I'm sorry he has to set it aside," Rosy murmured. Part of her thought it might be more important for him to come up with enchantments to help himself first if he wanted to be in the thick of it with Shaw, but she understood his desire to help the rest of the seniors with protective runes first.

Oluk shook his head. "He's passionate again, Rosy. He has so many ideas, for himself, for the others."

It *was* nice to see Einar back to his old self. Rosy wouldn't have called him passionate before until he'd suddenly been listless. Seeing him return to himself was heartening, even with the potential for war looming over them.

"That first week after Shantie returned was hard," Oluk admitted, the excitement dropping from his tone at the memory. "I think there was a part of him that was still holding out hope for a way to fix it. When Shantie confirmed what Yuyan had, that he'd never have full use of his legs again, it was like a part of him died. I was so afraid I'd lose him entirely. He was ready to give up there in that bed, until Shantie came in with the sketch of the wheelchair. Even then, I think he didn't want to believe that it would work. Not until it was built and he tried it out."

Rosy didn't know what to say to that. Luckily, it didn't seem like Oluk needed a reply, because he just shrugged and shot her a ruthful smile. "I slipped away to Multah just a few days before you and Toketie returned to school with Aklemin. They moved the market. I suppose you already know? The new market's not the same, but it made me feel . . . I don't know. Like there was hope, I guess? Like, no matter how things change, how much is destroyed, we can always build something from the ashes."

He reached into his pocket and pulled something out. Rosy took it when he offered and held it up to the light coming through the small stable window, trying to make out the details.

It was a necklace. Like the courtship necklace Oluk wore, the one Einar had given him some six months ago, this necklace was made of leather. But where Oluk's had been threaded with gold and visibly enchanted, this one ended with a single gold pendant etched with a rune.

"What does it mean?" Rosy asked. "The rune."

"Resilience. Perseverance." Oluk paused, then added, "Hope."

Rosy closed her fingers around the golden rune. It wasn't warm like the moonstone bones had been, but then, it didn't have any of Shaw's magic. Just Oluk's, if he'd been pouring energy into it like he was supposed to.

"It's beautiful," she said.

Oluk took the necklace from her and carefully returned it to his pocket. "Time is fragile. Mister Sorensen warned us back in the fall that we'd face hardship and we have, but I'm not naive enough to think this'll be it. I don't know how much time is left for us. However much I have, I want to be his. I'm going to give it to him soon. This weekend, maybe."

Rosy had a dozen statements on the tip of her tongue, but she swallowed them all down. Since Einar had been the one to court Oluk, by Oluk giving him a complementary necklace, he was telling Einar that he was ready to bond. Witches and familiars nearly always bonded young, and there was no reason for Rosy to tell Oluk it was too soon. He was right, after all. The future was uncertain, but it was clear that Einar and Oluk were dedicated to each other.

An ugly feeling, the one she didn't want to call jealousy, raged in her gut. The wolf in her heart howled, though not, she thought, in protest to Oluk's plan. The wolf knew what it wanted, and none of Rosy's arguments had ever swayed it. Aklemin was courting Toketie, and Oluk and Einar would soon be bonded. Where did that leave Rosy? Living out the rest of her life on the land Shaw had gifted her, forever the outsider to a place that had once been offered to her on a silver platter?

"I'm happy for you," Rosy said, because she wanted to be.

Because she had to be. Shaw had made herself clear. It wasn't Rosy's place to interfere with the royal entourage, not anymore.

THE NIGHT AFTER THE SECOND full moon assembly of term, Rosy sat in the bone familiars' suite staring into the fire. As he'd said he would, Oluk had asked Einar to bond a couple weeks prior. Einar had been delighted, wearing his new necklace proudly. They'd taken advantage of the assembly to announce their coming bonding ceremony and invite everyone at school to attend. It would be held next week, on the spring equinox. Toketie had accepted Aklemin's courtship in time to help the entourage plan the bonding ceremony while Rosy had distanced herself from it all, as Shaw wanted. She'd been spending more time with Jingyi and Chao just to fill the space, but even though she liked them, it still felt like loss.

Rosy pulled out the two necklaces she'd had Lilly make. Where Oluk's and Einar's necklaces were braided leather, these two were woven like the straps on Cow's fancy bridle. The weave was slightly different on each—one simpler, the other more ornate. Embedded in the center of the fancier one, the moonstone bone had swirls of silver thread tying it in place. The simpler one had silver thread ducking in and out of the weave, but the moonstone bone was held tightly by the leather itself. They were beautiful pieces. Rosy had been delighted when Lilly had finished them, imagining how beautiful the fancy one would look on Shaw's neck.

Now she wondered when she'd ever get to see it. Would the

Witch Queen of the Cursed Kingdom even have the time to visit a simple bone horse rancher, vassal of the royal family or not? The new land was closer to the Frozen Mountain than Forest's Edge, which would certainly make Uncle Inge and Uncle Chetwoot happy. Perhaps Oluk would join Toketie for once-a-year visits and give Rosy all the gossip from court she would pretend not to care about but secretly craved. Half the jarls' council would eventually be composed of her classmates.

Rosy watched the glimmer of firelight reflect off the moonstone bones, sitting alone in the center of the suite. She knew the entourage was gathered together in the library, making a seating chart for the coming bonding ceremony. Perhaps she should have gone with them and pretended to study something while listening in.

Several suitemates came and went as Rosy sat there, morose. She noticed them glancing from her to the necklaces and leaving once they realized what they were looking at. She barely cared what gossip would be flooding the school the next day, too caught up in her own misery.

The fire was just getting low enough that she was contemplating adding a log when Charles arrived.

"Heard a rumor you finally got a replacement necklace," he said, sauntering up. "There a reason you haven't put it on?"

"There is," Rosy said. Her voice sounded dull to her own ears. It didn't matter. She'd made her decision. She made it months ago, back when she'd first ripped Shaw's necklace off. She was who she was and she couldn't be who she couldn't be.

Shaw needed a familiar to stand at her side. Rosy would do what she could to see peace achieved, but what could she do when it came time for reparations and treaties and everything else? If there was to be a Familiar Queen of the Cursed Kingdom, then she could only think of one good choice to stand with Shaw.

"Charles," Rosy said, coming back into her body and glancing up at him. His hair was the same orange-red as the fire burning in the center of the suite. He'd been awful to her before, but his loyalty to Shaw was unquestionable. And he'd grown on her a bit since he stopped being such a bully. Grown on her like algae on the sides of a bathtub maybe, but she'd gotten used to its presence.

She would never accept Charles as Shaw's partner, but his cousin was a different story entirely. Emma Chambers had found her second shift over winter break, after spending the latter half in Gravestown with her aunt and Charles. Alongside her dog, she'd claimed the voice of a fox. Not a gray fox, like Jingyi, but an arctic fox—with its protruding bones blending seamlessly into white fur. Compared to Ragna, who'd just begun hearing the voice of a rabbit to complement her ermine shift, it was enough to mark Emma as the clear choice.

Emma was loud and commanding. She wasn't afraid to speak up. She wasn't afraid to fight. If her cousin and her aunt stood with her, she'd have significant political support as well. She was the right choice. Rosy knew that.

Why was it so hard for her to say it?

"Charles," she said again, then gave up on words. She handed him the necklaces.

Charles took them and turned them both over in his hands. "Not bad," he said. "Not bad at all, actually. Who did the leatherwork on these?"

Rosy almost answered, then shook her head. She couldn't let herself be distracted. "How would—What would— Would you be supportive if Shaw gave a courtship necklace to Emma?"

"Is that a joke?" Charles's tone was flat. If he thought it was a joke, he didn't think it a funny one.

"I'm going to give one of those to Shaw, to give to her. And the other for Emma so she can give Shaw the match when she feels it's right. Emma doesn't have to say yes, of course, but if she does . . . I mean, she'd be queen. And I know Shaw likes her."

That was, perhaps, an exaggeration, but Shaw obviously respected Emma well enough. Rosy had been observing their interactions for the entire term. She wouldn't have been as convinced Emma was the best choice otherwise.

"This is a test, isn't it?" Charles's face began to glow as red as his hair.

"No—"

"Because I get it. I know I was wrong, okay? I did bad things because of my jealousy and my anger and my inability to take a hint. I've learned my lesson. It doesn't matter. I know it's not going to be me, okay? You don't need go to rubbing this in my face—"

Rosy grimaced. That was what she was doing, wasn't it? "I didn't mean to make you upset. It was an honest question. Would you support Emma as Familiar Queen?"

Charles snorted. "Would I? Sure. In some world where you never came to Witch Hall. If Shaw chose my cousin over me, I'd probably get over it eventually. But that is not our world. Don't you think Shaw's already made her choice of partner clear, Rosamund Holt?"

That wasn't what Rosy had meant at all. "I can't be what you think I am, Charles. Shaw needs a familiar who's going to stand by her. On the battlefield and in court. Someone who can rally support and be a voice among the jarls and help her get through what's coming. It's not me. I wish—but it doesn't matter. It's not me."

"You're full of shit," Charles spat. "The same shit that made you rip off Shaw's necklace in the first place. I thought you'd have grown." He threw the necklaces back at her and stalked away.

Something about the way she had to scramble to pick up the necklaces off the ground felt like revenge. Luckily, the new necklaces were unharmed from their tumble on the floor. Rosy held them both tight to her chest and ran out of the suite after Charles. She needed to explain—make it clear that it wasn't even about her anymore. Shaw had made her choice too.

"Charles, wait!"

Charles didn't acknowledge her. Rosy ran faster and caught up with him at the edge of the eastern longhouse. She grabbed his arm to force him to stop, except he already had.

Rosy's instincts were too good to ignore a potential threat. She quickly turned to look at what had caught Charles's attention. It wasn't, as she'd immediately feared, anything to do with the war or Vetle coming to attack. It was two girls kissing. The taller one had the shorter backed against the wall of the library building. The shorter had her fingers woven in the taller's hair, pulling her closer. The girls separated for air, and when they met again, the kiss looked gentler.

"Oh," Rosy murmured. She knew those girls. Those were Yuyan's fingers, in Shantie's hair. That was Shantie's arm around Yuyan's waist.

"Are they really—" Charles began.

Rosy turned on him, all thoughts of the necklaces forgotten. "Don't you dare say anything. I know how you feel about those kinds of relationships. If I hear a hint that you've spread a rumor about them around school, just because they're both witches—"

"I wouldn't," Charles protested.

Rosy scowled. "Are you just conveniently forgetting what you said about Oluk and me last fall? What you said about my grandparents?"

Charles had the decency to look contrite. "I was just trying to make you mad. I don't actually believe that."

"Obviously a part of you does, if you thought to make it an insult."

Charles looked like he was about to argue, but then he looked down. "I know it wasn't right to say. I am sorry. And I won't say anything about them. Not until they're ready to tell people." He paused, glancing sideways at the two flower witches. "Though if they aren't ready, they shouldn't be kissing out in the open."

Rosy had no idea if Yuyan and Shantie were trying to hide this or not. She didn't know if they were actually together. If this was the first time they'd kissed, or one of many. All she knew was that both of them had been through too much to have this ruined by some misguided rumors. "Just keep it to yourself for now."

Charles glanced down at the necklaces still clutched to her chest. "I'll do it so long as you don't talk to Emma. It'll only make her mad. We all know how this is going to end."

Rosy stared after him as he stalked away again. Before she could protest that Shaw had already chosen a different ending, she heard Shantie call out, "Is that Rosy?"

Caught, Rosy walked over to the flower witches. "Hi. Sorry, I didn't mean to interrupt."

Yuyan looked a touch embarrassed, but she shrugged as if to say it didn't matter.

Shantie merely smiled. "Who were you talking to just now?"

"Charles. I was trying to . . ." Rosy trailed off, looking at Yuyan. She still didn't know what Yuyan knew of her relationship with

Shaw. The fake courtship. The real feelings. The distance Shaw had asked for.

Shantie looked between Rosy and Yuyan. "Why don't we go for a walk, Rosy. YuYu, I'll see you later?"

"Good night," Yuyan murmured, and made her escape inside library. Rosy heard Toketie's voice loudly arguing something about the proper distance between seat rows before the door closed behind Yuyan.

"Please excuse her, she's a bit shy," Shantie whispered.

"Can I ask?"

Shantie started walking in the direction of the dock, and Rosy fell into step beside her. "It hasn't been long. We weren't sure about saying anything, with all the preparations and the war hanging over everyone's heads. But with the bonding ceremony coming up, YuYu doesn't want to hide it anymore. She's going to tell Shaw and the rest tonight."

Rosy looked at Shantie out of the corner of her eye. "I'm happy for you both." She hesitated, wondering if it would be appropriate to say, but then forged on. "I think Guanyu would be too."

Shantie laughed. "I know he would. He said it himself. That's what his final message meant, you know."

"It is?"

"It sure is. That brat. He knew about my feelings for Yuyan long before I did. He tried getting me to tell her for years before . . . well, before everything."

Rosy took an extra second to process that information. "But what would that have meant? For you two?"

Shantie shot her an amused look. "Nothing like you're thinking. The way I loved Guanyu and the way I love YuYu, they're not so different. Guanyu always said it just meant my heart was big enough for both of them. I regret not going for it sooner. Not giving us the time to figure out what it would have looked like, all three of us."

They reached Witch Hall's small dock. Shantie sat at the end of it and stared out at Wimahl River. The reflection of the barely waning moon was distorted slightly by the gently lapping water. Rosy looked from it to Shantie. For all her apparent amusement, there was deep sadness in the lines around her eyes and mouth—as if she was fighting back tears. Sitting next to her, Rosy rested her shoulder against Shantie's in a silent offer of support.

"It could have been perfect, you know," Shantie said finally. "YuYu never wanted a flower familiar, but Shaw needs one for her entourage. If Guanyu was here—if he was still with us, he could have filled that role."

Rosy could picture it then. She had no idea if Shantie and Yuyan would have been able to bond on top of Guanyu's bond with Shantie, but even so they could have been together. All three of them, however they wanted. Shantie the permanent gate crasher of Shaw's entourage meetings. Rosy could just imagine how Shantie's cheer would have brightened the room. How Guanyu's sly humor and Yuyan's sarcastic quips would have played off each other.

"It would have been perfect," Rosy agreed, soft in the face of Shantie's sadness. Soft in the face of her own. Yuyan would have to choose a different familiar. One who might not understand the relationship between Shantie and Yuyan. Who might try to get in the middle of it. "There are familiars who don't want to bond at all," she said, thinking out loud. "Maybe one of them, at least, for the entourage . . ."

"Yuyan's working on it," Shantie said. "You'll just have to work to make sure that familiar doesn't feel excluded."

Shantie was speaking like Rosy would be in charge of the familiars in the entourage. "It won't be me, Shantie. But I'm sure Tokey and Oluk will do their best." Rosy hesitated, then pulled the necklaces out to show Shantie. "This was what I was talking to Charles about. I'm going to tell Shaw to consider Emma. I think she'd be a strong Familiar Queen. She won't be afraid to share her opinion with Shaw. To fight for what's right."

Shantie's expression didn't change. She barely glanced at the necklaces before focusing on Rosy's face. "Do you really think Emma is a better choice than the familiar already standing at Shaw's side?"

Rosy didn't understand why these people who'd seen her horrible mistakes firsthand would even want her to become queen. "I can't, Shantie. You get it. Out of all of us, I know you get it. I'm not strong enough."

"You're stronger than you wish to admit."

"I'm not! I've failed so many times. I've turned my back when I should have fought. I make mistakes. What will that mean if I become queen? Failure would affect more than just me or my immediate family. It would affect the whole kingdom."

The circles under Shantie's eyes looked like dark crescents made sallow by the light of the nearly full moon. "Failure is never getting back up. Never trying again. Your mistakes may weigh heavy, but they aren't yours to carry alone. You weren't the only one who could have done differently. Who could have saved Guanyu. I might have given up. I went home and I wallowed. But you and Shaw reminded me that pushing forward and living with that pain is worth it. There is strength in working through our mistakes, no matter how horrific."

Rosy closed her eyes, unwilling to be haunted by the pain on Shantie's face anymore. "I don't know what to do," she whispered.

A gentle touch forced Rosy to open her eyes again. Shantie had the tips of her fingers pressed against Rosy's hand, staring down at the necklaces. "Tell me something. If Shaw were just a normal princess, if this war didn't hang over her head like an ax over an execution block, what would you be doing with those necklaces?"

She wouldn't be holding them. If Shaw hadn't been named Death's Heir? If there was no curse wreaking havoc on Vinland? No potential for a war that might spread across the entire continent? Rosy could admit the truth she'd been hiding from for months—she would have accepted Shaw's courtship necklace the first time it was offered. She would have let herself fall for this girl who would be queen. She would have figured out how to support her politically, because it wouldn't have felt as dire. Because gaining the approval of the jarls' council wouldn't have been as important when they didn't have to depose the Witch King and stop, or fight, the war he'd begun.

"Shantie," Rosy said when the silence had stretched thin enough that it couldn't do anything except snap. The leather of the necklaces dug into her palms as she squeezed them tight, held them close. "I made another mistake."

"So fix it," Shantie said, and there was no trace of that laughing, cheerful girl Rosy had met all those months before. "Shaw's not dead. You still have a chance."

Rosy had many reasons to rage at her past self, but this one felt worse for how easy it could have been to stop. She'd had months and months to figure out what everyone else had seen so clearly. "She told me she was done," Rosy whispered, and it sounded like a door being shut.

"Perhaps she is," Shantie acknowledged. "Are you?"

Chapter 26

SHAW

THE SPRING EQUINOX DAWNED AT THE BEGINNING OF THE sixth week of term. There was just one month left until graduation. One month until I was crowned Witch Queen of the Cursed Kingdom and forced to face my destiny.

I wished that Einar and Oluk could have had the freedom to wait. It had been six months since they started courting and that wasn't an unreasonable time for a witch and familiar to decide they wanted to bond, but neither Einar nor Oluk were impatient people. I thought they would have enjoyed a longer courtship, slowly growing closer and closer until they felt that the only way they could bridge that final gap was to bind their magics.

That was not our reality. So instead, the rest of the entourage and I did our best to make the event special despite the quick lead time. I'd asked Shugh, the grandson of the jarl of Desertmouth, and his childhood best friend, Lei, to arrange transportation for Oluk's family from his hometown an hour south of Desertmouth to Witch Hall. I hadn't realized how many siblings Oluk had until we had to make the seating chart. He was the middle child of seven—and the only one with magic of the bunch. His three elder siblings were all obsidian miners alongside his parents, while the younger three had apparently been encouraged to go to school in Desertmouth to learn their letters and numbers.

I vowed to take the time to sit down with Oluk's family and discuss the needs of literacy among my people. To brainstorm ways to make education available for even the poorest among them. It was yet another reason to strive for peace—so that I could focus on making the Cursed Kingdom better for all of my people. What priority could I give public education if I had to lead an army of the dead on a battlefield some thousand miles away?

In contrast to Oluk's large family, Einar only had his mother. She was one of the wealthiest merchants in all of the Cursed Kingdom, with a hand in almost every market. It didn't take long for us to learn, upon her introduction to the Blackwells, that she actually owned the mine that Oluk's family worked in. Judging by the look that crossed Einar's face at that revelation, he would be having words with his mother before she went back home. Madam Ottosen lived in Solberg, a bustling trades town that sat in the southwestern corner of the kingdom, far away from the consequences of any less ethical business practices she may have implemented upon the miners and farmers and other workers of her vast business empire.

Einar and Oluk weren't allowed to see each other for a full day leading up to the ceremony, so Yuyan, Aklemin, and I took all our meals in the senior glass witches' suite with Einar and his mother while Rosamund and Toketie mingled with Oluk and his boisterous family. My biggest regret in asking Rosamund for space—and having her listen to my request so adamantly—was the visible strain it had placed on her friendship with Oluk. I was glad when Oluk had pulled Rosamund into helping for the last week leading up to the ceremony. We'd certainly needed more hands to get everything ready.

The morning of the ceremony felt nostalgic. It was rare to spend the day with just with my original entourage. A reminder of how far we'd come from those years when it was the four of us, sitting together by the fire and eating in comfortable silence.

"Are you ready?" I asked once Yuyan had left with our dishes and Aklemin had gone to take Einar's mother to her seat for the ceremony.

Einar gave me a rueful smile. "If I say *not at all*, you'll know it's not an insult to Oluk?"

I smiled back and shook my head. "Of course I'll know. You're so in love with that boy that it makes the rest of us look emotionless."

"There are more emotions than just love," Einar chided.

I knew that far too well. "I'm happy for you," I said to keep the peace. Taking cues from Oluk's own frustration, Einar had been vocal this past month about his dislike for Rosamund's distance—even after Yuyan had talked with him. Considering that Yuyan and Shantie were now happily in their own relationship, I understood his frustration. I was the only member of my own entourage left alone.

Einar would rather see me forge a genuine friendship with Rosamund than turn her away entirely. Perhaps he was right. I wasn't sure the distance was helping, or at least not like Yuyan had hoped it would. I was all too aware of the hole Rosamund's absence had left in my growing entourage.

"Oluk is everything I could have wanted for you, and for our entourage," I said, because I knew what was most important just then. "We were all fools not to spare him the attention to see it earlier."

"We were," Einar agreed. "Sometimes I wonder if we'll spend the rest of our lives discovering all the ways we were willfully ignorant to things we should have been aware of."

"That's why the royal family has an entourage. So that we may bridge the gaps between our understanding and the many varied experiences of our people."

"There are more experiences than just that of the magicals in our society," Einar murmured.

I thought of Oluk's family and nodded. "Yes, there are." I glanced down at Einar, realizing that he was trying to distract himself from the coming ceremony. "But today isn't about that. It's about you and Oluk."

Einar touched the golden rune dangling in the crevice of his neck, then carefully untied the necklace to hold in his lap. "Very well, Shaw. I'm ready."

The entire school was seated on the central lawn of Witch Hall. At the top of the hill, framed by Witch Hall's waterfall, the other senior glass witches had built a beautiful bonding arch constructed from juniper wood and absolutely covered in blooming honeysuckle. Against the pink-orange sunset, it was picturesque.

Yuyan, Aklemin, and I had all spent last night helping Einar decorate his wheelchair with long gold chains that swooped along the back and jingled pleasantly with each turn of the wheels. The three of us also went in together on a bonding-day present—supple leather gloves imbued with half a dozen enchantments to keep his hands from cramping as he cranked his chair or etched runes or crafted anything his heart desired to build.

Once we got past the back rows of chairs, I let go so Einar could take over rolling himself and went to sit next to the rest of my entourage in the front row. Oluk was already under the bonding arch, shuffling his feet nervously as he watched Einar come down the aisle between the seats. Einar and Oluk were dressed in new outfits just for the occasion. An embroidered green-and-gold tunic for Oluk and a fur vest over a mauve long-sleeved shirt for Einar. The soft orange of the dipping sun cast a golden glow across their faces as they faced each other.

"How is he?" I asked Rosamund with my eyes still on Einar and Oluk.

"He barely ate," Rosamund said. "But I think it was anticipation more than nerves."

Toketie shushed us. The musicians I'd hired began to play the traditional melody—a sweeping violin meeting a resonating bass. Slowly, Oluk walked through the arch. Einar pushed his wheelchair to match him. They passed each other just under the arch's center and then turned in opposite directions. They both made a loop around, then went under it again. As one, they stopped just in the center, facing each other. An infinity knot, completed together.

There was no talking in a bonding ceremony. There didn't need to be. Einar held both palms up, offering the necklace he'd been given. Oluk, in return, took off the necklace he'd worn since they began courting. He held it between his fingers as he lowered both hands, palms down, over top of Einar's.

Officially, this was the last moment where either party could back out. None of us were surprised when Einar and Oluk barely paused. Their hands separated with each holding the other's necklace. Oluk had to bend low so they could reach each other's necks. In perfect synchronization, they clasped the necklace on their partner.

I held my breath. It was the last part of the bonding ceremony that often tripped up potential partners. It wasn't unheard of for witches and familiars to need to try multiple times before the bond took.

Oluk shifted into his first shift—the plain glass garter that had caused so many to ignore the young familiar. As a snake, Oluk slithered up Einar's leg and draped himself over Einar's lap.

Einar cupped Oluk's head with one hand. I didn't know how he could do that and not worry about smothering his partner. I'd always been glad that even the smallest bone animals were large enough to hold without fear.

The glass witches watching the ceremony began to hum as one. All the glass familiars in the crowd shifted and added their hisses or clicks or rattles. Madam Bai's small green snake wrapped around Madam Xu's enormous white python, and they hissed together loudly enough to drown out Mister Xu's humming.

I knew what was happening under that arch, though I couldn't feel glass magic the way I could feel bone. Einar was doing his best to push his magic inside of Oluk. By shifting into his first animal form, Oluk was trying to open a pathway to accept Einar's magic into the depths of his heart.

I'd attended several bonding ceremonies, and this part always varied in length. I knew that the strength of the bond didn't truly depend on how quickly it snapped together, but that was a common misconception. It did often show true compatibility. I worried, briefly, how Einar and Oluk would feel if they failed on their first attempt to connect.

The worry was proven obsolete in the next minute. Einar broke out into a huge grin. Oluk shifted from garter to rattlesnake to tortoise—though that last one proved heavy enough that runes on the side of Einar's chair that prevented him from toppling over lit up to stabilize them. Oluk quickly went human and clutched his witch's shoulders. Both of them laughed.

I joined the rest of the crowd as we all began to clap. A few glass witches whooped in celebration, and Shugh led a round of hoorahs. I happily joined in.

THE CELEBRATION OF EINAR AND Oluk's bonding was expected to last the entire night. Though it was traditional for me to open any ball, as the highest-ranked student on campus, I insisted that Einar and Oluk do so tonight. They had to improvise a few steps because of Einar's wheelchair, but they looked in high spirits throughout and the crowd loved it. When the second song began, the field soon became overcrowded with dancing partners.

I chose to find a table under one of the pavilions instead of fighting through the masses. My entourage rotated between the dance floor and the table. Yuyan didn't like dancing, but she allowed Shantie to pull her into a couple of favorites. Aklemin and Toketie danced together for three songs in a row before letting the other ice witches and familiars take their turns. Oluk and Einar went for an hour straight, then joined me at the table to catch their breath.

No one came to ask me to dance. It would be impolite to do so, considering my status, and I'd never given anyone permission to break those rules the way Aklemin had with the ice familiars two years prior, claiming to be too lazy to be the asker. For myself, I'd always been the one to ask my entourage or the various heirs or, very rarely, a few bone familiars over the years.

Today, I sat at the table with a full cup of water in front of me, even as my friends finished their breaks and went back out to keep dancing.

Rosamund stumbled over to our table, flush from an exuberant dance with a group of bone familiars. "I haven't seen you dance once tonight, Shaw!" she exclaimed. "Come on, the set list says our song is next."

"Our song?" I asked, refusing to listen to the extra thump my heart tried to give.

I wondered if Rosamund had drunk some of the spiced cider, but the look she gave me made me think she was well aware of what she had said. The stubborn glint in her eyes that I'd always found unreasonably attractive had returned sometime in the last week. I didn't know what it meant, or why it had only come back now.

"Dance with me?" Rosamund asked, more intentional now. Soft but not gentle. There was a deadly edge to her voice, like she was preparing to unsheathe a weapon.

I stood and held out my arm. Rosamund took it and pulled me to the edge of the dancing area, away from the mass of bodies in the center. We got into position just as the next song began. It was the song we'd used to open the floor at the autumn equinox ball six months prior. *Our song*, Rosamund had said.

"Do you believe in inevitability?" I asked, bowing in time with the music.

Rosamund curtsied. When she rose from it, she said, "I think things are only inevitable when we think they are."

"Self-fulfilling prophecies," I said.

"Exactly."

The first verse began. Rosamund danced away from me. I watched her go until my music cue, then stepped after her. Once we were in line with each other, we swayed left, right, and then circled each other. Our hands brushed, warm tingles flickering up my arm.

"You didn't ask Emma to dance," Rosamund said. "I was watching. Not Emma or Charles or Ragna."

"Why would I ask any of them to dance?"

"Because you want a partner," Rosamund said, sharp as a knife.

It was my verse to run away, so I did. I danced off the area of the field meant for it, to the edge of the waterfall's creek.

Rosamund chased me like the wolf she was. We swayed and circled and touched again.

"You had years to choose a familiar before I came to school," Rosamund said. "You told me yourself, didn't you? When you asked me to keep your courtship necklace. You said there was no one at school you wanted."

"No one except for you," I said, because Rosamund seemed determined to have this conversation. At least we were now far enough away that I doubted anyone could hear us.

Rosamund took the third and final verse to hop across the creek into the woods east of campus. I chased after her. The music was nearly too far away to make out, but I swayed and circled from memory. We ended with a bow and a curtsy and stayed there, frozen like a painting, for a beat too long.

"You gave me your apologies and wouldn't let me say my own," Rosamund said, lifting from the curtsy to take one step closer to me. I resisted the urge to back away. I'd always been taught to stand my ground when faced with a predator.

"I don't need your apologies," I said.

"I'm a coward, Shaw. I've been one for so long, it's hard to find my bravery. No, it's my turn to speak, please," she added when I opened my mouth to protest. "I need to tell you something I should have told you months ago. Something I should have been brave enough to say when you asked instead of pretending to sleep to get out of answering."

My breath caught in my throat. The only question I could remember asking when she was sleeping was that one in the obsidian mine. It ripped out of me again, entirely without my say-so. "Am I your pack, Rosamund Holt?"

Rosamund let out a little laugh like I'd startled her. "You're so much braver than me. I admire that about you. Yes, Shaw Colchuck. You're my pack. You and your entourage. I was foolish to believe I could ever walk away from you all. These last weeks have been miserable. I tried giving you space, I really did, but I don't want space from you."

The hope that had begun to ignite in my chest began to sputter. "I didn't mean for you to distance yourself completely. I know you're friends with my entourage, and they with you. You'd always be welcome among them, if only because your cousin is one of ours now."

"I appreciate that, but don't misunderstand me on purpose." Rosamund gave a little stomp of her foot, almost like an impatient horse. "You asked for distance, but maybe I needed it too. I apparently wasn't going to figure myself out any other way."

"Rosamund, don't be cruel," I said. What was it about this familiar that could reduce me to begging, where no one else ever managed it? I didn't want to hear her tell me that we should try our hand at true friendship. Even if Einar and Oluk and Toketie would celebrate the thought, I couldn't stand to hear it. Not tonight, on the heels of a bonding ceremony so beautiful it had made me long for things I would never have.

"Oh, Shaw," Rosamund murmured. "I really haven't been kind to you, have I?"

"All part of your charm," I said wryly. She hadn't given me any consideration from the start, but then, I hadn't given her much reason to. Not before. Perhaps not even now, weeks after I'd asked her to go away just to spare my own feelings.

"No," Rosamund said, as if she could read my thoughts on my face. "You deserve so much better. I don't know that it's me, to be honest. I still think you could do better for a partner and a fellow queen. But when Froya asked Aklemin to respect Toketie's choice, it made me realize I never respected yours. I've been holding myself back out of fear. But I'm done running."

"What are you saying?" I asked, because I had to. Because I couldn't stifle the roaring hope in my chest any longer.

Instead of answering, Rosy reached up with both hands and pulled me down for a kiss.

I wasn't strong enough to pull away once my lips were on hers. I surged closer instead, wrapping one arm around her waist and the other around her shoulders so that I could clasp a hand to the base of her head. Her lips were winter-chapped, but she tasted like berries and cream. I chased the taste into her mouth, wanting to devour her. If this was to be my one chance, I would remember it forever.

She pulled back to breathe, and I opened my eyes to the sight of hers filling with tears.

"I love you, Shaw," she said, voice thick. "I'd want you even if you were a simple horse seller I met at Gravestown's market or a small-town witch who'd never even been invited to Witch Hall. But I want you now exactly as you are. As Death's Heir and future Witch Queen and everything in between."

"Rosamund, Rosy, my love." I couldn't stop my voice from shaking. Or maybe it was my body that shook—all the repressed feelings driving through my blood and my bones like a flood of winter melt. "Please tell me you're being true. Let me give you a new necklace and tell me you won't tear it off this time. I won't be able to go through that again. Not now, not after everything."

I knew I couldn't make her promise. A courtship wasn't forever, not like a bond was. She had every right to remove my necklace. Not to tear it off and throw the broken pieces at my face, perhaps, but she was always allowed to return it to me.

Except, even despite my unreasonable request, Rosamund was smiling. "How about I give you the necklace this time? I know it's not proper, but you already courted me. Isn't it my turn?"

"I never completed my courtship. I still have a third gift to give you."

"Shaw, you gave me the moonstones and a huge plot of land and a horse to pasture on it. You have more than exceeded the courtship expectations."

"We weren't courting then," I said stubbornly. I wanted the chance to do it right this time.

"We can court each other," Rosamund replied indulgently, leaning up to give me another kiss.

"If you insist," I conceded. I kissed her again, relishing that I was allowed to. A thought occurred to me, and I pulled back. "Wait, were those rumors that you had a new necklace made true?"

"Yes. There's two actually. Come with me, I'll show you." Rosamund tugged me to follow her.

I nearly let her pull me, but propriety won out. "We shouldn't leave Einar and Oluk's party without saying goodbye."

"Didn't you see them sneak off half an hour ago?" Rosamund

laughed at my disgruntled expression—I hadn't, in fact, noticed that. "It *is* their bonding night, Shaw."

She was right, and I let her own giddiness sweep me away. I grabbed her hand and entwined her fingers against my own. "I think you need to let me resume my courtship. Tradition says we'd have to do the usual week of silence if you offered me a necklace instead."

"Fine, you win." Rosamund began walking determinedly toward the bone familiars' suite. "I still say you've given me all three of the courtship gifts though. So I can give you the bonding necklace whenever I want."

"Take your time," I said, tone dropping to show her that I was serious. "I know the future is scary, but I want you to be sure of us before you commit to anything." I might be able to survive Rosamund removing my courtship necklace, but the thought of her running away from a bonding arch was unbearable.

Rosamund stopped walking so suddenly I nearly ran into her. She turned, twisting our hands up so they were clasped between our chests. "I am sure," she said. "You're my pack, and wolves mate for life."

I remembered General Holt and Ylva's ghosts floating together at the heart of the Forest, still besotted after decades of life and years of death piled upon them. "I love you," I said, though three simple words didn't seem enough to encompass everything I felt. "Rosamund Holt, I can offer you all this kingdom has, every courtship gift you could ever want and then some, but in truth, what I have to give is only my own heart. Will you accept it?"

Rosamund's smile was like summer, and it melted all the ice still lingering in the shadowed corners of my heart. She leaned forward and whispered against my lips, "I will."

Chapter 27

"About time," Charles remarked as Rosamund and I passed him on our way to breakfast the next morning.

After years of seeing only the deferent version of Charles Almstedt, it was refreshing to be faced with snideness—even if the snideness was directed more at Rosamund than at me.

"Yes, yes, you were right, I was wrong," Rosamund replied, rolling her eyes. "Go away, Charles."

Charles pranced off like the stag he was, a smug smile still gracing his lips. I leaned in to press a kiss to the baby hairs frizzing out around Rosamund's temples. "I love it when you take charge," I murmured.

Rosamund rolled her eyes again, this time at me. "I need tea." She pulled away and retreated to the food line. The back of her neck was flushed pink.

I chose not to follow her, heading first to the table where Aklemin, Yuyan, Toketie, and Shantie already sat. Einar and Oluk were nowhere to be seen, but that was hardly surprising. No one could expect them to be on time for breakfast the day after their bonding ceremony.

"My brother's wife made the necklaces," Toketie said as I sat down. "Rosy helped design them, but my sister-in-law's the one who actually made them."

"She's a wonderful craftsman," I responded. "They're both beautiful pieces."

"Has Miss Rosy already tried to give you the other one?" Aklemin asked, a touch amused.

I glared at them, though my heart wasn't in it. "I wouldn't let her. Not yet. I'd like to give Einar and Oluk at least a couple weeks before upstaging them with my own bonding ceremony." Despite the levity in my words, I still worried over Rosamund's desire to give me the bonding necklace so quickly. Months of heartache could not be soothed so easily, and a part of me might always fear her leaving again.

Aklemin hummed, as if they were holding back a comment.

"I'm glad it worked out, Shaw," Yuyan said. "Really glad."

A smattering of applause rose up from the dining hall. I looked over to see Einar and Oluk coming through the double doors. Even from this distance, I could see the pink that spread over Oluk's cheeks at the attention.

"Guanyu wanted to have our bonding ceremony at school," Shantie murmured as the applause died away. "I managed to convince him that I'd rather do something small, but . . ." She trailed off, obviously unwilling to continue.

I'd been one of the few invited to Shantie and Guanyu's ceremony. I'd gone mostly to keep Yuyan company. It had been a small event—just a handful of students and Shantie's and Guanyu's families. Still— "It was lovely," I told her sincerely. "There is no shame in a simple bonding ceremony, especially not one as beautiful as yours, I promise."

Shantie gave me a small smile. Yuyan stood. "I'll get you some more tea," she said.

I watched Shantie watch her go, wondering if she was offended at Yuyan's lack of comfort. But when Shantie turned to see me looking, she merely shrugged. "She's always had horrible bedside manners, hasn't she?"

"The worst," Aklemin agreed, so dramatically that it made Shantie snort with laughter.

"Not everyone shows their care in the same way," Toketie said softly.

"No, of course not," Shantie said. "I've known YuYu for many years. She'll bring me tea exactly how I like it. I also know that, if Guanyu were here instead of me, she'd do the same for him. That's her version of care, and it's part of why I fell for her."

Rosamund approached the table with a plate full of breakfast and two steaming mugs. "Here," she said, handing one to me. "They didn't have the lemon-ginger blend you like, but I think this one's your second favorite."

I took the tea and smiled down at my reflection on the surface of the liquid. "Thank you," I murmured. "I'm going to join Einar and Oluk in the food line. Does anyone want something else?"

Aklemin, Shantie, and Toketie all shook their heads. Rosamund set her own overflowing tray down on the table and waited until I got up before climbing over the bench. She began to attack her food like a ravenous animal, and I resisted the urge to kiss her head again, overflowing with indulgent joy.

There were several students in line behind Einar and Oluk, but they waved me to pass them. I thanked each of them—making two of the younger students giggle—as I took the spot behind my friends.

"Good morning, Shaw," Einar said placidly.

"Good morning," I replied. "I'm sure you're tired of hearing it by now, but I do want to give you both one more congratulations. It was an honor to be a part of making last night happen for you."

"Shugh ran to tell us about Rosy's new necklace as we were getting ready this morning," Oluk said. "So I guess last night was good for everyone."

If I had been given an ounce less court training, I might have blushed. "Yes, well . . ." I looked back to where Rosamund sat at the table, surrounded by the other members of my entourage. She was laughing at something Aklemin was saying while Yuyan buried her head in her hands in exasperation. "She fits."

"She does," Einar agreed.

"And she makes room for others," Oluk said. He accepted a spoonful of eggs from the students on serving duty. As he turned away to head back to the table, he added, "I'd resigned myself to war, you know? Given up hope that I'd be able to do anything after graduating Witch Hall except enlist in the army. But now we have a real chance of giving the younger students a choice in their future. Because she chose to fight for peace, and you chose to listen. I'll always be grateful for that."

I SUMMONED MY CLASSMATES TO the seniors' corner during the third and final full moon assembly of term. The last week of school was quickly approaching and, with it, graduation. All the jarls had elected not to come for the assembly since they would gather instead for Witch Hall's graduation ceremony, as they always did. Which meant tonight was the perfect opportunity to make a plan for how to convince the jarls' council on the subject of peace with Vinland.

Rosamund and I stood together facing the heirs—a pair, a united front, partners, just as I'd always dreamed.

"Next week, the jarls' council will come to Witch Hall to watch the graduation ceremony. After, they will approve my to claim the Witch Throne and announce the day of the coronation ceremony," I said. "They will also discuss declaring war with Vinland."

"We can't let them," Rosamund continued, jumping in at my pause like it was natural. "We have to convince them that peace is possible."

"At minimum, we must delay them until we have time to negotiate with Prince Vetle," I added.

"What do you need us to do?" Charles asked.

I remembered having a similar conversation with Charles, Froya, and Kwaddis leading up to Candlemas. This felt different. All the heirs were here, sitting in the front, while the rest of the seniors who'd chosen to take Advanced Combat with me this term sat at the tables behind them. Everyone understood what was at stake, and had put their blood and sweat into preparing for what was coming.

After half an hour of talking strategy with the assembled heirs and other seniors, I dismissed them to go enjoy their final assembly of our time at Witch Hall.

"Chao," I called before he could leave with the rest. "If you have a moment, we should talk."

Chao redirected to my side without hesitation. Jingyi followed at his heels. I didn't bother asking the bone familiar to leave—his support of his witch was stringent, and he wouldn't go unless Chao wanted him to.

I'd been putting off this conversation, primarily because I struggled to predict how Chao would react to it. His mother was on house arrest with my father, but my entourage and I knew that Chao's father was our most likely opponent in our approaching fight for peace. I'd written back and forth with the jarls several times over the term, and as expected, Bao had never replied to the trial summons. The jarls couldn't put out an official wanted notice without revealing the treason to people at large—something they wished to avoid—but the various companies of the army were on alert for any sign of him.

"I need to tell you what Aklemin saw in the Candlemas vision," I began. "And what we believe will happen because of it."

"Don't try to spare my feelings, Shaw," Chao said. "Not now. I know it's arrogant to call us the same, but I was there. I know how hard it must have been to speak against your own father. I want to believe that my parents were just manipulated, that they didn't really understand what the Witch King was working toward, but that's childish."

I gave Chao a wry smile at that. "I wish we could afford to still be children. But we can't. And your father is the only member of my father's entourage left unaccounted for."

Chao clenched his jaw, until Jingyi hugged him from behind. He let out a long, steadying breath. At my side, Rosamund stepped close enough for me to smell the faint hint of vanilla and pine that drifted off her cloak.

"What is he going to do?" Chao asked.

I told him, because out of everyone, he deserved to know. When I was done, Chao nodded once. "We've trained for months now to fight with you, *for* you. I won't hesitate just because it's my own father at the helm. It's . . . Shaw, it's ridiculous, isn't it? How could they possibly think any of this was a good idea?"

"Our parents want what's best for us," I said. "Only, what they believe is best is not what we do. Is not, I think, what's best for anyone except the rare few who will benefit. I will not lead so selfishly. For all their arguments, I have to believe there is a kinder way to rule that leads to a better future for everyone."

Chao glanced to my left, to where Rosamund stood. "I have faith that you both can find one."

"Always knew you had what it took," Jingyi whispered to Rosamund. "I love being right."

Chao laughed and twisted around to pull Jingyi to his side. "Enough of that. We should go make an appearance at the feats."

"As you say, Chao-er," Jingyi said, the picture of innocence.

Rosamund and I watched them go, bemused.

"I think you doubt how loyal your classmates are to you," Rosamund said once they were out of sight. The seniors' corner had emptied entirely.

"I don't believe I've done much to earn their loyalty," I admitted. "Only that this war has hung over all of us so long that any chance to prevent it is worth trying for."

Rosamund shook her head. "No, Shaw, that's not it at all. I avoided coming to Witch Hall for years because of my fear. I saw the damage war could do, and I was terrified of it. And in a handful of months, you made me reconsider. Do you want to know the real reason I ran away when you offered me the army contract?"

I wasn't sure I did, but Rosamund was forging ahead before I could say so.

"I ran because I could see myself fighting. I could picture what it would be like, following you into war, and a part of me wanted it. I'd let Guanyu die due to my own cowardice, and I regretted it so severely it was killing me. But it's so easy to trust you, because you will never ask your people to do things you wouldn't do yourself. You may send your classmates to battle, but you will be there fighting alongside them. I promised to be your weapon as penance, even though it would have destroyed me. And instead you've found a new path that I can actually be proud to fight for. *That* is why we're loyal."

Throughout Rosamund's little speech, something began to build in my chest. Bigger and bigger, until my lungs felt so tight that I could barely breathe. Rosamund believed in me so strongly that I couldn't help but want to be better. To live up to this fantastical image she had of me.

"I'm not the only one who inspires loyalty," I said, choking on the words.

Rosamund huffed a bit, obviously not interested in hearing any compliments to her own inspiring presence. She reached up to rest her fingertips gently against my cheek. Tingles of warmth shot through me as our magics mingled.

"I want to bond with you," she said, soft and sure. "I know you're afraid I'll regret it, but I've never been so sure of anything in my life."

The thing was, I knew bonding with Rosamund was the most practical solution to a whole host of potential issues. The necklace she wore would help combat her feral rages, but it wasn't infallible. What if it was ripped away or otherwise destroyed? And bonding with her would increase my own powers tenfold. We wouldn't need to be touching for me to access her magic, which would give us significantly more flexibility if this turned into a true battle.

Only, I didn't want us to bond because it was the practical

thing to do. I spent years searching for a partner who could fill all the practical requirements of the Familiar Throne, but deep down I've always wanted someone whose real desire was simply to be with me.

I put my hand over Rosamund's fingers, clutching them tightly until I couldn't tell which one of us was trembling. I said nothing, but I leaned down to kiss her and she seemed to accept that was all the response I could give her.

By the time graduation dawned, the perennial trees had regained their leaves and the first flowers were beginning to bud. Spring had overtaken the land. There were no more barriers to another attempt at invasion—or to Bao Hu's reply to one.

The graduation ceremony was a pompous affair. The Witch King normally came down from the Mountain to preside, but of course he was absent this year. Jarls Falk, Tenas, and Almstedt took turns giving the commencement speeches inside the crowded dining hall as all the students watched. The round tables the teachers normally sat at had been taken over by the rest of the jarls' council, leaving the teachers to stand on the makeshift stage that had been assembled for the ceremony.

The seniors and I stood along the wall near the doors of the dining hall, waiting for our turn to come to the stage. Rosamund kept fidgeting next to me. I reached out and rested a hand at the nape of her neck, letting my touch soothe her as much as it soothed me.

"I never thought I'd be here," Rosamund murmured as Jarl Tenas droned on.

"Well, you never planned to come to Witch Hall."

"Exactly. I was happy with Gran. Well, as happy as I could be, with her imprisonment. But Shantie reminded me that we can't live our lives constantly regretting the what-could-have-beens. We can only move forward with what we can do now."

Jarl Tenas finally concluded his speech. I reluctantly removed my hand from where it had been stroking the woven leather of Rosamund's necklace so I could clap along with the rest of the room.

"I'm glad you're here, Rosamund Holt," I whispered to her. "My what-could-have-beens would have been much worse without you."

Jarl Falk stepped forward. "We will begin with the ice witches and familiars. When you hear your name, please step forward to receive your graduation medal."

They opened a copy of the Witch Hall graduates tome that listed every recorded graduate of the school since its founding. All of us seniors would have been added to it that morning just before the ceremony, once Madam Kawak had confirmed our grades and senior projects. With the mess that had been the second half of our senior year, several seniors had struggled to complete their projects—but we'd all banded together to help each other this last month. Not a single senior had failed to graduate in the end.

With every student and teacher at school in attendance, the applause was loud and sustained. You could barely hear Jarl Falk as they announced the names. The order was, as always, first familiars, then witches. Ice, then glass, then flower, and finally bone.

Within each category, names were announced in reverse order of rank, so that the most politically powerful received the final medal and spoke a couple words to give thanks for their group.

Toketie Holt was the very first name called, sparking murmurs among the rest of the school. She wore Aklemin's courtship necklace, but by law she didn't officially take on their status until bonding. Toketie didn't seem to care as she walked onto stage with her head high to receive the very first graduation medal of the year. The rest of her suitemates followed as Jarl Falk read the names, ending finally with their own daughter, Froya Falk.

Instead of saying her words, Froya gestured for Toketie to come to the front of the stage with her.

"The ice familiars are grateful to all of our teachers and our classmates for these years at Witch Hall," Toketie said, loud enough to be heard over the sudden murmurings of surprise. She turned to a table of jarls and curtsied. "Thank you."

Froya nodded to her parent and walked with Toketie to the corner of the room where the rest of the ice familiars waited. It took Jarl Falk a second to recover before they began to read the names of the ice witches.

When it was Aklemin's turn to speak, they said, "I too am grateful for all our classmates. The future has long sat darkly upon our horizon, but hope, I've found, can arise from unexpected places and in unpredictable ways. There is brightness rising over the horizon now, and I, for one, cannot wait to see what colors it brings to our sky."

Aklemin's words sparked a memory I'd long forgotten. Of the procession through the small town of Forest's Edge. I remember how Aklemin had been captivated by a girl struggling with a temperamental bone horse at one of the quaint little market stalls.

I think it has a certain charm, they'd told me. *Like a candle in the darkness. A streak of sunlight after a thunderstorm.*

There were still storm clouds gathering, but I had to hope we would be strong enough to weather them until blue skies returned.

Jarl Esalth was next, to read the names of the glass students. Oluk was the last in that group. He'd practiced with Einar several times over the last week, and I was proud to see him deliver his thank-yous with only one small, nervous stutter. "The best lesson I learned from my time at Witch Hall is that perseverance does win out in the end," he concluded. "I'm proud to be among classmates who have faced some of the worst things the world has to offer and, instead of crumbling under the pressure, have rallied together to face them again."

Madam Bai actually whooped instead of clapping when he finished.

The stage had not originally been designed for a wheelchair like Einar's, but Mister Jostein had helped build a ramp on both sides so there was no issue when Einar's name finished up the glass witches' group. Because he was seated, I could barely see him over the heads of all the students seated in the dining hall in front of me. But I heard Einar's deep voice clearly as he expressed his gratitude: "For all that has changed, we have found strength through our bonds with one another. Not just those of a magical nature, but those of the more esoteric kind that may be nurtured through companionship and trust. May those bonds continue to grow with time and dedication."

I clapped especially hard for that one.

Jarl Tenas returned to the stage next to announce the flower familiars and witches. Like Froya, Kwaddis did not step up to give the thank-you. Instead, he nodded for Lei to take the center stage.

"Kwad—" Jarl Tenas began.

Kwaddis shushed his own father.

"I'm thankful for the years I've had at Witch Hall," Lei began. "As many of you know, I used to hate that I was a flower familiar. When my best friend discovered he was a glass familiar, I was determined to follow him. I am grateful to my suitemates for giving me a home despite how I behaved those first few years. I'm grateful too that even though we can't bond, Shugh has agreed to marry me anyway."

Shugh Esalth grinned as everyone turned to stare at where he was standing with the glass familiars.

"And I'm grateful that Yuyan has asked me to take on the role of flower familiar in Shaw's entourage, because that gave me the rank to be able to propose to Shugh, since he apparently was never going to do it."

"Hey!" Shugh protested. "I was working up to it!"

The hall exploded in laughter.

"Did you know?" Rosamund asked me quietly. She wasn't the only one visibly shocked by Lei's declaration.

"Yuyan told me last night," I said. I hadn't been convinced Lei was a better choice over Kwaddis, but I hadn't said anything because I'd given Yuyan permission to do what she thought was best. Now, after hearing Lei's speech and seeing how Kwaddis cheered, I was mollified. I would accept Lei *and* Shugh into my entourage meetings, just as I'd accepted Shantie. It wasn't traditional, but I'd long since decided tradition wasn't always right.

The flower witches went much more smoothly than the familiars. Yuyan gave her gratitude in just a few sincere words, then went to rejoin Shantie and the rest of the flower witches. Shantie entwined her fingers in Yuyan's.

Jarl Almstedt stepped up onto the stage last. Rosamund's name was the first called, to the obvious surprise of most of the school.

Had they already forgotten that Toketie too had gone first? For all that Rosamund had stepped up into her place as my partner, she wasn't officially heir to the Familiar Throne until we bonded.

Charles was the last to receive the medal for familiars. Jarl Almstedt whispered a few words to her son as she placed it over his head. Whatever she said made Charles shake his head. I thought we all knew what was about to happen. If nothing else, Jingyi's broad grin was a clear sign that he expected it.

"Rosamund," Charles called, gesturing with a single finger for Rosamund to come back on the stage.

Rosamund squeezed Charles's arm as she passed, and he held his head high as if he'd been craving that tacit approval.

"I came to Witch Hall far later than I should have," Rosy began, a touch hesitantly. Unlike Oluk, she hadn't practiced her speech, at least not in my earshot. "I spent many years hiding who I really was out of fear. I made a lot of assumptions about Witch Hall and my fellow students. I know I've frustrated most of you in my short time here."

There was laughter at that, especially among the seniors.

"All of us!" Charles shouted back, and even more laughter erupted. A few of the teachers, Madam Bai among them, joined in.

Rosy smiled, and her next words came louder and more confidently. "I'm so grateful for the friends I've made here. For the teachers and the classes that taught me things I hadn't realized I would need, but that I now can't imagine forgetting. And especially to Shaw."

Across the dining hall, I met Rosamund's hazel-green gaze.

"Thank you for being willing to listen. For being willing to change. The path we're taking isn't easy, but it's the right one and I'm proud to walk it alongside you."

I touched my fingers to my lips, unsuccessfully hiding a smile.

I didn't have to wait long before it was my turn to walk up onstage after the rest of my suitemates. I lowered my head so that Jarl Almstedt could put the final graduation medal around my neck, then turned—not to face the rest of the dining hall, but to face the wall where all the seniors waited, graduation medals gleaming on their chests.

"I'm grateful to all of you. For believing in me. For trusting me, even when I didn't trust myself. I'm grateful to you for fighting beside me, in whatever manner you've chosen to do so. I can't guarantee a peaceful future, but I can guarantee that I will fight for one. I will fight for us, because we deserve a chance to live without war."

I bowed to my classmates, even though it put my back to the jarls' council. When I rose from my bow, I saw the seniors all bowing and curtsying back. Only Rosamund didn't—standing in the front of the seniors like a waystone guiding my path forward.

I kept my eyes on her as I said one final thing. "Tonight, after the graduation feast, I would like to invite each of you to the bonding ceremony of myself and Rosamund. You have supported us throughout our relationship, even when that support may have seemed foolish, and I can think of no better way to repay you than to show you how far your support has brought us."

It was a good thing that everyone's eyes were on me, because the cheers drowned out Rosamund's gasp of surprise. I nodded to her. I had decided. On the eve of change, I would hold on. I would complete the claim that I'd begun nearly nine months prior. I would trust in Rosamund, as she trusted in me, and we would face the future together.

Chapter 28

THE JARLS' COUNCIL STAYED BEHIND AS THE STUDENTS headed off to finish packing. While some students had already left, most had stayed to watch graduation. There would be a send-off feast tonight, and then everyone else would leave the following morning. Some of the seniors would head home to celebrations with their families and hometowns, proudly showing off their graduation medals and their new place among Witch Hall's alumni. Most of the seniors—those who'd promised to fight with me—had already decided to stay at Witch Hall instead for an extra week of preparation. Beltane rapidly approached, and I was simultaneously ready to be done and dreading the conclusion.

The newly graduated heirs joined their parents at the round tables at the rightmost end of the dining hall—Charles with Jarl Almstedt, Kwaddis with Jarl Tenas, and Froya with Jarl Falk. Kalitan took a seat next to her brother, while Shugh sat near his grandfather. Lei hovered around Shugh's shoulder. Chao and Jingyi stuck to the wall as if unsure of their welcome. Powish and a few of the younger heirs hesitated at the door, but their parents sent them away—something I approved of. Leave the talk of war to the adults, which I and the rest of the seniors now counted among.

I stood just in front of the stage with Rosamund at my side.

Aklemin and Toketie were perched to our left, and Einar and Oluk on our right. Yuyan and Shantie took places on the wall next to Chao and Jingyi, as if to offer silent support to Chao's presence in the room despite his traitorous parents. I planned to have the council appoint Chao as the new Jarl Hu as soon as I was crowned queen. Aklemin would need to be named Jarl Alki as well, which would put two people on the council I could trust from the very start of my rule. That was a comforting thought.

"Esteemed jarls," I began. "I stand before you as a graduate of Witch Hall. Do you confirm my status as heir apparent to the crown of the Cursed Kingdom?"

"We confirm it," Jarl Falk said.

"We made the Witch King sign a letter of abdication before we left the Mountain," Jarl Tenas added. "We will cite health concerns for why he isn't present at the coronation ceremony, then crown you as Witch Queen."

It was a decent excuse. My father would live under house arrest for the remainder of his life, so there would need to be a reason given to explain his complete withdrawal from society. That wouldn't explain Jarl Alki's, Jarl Hu's, or General Tepeh's arrests though.

I'd worry about that problem later, after I was crowned. There was a far more pressing concern.

"And the Royal Company?" I asked. "What did the council decide about them?" The deliberations had still been ongoing during the last letter I'd received.

"Though they cannot be charged with any crimes, as they were following orders, the members of the company have been disbanded and split among the squads and platoons of the other companies. We plan to re-form the Royal Company after your coronation," Jarl Almstedt explained.

"What of Jarl Anders's platoon?" I pressed. "Those who physically crossed the border to slaughter innocent Vinlanders should at least face dishonorable discharge from the army."

I'd said as much in my last letter, but I could see on the jarls' faces that they disagreed.

"They were just following orders," Jarl Falk repeated.

"Bibi," Froya protested, but her parent didn't even look at her.

"And Bao Hu?" I pressed.

Several jarls looked over at Chao. Jingyi pressed closer to his witch, scowling.

"He has not been located," Jarl Tenas admitted. "But he will not escape justice."

I glanced toward Aklemin in time to watch them wander over to the tea table. They normally drowned their tea in honey, but it seemed the jarls were stressing them out enough to need a stronger brew.

"As I explained in my letters, the Candlemas vision gave evidence that Bao will attempt to complete what my father began," I said. "It's not enough to covertly search for him. What has the council decided on the matter of Vinland?"

"By your own admission, the land has been cursed," Jarl Almstedt said. "You can't mend an egg that's already cracked. Soon enough, the inside will rot."

"The emperor is not convinced by his son's thirst for revenge," I argued. "We need only to convince Vetle to give up his quest for vengeance, and we can broker peace with the empire. None of us want to face the fury of the Empire of Vinland. If there is a way to save our people that trauma, should we not pursue it?"

"And how do you propose we do that?" Jarl Falk asked. "Spring is here, Princess. War will soon be upon us."

"If there will be war, then I will fight in it," Kwaddis said.

"Son," Jarl Tenas protested.

"As will I," Froya said.

"You no longer have a contract with the army!" Jarl Almstedt protested.

"No, but I have loyalty to my queen," Charles replied. "We will all fight. If you will send our queen to war, then we will follow her." Kalitan and Shugh nodded.

"Give us until Beltane," I said before the jarls could argue more.

"We don't have until Beltane," Aklemin stated.

I spun to look at them, still standing by the tea table. They'd drained their cup empty of all but tea leaves, and now stared down at it with an emptier expression.

"Your father and his entourage have escaped the Mountain," they said, almost monotone, as if they were reading from a script. "I see them meeting Thane Anders's platoon across the river. The prince readies another group of warriors to attack, and they mean to intercept him."

My heart had sunk into my stomach. All term I'd been preparing to face Bao and a handful of deserters, but to have to face my father and his entire entourage? I wanted to rage at the jarls for not securing their prison properly, but there was no time for anger—only practicalities.

"Beltane's more than a week away," I said.

"Yes," Aklemin agreed. "Your father won't dare to wait. The magic of Beltane would make it easier, but Bao has not been idle. He shrouded himself in bone magic so I couldn't scry him, but it's clear now. They will do the ritual as soon as the prince is in their possession. We must move now if we've any chance to stop it."

I closed my eyes, as if that could block out the truth Aklemin had just said. "We *must* stop them, or there will be no more chance to halt this war."

"I'll get the other seniors," Charles said, standing.

"Charles!" Jarl Almstedt snapped. "Sit down this instant."

Charles spun on his mother. "No, Mother. I promised to fight with Shaw, and I plan to."

"It's not worth it!" Jarl Almstedt yelled back. "She's already chosen that wolf familiar."

"I'm not doing this because I want to bond with her!" Charles shouted back. "You taught me to always stand up for myself. It took me far too long to realize that standing up for myself means standing up for others too. I will fight because fighting is the right thing to do, and I don't care if you disagree."

Kwaddis had also stood, but he stayed at the table staring his father down. "If we don't try, then we're telling everyone who's already died that they didn't matter. I won't do that either. Our own people deserved better than to have been sacrificed for a warmonger."

Jarl Tenas sputtered like a gaping fish as he stared up at his son, but Kwaddis did not stay at the table for him to collect himself enough to argue.

Froya slipped around her parent too. Jarl Falk tried to catch her attention, but she ignored them just as they'd ignored her earlier. "Come, we must get ready," she told Charles and Kwaddis, who immediately went to follow her.

Lei and Shugh hurried to join the procession of heirs leaving together in defiance. At least the jarl of Desertmouth looked like he approved. He nodded to his grandson, and Shugh stood straighter at the acknowledgment. Kalitan hugged her brother before following.

"Rosamund," I began.

"I got this," she said. "Charles, let Froya tell the others what's happening. I need you and Kalitan to get the shields and weapons into the boats. Lei, grab the food and water packs. Kwaddis, you're in charge of the potions and medical supplies. Shugh, those traps the glass witches made."

No one hesitated—setting off immediately. My entourage flocked after Rosamund, followed by Chao and Jingyi. I heard Rosamund direct them to their own tasks as I turned my attention back to the jarls.

"Princess—" Jarl Falk began to protest.

"I will soon be your queen, and I would have you respect me as one," I interrupted. "I cannot fathom why you would all rather prepare for war than try for peace. Is it because you assumed your own children would sit safely home while you send soldiers across the border to die in your name?"

"It's only natural to want to see our heirs safe," Jarl Tenas said. "We know the dangers of war!"

"As do we," I replied pointedly. "Your children follow of their own accord. They are all adults, they may make their own choices. If you can't trust them now, would you ever be able to trust them to take your seats on this council?"

"You're all so young. Don't throw your lives away over a fool's hope," Jarl Falk pleaded.

"Better a fool's hope than assured destruction. I will fight this war, but I will do so only after I have exhausted any and all attempts at peace."

"Your grandmother tried the same thing," Jarl Esalth, the old jarl of Desertmouth, said mildly. "And she was vilified for it."

She had been. I'd bought into the rhetoric myself, all my

childhood. Only now, faced with the realities of my own war, did I finally understand her. "So be it. I'd rather be vilified for kindness than for bloodthirst."

That, at last, seemed to get through to the jarls.

"I'll send Multah's Company after you, but they'll be a day behind," Jarl Tenas said.

"Reinforcements may very well be needed," I replied gratefully.

"The rest of us will wait in Multah with Jarl Tenas for your return," Jarl Falk said. "Do not risk your lives needlessly. If there is to be war, then we will all prepare for it together. But if there is a possibility for peace . . ." They looked across the round tables at their fellow jarls.

Jarl Tenas nodded. "Then we would welcome it," he said.

"Good luck, Shaw Colchuck," Jarl Almstedt added, weariness weighing down her tone. "You carry with you the future of the Cursed Kingdom."

I thought of Rosamund and my entourage and the rest of the seniors who'd agreed to fight for peace with me. "I don't carry it alone."

ROSAMUND FOUND ME IN MY suite, packing my bag. I didn't know how long we'd be in Vinland, but I'd learned to prepare for any eventuality. We'd keep the bags on the boats once we docked, but at least we would have them ready if this turned into a longer quest.

"Everyone's nearly ready. I told the others to make sure they eat something. We'll need the energy." Rosamund held out a bowl of stew. "Luckily, Madam Xu was nearly done preparing lunch."

I took the bowl. The meat was still steaming, so I blew generously before taking a bite and even then it was hot enough to scald my tongue. I forced it down and spooned another bite.

"You said tonight," Rosamund began. "That is, if you meant it—"

"I love you," I said. "We may not have had a conventional courtship, but I would happily keep you at my side forever, Rosamund."

Rosamund leaned in, and I had to lift the bowl of stew out of her way so she could lean against my chest. "I'm scared, Shaw. What if we're too late? What if the war is impossible to stop?"

"Then we will end it quickly and save our people as much hardship as we can," I said. "I know you're afraid of going feral. I'm sorry that I didn't say yes to you sooner."

If I'd just done as Rosamund had wished and bonded with her sometime in the last few weeks, she might have felt more confident going into this battle. I might have as well, with the strength of Rosamund's magic flowing through me.

Rosamund shook her head, rubbing her face against my shoulder as she did. "The necklace helps. I won't be a burden."

A burden? How could she even think that? I pulled back so that I could lift her chin up and press a hard kiss to her lips. "You never could be," I said once we had separated again. "You're everything I've always wanted, Rosamund Holt. I'm proud to face my future at your side."

Rosamund smiled and pulled away from me long enough to grab something from her pocket. It was the necklace—the one that complemented hers. "Will you wear it now?" she said. "Even if we can't bond tonight, I want to see the promise of what's to come."

I could tell that a part of Rosamund feared it might not come. Either I would change my mind or one of us would be killed or the war would begin and there would be no time for it. My own fear was simpler—I could not bear to be separated from her any longer.

I leaned down so that Rosamund could clasp the necklace around me. She had already pushed her magic into it, and the warmth that spread across my neck was more than welcome.

"I promise you, the moment this is over, one way or another, we will lay claim to each other," I murmured. "Let the jarls plan some big bonding ceremony when there's time for it. We don't have to wait. I will bond with you before our entourage and the seniors who've volunteered to fight with us."

"When?" Rosamund demanded.

"Tonight," I said, because I had promised that I would and I couldn't imagine turning back on my word now. Not with the warmth of Rosamund's magic tingling over my skin. It might take days to stop my father or it might take hours. Either way, I would carve out time tonight to bond with Rosamund before the eyes of our friends, and we would face our future as one.

It was early afternoon when we loaded the boats docked at Witch Hall's little pier and began to row toward Vinland. I sat in a longboat with my full entourage. Einar, Oluk, Rosamund, Aklemin, Yuyan, Shantie, Lei, and Shugh were all rowing, while Toketie flew over our heads and I sat at the rear, just behind Einar's stored wheelchair. All around us, the other seniors who'd promised to fight at my side were in boats of varying shapes and sizes—ranging from ferry rafts to canoes.

Petals floated in the reflection of sunlight on the surface of the river. It was unusually still—barely any current running through the center. We headed east through the gorge. Aklemin's scrying had revealed that Vetle planned to attack Desertmouth, and that my father was set to intercept him on Vinland's side of the river before he could.

I could tell the rowing was laborious from the sweat that began beading at Yuyan's forehead. She rarely sweated, and it was still cool enough that I was especially surprised to see it. I hoped the rowing wouldn't wear everyone out before we even got to the fight.

"Push!" I called, and the oars sliced through the water. "Push!"

Someone was whistling—but it wasn't in rhythm with the rowing. I turned in my seat, looking left and right to figure out which senior was making the noise. The basalt cliffs of the gorge loomed on either side of us. The whistling echoed off those canyon walls, seeming to come from all around us.

"Shaw, something isn't right," Lei said from her seat at the front of the longboat.

"Halt!" I called.

As soon as we stopped rowing, the boats slowed to a complete standstill. Outside of the slight bobbing as the seniors shuffled on their seats, the boats did not move an inch. The whistling grew louder.

"Is that . . . ?" Kwaddis said from the canoe to our left, but he didn't finish his thought aloud.

I carefully stood on the stern of the longboat so that I could peer over the heads of my classmates. There was a small cluster of orchids floating in the water just before us. Orchids with fully blooming petals puckered up just like lips. Whistling.

We weren't far from the end of the gorge where Rosamund and I had made our mad escape from Vinland months before. I remembered suddenly those vines that had wrapped around my leg. I'd been too distracted by the cold and shock to make note of it at the time, but I'd never known vines to grow within Wimahl River. Nor were orchids known for sitting on top of the water like lily pads.

"Lei, Kwaddis, go together and dive to the riverbed. Tell me what you find," I said.

Lei handed her oar to Shugh, and Kwaddis to Charles. In unison, the two jumped into the river—shifting into fish forms before they even hit water. There was a tense silence as we waited for them to surface. Silence, except for the incessant whistling of the orchids.

Lei was the first to surface. Shugh reached down to scoop her flower bass up by the middle so she could shift back in the boat. Kwaddis followed soon after.

"It's like Lake Bloom," Lei said even as Kwaddis was shifting back.

"It's worse," Kwaddis added. "There's a veritable jungle under there."

I closed my eyes to block out the icy-hot anger that flowed at the image. This wasn't like the Frozen Falls or Ghost Town. My father had somehow succeeded in cursing Wimahl River. Flower magic had been the weakest of the four in the Cursed Kingdom, but I doubted it would stay that way for long. The curse must have already spread from the part Rosamund and I had encountered several months prior. How far would it go? What if it took over the entire river and flowed toward the bay? I wondered, with just a touch of hysteria, if I would see a whale familiar appear in my lifetime.

Flower magic growing more powerful wasn't inherently the issue. The problem was how dangerous these cursed lands were to those who didn't hold their magic. Wimahl was a huge center of commerce. What had my father been thinking? Cursing the river was just as likely to harm the Cursed Kingdom's own trade. But then, Aklemin's vision told us how little he cared for that. All he seemed to want was for magic to spread and spread and spread until nowhere on the continent was untouched by it.

"I need all the flower familiars to help lead us through this," I said. "We must get to the Vinland shore before the prince is overtaken."

My leg ached with the memory of the vines that had tried pulling me into the freezing depths, but luckily the new Flowering River didn't seem to care for the boats floating atop it. The unnatural stillness and haunting whistles receded once we reached the end of the gorge. To our right was the small village where the weaver Arud had offered us sanctuary. Past it, I could just make out the edge of Desertmouth.

Toketie circled back and landed on the open seat in the center of our longboat. She shifted to report, "The fight's already begun! But, Shaw, there are archers on the beach. If we come up that way, we'll be shot down before we can dock the boats."

A year ago, I would have pushed forward regardless. We had enchanted shields that would block most of the arrows—but I knew it wouldn't be enough to cover everyone.

"Shaw!" Chao called.

I looked to where he pointed. A ghost was floating over the water. No, not a ghost. An angry red spirit. I reached to put my hand on Rosamund's shoulder so she could see it too.

"Isn't that . . . ?" Rosamund began.

"Yes," I agreed. It was the same ghost we'd seen in Vinland. The one who'd tried to possess me after we'd fled Vetle. For a second, I remembered how it had felt to choke on her. Then I raised a hand and soothed her anger away. She floated closer to our boat, placid once more.

"We're here to rescue the prince," I told her. "Can you show me where he is?"

The ghost said nothing, but she drifted toward the Vinland side of the gorge.

"Follow her!" I commanded. "Bone witches, direct the boats."

The ghost didn't lead us to the shore. She floated back into the gorge itself. Toketie shifted into the goshawk and flew ahead. Though she couldn't see the ghost, she could at least scout in the direction we were going.

"We don't have time to go all the way around!" I called to the ghost as we backtracked farther.

But the ghost had already stopped along the cliff face on Vinland's side. I stood, trying to see why. There was a strange crevice in the gorge where water swirled and splashed against the rocks.

Toketie returned, flying out of that crevice to land back on our boat. "There's a cave," she announced, loud enough for everyone to hear.

I directed us to row closer. Luckily the river current was sluggish enough that the swirling water wasn't dangerous. There was indeed a cave inside that crevice, hidden behind the jutting rocks at the base of the basaltic cliff side. It was half submerged by the river, but it was wide enough for a longboat to fit, even with the oars, and tall enough that we'd only have to duck a little. The ghost had already disappeared inside.

"Aklemin?" I asked.

The ice witch stared down at the too-calm surface of the river, obviously scrying something. "It may be our best chance," they said finally. "At the very least, we'll have the element of surprise."

"Make ready," I called to the seniors. "Froya, I want your boat to lead the way."

Froya was in one of the smaller boats, and as an ice familiar, she had the best eyesight among our group. The other boats waited at the entrance until Froya flew out a few minutes later. She circled the air in front of it a few times to get our attention, then flew back inside. It was safe enough to follow.

"Slowly now," I directed.

We rowed inside.

Chapter 29

There was something eerie about the cave, though I didn't know if it was my nerves, magic, or common sense telling me so. We rowed until we were far enough from the entrance that it was hard to see, then idled until our eyes adjusted.

Rosamund got tired of waiting and shifted. I couldn't see exactly what she shifted into, but she made a large splash as she jumped into the water. She came back about five minutes later, clambering over the side of the boat as a bedraggled raccoon.

"It's close," she said once she was back on the boat. "The water recedes up ahead."

By that point my eyes had adjusted just enough to make out the cave walls, so I called for the rowing to start again. If Rosamund hadn't told me about the water receding, I may have just thought the cave was growing larger. But it didn't take long before the oars began to scrape against the bottom. The first group had dragged their boat entirely onto land, leaving the gentle slope for the other boats. A few of the stronger seniors jumped out once the water was just about waist height and helped pull the boats until they beached. We all had to disembark to get the boats high enough on the cave floor that they wouldn't slide back into the water. I helped Oluk grab Einar's chair from the back of the boat. Together, we supported Einar lifting himself off the boat's bench and onto the seat of his wheelchair.

"Make sure you have what you need for a fight. Those with swords, keep them drawn," I told the rest. Madam Xu had somehow procured a few dozen real swords for us to take, despite the vague legality of it. I doubted the jarls' council would care, not under the circumstances.

I took the front of the group with Rosamund. The cave was still giving me an eerie feeling. My eyes had fully adjusted now or else it was lighter in this section of the cave, because I could see the walls and ceiling fairly well. The stone was the same black basalt as the cliffs, but it was smoother than the weather-worn rocks outside. It was also, I realized after a few minutes of walking, a near-perfect circle.

"Oh," I whispered. "A lava tube."

"A what?" Rosamund asked.

She wouldn't have been in the class we'd all taken a few years prior on the formation of the landscapes of our kingdom and beyond. "They form near volcanoes," I explained. "They're rare though. I never knew there was one just across the border here."

"I visited a lava tube farther north in Vinland when I was a small boy," Einar said. He was letting Oluk push him so he could safely carry his sword. "This one is strange. It almost feels . . . alive."

"I feel it too," Oluk said. "Like something's poking me."

I stopped, forcing the entire party to stop behind me. "Does anyone have a light?"

"I do," Chao offered. He pulled a torch out of his bag and a set of matches. Once it was lit, he held it up as if to hand it over to me.

I didn't take it. My eyes were caught on the ominous sparkle that lit up all around us like stars in the night sky. What I'd assumed was basalt walls was actually obsidian glass. But unlike the obsidian sand of the Desert or the larger obsidian boulders that encircled it, this obsidian was entwined with blue-and-green flecks that reflected the torchlight in a thousand tiny pinpricks. Even as I watched, those glittering specks seemed to move—like the glass was rotating into swirls along the walls and ceiling.

"Einar, Oluk, I need you to lead us out," I said slowly, as if the cave was an animal I was trying not to spook. "The rest of the glass witches and familiars, spread out among the group. Shugh, can you take up the rear and make sure no one gets left behind?"

"Oh," Shugh said, figuring out what I had. "Right, yes."

Oluk pushed Einar to the front. I walked to their left and just slightly behind. Still close enough that I could see as Einar closed his eyes and began to mouth indistinguishable words.

"We really should have expected this. It was the only one we were missing," Rosamund said, obviously trying to keep a light tone. "What should we call it? The Glittering Cave?"

"The Glass Cavern," Oluk offered.

"I don't think that's fair," Toketie complained from somewhere behind and to my right. "You've got the Bone Forest and the Ghost Town. The Obsidian Desert and the Glass Cavern. Lake Bloom and the Flower River—"

"The Flowering River sounds better," I said.

"Oh, I like that," Shantie agreed. "YuYu, don't you think that's nice?"

"It's fine," Yuyan said. "They're all a bit ridiculous, anyway."

"The point is," Toketie continued, "they're all distinct. And yet you named that cursed waterfall the Frozen Falls? We already have a Frozen Mountain!"

"Yes, but Ice Falls doesn't roll off the tongue, does it?" Aklemin countered.

"Aklemin, you're supposed to be on my side."

"I'm with you, Tokey," Froya said. "Though if we're being honest, I'd rather we rename the Mountain."

"Mount Icicle," one of the ice familiars chimed, then snickered. This set half a dozen other seniors off into a flurry of suggestions.

A loud crack reverberated around us, silencing everyone immediately. I wasn't the only one giving the cave nervous looks. The Obsidian Desert would have swallowed us whole by now, but either the presence of the glass witches and familiars or the presumed youth of this cursed land meant that it wasn't doing much more than making headache-inducing patterns in the glittering obsidian.

"I can hear something," Rosamund whispered, sounding unerringly loud against the soft shuffle of feet along the smooth floor of the cave. "People. They're arguing. It's— Yes, that's Thane Anders."

Ahead, I could just barely see a patch of light. The other side of the lava tube. I waved for Chao to snuff the torch. The seniors didn't need me to tell them anything. We'd drilled enough. The most confident fighters carefully shuffled to the front of the group. I fell back to the center, leaving the flower and glass witches and other support to stay behind me. Shantie took over helping Einar while Oluk shifted into his rattlesnake and Rosamund into her wolf.

The group crept forward. I started being able to hear what Rosamund had. It was definitely Thane Anders. "The king needs your help," he was saying.

"Everything will fall apart if we don't figure out the problem with this cave," General Tepeh responded, audibly annoyed. "I told David it was too close to where Agalax planted those seeds."

"The waterfall's barely holding on too," Thane Anders retorted. "It's good enough. So long as there's something to grab on to, and there is. Sir, Vetle's gone berserk. We need you."

"Very well. Let me just—" They didn't finish their statement, but a second later, there was a crunch like glass breaking underneath an immense weight. The blue-and-green obsidian specks began to twist into veins.

Rosamund straightened up. "They left," she said.

"Einar," I said. "What did they do?"

Einar didn't respond. I turned and found him red in the face, like he was attempting to lift something heavy. "I can't—hold much—longer," he said, panting for breath.

"Go!" I shouted to the seniors, and we all rushed for the exit.

From the ceiling of the Glass Cavern, a green stalactite twisted down in a corkscrew. More stalactites grew rapidly. Green and blue and solid black.

"It's out of control!" Shugh yelled.

Rosamund was running just in front of me. I watched, horrified, as under her feet a massive glass stalagmite grew out of the ground. She had to shift into her squirrel form to save herself from being impaled by the shining green tip. Somewhere behind us, there was a crash as one of the stalactites broke from the ceiling. I glanced back, heart in my throat, in time to see the seniors underneath scatter out of its way. It shattered onto the floor in a thousand shards of glass, pelting everyone nearby.

Just as suddenly as it had started, the Glass Cavern stilled.

"I have it," Einar said, only slightly less strained. I looked to see that Oluk had climbed over his shoulders as a snake, obviously helping anchor his magic.

"Wait!" I called. The first of the seniors had reached the exit, but it would be foolish to flee from the Cavern only to find ourselves in the middle of battle. "Aklemin, grab Einar's chair so Shantie can help with healing. Yuyan, how are the injures?"

"Nothing vital," Yuyan said, already at work removing a large shard of glass from Froya's arm.

"Form lines at the exit. We leave as a unit," I commanded, and despite the moment of terror, no one balked.

I began to hear the shouts from outside as I reached the exit of the Glass Cavern. It was fortunate that the Vinlander battle cries were so loud or someone might have heard us yelling inside the Cavern.

"Our goal is to stop the soldiers. Don't turn your backs to the Vinlanders, but try not to attack them either. With any luck, they'll see we're here to help and leave us be."

Shantie and the other flower witches rotated around, offering potions to drink and using their magic to warm up our muscles. Shantie pressed a hand to my shoulder as she passed by, and I felt a burst of energy like I'd just started taking Cow through her paces—warm, energized, and anticipatory.

"This isn't like the tests the general gave us during winter term," I continued. "This isn't for a grade, isn't some combat game. Assume every single person out there is willing to kill you, and do what you must to protect yourself. Are you prepared?"

"Yes," Charles said.

"I'm ready," Kwaddis said.

Froya rotated her arm to test how well Yuyan had healed it, then nodded.

"Shaw, I can't hold this forever," Einar said.

"Charge!" I called, and together we broke through the gloom of the Cavern into the bright light on the other side.

The landscape on the other side of the Cavern could only have been described as chaos. We'd arrived in a grassy ravine that gently curled down toward the river, with the gorge's cliff walls on one side and a steep, pine-covered hill on the other. Thane Anders's platoon had formed three solid lines, their backs to the shore as they pushed forward into the ranks of the desperate Vinland warriors.

The smell of blood was so pungent that I wanted to turn my face away from the wind, but that would take my eyes off the battlefield. The groans of the dying followed, half hidden behind much louder shouts—tactical commands mixing with battle cries.

"Shields in front!" I called. "Ranged, get ready! March!"

We marched as one—fifty newly graduated witches and familiars on a quest to save our people and our futures. It wasn't long before we were spotted by Vinlanders and soldiers both. The Vinlanders cried out in alarm, obviously anticipating being crushed on two sides. But my platoon marched south, heading for the soldiers' unprotected flank.

"Hold the line!" General Tepeh commanded. "Third squad, wheel about!"

A group of soldiers broke off, re-forming as a new line to face us. We had the advantage of height, since the Cavern had deposited us at the top of the ravine slope. I looked over the heads of the soldiers to meet General Tepeh's furious eyes.

"Take care not to hurt the jarls' heirs," General Tepeh commanded, fury freezing into pragmatic ice now that they'd realized the situation. "They'll be valuable hostages to keep the council in line once we're through."

Implicit in those words was the fact that any student who wasn't heir to a jarl could be killed without consequence. I would not let that happen. Last time I'd faced General Tepeh had been a disaster, but I was not the same girl I'd been, nor the same woman I could have become. I would neither sacrifice my people nor see the Vinlanders sacrificed in their stead.

The soldiers attacked, and we responded with enchanted shields and bespelled arrows. Familiars struck at the soldiers from behind the protective barrier. Unfortunately, our enemy was just as proficient and significantly more experienced. None of the soldiers' blows were getting through our defense, but ours weren't getting through theirs either.

The same could not be said for the Vinlanders. They might have had the strength in numbers originally, but they were faltering even against the half platoon still hammering away at their disorganized line. I looked but couldn't see Prince Vetle among them. My father too was missing, along with the rest of his entourage. I didn't know how long my father's intended ritual would take, or even if they'd already captured the prince to begin it, but I knew that our time was limited.

There were corpses littering the ravine. I grabbed as many as I could and passed them off to Chao and Kalitan and the other bone witches who had practiced so hard to be able to use necromancy when we needed it most. Even as I worked, more Vinlanders fell to Accursed blades. I threw what ghosts were made back into their bodies and pushed them to fight against the soldiers still attacking the Vinland warriors.

A high-pitched shriek broke my concentration. I turned to find the ghost of the Vinlander woman we'd followed. She hovered around the northern end of the ravine—far from both active combat zones. She shrieked again, shrill as a hawk and twice as loud. Was she calling for me to follow her? She'd been able to lead us here—and she'd led Rosamund and me to the Ghost Town before. Was she trying to lead me now to wherever my father had taken the prince?

Another Vinlander dropped, the fresh wave of death rushing

over me like wind before a storm. I couldn't concentrate on the ghost or the prince until I dealt with General Tepeh and the soldiers they commanded.

I turned my attention back to the battle. The corpses were beginning to make a difference now. The Vinlanders who remained seemed to have realized the dead were there to help, and were actively using them as shields to strike at the soldiers. In fact, the ranks of soldiers had thinned significantly. The tide had turned enough that the Vinlanders might be able to push toward General Tepeh's half soon so that we might envelop them on both sides.

Something nagged at me. I scanned the soldiers struggling against the renewed Vinlander threat, and then at General Tepeh's group trading unsuccessful blows with my classmates.

"Aklemin!" I called. "Where's Thane Anders?"

They swirled the water inside their scrying bowl twice before peering into it, then up at the sky. "There!" they yelled, pointing to our right.

The only thing to the right was the beach. I looked but couldn't see anything, or anyone. I didn't doubt Aklemin though. This was obviously the ploy. I didn't know how General Tepeh had given the order without my noticing, but it was obvious they must have decided to sacrifice a dozen or so soldiers to the Vinlanders for a chance to quickly deal with the threat my own arrival had created.

"Rosamund, take your group south! There's a squad coming from the beach to flank us."

Rosamund howled, summoning the group of combat-oriented familiars I'd put her in charge of. The small group veered right just in time. A squad of soldiers burst through the patch of trees hiding the western side of the shore from view, led by a massive ice eagle—Thane Anders's shift.

The shield wall was in a stalemate, but the same could not be said for the charge to the west. "Yuyan, Shantie, be ready!" I yelled as I felt the first wave of death from that direction. I couldn't look to see if it was a classmate's or a soldier's. All my focus was on General Tepeh, who had lifted both hands toward our shield wall.

"Einar!" I called in warning.

"I see it," he called back.

"Pull back!" I commanded.

Like we'd practiced, the shield wall, the archers, and the small but deadly familiars who could slip between them, all took carefully measured strides backward. I was farther away, slightly above them on the ravine slope, so I had the perfect view to watch the retreat. The line of graduates made it about twenty feet before General Tepeh called for a charge. They were obviously unwilling to let go of the chance to catch the group off-balance.

The first line of soldiers raced to overwhelm the retreating shield wall—and in doing so fell for the line of traps that had been so carefully laid beneath the shield wall's original position. They went down so quickly that the second line didn't even have time to notice before they too were caught in the spell.

Rosamund had been the one to suggest the trap, taking inspiration from the tabards worn at page duty. Einar and the other glass witches had refined it with Mister Xu's support, until the runic line on the ground worked like a net that forced anyone who stepped over it to their knees. And unlike the page duty tabards, this trap lasted far longer than a minute.

"No!" General Tepeh cried. They redirected their energy to the trap, obviously intent on dismantling it.

Kalitan, who'd been huddled to my left with the other bone witches, twitched toward me. I held out a hand, assuming she was struggling to keep control of the corpse I'd given her, but what she passed over to me was just a single ulna bone.

A bone, my sixth sense told me, that hovered only a foot from General Tepeh's back. By sending Thane Anders off to flank us, General Tepeh had left their own back unprotected. The few soldiers they'd left to defend against the Vinlanders had nearly all been sacrificed by now. There was no one to cry out a warning about that sharp piece of an arm that Kalitan must have pried loose from the corpse I'd given her to control.

Kalitan looked at me and nodded once. She was giving me the choice.

I curled my fingers toward my palm, pulling the bone toward me.

General Tepeh was too far away for me to hear their gasp of pain, but I could see them drop to their knees. See the tip of the bone work its way out of the hollow of their neck. See the spray of blood that came after the bone pulled free.

A deep sadness bubbled up in me as I watched my father's glass witch die. Not for Tepeh themself, but for the realization that it was never going to end any other way. My father and his entourage had gone too far in the name of a vision that I didn't even want. They weren't going to back down unless we forced them.

I'd promised myself that I would save everyone I could, but General Tepeh had told me that sacrifices were necessary. In the end, perhaps they had been right.

"Rest in peace, Kiwa Tepeh," I murmured.

"Shaw!" Toketie cried out. "Over there!"

I tore my eyes away from General Tepeh's corpse to look where the ice familiar pointed. General Tepeh's death must have removed the enchantments they'd placed on the area to divert our attention. There, at the northern end of the ravine where the Vinlander ghost still wailed, I could now see my father and Bao Hu standing with their arms raised, chanting. In between them stood Jarl Alki, holding a struggling figure tied in several layers of rope. Prince Vetle, still miraculously alive—for now.

"Aklemin, I need you to take command," I said. With General Tepeh dead and Thane Anders occupied, I was more confident that my classmates could handle the soldiers who remained. "Chao, Jingyi, you're with me."

"Shaw, wait," Einar called. He turned in his chair so that he could toss something in my direction. I caught it out of the air. It was a string of bones connected together by a knotted rope. Each of them was covered in carved runes.

"I made some tweaks to our winter midterm project," he added when I'd looked back at him in confusion. "It should activate as soon as you add your magic."

"You're a lifesaver, Einar," I said, and hoped that my words would count as prophecy. "Jingyi, we need a distraction," I told the fox as Chao and I rushed toward our fathers—both still caught up in the ritual they were attempting.

Jingyi darted ahead. She reached the witches before Chao and I were even close and didn't hesitate before scaling up Bao's side. She bit him hard on the chin, and he fell back in surprise.

My father wasn't so easily deterred. He continued chanting, speaking louder as if to make up for Bao's absence. I was still a hundred feet away, but I could almost feel the buildup of energy boiling below my father's feet. The ritual was reaching something of a crescendo.

And then the words stopped and Jarl Alki handed my father a ritual athame.

I threw the strings of bones. Prince Vetle screamed obscenities.

The ghost wailed. Jingyi leaped at Jarl Alki, making him pull away, but not before my father grabbed the athame and held it high above the prince's chest—ready to cleave it into his heart.

The string of enchanted bones encircled Prince Vetle's struggling form. I pushed my magic through it, straining to somehow activate the spell without physically touching the bones.

Then my father's athame came down—and bounced off an invisible wall.

I nearly collapsed to the ground in relief. Only momentum kept driving me forward. My father tried again to attack the prince, only for the magical prison Einar and I had designed to deflect him. Vetle was safe now. Only a bone and glass witch working together could undo what we had created—and General Tepeh was dead by my own hand.

"Father!" I shouted to get his attention. "It's over now. You cannot complete your ritual. Surrender, and we will return to the jarls' council together."

Somewhere to the right of us, I caught a glimpse of Chao attempting to reason with his own father. Jingyi must have chased Jarl Alki off, because neither was in my line of sight. I resisted the urge to glance back at the battlefield far behind us.

"No, my dear, I cannot surrender here," my father replied. It seemed as though the lines on his face had only grown deeper in the past three months. His shoulders were folded in, like his posture could no longer hold up against the weight of his imprisonment. "If only it hadn't come to this."

"You're the one doing *this*," I responded, equally furious and hurt. "Don't act like your hand is being forced."

"But it is," he said. "I know you're frightened. I realize now that I pushed you too soon. But your destiny is so much more wonderful than the war you rage against. You mustn't let childish fears get in your way."

"I'm not afraid," I said, and it was the truth. Fear had fled once I'd managed to save Vetle. "I just don't understand why you would do all this. Can't you see how dangerous it is? You know how terrible transmuting rituals are. What could the cost be to curse an entire continent with magic?"

"Not an entire continent. Not yet. That will come, my dear, when you realize the need for it. Just this piece is enough. A single life for a magical sanctuary. The Cursed Kingdom has never been big enough to hold its own, but I will see to it that we have that power. That *you* have that power."

"Mother knew, didn't she?" I said, sharp as the athame my father still held. "*My daughter, you are Death's heir. Hold your heart close, else you lose it to Death's greedy maw.* I am your heir, Father. You would have me destroy everything, to fulfill your own greed."

"My greed?" my father said, as if the thought was ridiculous.

"You've inured yourself to the true cost of what you plan to do. You say all it takes is a single life, but already hundreds have died in your name." I glanced at where the Vinlander ghost floated just behind Vetle's bound form.

Vetle had managed to sit up and was working furiously at the ropes that tied him. He saw me looking his way and glared, but he wasn't shouting at us anymore. He was listening. Perhaps he could be swayed, if he understood that everything that had been done to his people had been the work of my father's mad vision, instead of the will of the Cursed Kingdom at large.

"It's too late. We've come too far." My father sounded so horribly sad. If he were a different man, I might have expected him to begin crying. "I will show you the power of a single sacrifice."

My head snapped back toward my father even before my mind realized what he was saying. "Wait!"

The Witch King smiled gently at me, ritual athame lifted in front of his face like an offering to the sky above.

"My final gift to you, my dear," my father said.

"Stop!" I lunged forward, hand outstretched.

It was too late. My father switched his grip on the athame and, in one dismayingly fluid motion, slit his own throat.

Chapter 30

ROSY

Many years ago, Rosy had learned the reason for her grandmother's nickname. Ylva the Red Wolf, for the blood that would soak her pale fur as she carved a path through the invading Crusaders. As a bone wolf, Rosy was twice the weight of an average person in a combination of solid muscle and exposed bone. But most of all, she had the wolf's instincts—and wolves always went for the throat.

Rosy had trained all term alongside the familiars who followed her to intercept Thane Anders's charge. She didn't want to kill, but she refused to allow another one of her classmates to die because of her own hesitation. She threw herself against the soldiers as a wolf among sheep.

Swords stabbed and sliced, trying to find purchase against her thick fur and patches of bone, but Rosy was more than just the wolf. She shifted to badger and raccoon, jumped aside as squirrel and weasel, then threw herself at them from behind as the wolf again.

She kept her ears primed. All it took was one cry of pain or animal squeal. She disengaged from the soldiers she was fighting, scurrying under them as the mouse or barreling through them as the horse to get to the classmate who needed her help. Each time, her classmates converged on her, their own animal forms disguising hers so that the soldiers couldn't gang up on her before she moved on to the next.

Emma-the-fox yipped as one of the soldiers stepped on her tail. Rosamund threw herself at his face as a raccoon to give her enough time to shift. Once Emma was free, she went mouse to climb to the crest of the soldier's head and survey the fight. Several of the soldiers were shifted too, but they obviously hadn't gotten Madam Xu's lessons in how to consistently switch form to confuse one's opponent. Her strategies for the other familiars seemed to be working well.

Before Rosy could leap back into battle, she found herself airborne. She shifted squirrel instinctively, since it was her form most comfortable being at such heights, only to feel talons squeezing her tight. She went horse to force the bird to drop her, then squirrel again once she was in free fall. She just barely managed to catch herself on the branch of a nearby tree, but the impact was enough to knock the wind out of her.

Before she could recover, Thane Anders swooped around to try again. He was a massive ice eagle. Not a golden eagle like Froya, but a bald eagle with a head full of ice-encrusted white feathers. It made him easy to spot at least as he reached for her with talons outstretched.

Rosy scurried around the tree, and Thane Anders swooped by. She judged the distance from the tree back to the mass of soldiers and familiars fighting. As a squirrel, Rosy leaped toward the ground. But squirrels fell slowly, even bone squirrels, and Thane Anders must have caught a wind current strong enough to twist into another dive. She felt the prick of talons close around her neck, one of them catching on the edge of her necklace.

She hesitated, worried shifting would cause that talon to rip the necklace off instead of just pulling it free. Her fear of going feral was deeply ingrained, but Shantie's return had been a blessing in more ways than one. She'd gotten the ingredients to remake the final test of her feral aid potion. Rosy had made sure to drink it before they loaded the boats earlier that afternoon. She would hate to lose the necklace for other reasons, but she was in complete control of her animal voices.

Thane Anders's talons were moments away from piercing her side. She shifted wolf, sank her teeth into one of his wings, and let both of them fall.

Familiars stayed in the form they were shifted into upon death. She wasn't sure if that made it better or worse, seeing the mangled eagle that remained on the ground after she shakily climbed to her feet. Her hands went to her throat, double-checking the necklace was still intact. The warmth of Shaw's magic pulsed back at her, and she sighed in relief.

"Rosy," Aklemin cried. "Rosy!"

Rosy glanced around the battlefield. Charles had taken the lead on defending their classmates against the western squad when Rosy had been forced to deal with Thane Anders. She spotted Oluk's rattlesnake shift sliding through the muck at the bottom of the ravine and knew he was coming to help handle the remaining threats.

Shifting to deer, Rosy darted toward the other side of the battle where Aklemin was still frantically calling for her. Toketie was at their side, holding them up, though Rosy couldn't see any visible injuries.

"I sent Yuyan ahead already," Aklemin said once Rosy was close enough. "Shaw needs you. Quickly. It's the only way."

Rosy looked and saw that Shaw had somehow ended up at the northern end of the ravine. She seemed to be talking to her father. Yuyan was sprinting over. Rosy didn't bother asking why. She bolted after Yuyan, shifting horse, then back to deer when the mud at the bottom of the ravine proved too slick to keep her footing.

"Re-form the line!" Aklemin called behind her. "Protect Shaw! Protect Vetle!"

Rosy couldn't see it, but she heard the muffled shouts as her classmates retreated into formation, standing between the northern side of the ravine and the remaining soldiers. Yelling filled the air. In order to re-form the line as Aklemin had directed, her classmates would have to break the shield wall—lessening the protective enchantments until the line formed again.

Toketie let out a high-pitched shriek, like an echo of that moment years ago when Gran had attacked her. That was her cousin's shriek of fear. Of pain.

Time seemed to slow. Rosy was frozen there, halfway through a leap. She'd nearly reached Yuyan, who herself had nearly reached Shaw. The Witch King was just ahead, a ritual athame pressed against his own throat. He was smiling.

Behind her, her cousin was in danger. Her classmates had fallen into chaos, trying to organize into a cohesive unit again, but the remaining soldiers were leaderless and desperate. Had they pushed to destabilize her classmates' uncertain lines before they could form again? What if the surviving Vinlanders had decided to take advantage of the new formation and attacked her classmates' exposed flank? What if Toketie even now lay dying?

But Aklemin was back there. As were Oluk, Einar, and Shantie. Even Charles and Froya and all the others. Toketie was not alone. In front of her, Rosy watched Shaw reach out, unsuccessfully, to stop her father from sacrificing himself, and knew her choice was no choice at all.

Yuyan was at the Witch King's side a second after he collapsed. Her hands clasped tight over the open wound in his neck, pressing down even as she glowed with flower magic.

Rosy nearly collided with Shaw in her attempt to get close. She shifted back in time to grab Shaw's elbow before she too could collapse.

"Tell me you can save him," Shaw begged.

Yuyan's face was far too pale. "He hit a major artery. I'm losing him, Shaw."

"Keep trying!" Shaw yelled.

"Why did he—" Rosy tried to ask.

"The ritual," Shaw said. "He couldn't get to Vetle, so he chose to sacrifice himself instead. If he dies, it's all over."

"What will it do?" Rosy pressed. "What exactly? You saved the prince, the war hasn't started. What can this ritual make happen?"

"It's a gift, to our children," Bao Hu said. Rosy turned to see that Chao had managed to force him to the ground. He held both his father's arms tightly behind his back, even though Bao didn't appear to be struggling.

"What kind of gift requires human sacrifice?" Rosy yelled.

"Tell us, Baba, please," Chao said.

Bao hesitated, watching how Yuyan clutched the Witch King's neck tighter, blood seeping unendingly through the cracks between her fingers.

Shaw stepped between them, forcing the other bone witch to look at her instead. "If it's for us, don't we deserve to know?" she said, voice tight.

"We seeded the lands so that they might become extensions of those in our Cursed Kingdom," Bao finally answered. "The ritual will guide the hearts of the cursed lands to take root in these hollowed grounds and see them as part of itself."

"But that won't work!" Shaw argued. "All that will do is encourage the lands to want to bridge the distance between their pieces so they can be whole."

"They're too close," Rosy said, remembering what General Tepeh had told Thane Anders in the Cavern. "They won't even be able to make a bridge without colliding with each other. What will happen then?"

"It will work," Bao said stubbornly. "There are half a dozen burial mounds in Daming with active bone magic. Any bone witch can tell you they are the same."

"Baba, you told me yourself that they each have their own name, their own identities," Chao protested. "They're not one singular entity spread over thousands of miles."

"The theory is sound. It has to work," Bao said, trying to peer around Shaw to where Yuyan still struggled to save the Witch King. "It's too late to stop it now."

"No, no, no," Yuyan mumbled, getting louder with each repetition.

Death washed over them all, simultaneously. Rosy winced, Chao swore, and Yuyan gave a strangled noise of frustration. Shaw kept her back to her father's fresh corpse, covering her ears like she was trying to drown out screaming.

In the wake of the Witch King's demise, energy began to gather like a great beast somewhere far over their heads. The pressure the coalescing energy exerted on the ravine was enough to make Rosy's ears pop.

"What in the name of the gods—" Vetle shouted.

"There's no time," Shaw said. She held out a hand, and Rosy grabbed it like she was dangling from a cliff and Shaw's hand was the only thing to keep her from falling.

"What do we do?" Rosy asked. Bile built in the back of her throat. What *could* they do? The energy was gathering above them as the largest, darkest storm cloud she had ever seen. The Witch King had played a winning hand, and they were all out of cards.

"No," Shaw said, as if in response to Rosy's thoughts. "I won't let it end like this. Help me."

Rosy tightened her grip until she could almost feel all the bones in Shaw's hand. "I'm here."

"I need an anchor," Shaw said, desperate, like Rosy might deny her.

Rosy shifted into her wolf in response. Shaw placed her hands on either side of Rosy's face, and then the warmth flooded through her as Shaw's magic rushed into her body. Shaw had pulled on her magic before, but it hadn't felt anything like this. A torrent of fire threatened to burn her from the inside out.

It's Shaw, Rosy thought. This was no rampaging wildfire, but the essence of her witch. All her logical practicality and ice-cold fury and noble dedication. The core that had made Rosy simultaneously hate and admire her until love won over everything.

Rosy sank into that heat, pushing with all her might to match it. She couldn't tell exactly what Shaw was doing, but she could feel the enormity of it through the tenuous connection their touch had created. As if some great monster's shadow had been cast over the entire kingdom and Shaw was a single speck upon the ground crying out for its attention.

"It's not enough!" Shaw cried. "More, Rosamund, *please.*"

Rosy was giving everything she had, but it was like she was

attempting to drain a lake with only a cup. She needed to break the dam between her and Shaw. Needed to remove that final barrier that not even touch could overcome.

Rosy had read up on bonding in preparation for Oluk and Einar's ceremony. They didn't have a bonding arch, but that was just ceremonial. The most important part of the ceremony was willing intent, and the successful joining of magic. Rosamund was already shifted into her wolf—her first form—and Shaw's magic already mingled with hers. They were so compatible that sometimes she thought all it would take would be a single push, and so she pushed now.

The voices in her heart began to sing. Like the Forest's song after Samhain, they joined together to call Shaw home. One by one, Rosy shifted, and Shaw just barely managed to keep hold of her through each. From wolf to horse to mouse. Squirrel and raccoon and deer. Rabbit, weasel, and even her otter—a voice she'd thought lost to her after Guanyu's death. The last to come was the badger. Her connection to Pops just as the wolf was her connection to Gran. Every single shift rose to the call and joined their voices into a chorus inside of her heart. Shaw's magic swelled in response, coming to harmonize with the symphony inside her.

Just like that, the bond settled into place. The torrent that had been Shaw's magic banked into a pleasant warmth. Rosy imagined it as a fireplace at the center of her heart, where all her animal voices could nestle around in safety and comfort.

Shaw's hands fell away. Rosy shifted human, and as she settled back on two feet, she could feel Shaw's awe echoing up from that fire in her heart. Like one of her voices but louder somehow. More deeply entrenched than even her wolf.

"Oh," Rosy said, holding a hand to her chest. "I can hear you."

"Rosamund, you—" Shaw's hands returned to the sides of her face. It felt different on her human cheeks than on the wolf's fur. "How—"

"I'm here. I'm yours." Rosy kissed Shaw just once on the lips because, despite the feelings welling up inside her, it was neither the time nor place for more. "Everything I am, I give to you freely. Use it to save our kingdom, Shaw."

Then she shifted back into her wolf and stoked that fire in her heart back into an inferno. She envisioned it like an eruption—a hot blast of energy that poured out of her. This time, there was nothing blocking the lava-hot landslide of her magic from flowing directly into Shaw.

Chapter 31

SHAW

IT WAS SHOCKING HOW ONE SINGLE MOMENT COULD CHANGE everything. Like it had when the Vinlanders attacked Multah's market. Like my father saying that war with Vinland had always been my destiny, or Aklemin revealing the real truth about my future. Like it had mere moments ago, when my father chose to sacrifice himself instead of surrendering and completed the ritual I had tried so desperately to stop. Like it had again, just now, when Rosamund opened herself up to the bond she'd once tried so hard to flee from.

Rosamund's magic was a balm against the horror in my soul. My father was dead. My kingdom was on the brink of war. My power was fleeting against the strength of the ritual.

I would not, could not, stop it. Bao had been correct—it was too late for that now. But neither could I let it do what my father had originally intended. Aklemin had made the consequences clear enough, and my imagination did the rest. Only destruction would follow creating such massive wells of magic, stretched over such large distances.

Rosamund's concern about their closeness to each other was rattling in my head. Einar and I had proven with our magical winter midterm project that the different magics *could* mix. Not easily, and not without intent, but what if this ritual created enough of a pathway for them to do so? What unholy monstrosity would become of the magical lands of the Cursed Kingdom and the newly cursed lands in Vinland? Would I even have a kingdom left to rule anymore? My father's vision had been so focused on my ability to conquer the entire continent that he'd neglected to care for what that might do to the ancestral homeland of my people.

The Vinlander ghost was still wailing, her voice mimicking the howling wind that had begun to streak across the ravine in response to the great storm of energy gathering above us. I wished I could spare the time to force her to fade, because she was not helping my ability to concentrate.

But I had never been someone who struggled with distraction in the face of duty. I pulled as much of Rosamund's magic as I could handle inside of myself, let it build and build and build until I couldn't fathom holding any more.

The cloud of ritual magic had begun to swirl. Massive arms of storm clouds reached south, toward the Cursed Kingdom. I threw both my hands to the sky, relying on Rosamund to lean against me so that I could cast my magic higher than I'd ever cast it before.

In my mind's eye, I passed over my own kingdom like a bird. I saw the surface of Lake Bloom boil, bubbling over its own shores. Saw the great boulders of the Obsidian Desert crumble into even larger black dunes. Saw the bone pines of the Forest stretch themselves up toward the sky, tall enough to overtake even the original heart pine. I circled around to the Frozen Mountain, to the massive glowing glacier at its peak, and watched it begin to creep closer to the royal palace and Falconridge below it.

Only, there was a figure standing in the glacier's path. A glimmering translucent figure.

Mesachie, my many-times ancestor, stood in the increasingly small gap between the bottom of the glacier and the palace's outer walls. I reached out to her.

"Grandmother," I called, though of course I was too many miles away for her to hear me. "I need your help."

Mesachie kneeled down at the edge of that ever-growing glacier like a memory of her ancient sacrifice. Her ghostly form flickered blue. Ghost gave way to spirit and I thought my ancestor lost to her misery, but when the spirit spoke, it was clear enough for me to hear.

"Let me in, grandchild," she said. "I will guide you."

I didn't hesitate. I imagined swooping down from the arm of the storm, riding the glacier until I reached Mesachie's side. She closed her eyes, her blue so bright now that it nearly overtook the shine of the glacier's ice magic, and we collided.

My ancestor's spirit rode the thread between my magic to my body. I waited for the pain to come as she settled under my skin, but it was nothing like how I'd felt when that Vinlander's angry spirit had possessed me. Maybe it was my new bond with Rosamund, or maybe it was Mesachie herself, but though she'd become a spirit of deep sadness, all I felt was the same determination to see my kingdom saved.

Lands given life by magic are uncontrollable, Mesachie said, and it was as if she spoke inside me. Her words were not words so much as concepts forming directly in my mind. *But these lands are not unreasonable. It is the witches and familiars who give the land its identity. And so the magic builds with them, not over them.*

I thought of the Bone Forest. The way it always seemed to welcome me. I remembered the rattling of bones at the heart pine where we'd done the Samhain ritual. I thought too of how I'd first met Rosamund—the raging bull moose the Forest had sent in our direction, as if to force us together.

"I understand," I said, and together Mesachie and I sent our magic back to the kingdom.

We went first to the Bone Forest. My bond with Rosamund thrummed, and it was almost too simple to use her magic to reach out to the Forest itself. I saw in my mind's eye that the trees around the Ghost Town had begun to grow skeletal. Just like how Rosamund was able to pull the Bone Forest's fog into the Town to help us escape Vetle, fog now rolled across the ground entirely of its own accord.

"Vetle, listen to me," I said, though I didn't dare open my eyes to look at the prince. "Tell me about that town. The one where you attacked us."

"Why should I—"

"Give me a chance to save our people!" I shouted. "Tell me now, before it's too late."

There was a pause. I saw the pines of the Bone Forest begin to shake, and the pines around the Ghost Town begin to mimic them. The Vinlander ghost's wailing turned into a soft croon.

"Its name was Leifsburg," Vetle muttered, only barely audible over the wind. "And it was where my Lyssa was born and raised."

Vetle grew louder, talking about the ancient town hall where he'd gone for a meeting, and the young woman he'd met there. How she'd pulled him through the quaint market where her family sold their wares. How they'd walked together through the streets where she'd grown up.

As he talked, I pulled at the Bone Forest. Reminded the land that its heart was that of a great pine, not a desecrated village. The Bone Forest began to calm, and so I turned my attention to the Town. The energy of the ritual branched, one piece staying with the Forest, and the other swirling around this new land. The Ghost Town began to speak. Unlike the Forest's song of whispering pine needles and animal cries, the Town spoke in the drumming of footsteps and the creaking of lumber. I encouraged the energy to echo that sound, until all the buildings of the Ghost Town rumbled together.

"The Cavern now," I said. "That lava tube."

The Obsidian Desert was not nearly as receptive to my magic as the Forest, but I called on it to remember me. To remember the sandstorm it had created, to protect Rosamund and me from Vetle's pursuit. Surely it didn't want to stretch itself so thin? How far would its sand truly reach, if it had to cover such a great distance? I argued for it to turn its attention to the abandoned quarry Rosamund and I had sheltered in, and saw through the energy of the ritual as the Desert pulled away from the distant Cavern to do just that.

Vetle talked about the lava tube with less enthusiasm than he had the town of Leifsburg but less pain too. I'd gotten used to the touch of glass magic through my project with Einar, which helped. The Cavern was glittering in pride as Vetle talked of its appeal. Even among lava tubes, this one was unique. The emperor himself had visited it the last time he'd come to this side of the empire and taken home a piece of it as a souvenir. I pulled another slice of the ritual's energy to feed the Cavern. It whirled in joy as its multicolored shards of glass began to glow with power.

"The River," I said next.

I had less experience with flower magic than with glass and had barely spent any time at the shore of Lake Bloom. The Lake was still boiling over. Its water had begun to flood the nearby houses. I tried desperately to pull back the energy of the ritual, but it resisted me. Mesachie chided from within, reminding me I needed a direction for the magic or the ritual would overpower me.

A chittering noise came across my bond with Rosamund. She pushed a memory at me, of a bone otter swimming playfully alongside a huge flower salmon within the depths of Lake Bloom. Guanyu's salmon. I remembered then that Shantie and Guanyu's bonding ceremony had taken place on the shore of the Lake. I pictured their beautiful bonding arch, covered in pink and purple flowers that matched the lily pads floating serenely on the Lake's surface.

The Lake did not want to settle back like the Forest and Desert had. It had been confined for so long within the bounds of its small shoreline. It wanted freedom—wanted to taste the open water. The River too was beginning to boil in response to the Lake's rage. The wind from the ritual's storm whipped so fiercely that a tree branch came crashing into the ravine. I nearly opened my eyes at the sound, but Mesachie's spirit smothered my instinctive fear.

Connect them, Mesachie urged. *Let the ritual do as it wishes, just this once, but guide the Lake to do it safely.*

Lake Bloom was a lot closer to the Flowering River than any of the other lands were to each other. I urged the Lake to stop overflowing and instead turned the energy into a concentrated torrent to carve a channel through the center of Multah. I pushed it as deep as I could, churning up dirt and cobblestone. The edges of the new canal crumbled inward, until a true bank began to form. The canal shot through the old market in the center of the city and kept going. The citizens of Multah shouted in fear, but the carving was slow enough that they could get out of the way as the canal pushed down the main street all the way to the docks. I had to struggle at the end to curve the canal around a group of town houses, but at last it broke into the shore of the river between two of the dock's piers.

The ritual rejoiced. The heart of the Lake overtook the infant River. The orchids whistled in time with the croaking frogs. Vines began to creep along the floor of the new canal, stabilizing the edges of the channel.

The ritual was not finished though. There was still one more land it wished to connect. I turned my attention to the Frozen Falls and saw that they were glowing with the same ferocity as the Mountain's glacier. The glacier itself had collided with the palace walls and did not seem like it would stop until the entire palace was encased in ice.

Unlike the new home of flower magic, the Mountain could not be allowed to overtake the Falls. Ice would suffocate everything in its path in an attempt to connect the two pieces. But ice magic was the antithesis of bone magic. I tried as hard as I could to get the Mountain to focus on me, but it would not listen.

Let me, Mesachie's spirit said.

The Frozen Mountain was the largest of all the wells in the Cursed Kingdom. Compared to it, the small little waterfall was insignificant. Mesachie urged it to settle back into its rightful place, looking over the Cursed Kingdom for which it existed. The Mountain let out a long, windy sigh. The glacier stopped its downward descent, clinging to the southern walls of the royal palace like a hug.

"Tell me about the waterfall," I demanded, then realized there must be dozens of waterfalls in this area of Vinland, just as there were in the Cursed Kingdom. "Have you seen it? The one my father froze with ice magic, northeast of here?"

"I know it," Vetle said, and his voice was hard. "Love's Light, we used to call it, for it was where all the people of the western provinces made their forever promise to each other. The mists made rainbows of the afternoon sun and reflected those colors on the surrounding cliffs. That light is forever trapped beneath the cursed ice now."

But it didn't have to be. The Frozen Falls listened with curiosity. The Mountain had retreated under Mesachie's gentle touch. The last of the ritual's energy began to rain over the Falls. It caught those droplets against the moving ice of its frozen waterfall and held them there like tiny prisms. The time was approaching late afternoon, and the sun was in the perfect position to catch on those droplets. Rainbow shimmers began to appear over the cliff face.

I'd done it.

I slowly opened my eyes and had to blink several times to clear the blurriness of my vision. The storm above was gone, the ritual subsided. Four lands had become seven—each unique. Stronger than before but stabilized now. My people were safe, at least from that threat.

A pulse of Rosamund's magic shot through our bond, and then Mesachie's spirit detached. I raised my hand to soothe her back into a ghost, but the blue did not drain away. I tried again, more deliberate this time. My magic felt strained, like a muscle I had overused, but calming spirits was a basic skill for bone witches. I should have been able to do this.

Still, Mesachie remained a spirit. Her human shape began to break apart, leaving an amorphous mist of blue.

"No, Grandmother," I protested, and somehow this, above everything else, was enough to bring tears to my eyes. "Stay with me. You've been here so long. Don't let this be the end."

The spirit drifted closer to me. Rosamund growled, like a warning, but I couldn't resist reaching out to touch the edge of that blue mist. It clung to my fingers for just a second, a soft kiss goodbye, and then the blue mist became small motes of light—and my ancestor faded away.

I swallowed down the sob that wanted to erupt. It wasn't fair. She had already sacrificed herself to save her people once, and now my father's ritual suicide had caused her to sacrifice herself again. How many hundreds of years had she watched over her descendants? No longer would she linger, an unseen force upon the Mountain guiding us home.

Rosamund shifted, and I clutched at her. I wanted so badly to collapse against her chest. To cry like a child, free to grieve without consequence. A part of me was aware that I was using my grief over the loss of Mesachie to reflect the grief I wasn't sure I was allowed to feel over the death of my father, but that was a burden I would have to face another day.

I couldn't let myself drown in sorrow. Not here, not yet. Bao was demanding an explanation, obviously aware that I had done *something* to the ritual. Vetle's own demands were nearly loud enough to drown out Bao's.

I wiped my eyes on Rosamund's blouse, then pulled away. Rosamund entangled our fingers, offering silent support, as I turned at last to face the prince of Vinland.

Vetle had managed to work himself free of the ropes. He pounded unsuccessfully on the invisible wall of his prison, only to stop as he saw me turn his way. He threw back his shoulders. "Let me free."

"I will," I said, and my voice croaked. I cleared my throat. "Once you agree to lay down your arms. The man responsible for your people's suffering is dead. The ritual he would have used to destroy your lands is conquered."

"And the curse he placed upon my lands?" Vetle spat.

"Magic has seeped into the very pores of Vinland, and there is no way to remove it now," I replied. "But the lands can be reasoned with. Magic is a tool like any other if your people learn to make use of it. Help me foster peace between our kingdoms, and I will do everything in my power to aid you."

I knew I would have to offer some kind of education in the reparations I sent to the emperor. It would be irresponsible not to. Witches and familiars had always existed in Vinland—though many had immigrated to the Cursed Kingdom over the years—but with the new proximity to cursed lands, the number would increase dramatically.

First, I had to convince Vetle to put aside his desire for vengeance.

I stepped closer to Vetle's prison. He snarled at me, obviously unwilling to be soothed by my words, but he didn't give verbal protest. His attention seemed to have been caught by something over my left shoulder. I looked, but the only thing there was the Vinlander ghost.

I turned back to Vetle, a suspicion growing. Something that had been bothering me for months returned to the forefront of my mind. The way Vetle had reacted during the attack at Goose Point, almost as if he'd been able to hear what the ghost of Squad Leader Moolocks had been yelling. And again, how he'd reacted to the threat of the Vinlander ghost when she'd turned into an angry spirit and tried to attack him at the Ghost Town.

"Do you see her?" I asked, stepping aside so the ghost was directly in the prince's line of sight.

Vetle didn't respond the way he would have if he didn't. He said nothing, but he tore his gaze away from the spot where the ghost floated to meet my eyes as if I had caught him doing something he shouldn't have.

Every time I'd encountered Vetle, she'd been there. She must have haunted him for months. Always caught between mournful ghost and angry spirit.

"Who is she?" I asked, softer. Pulling upon all my training as a bone witch.

Still, Vetle did not speak. But I thought I knew the answer.

I looked over at the ghost. "Lyssa," I said. "Will you come closer?"

The ghost flickered red. I soothed her, and unlike with Mesachie, my magic did as I'd intended without issue.

"My love," Lyssa crooned, floating to the edge of Vetle's prison. She reached out, but it seemed the combination of glass and bone was enough to repel ghosts too. Her translucent fingers rested against the invisible barrier.

No wonder Vetle was so focused on revenge, if his lover had been one of the people killed. Perhaps that was the whole reason my father had targeted the town of Leifsburg.

"You're a bone witch," I observed, for only bone witches could see ghosts as well as he so obviously could.

"I'm no witch," Vetle said, though his protest was weakened by his fixation on the ghost of his dead lover. "I've been cursed. Twice now this abomination masquerading as my Lyssa has tried to kill me."

Lyssa's ghost moaned, and the red returned. I quickly soothed her again.

"She's angry," I said. "She follows you because she loves you. As a ghost, she doesn't want to hurt you, but as a spirit, she's instinctively drawn to possess bone witches. *That's* what almost killed you."

It was a miracle that he hadn't been, if she had managed to possess him twice already. If anything, Lyssa's love for him must have been enough to keep the possession weak so that he could escape her.

"She nearly killed me too," I added. "We bone witches are weak to it. That's why we need training. You can learn to soothe the emotion overwhelming them so that the ghost remains in control."

"My love," Lyssa crooned again. "Oh, my prince, please forgive me. I never wanted to hurt you. Never you."

"She's hurting," I said, because devolving into a spirit was a painful process for ghosts, and this one had been stuck in a halfway state for far too long. "You are a bone witch, Prince Vetle, and that is a special gift. It means that we can help our loved ones move on, even in the face of tragedy."

Lyssa's croon became a shriek. The red overtook her again, faster this time, and once more I soothed it away.

"Her anger is warping her. She will lose what's left of herself if we don't do anything. Bone witches are able to help the dead find peace. Will you let me show you?"

Vetle was caught in the siren call of the dead now. Lyssa pressed her whole hand to the barrier between them, and slowly he lifted his to match it.

"Shaw," Rosamund whispered. "Einar's here."

I glanced over to see Einar struggling to push his wheelchair over the uneven slope of the ravine. Rosamund left my side to go to him and help get his chair the rest of the way.

"Aklemin sent me," Einar whispered, though he hardly needed to. Vetle wasn't paying either of us any attention.

"My love," Lyssa was saying over and over again. For the first time since I'd seen her, she flickered the deep blue of sadness instead of the red of anger.

"It's really you?" Vetle asked. He was so tense that his pale skin had turned pink with strain, but his eyes were transfixed on the ghost. "You're really my Lyssa?"

"I'm yours. Always yours, forever and a day, like we promised," she said.

The blue came back, darker and deeper than before. I raised my hand to drain the emotion, then paused. "She needs to be soothed," I said. "Will you try?"

"How?" Vetle asked.

I tried to think back to my earliest bone witch lessons at school. "Imagine wiping her sadness away. It's heavy, weighing her down. Pull it off so she can be free."

With a shaking hand, Vetle did as I asked. I felt a tendril of what had to be his magic reach out and latch on to Lyssa's sadness. Surreptitiously, I gave a small tug of my own to help him. It wouldn't do for him to fail his first attempt at actually using bone magic.

His eyes widened in obvious surprise as the blue faded away, leaving Lyssa with only that beautiful translucent shimmer of a ghost.

I knew that in order for trust to be earned, it first had to be given. I'd given Vetle a reason to stay his hand. Even so, the thought of letting him free now, when my glass witch was nearby and even more vulnerable than the first time Vetle had nearly killed him, made me want to vomit.

Einar reached down to touch the nearest engraved bone, then looked up at me with an expectant air. I swallowed down my bile and joined him. Together, we pulled our magic back from the prison—and the barrier fell apart.

Vetle let out a small cry as his hands pushed through the air, clasping for Lyssa's, only to fall through her ghostly form.

Rosamund stiffened—the only warning I got before a bone leopard launched itself from the nearest tree, directly for Vetle. Jarl Hu had obviously been lying in wait. Perhaps my father had even foreseen this chance for his plan to fall apart and had instructed her to hide until Vetle was released from his protective prison. Her claws were outstretched, fangs bared. All she needed was one good swipe, and any chance at peace would be gone forever.

No! I didn't know if I screamed it or pushed it through our bond, but either way, Rosamund reacted just in time.

Bone wolf met bone leopard in midair, and they both fell away. I barely had any magic left, but I pushed what little I could to Rosamund, giving her the energy she needed to overwhelm the leopard.

Rosamund wasn't alone either. Einar threw the string of engraved bones at Chao. Yuyan had taken over holding on to Bao's bonds so that Chao could rush over to where his mother and

Rosamund rolled against the ground, biting and clawing at each other.

I sent the image of it through our bond, and Rosamund leaped back just in time. Chao encircled his mother with the bones, and the prison reactivated. The leopard familiar yowled in protest as her claws scratched uselessly against the invisible wall.

Like an untrained bone witch too caught in the call of the dead to care about the rest of the world, Vetle had ignored the fight completely. He was completely transfixed by the ghost of Lyssa.

"Can she stay like this? With me?" Vetle asked.

I pressed a hand to my chest to try to calm my racing heartbeat. "Not unless you want to lose her all over again. Eventually soothing away the anger or the sadness won't work anymore. It's best to help her move on now, while she's still herself."

Some ghosts were more stable, like Mesachie had been, but Lyssa was obviously not one of them. Lyssa began to cry dark blue tears at my words. She didn't want to move on, which made her the worst type of ghost to deal with. I worried that would make Vetle angry, but somehow her tears seemed to give him strength. He couldn't touch her, but he hovered his hand just over her cheek.

"Be brave, my love," he said. "I know it's hard, but I won't let you hurt anymore. I'm sorry I've let you suffer for so long."

"I miss you," Lyssa wailed. "I don't want to leave you."

"I'll think of you every day," Vetle promised. "And when I die, I will join you in the halls of our ancestors."

I said nothing about Vetle's belief. He'd learn soon enough, if he honed his new magic, what happened to the dead. His words seemed to calm the ghost at least.

"I'll wait for you," she vowed, a twin to his own promise.

She'd already begun to fade, the edges of her essence drifting away. Vetle touched the glowing motes, shuddering in obvious anguish, but didn't take his gaze away until the last specks of her light flickered one more time and disappeared.

Only then did Vetle turn his attention to the bone leopard pacing in small circles inside the prison and to the bone wolf studying it from the other side of the barrier. Chao had stumbled to his knees at Rosamund's side and was whispering pleas for his mother to stop, *just stop*.

Finally, Vetle looked at Einar.

"What type of magic is this?"

"Glass and bone working in tandem," Einar replied. "For the universal truth has always been that people are stronger when they work together."

Vetle frowned but didn't argue. His eyes lingered over Einar's wheelchair. I wondered if he recognized the boy whose life he'd so permanently altered.

"Look there, and perhaps you'll see," Einar said gently. He pointed down the ravine.

Vetle and I both turned to look. The battlefield had changed from how it had been when I'd gone to confront my father. The line had moved down into the middle of the ravine, only they weren't in the formation I would have expected. Like a strangely mirrored image of the battle at Goose Point, my classmates and the remaining Vinland warriors were standing shoulder to shoulder, holding off what was left of the platoon of soldiers.

The rest of my entourage stood in the back. Jarl Alki must have gone in that direction after Jingyi had chased him off, because he was collapsed in a heap on the ground behind Aklemin. Toketie was glaring down at him, as if just daring him to get up so she could finish him off. She was bleeding from the shoulder, but Shantie was already working to heal her.

Even as we watched, the line composed somehow of both our people worked together to encircle the last of the soldiers. Oluk shifted from rattlesnake to human and said something I was too far away to hear. One by one, the soldiers dropped their swords and crossed their arms in front of them in surrender.

"Very well, Princess Shaw of the Cursed Kingdom," Vetle said. His voice was the slightest bit shaky. "You will have your precious peace. Just so long as you teach my people how to live with magic as yours do."

I nearly couldn't believe it. My heart had not stopped pounding. I almost expected another of my father's entourage to burst out of the woods to attack us again, though I knew that was impossible. Jarl Hu and her witch were both bound. Jarl Alki was either dead or unconscious. General Tepeh had been killed by my hand, and my father by his own.

"Magic can do a lot for a kingdom, Prince Vetle of Vinland," I said finally. "Perhaps your father can be convinced of that."

Vetle stared down at his hands. "Teach me how to raise an army of the dead to beat back those damn Crusaders, and he will be more than convinced."

That was a much harder prospect, but I thought of the Ghost Town and Vetle's connection to it and nodded. "I'll do what I can."

I knew how succession worked in Vinland—knew it was by the emperor's choice who among his children would succeed him, not by birth order. Would the Vinlanders rally behind a prince who used magic to win their war with the Colonies? What would that do for the acceptance of magic in Vinland?

I would not conquer anyone, but that didn't mean I couldn't

show the continent just how useful it would be to allow magic to thrive. Perhaps Vinland and the Cursed Kingdom's peace would lead to an even stronger future than the one my father had killed to create, and died to maintain. A future where magic ruled alongside those without. Where witches and familiars were both welcome and accepted. A future I could look to, for the first time in my life, with joy.

Chapter 32

"Ready?" Rosamund asked.

"No," I replied. "Are you?"

"No," Rosamund echoed, smiling a little.

It was the day of our coronation. I'd managed to convince the jarls to include Rosamund in the coronation ceremony, though they'd wanted to wait until after our public bonding next month. I hadn't allowed it. The rushed and unintentionally private nature of it aside, we were already bonded. Our kingdom had waited long enough for someone to sit on the Familiar Throne.

"Rosy!" Toketie called. "Shaw! Come out here a second?"

Rosamund opened the door to the inner chamber we'd been getting ready in and walked into the parlor. I heard her give a little "Oh!" of surprise, so I hurried to follow her.

Rosamund's entire family waited for us, standing among the dark blue couches and chairs that littered the parlor of my suite of rooms in the royal palace.

"Look at you, baby," Rosamund's mother said, holding her daughter by the shoulders so she could look her up and down.

Rosamund did look gorgeous in her brand-new white dress embroidered with all manner of bone animals, the most prominent of which was the stylized bone wolf leaping across the front skirt. My own outfit had a matching bone wolf, though it had been embroidered on the back of the long robe I would wear over my black doublet.

"Your grandparents would be so proud of you," one of Rosy's uncles whispered, obviously trying to hold back tears.

At his words, Rosamund's own eyes grew wet. She pulled away, dabbing her eyes so as not to mess up the makeup Toketie had made her wear.

"I need to introduce you all to my witch," Rosamund said. "Shaw, meet my family. Family, this is Shaw."

"We have already met," I remarked, wryness covering my sudden nerves. What if Rosamund's family didn't approve of me? After everything that had been done to them in the name of my father's war, I wouldn't blame them for being apprehensive.

"Not like this, not as one of us," Rosy insisted, accompanying her words with a pulse of reassurance through our bond.

"Welcome to our family, Shaw," Rosamund's mother said. She reached out, arms open, and I nearly didn't realize until it was happening that she wanted to pull me into a hug. I leaned forward, more hesitant than I should be, and hugged her back.

I had never been hugged like this before—warm and welcoming. A mother's embrace. I had to swallow down my own tears, blinking heavily to conceal them.

"Thank you," I said as she finally let me go. "And I am sorry to be taking your daughter from you."

I meant to go on, to make it clear that Rosamund would be able to take all the time she wanted to visit them at their new house, but Rosamund's other uncle scoffed before I could.

"Nonsense!" he exclaimed gruffly. "You've taken nothing from us."

"If anything, we've just gained another niece," the first uncle added. "And this one is going to be a queen. The neighbors will be so jealous."

Toketie raised her eyes to the ceiling in response to her dad's words. "Rosy's also going to be queen," she reminded him.

"Ranch hand or soldier or queen, it's never mattered to us," Rosamund's father said. "So long as you're happy."

The emotion that flowed through me from our bond could be described accurately as overjoyed. "I am," Rosamund said.

"We both are," I agreed.

We stayed for a few minutes longer. I got the chance to meet Solemie's new wife and thank her for the beautiful necklaces. Lilly, as she'd told me to call her, waved off my thanks. "I've already gotten a dozen requests for courtship and bonding necklaces by your classmates," she said. "I might have to take on an apprentice soon!"

Toketie rushed her family away soon after to go get seats for the ceremony. No, not just her family. Our family. I had lost my father, but I had gained so much more. Rosamund's parents and cousins and uncles would never be able to replace him, not truly, but I didn't need them to. I was ready to learn a new type of love—a softer kind.

I held out a hand and Rosamund took it so that we could walk together to the waiting chamber outside the throne room and stand there until the jarls were ready to call us inside. A great clamor of voices was coming through the other side of the heavy wooden doors in front of us, quieting down a few minutes later as the jarls began the ceremony.

"I love you," I whispered as I waited for our cue to enter. "I'm glad you're here with me, Rosamund Holt."

"You should be glad I love you too, Shaw Colchuck," she said, equally as soft. "I'd be running away otherwise."

"No, you wouldn't," I said, utterly certain. "Not anymore."

She smiled at that and agreed, "Not anymore. Not ever again."

The doors to the throne room opened as our names were called in tandem. Hand in hand, Rosamund and I walked inside.

THE END

Acknowledgments

This book has been a labor of love and I need to thank everyone who had a hand in it.

First to my amazing editor, Holly West, who stuck with me through all the many drafts of this story until we landed on the best way to conclude Rosy & Shaw's journey.

To the readers who gave notes on those drafts, including but not limited to Clare Edge, Rachel Diebel, and Mary Lusebrink.

To Lara Ameen, for being so supportive, for educating me on aspects of using a wheelchair I couldn't discover through research alone, and for combing through this manuscript looking for any microaggressions around disability.

To Rich Deas for the absolutely stunning cover and to his design team, the marketing team, and everyone at Feiwel and Friends who helped with the production of this book.

To my parents, for their unending support of my long-standing dream of being a published author.

To my girlfriend, my brother, and my best friends for sitting through so many brainstorming sessions.

To my agent, Mary C. Moore, who always has my back.

And finally to the high schoolers I work with who prove to me every day that teenagers have so much capacity for change, strong moral and ethical opinions, and so much bravery even in the face of life's many hardships.

About the Author

Jasmine Skye is a queer-romantic, gray-ace, bigender fantasy author who earned an MFA in creative writing from the University of Southern Maine's Stonecoast program. The author of *Daughter of the Bone Forest* and *Daughter of the Cursed Kingdom*, s/he especially loves to create magical worlds where LGBTQIA+ heroes persevere through hardships to claim their own happy endings. Jasmine has a small menagerie of pets and a collection of hobbies, including cosplay and figure skating. When s/he's not writing, Jasmine does STEM outreach work with high schoolers across Texas.

Thank you for reading this Feiwel & Friends book.
The friends who made

Daughter of the Cursed Kingdom

possible are:

Jean Feiwel, Publisher
Liz Szabla, VP, Associate Publisher
Rich Deas, Senior Creative Director
Anna Roberto, Executive Editor
Holly West, Executive Editor
Kat Brzozowski, Senior Editor
Emily Settle, Senior Editor
Dawn Ryan, Executive Managing Editor
Kim Waymer, Senior Production Manager
Foyinsi Adegbonmire, Editor
Rachel Diebel, Editor
Brittany Groves, Assistant Editor
Ilana Worrell, Senior Production Editor
Mariam Chaduneli, Production Editorial Assistant

Follow us on Facebook or visit us online at fiercereads.com.
Our books are friends for life.